CHRIS RYAN

LAND OF FIRE

arrow books

15

Arrow Books
20 Vauxhall Bridge Road
London SW1V 2SA

Arrow Books is part of the Penguin Random House group of companies
whose addresses can be found at global.penguinrandomhouse.com

Penguin
Random House
UK

First published in Great Britain by Century in 2002
Published in paperback by Arrow Books in 2003

www.penguin.co.uk

A CIP catalogue record for this book is available from the British
Library.

Typeset by SX Composing DTP, Rayleigh, Essex

Penguin Random House is committed to a sustainable future for our
business, our readers and our planet. This book is made from Forest
Stewardship Council® certified paper.

MIX
Paper from
responsible sources
FSC® C018179

Printed and bound in Great Britain by Clays Ltd, Elcograf S.p.A.

ACKNOWLEDGEMENTS

To my agent Barbara Levy, editor Mark Booth, assistant editor Hannah Black, Charlotte Bush and the rest of the team at Century.

ONE

'Air raid warning red!'

Autumn in the South Atlantic. 3.32pm on 25 May, a bright, cold afternoon in the narrow inlet of San Carlos Water, East Falkland. The alarm call sent a shiver through the British fleet – and my war turned bloody.

This was Argentina's national day. In enemy sorties before lunch, missiles from HMS *Coventry* had shot down two A4 Skyhawk bombers over the sound, with a third destroyed by small-arms fire. But an hour later the bombers had returned to exact revenge, damaging *Broadsword* and hitting *Coventry* with three bombs, capsizing her and killing nineteen men.

Now the bombers were back again.

This new message meant that the long-range radar of a ship on the forward picket line had detected hostile aircraft in descent towards the island on a strike mission profile.

Minutes earlier a Sea King helicopter from HMS *Invincible* had set me down on the main deck of the SS *Northland*, a 15,000-ton roll-on roll-off container ship. There were four of us there from D Squadron SAS, under the orders of my brother, Troop Sergeant Andy Black. The other two were Tom – one of my great mates, a huge and unflappable Fijian corporal – and Doug Easton, the troop troublemaker, who had just made selection. Doug was a bullet-headed tearaway from east London, violently aggressive and forever forcing his opinions on people. He and I had never hit it off.

The squadron was scheduled to undertake a major operation in the next couple of days, and now we were hunting for a missing container of stores. Some clerk in Portsmouth had screwed up on the cargo manifest and our vital laser target designators had ended up on the wrong ship. I was twenty years old, and the operation would be my first time under fire in a real war; so I was quite nervous about how I would perform in a major action.

A stench of diesel and avgas. The cavernous main hold was jammed with giant helicopters and massive crates holding spare engines for Harrier jump jets. Teams of RAF technicians – 'crabs' in our language – were labouring to bolt the rotors into place on a twin-engine Chinook. Andy sent Tom and Doug forward, and took me aft with him to check the lower vehicle deck. He purposely wanted to keep me apart from Tom – when the order to leave for the Falklands came through, Tom and I had been out drinking. We had ended up pissed in some stinker's house and missed the flight out to Ascension Island with the rest of the squadron, and had to catch a later plane – Andy hadn't forgiven me yet. A veteran of the Oman campaign, he sported the droopy tash and long hair of a seasoned SAS operator, and took no nonsense from anyone, officer or ranker.

As we searched for a stairwell we met a couple of airmen coming forward. 'How do we get down from here?' Andy asked. One of the men jerked a thumb over his shoulder and hurried on without stopping.

'Fucking crab,' Andy grunted. 'Shitting himself in case the Argy planes come back.'

You couldn't exactly blame him, though. It was bad enough being on a troop ship, but with holds full of fuel and ammunition these guys were sitting on a bomb – literally.

The war at this point was becoming very real. I had seen enemy aircraft blown out of the sky over the anchorage, and ships burning from missile hits.

We clattered down into the bowels of the ship. The lower deck was shadowy, crammed with long lines of all-terrain vehicles, Land Rovers and eight-ton medium trucks packed to the roof with stores and chained to the deck by their axles.

'Take fucking hours to search this lot,' Andy said. 'We'll need more light. Hang on here, Mark, while I go back for a couple of torches. And keep your eyes open for anything worth nicking – if the crabs haven't got there first, that is.'

Hampered by my bulky life vest, I squeezed past a rank of bucket loaders belonging to the Royal Engineers and a grim contingent of battlefield

ambulances. From up above came the sounds of a
Tannoy blaring: probably another aircraft warning –
the Argies were throwing their full weight against the
landings.

Andy returned with torches, and we set to work. As
we moved along the lines I was quizzing him about the
forthcoming mission. Rumour had it the squadron was
to send a patrol into the Argentine mainland. If true, it
would be a major escalation of the war. I knew Andy
was bothered by it because it was a four-man patrol, and
I was listed number six in reserve – which meant I was
unlikely to be picked, a fact that was pissing me off a lot.

I made out four of the squadron's trucks among a fleet
of BV lightweight tracked vehicles – the kind that can
go across the ice cap if you need to. The first contained
bivvy bags and groundsheets, as listed. I counted the
bundles as best I could in the semi-dark. The canvas flap
at the back of the second truck was partly unsecured,
and I squirmed underneath to take a dekko inside. Jesus,
I thought disgustedly as I played the torch around. The
neat packs of arctic clothing and spare sleeping bags had
been hollowed out in the middle to make a hiding
place, and some pisser was kipping down in there. I
pulled the canvas back for a better look. Whoever it was
had dug out a sleeping bag and there was a torch ready
to hand, an army-issue water bottle and the remains of
a meal from a ration pack. Fucking crabs, I thought,
they get better fed than we do, and still they nick our
grub.

Feeling around among the bundles, I turned up a

camera and a miniature tape recorder, quality-looking items both. Along with them was a piece of electronic kit I didn't recognise, a flat grey plastic box around six inches long by two-and-a-half wide, with an extendable aerial like a transistor radio but no tuning dial, only a tiny red button that glowed to show it was switched on.

I was about to go back and show Andy what I'd found when there was a rustling noise from the front of the truck. A rat after the remains of the food? But it seemed like too much noise for a rat. A man – and whoever had been living here was still around, by the sound of it.

Right, I'll have you, I thought, and launched myself across the piled stores. There was a frantic scuffling as a body tried to get away. I got a hand around a limb in the darkness – arm or leg I couldn't tell.

'Come on, get the fuck out of there,' I said, heaving.

A foot came out of the blackness and connected with my face with a force that rocked my head back against the steel frame of the roof. The torch went flying and the crack I'd taken felt as if it had broken my jaw. My head was singing and I could taste blood in my mouth. I was angry now.

OK, I said to myself, if that's how you want to play it, fine. I let fly a punch with all my twelve stone behind it. My fist connected with something solid. There was a gasp and a whimper and the struggles ceased. This was better.

Locating a foot, I dragged my opponent into the half-light near the truck tail to take a look at him. The guy was wearing army combat fatigues. I'd been expecting a crab or a sailor – maybe he'd nicked the gear too. He was so slight he looked more like a boy than a man. 'Who the fuck are you?' I demanded.

The little bastard struggled violently and tried to knee me in the groin, unsuccessfully. I figured he had to be some kind of cabin boy, someone from the crew – probably scared to death by the bombing, hiding down here when he should be topsides.

He twisted like a snake, diving under my arm to reach the roof flap. I was ready for him, though. Flinging myself after, I dragged him back, rolling him over and pinning him down. He fought and squirmed; it was a while since I'd fought with a kid his size, and it didn't feel right somehow. I was worrying I'd break a bone or something. Eventually, though, I got him pinned down by sheer weight. I straddled him between my knees and laced his hands across his chest so he couldn't move, though he continued to snarl and wriggle like a wildcat.

'What's your name then, arsehole?'

His response was to spit in my face. I cuffed him a couple of times across the mouth to teach him manners, and he shut up. His wrists were so thin I could hold them together one-handed while I searched his tunic for ID.

It was while I was patting him down that I realised something was wrong – and not in the way I had been thinking before. In addition to a combat jacket several sizes too large, he had on a roll-neck sweater with a T-shirt underneath. Ignoring his squirmings I pulled these up – to reveal a narrow ribcage and a flesh-coloured sports bra hiding a pair of adolescent tits.

My cabin boy was a girl.

I let go her hands and sat up. The torch was lying nearby and I snapped it on – definitely a girl. The dark hair was ragged and plastered to her grimy face, she was unkempt and pale – but the dishevelled appearance and dirt could not disguise the fineness of the features or burning intensity of the eyes. A bit younger than me; seventeen or eighteen at a guess.

There was a reddening mark on one cheek where I had hit her. I reached down to touch the place. Her eyes flashed hatred. A hand swept out of the gloom, fingers curled like talons to rake my face, but I knocked the hand aside. 'I didn't mean to hit you!' Well, I hadn't – I'd thought she was a bloke. 'What are you doing down here anyway?'

'*Bastardo!*'

A girl, I was thinking. How she had got here I couldn't imagine – unless maybe she was some crab's bit of fluff smuggled aboard at Portsmouth. I hadn't seen a girl in six weeks. We'd heard rumours that a few were serving on the *Canberra*, but we'd never got near enough to find out. Or could she be a journalist stowed away on board to get a scoop on the campaign . . .?

Then it dawned on me that she'd spoken in Spanish. I ran my gaze around the nest in which she had been lying up, taking in the items I'd found – the camera, the tape recorder, the radio-type device.

And it hit me. Jesus, I thought, the bitch is a spy. She's down here vectoring the bombers in on us.

That moment she flew at me again.

I called Andy over. Even against the two of us she continued to put up a fight; she could kick and punch like a bantamweight. My teeth were aching and Andy took a poke in the eye that left him gasping, but eventually we got her tied down with some straps off a vehicle, and Andy told me to watch her while he went off to find the ship's ops officer.

After that, everything started to go ratshit. The ship's captain and the ops officer took one look at the girl – still spitting and snarling – and the kit she had with her, and told Andy and me that on no account should we talk to anyone. I described to them the scene in the back of the truck, how I'd guessed she had a homing device – which was what it seemed the thing was – and there were long faces as the officers tried to figure out how an enemy agent had managed to breach their 'impenetrable' security cordon. No one knew how she had got on, or whether it was at Portsmouth or Ascension Island where the ship had stopped en route. Small wonder we had been taking such losses to air attack.

By this time they had brought a couple of seamen down and told them to get the kit off her. These boys set to work grinning. The prisoner fought and kicked, but it didn't do her any good. In a trice she was shackled to a bulkhead and every shred of clothing was ripped away. It was freezing cold down below decks, but in the overhead light her olive skin was beaded with sweat.

Front on, she looked pathetically young and emaciated. I felt no anger now, only pity and disgust. I wondered what they were going to do with her. This was war, and in war spies are shot. I knew the procedure. I'd been through it myself on an escape-and-evasion exercise during the SAS initiation test in the Brecon Beacons before the war. Next she'd have the full treatment: the body cavity searches, the physical and verbal abuse, the threats, the hooding, and banging on the walls and door to induce disorientation. I could have told them they were wasting their time; she was never going to talk – but it wouldn't have done any good.

The two seamen stayed in attendance to see that she didn't kill herself. Though God knows how she was going to manage that, the way they had her trussed up.

I felt sick as we climbed back topside, the captain explaining that we weren't to talk about this, not to anyone. It was all top secret. In other words, a cover-up was in force. We were to forget the girl, forget the homing device – none of it had ever happened. But I couldn't get the image of her spread-eagled against that bulkhead out of my mind.

Tom and Doug were waiting on deck. The ops officer told us to get our kit together before our regimental helicopter flew us back to rejoin the unit.

That was when all hell broke loose.

TWO

The attacking aircraft were A4 Skyhawks belonging to the Argentine navy based at Rio Grande on Tierra del Fuego. Equipped with a pair of 500lb freefall iron bombs each, the planes' targets were the closely packed transport vessels moored in the narrow inlet of San Carlos Water off the beachhead.

It was a dangerous mission. Our ships were protected by radar-controlled anti-aircraft guns and state-of-the-art missiles, including the deadly Sea Dart which was carried aboard the Type-42 destroyers positioned at the mouth of the inlet. The Sea Dart was a fifteen-foot-long missile weighing half a ton. On firing, the rocket booster accelerated it up to twice the speed of sound within three seconds, and it could pluck an aircraft out of the sky at forty miles' range. By this stage of the war the Sea Darts had claimed three attacking jets, and the pilots were under no illusions as to the risks they faced.

But the Sea Dart had one weakness. It was primarily designed to fight the Russian navy in an open-sea war. But against a low-level target, operating against a background of clutter from the land, it was less effective. And this afternoon the Argentines had exploited that weakness to deadly effect. Screaming off the land at near wave-height, their aircraft had hit the destroyer HMS *Coventry*, capsizing her with a loss of nineteen men.

The catastrophe left a yawning gap in the air defences of the San Carlos beachhead. The only guard vessel left was the smaller frigate HMS *Broadsword*, herself damaged in an earlier attack. Her Sea Wolf missiles were of an advanced type designed to counter sea-skimming missiles fired by submarines, so new they were still under test. They were highly accurate, but their range was just two-and-a-half miles: no time for a second shot.

As the low hills and fractured coastline of the islands loomed ahead, the lead aircraft dropped to three hundred feet and commenced its run up the coast. The pilot twisted and turned his craft, weaving among the valleys. His instruments would be able to detect the pulse of enemy radar beams feeling for him, striving to pick out his plane from the jumble of returning echoes bouncing off the hillsides.

Travelling at 500 knots, the four aircraft split into two sections for the final attack to divide the gunners' attention. The lead aircraft appeared to be heading directly for the centre of a massed group of store ships.

An urgent warning pealed from the on-board speakers: 'Air raid warning red!' There was a panicked rush for the upper decks by some of the civilian seamen. They had seen the *Coventry* turn into a fireball and go down, and they didn't want to be caught below when it happened to their own ship.

From previous drills I knew we had about a minute and a half from the warning before the bombs started to fall. I looked towards the south-west and saw a dark shape loose itself from the land and come streaking down the sound. The next instant the twin 20mm WW2-vintage Oerlikons opened up, *bam, bam, bam, bam*. From all around, guns on ships and land were firing and the air was full of smoke bursts, but the planes flew on unscathed. I saw a rocket plume flash up from one of the hills. Someone having a go with a Blowpipe, but Blowpipes didn't engage crossing targets well and this one ran wild on to a hillside.

Four-and-a-half miles out, and the lead planes were so low the wash from their jet engines was striking spray from the surface of the inlet. The firing became a crescendo. The racket was unbelievable; the deep boom of the 4.5-calibre main guns of the warships was joined by the hammer of cannon fire and the shrill stammer of GPMGs. But all the gunfire seemed to be falling short, bursting in front of the planes and making the water dance. To me, watching from the deck of the *Northland*, it seemed incredible that planes could fly through flak that thick and survive.

The ships that had way on them were manoeuvring frantically to get clear. *Northland*, though, had no steam up. She was a sitting duck. Four hundred yards short, the pilot of the lead Skyhawk released his bombs. I saw them fall clear, dropping towards us as the jet screamed away overhead, two black dots growing larger by the second, and I thought, fuck, they're coming right at us.

We were the target. Doug had thrown himself flat on the deck; he hated air attacks and didn't like ships much better. I was thinking, this is where we all die – yet I couldn't tear my gaze away.

The first bomb hit the water twenty yards from the port quarter with a mountainous splash. 'Missed, you bastard!' I shouted aloud. I knew that these bombs had a delay function, an impeller in the tail that had to spin a set number of turns after dropping to release the firing pin, so that it could move forward on impact and trigger the detonator. Flying so low meant that they had to be released at exactly the right moment or the sods wouldn't go off.

It was my last coherent thought before the world burst in around me.

In fact the first bomb flew so fast I didn't have time to see it bounce off the surface like a skimmed stone and strike the ship's side, piercing it. It passed upwards through the engine room, killing three men, and emerged through the deck without exploding.

I don't recall anything of the impact because a fraction of a second later the second bomb struck us amidships, and this time the impeller did its stuff. The firing pin released and the bomb exploded in the main hold with a force that burst open the deck where I was standing and threw everyone nearby off their feet.

I remember a bright flash and then I must have been knocked unconscious for a few seconds. When I came to I was lying on my front. My clothes were blackened and I was surrounded by smoking wreckage. The decking was all ripped and a roaring jet of flame licked upwards. Ammunition was popping off down in the holds, punctuated by the heavier *whoomp* of petrol tanks going up.

I stood up, and realised the ship had taken on a list. It was like walking uphill. A hand grabbed me; it was Andy. His hair was all singed and I remember wondering if mine was the same. He was shouting at me but I couldn't make out what he said because of the noise and because the explosion had left me temporarily deafened. He thrust a survival suit into my hands and pointed to the side. Time to abandon ship. A survival suit was a once-only garment you pulled on over your outer clothes before jumping into the water. Its seals were supposed to keep you dry and alive long enough to be rescued – provided help came pretty quick. Without a suit the average person had a fifty-fifty chance of swimming fifty yards in these waters before hypothermia got him.

I was about to put it on when I saw the two seamen who had been guarding the girl come tumbling up a companionway from below. There was no sign of the girl with them. The bomb must have shattered the lower deck level and those guys had legged it. They weren't about to risk their lives for the sake of a spy.

I don't know why I should have done either, unless it was because I was the one who had found her and started it all. I looked around for Andy but he had disappeared. Presumably he figured I could look after myself. The ship didn't seem to be about to go down

14

this second and the fire hadn't reached the forepart yet. I decided I had a good chance to reach her and fetch her out.

In a way it was easier than I had thought. I nipped down the ladder on to the cargo deck level. There was a lot of smoke eddying around but no actual flames yet. One guy passed me carrying a kit bag; he must have been back to his cabin. I went down two more ladders. The emergency lights were on here, but there was less smoke. All the alarm bells were ringing. The noise of firing was muffled but I could hear big thuds of mortar bombs or gas tanks going up, which kept me moving forwards and down. The tilt on the deck didn't seem to be getting any steeper so I figured I wasn't about to drown yet.

When I reached the stern, there she was where they had left her, still lashed to the ringbolts. I ripped off the hood and untied her wrists and she sagged against me like she was all in. Her clothes were in a heap on the deck. I started pulling them over her arms and legs. There didn't seem much point in rescuing her if she was going to die of cold the second I dropped her in the water. She got the message and inside a couple of minutes I had her more or less dressed. I gave her the survival suit – it made one less thing to carry – and hustled her back to the ladders.

There seemed to be a lot more smoke and heat around now. Also the angle of the deck was suddenly worse. I pushed the girl ahead of me up the ladder. She had either recovered some of her strength or she was scared, because she went up like a squirrel. I guess after six weeks aboard she knew her way about.

Half-way up the next ladder conditions were vile. Flames were spreading into the stairwell. The ladder had broken free from several of its supports and swayed ominously as we went higher. The girl was slowing down because of the flames. I was having to climb one-handed, using the other to push her on. Another explosion shook the hold – more ammunition going up. Bits of debris were raining down from overhead and the bulkhead next to the hold was smoking or steaming, I couldn't tell which. I concentrated on trying to breathe in shallow gasps to keep the smoke out of my lungs. The ladder seemed endless and the handrail was hot to touch.

Somehow we reached the landing at the top, only to find the door leading out on deck wouldn't open; the watertight latches were closed fast. Some bugger had sealed us in to die.

The girl was going limp as she suffered the effects of the smoke. I propped her up against the wall and took a hold of the top latch. It didn't budge. Heat or the ship's list must have wrenched the frame out of true. I looked around but the passage behind was filling with flames. There was no other way out. I heaved on the latch again and was rewarded with a slight movement. A series of violent tugs at last worked it free. Now for the bottom latch. This was worse. It was so tightly jammed nothing I did seemed to make it move. Inky smoke was belching up the stairwell, making it impossible to breathe. In desperation I pounded on the steel door with my fist.

'Let us out, you fuckers!' I might as well have been pissing into the wind for all the chance there was of being heard.

I grabbed the handle of the top latch again with both hands, swung myself out over the stairwell and crashed both legs together against the jammed hatch. The impact jarred my spine but I thought I felt the latch move. I pushed off again with my feet, praying I wouldn't somehow fall off and drop twenty feet into the burning hold, and gave a second mighty kick – and this time the handle snapped free with a clank.

Out on deck things weren't a whole lot better, except that it was possible to breathe more freely. The ship was burning furiously amidships and listing heavily. Secondary explosions were shaking the hull as fuel tanks continued to detonate below decks. It was obviously only a matter of minutes before she was going to go down. A few disciplined types were trying to run hoses into the flames but most of the crew were launching life rafts and jumping overboard in their haste to get off in case she blew. Many of the floats were overcrowded and men were being washed into the sea. A frigate nearby had boats in the water picking up survivors, and helicopters were swooping down to pluck people off the deck.

I pushed the girl ahead of me along the deck. Now I could hear men screaming down in the hold. She stood, swaying with exhaustion, surveying the scene of devastation. In her eyes was a glow of triumph. Something inside me snapped. They could be my mates down there. I seized her by the scruff and forced her to the edge of the shattered deck, made her look down into the inferno. 'Now it's your turn!' I yelled.

A hand caught my shoulder. It was Andy again, his face blackened by smoke and flames. 'What the fuck are you doing, Mark?' he yelled. 'Come on, we've got a boat waiting.'

The adrenalin rush had left me light-headed. If she was a spy, then this girl was more valuable alive.

I was turning back from the fire when the ship gave a sudden lurch that sent us all sprawling. A burst of flaming smoke spewed out from the burning hole amidships. I felt my hair crackle. Andy pulled me to my feet and dragged me back out of harm's way.

Gasping, I looked around. 'Where's the girl?'

But she was gone.

THREE

The capsized hulk of the *Northland* was still visible out in the sound the next morning. How they had managed to stop her sinking I couldn't think. There was a big tug fussing about; maybe they intended towing her out to sea to clear the way for other vessels. The sun glistened on a big oil slick that was being washed in towards the shore.

Andy and the rest of us had got off the wreck with no trouble. He had found us places in a lifeboat but, as we were about to get in, a Wessex helicopter had come spinning down, lifted off our whole party and dropped us on to *Fearless*, our own ship, with minimum fuss. What had become of the girl I didn't know. Maybe she had been rearrested or else drowned. Either way, I had done my bit.

Andy was pissed off with me though. All he could think about was that the quartermaster was giving him grief because we had failed to bring back his precious laser target designators. Andy reckoned it was my fault for getting tangled up with the girl. He wouldn't listen when I pointed out that we had never located the missing container, and so had no idea if the fuckers were

ever aboard the *Northland*. As far as big brother was
concerned I had screwed up yet again.

Right now Andy was in the CO's office, a Portakabin
welded to the after deck, with Captain Guy Litchfield,
our troop Rupert, being briefed by the ops officer on
the forthcoming mission. Apparently this was a proposal
to insert an observation team on to the Argentine
mainland at Tierra del Fuego to mount a watch on the
big airbase at Rio Grande. Overnight the operation had
firmed up to the extent that it now had a codename:
Dynamo.

At least, that was the rumour. Officially we had been
told nothing, but three members of the squadron who
had been on Invincible reported seeing a Sea King being
stripped out and fitted with ultra-long-range fuel tanks.
Andy knew more, but he wasn't telling. I already knew
he didn't want me along.

Either way it was clear we would be going into action
soon.

We were in our bunk room on the assault ship with
the pipes gurgling overhead, busy shaking out our
equipment, checking batteries on the night sights and
missiles, bugging Cyril the quartermaster for more
grenades and pistols to replace a bunch of weapons that
had gone missing. Some of our arctic clothing had been
lost and no one knew how it was to be replaced. The
good news was that the squadron had received a
consignment of the coveted 203 from America, the so-
called 'over and under' Armalite with a grenade
launcher slotted underneath the rifle barrel. We had

been screaming for these for over a year, and they were like gold. Their sudden arrival was an indication of the importance attached to this mission.

'How many Claymores?' Tom, the Fijian, asked Cyril. Claymores were American anti-personnel mines that could be deployed quickly to discourage pursuit. 'One each,' Cyril told him. Cyril was a small, curly-haired sergeant who had damaged a leg on an op over the Norwegian border into Russia at the height of the Cold War and been relegated to light duties.

Taffy was our junior sergeant and doom merchant. 'There's a full battalion of Argy marines guarding that airfield, so I hear.'

'Fuck them,' Tom told him happily. 'I faced more than that in Oman.'

'Yeah, but they were rag-heads,' Doug put in with a jeer. Tom was a legend in his own right in the regiment for the time he had defended the base at Merbak from an attack by thousands of rebels. He had ended up working a 25lb howitzer alone, firing it at point-blank range. By the time reinforcements arrived he had been wounded in every limb and was still firing.

'Tom's seen more action than you ever will,' I told Doug.

'Yeah?' he said. 'So how come the two of you tried to miss the flight out then? No stomach for it?'

Tom didn't rise to Doug's baiting though. He was so good-natured he was next to impossible to needle. You'd have to push him to the limit to get him riled – but then it was hard to cool him down.

It seemed to be accepted that I was not to be a part of this mission. Andy had always done his best to look after me in training, and found it hard to stop now. But I hated being singled out and did my utmost to avoid it. The other guys knew this perfectly well.

I was an afterthought, fifteen years younger than Andy. Our father had died when I was ten, and Andy substituted himself in my upbringing. He was determined from the start that I should make something of my life and spent the little bit of capital my father left putting me through private school, an advantage he had never had. He was furious when I signed on for the army. He said he had hoped I would go to university. I explained that I wanted to live life, not read about it. There was another row when I applied to join the SAS. The least I could do, he thought, was get a commission and become an officer. He said it was unfair on our mother to have both her sons at risk.

Andy arrived with Guy, the Rupert. They had come to give us our briefing. We locked the door and settled down on the bunks to hear what they had to say. Guy was typical of the Ruperts we got – a big, tall rugby player who'd been promoted up to captain from lieutenant on joining the Regiment. Ruperts normally serve two-year hitches and then go back to their units, taking their new skills, if any, back with them.

Guy started off. 'Shall I give the orders?'

'No,' Andy told him shortly. 'I'm in charge. You're just a spare gun.'

Guy's jaw dropped. It's a big culture shock for young

officers to come into the SAS and find they are a lot less important than an experienced NCO.

Before Guy could speak Andy went on: 'You sit there by Mark. The two of you should have plenty to talk about.' This was supposed to remind the others I had been to private school. I shifted up to make room on the bunk for him. Doug squeezed in on the other side. Opposite us were Tom and Taffy, with Andy on the outside nearest the door.

'It's an OP job,' Andy said. An OP was an observation post, holing up somewhere, watching and reporting back. It was a task we practised often.

'Where?' Taffy asked.

'The Argentine mainland, Tierra del Fuego,' Andy answered.

So the rumours were true. This meant a big increase in the scope of the fighting. Until now the hostilities were supposedly limited to a 200-mile exclusion zone around the islands.

'The Argy air force is sinking our ships faster than we can replace them,' Andy went on, 'and the Navy is shit worried.' He looked at the three of us who'd been on the *Northland*. We didn't need reminding what it was like to be bombed. 'Our target is the big airbase at Rio Grande. We infiltrate by helicopter under cover of darkness, set up an OP, and observe and report enemy aircraft movements: time out, course and direction, numbers and weapon loads. The usual kind of thing. Fleet also wants to know how many make it back so they can estimate the attrition rate of the defences.'

'How long do we stay?' Taffy wanted to know. Taff always got nervous before a mission.

'Until the war ends, stupid,' Tom retorted in his thick accent. Tom wasn't worried one bit by the prospect of landing in the middle of enemy territory. The longer the better, so far as he was concerned. He was genuinely without fear.

Now Doug was giving Guy a hard time, shouldering him off the edge of the bunk. 'You've got balls to say you're in charge, when this is your first mission.' His mean little eyes squinty with amusement. Doug loved picking on people, and he knew Guy's dignity as an officer wouldn't let him fight back.

'What about exfil?' I chipped in.

Andy gave me a hard look. It said, you aren't going on this trip, little brother, so why ask? Eventually he said, 'That's still to be decided. It depends what we find out. They may send the helicopter back or a submarine. If necessary we can always tab out for the Chilean border, fifty miles west.'

'What's the country like?' Taffy wanted to know. He was our Stinger missile operator and would be carrying one of the biggest loads.

'Pampas and moorland mainly.' Andy grinned. 'Just think the Brecon Beacons in winter and you'll know what to expect.'

'Shit!' someone said and there was a general groan. The Brecon Beacons in Wales were our regular training ground. Soldiers had died out there of hypothermia and exhaustion.

Andy took us back to specifics. The helicopter would drop the patrol off north-west of the base. It would work its way up to the perimeter during darkness and establish a lying-up point with a forward OP. The OP would have the main runway under constant surveillance.

'Taffy, you'll be on the gimpy with him.' He jerked his head at Guy. 'Doug, you'll carry the signal kit.'

I waited. Then, 'That it?' I said. 'What about Tom and me?'

Andy shook his head. 'I told the OC we could do this with just the four of us.'

Anger shot through me in a hot rush. 'Fuck you!' I told him. 'You can't run a proper OP on enemy ground with just four men.'

Andy smiled at me grimly. 'That's the decision. You'll just have to lump it.'

Unexpectedly Doug backed me up. 'Why not take Mark instead of the Rupert? What's the use of an officer on a mission?'

'Because we need him to sign the claims cheque for equipment,' Andy said, and Doug grinned at the joke.

All this was making me madder than ever. I jumped up with my fists balled. 'You bastard!' I screamed in Andy's face. 'You treat me like a kid because you're scared I'm better than you.'

Andy was on his feet in an instant. 'Let's see you try it then, little brother.' We glared at one another, hatred flushing our faces. I was taller than Andy but he had the weight. I was quicker though, with a longer reach, and if I could get the first blow in . . . It was just like the start of all the fights we'd had as kids, when he would thump me for daring to defy him.

But Guy shouldered his way between us. 'Knock it off,' he snapped, 'the pair of you. This is a briefing. It's no time for stupid squabbling.'

Andy's eyes were hard with rage. But Guy was right. This was no time for a fight and the CO would be pissed off if he got to hear of it. With an effort Andy relaxed his fists. 'You do as you're told, boy,' he spat between clenched teeth. 'You had your fun today. Now it's someone else's turn.'

I turned away and looked at Tom, sitting quietly on his bunk. He was the best man in the squad, and everyone knew it. 'You're crazy leaving Tom out because you're so fucking jealous you can't bring yourself to take me along. If you won't see reason, I'll go to the OC myself,' I shouted, storming out.

'That's right,' Andy jeered after me. 'And while you're at it, put in for a commission, why don't you?'

Up on the deck I breathed in the cold air, shaking with anger and humiliation. It was as though Andy was determined to frustrate my attempts to prove myself a soldier and a member of the Regiment. He wanted to keep me always in his shadow.

Carrying my grievance to the OC was an empty threat, and we both knew it. No officer would override the decision of a senior NCO in charge of a patrol on selection. Andy had chosen his three team members to accompany him, and that was that. As far as he was concerned I could spend the war kicking my heels.

I saw the four of them trooping up the stairs, making their way aft to the Portakabin for the OC's briefing. Fuck them, I thought. In my anger I was hoping they'd all get cut up by the Argies and serve them bloody right. Tom and I would stay behind and get drunk. That was something we were good at.

Tom was unfazed at being left behind. 'There'll be plenty more battles,' he observed. He'd scarfed us a can of lager each from the mess, and we cracked them open. I took a deep slug and sat back, feeling my anger slowly ebb away. I envied Tom his placid outlook. He hadn't much education but he never let it worry him. He just took life as it came, one day at a time. He had done a lot of fighting but he would probably never make better than corporal – and he was quite content with that. He lived simply. In his quarters in Hereford there was no furniture; his family sat around on the floor watching television and drinking beer, and they were happy too. I wished I could be more like him.

We had just finished and were crumpling our cans when Taffy stuck his head round the door. 'Change of plan,' he grinned. 'The OC wants you in the cabin pronto. They're upping the team to six and you buggers are coming with us.'

FOUR

The OC's office wasn't much larger than our bunk room. It had no windows and there was a permanent guard on the door. Major Clayton's regimental nickname was Claymore, and he was one tough-looking bastard, with pouched eyes and a reputation as a hard drinker. His junior officers used to take it in turns to sit up, at nights, keeping him company, and he could drink any of them under the table.

I was glad Andy had a pissed-off look. He'd been made to eat his own words, and serve him right.

I took my seat, feeling completely keyed up. This operation must be important, I reckoned, for the OC to override the decision of a senior NCO.

When the door was locked behind us again, Claymore launched into his briefing. The objective was to destroy the Argentine bomber capability. There were particular fears over the Exocet AM-39 air-launched missiles, which were evading our most modern defences. 'If the Argies should succeed in sinking either of the aircraft carriers, *Hermes* or *Invincible*, then the task force would no longer have an air defence worth the name. Effectively the war would be lost. One missile hit is all it takes.'

That sobered us considerably. With more than 2000 troops ashore we had pretty much assumed the war was as good as won – and here was a senior officer telling us we were up shit creek.

'According to intelligence,' Claymore continued, scowling at us, 'the Argies have only a handful of missiles left, and no more than five of the Dassault Super Etendard bombers capable of launching them. They're doing their best to buy replacements on the world market and our agents are attempting to block them, but that's another story. The point is each of those missiles is sufficient to sink a ship. The threat has to be neutralised somehow. And that's our job.'

At a sign from him, the operations officer, a gaunt-faced major in his thirties, uncovered a map of the southern tip of the South American continent. 'Now, we believe the bombers and their missiles to be currently stationed at Rio Grande on Tierra del Fuego, an island which as you can see belongs partly to Argentina and partly to Chile. Rio Grande is approximately 350 miles distant from Port Stanley, so the bombers can make the round trip with air refuelling.'

He paused to let this sink in, then continued. 'The decision has been taken that the SAS should mount an assault on the base with the objective of destroying the bombers and missiles.'

Tapping the map with his pointer, he proceeded to expand on the plan. 'D Squadron is currently embarking for Ascension Island. There the squadron will transfer to a pair of C-130 transports. They will fly in at low level below the radar net, and approach the base from the north-west to make a surprise landing on the main runway.'

As we listened, amazed, he explained how the planes would lower their tail ramps and, before the defenders had time to react, the SAS would race out from the aircraft in their heavily armed Land Rovers. 'Troops One, Two and Three will fan out across the base to attack the aircraft in their revetments, while Troop Four will storm the officers' mess and shoot down the pilots and crews found there.'

I sat up, electrified. Infiltrating an OP into enemy territory to report back on aircraft movements was one thing – the Argies might well anticipate some such move on our part. But a full-blown attack at squadron strength was an enormously ambitious plan. It was a classic mission, the kind that had made the Regiment's reputation in the Second World War. If successful it would be a huge blow against the Argentines and quite possibly end the war.

'Your role in this is vital,' Claymore continued, sweeping us with his bleak gaze. 'You will provide advance reconnaissance for the main party. It will be your job to identify the targets and report on aircraft movements. You will note the position of anti-aircraft defences and prepare the way for the attack by neutralising them at the appropriate moment.'

Now I understood why Tom and I had been called in. That last line gave it away. Our section's part in the mission had been upgraded from simple recon to playing a major role in the attack. As a sniper it would be my job to take out the enemy AA gunners as the transports were lining up for their landings.

Elated as I was to be part of the mission, I couldn't help thinking of the risks. The C-130 Hercules were our standard transport – big lumbering beasts, capable of carrying a hundred paratroops. If the element of surprise was lost they would be sitting ducks. Surely an air strike by the task force's Harriers – guided to their targets by us on the ground – would be a better option?

Extraction was going to be the biggest problem. Assuming the Hercules were undamaged, the plan called for them to refuel at the base then fly the surviving members of the squadron, us included, back to the Falklands. Taffy nudged me. 'It's a fucking suicide mission. If either one of the bleeders is hit that leaves you and me yomping fifty miles to the Chilean border with half the Argentine army at our backs.'

But I wasn't worried. Infiltration by night, lying up in concealment observing enemy dispositions, then guiding in an assault force – this was the kind of mission we had trained for. And I was a trained sniper. I could pick off a target at 600 metres. A single armour-piercing bullet would destroy a missile as effectively as a bomb. Even the tab out to the border didn't alarm me. We exercised that kind of trek often enough on our training area in Wales. I was confident I could handle it.

The operations officer took over the details. Rio Grande lay close to the sea, and the obvious way to insert a clandestine team ashore was by submarine.

Unfortunately the only submarine available was a nuclear boat, and it was too big and too valuable to be risked so close to the Argentine coast. So it would have to be an airdrop. We would be going in by helicopter.

There was a pause while the Navy crew of the Sea King assigned to us was called in to join the briefing. For security they were to be kept in the dark about the main mission so they wouldn't be able to blow it if captured. The pilots and their navigator took their seats, looking nervous.

The ops officer explained that we would embark on board the carrier HMS *Invincible*. '*Invincible* will close to the coast during the night for maximum range and fly the party off. The plan is to fly a course for the Beagle Channel at the southern tip of Tierra del Fuego, where the Chilean border comes down to the Atlantic coast. The helicopter will then turn northwards and fly up the border, keeping to the Chilean side, and approach Rio Grande from the west.' He coughed and continued. 'After setting down the recon party, it will fly on out over the sea.'

'What happens then?' Taffy asked.

'The team will have been dropped close to the Argentine base. You will then work up to a point where you can keep the runways under observation and establish an OP.'

'And what about the Sea King?' Taffy persisted. 'Suppose we have to abort, does it have fuel to bring us out?'

The ops officer exchanged glances with Claymore.

Both looked unhappy. The ops officer swallowed. 'Negative,' he said. 'Once you've reached the coast the Sea King will have insufficient fuel to reach the fleet. It will fly as close in as possible and ditch in the sea. The crew will be recovered by Search and Rescue.'

There was a pregnant silence. The helicopter crew were staring at the table. They didn't like the prospect one bit. Shit, I thought. If anyone had drawn the short straw on this mission it was these three. Ditching a helicopter in the South Atlantic swells probably gave them a fifty per cent chance of survival if they were lucky.

'Why not fly back to Chile and land there?' I suggested. The Navy guys looked up. The same idea must have occurred to them.

The ops officer shook his head. 'Too risky. Could blow the main operation.' He put on a cheerful aspect. 'Don't worry. The Navy takes care of its people. There'll be a frigate on standby with a helicopter to pick them out of the water.'

I looked at the crew. They were staring at the table again. I could read their expressions as clearly as if they had spoken out loud. That Search and Rescue helicopter would recover their bodies.

That was the way it was going to be, though. There was no argument. This was wartime and some missions are tough.

The briefing continued. We covered details of the flight: where to set down; what to do in the event we were detected on the run-in — which basically amounted to aborting the mission and heading for Chilean territory.

Major Clayton stood up again. Realising that morale was in danger of slipping, he treated us to a short pep talk. The mission was vital, he stressed. It was of crucial importance that the bombers and their missiles be destroyed. 'Otherwise the task force could sustain hundreds of casualties and the war be lost.'

The Navy crew went out, and we went through communications procedures, recognition codes with the assault force, how to link up and what our role would be in the final attack. We also touched on escape and evasion in the event we had to tab out on foot. There was a British agent providing intelligence in the area. He had been alerted to set up a ratline across the border for us. We discussed a procedure for getting in contact with him and a rendezvous point.

At the back of my mind all the time was the thought of those Navy guys flying off after leaving us, knowing they were going to almost certain death. Our job was a picnic compared to that.

'This mission stinks,' Taffy muttered as we filed out. 'Those bleeders in the Hercules don't stand a chance. By the time they reach Argy airspace they'll be committed. They won't have fuel to return. If they're picked up on radar they'll have no choice but go in. If one of the planes makes an error and has to circle round for a second attempt those Argy marines will blow it out of the sky.'

I shrugged. What could we do? 'You heard what

Claymore said. Either we go in or a couple of carriers get burned.'

'Fuck to that,' was Taffy's reply. 'We're talking about an entire squadron getting wiped out.'

Andy overheard this and came down on him like a load of bricks. 'Shut the fuck up, you hear? It's not your business. We carry out our mission and that's an end to it. If the main mission is successful we fly out with the rest of the squadron. If it goes pear-shaped and we have to tab out, fine. We'll do it, no sweat. And if you're gutless, say so now and I'll have you replaced.'

It was put up or shut up and Taffy backed down. He was a doom merchant, but no coward. Andy moved away without speaking to me.

Doug was following behind and had heard the exchange. 'What's the matter, Taffy, you scared or what?'

Taffy grunted. 'Fucking rookie, you think you know it all.' We stepped out through the door on to the open deck and he had to shout to make himself heard against the wind. 'Well, I'll tell you something else. A couple of blokes from B Squadron flew in from Ascension this morning. According to them the OC of D Squadron was RTU'd over the weekend and his sergeant major with him. And you want to know why? Because they told the Headshed this mission was a one-way ticket and that none of the guys would be coming back. So they were both replaced.'

Doug and I both stared at him. 'Fucking hell,' Doug whispered. To replace an OC and his senior NCO on the eve of a major operation was unheard of. I couldn't imagine how the situation would have arisen. It was part of the SAS creed that nothing was impossible to determined men. To admit otherwise was tantamount to mutiny. The OC concerned must have felt he was being asked to send men to certain death. For the first time I felt a sense of real unease.

Taffy saw he had us worried and grinned sourly. 'Bet you that assault never goes ahead. We'll be stuck out there on the mainland, all to no purpose. And another thing,' he added, dropping his voice as we moved into the lee of the superstructure, 'that talk of your brother's about flying out with the rest of the squadron is just bullshit. The only way we're getting home is on our own feet.'

FIVE

Final preparations started immediately. The aircraft carrier *Invincible*, escorted by a single frigate, would transport the recon team with its Sea King in towards the coast during darkness and fly them off at midnight. That meant a great deal of cross-decking of supplies, and we were taking a mountain of kit along. The Navy people all seemed to know their guys were not expected to make it back and were blaming us. There was a generally bad atmosphere and non-cooperation on all sides. We wouldn't have anything to do with them, and they weren't having anything to do with us.

Our kit went over first. It took a long time to get everything together. We had Norwegian arctic warfare clothing, Goretex bivvy bags, night-vision scopes, weapons, satellite communications equipment, food, ammunition and surveillance gear – enough to enable us to carry out our mission and survive for two weeks in the tundra if need be. Each man would be carrying his bergen, plus weapons and his share of kit, a load of 120lbs in most cases.

It was late afternoon by the time we were ready. The carrier with its escorting frigate was already out of sight to the south-west, proceeding towards the Argentine coast.

As well as the six of us there were eight other guys making the crossing, six of them SAS from another troop who were being positioned for another mission against East Falkland in two days' time. One of them, Nick Brown, was a mate of mine, a fellow Scot from Fife with white Celtic colouring and blue-black hair. We'd completed the induction course together and been friends ever since. Nick was a family guy. He was looking forward to going into action, but worried for his wife and kids in case anything happened to him.

The helicopter reappeared and touched down on the heaving deck. It had refuelled on the carrier. We piled in and it lifted off directly. We sat on narrow seats along the side of the cabin, facing into the centreline. I was sitting next to Nick with Tom on the other side, and Andy sat opposite with Taff, Doug and Guy. The rest of the guys were back in the tail. Our huge bergens were stacked down the middle between the two rows of seats. The pilots and navigator were on the flight deck, which was accessed through a hatch forward and up a few steps. Even with the side door shut the noise in the confined space was deafening.

We had barely cleared the deck and were coming out of the hover, moving over open water, when there was a loud bang overhead. A terrific concussion shook the helicopter and a shower of heavy impacts hammered the fuselage. In the same instant the aircraft lost forward speed and lurched towards the sea.

As the cabin tilted, I grabbed the straps holding me into my seat and braced my feet for a possible crash. The helicopter wallowed for a second or two, and for a moment I thought it was recovering and would put back to the ship. I guessed there had been an engine failure. But the next instant the fuselage dropped like a stone, so fast I felt myself lifting out of my seat. We hit the surface with a bone-jarring smash and rolled straight on to the starboard side, so that I was hanging up in the air from my seat belt straps. Water surged violently into the cabin and in no time at all it was over our heads.

We had all trained for this. Many of our exercises had been helicopter-borne, and we had all spent time on the simulators – they strap you in a large box, turn it upside down and dunk you in the drink. It had been drilled into us that speed is vital in this situation. Helicopters all behave the same way on a ditching: their engines are on top, so they turn over and sink like bricks. The only chance is to get out fast.

The water was shockingly cold. It seemed to strike straight through to my bones. We would die quickly from hypothermia – if we didn't drown like rats trapped in the sinking fuselage.

A heavy weight was pressing against my arms and legs, pinning me against the seat. It had to be the bergens – they must have rolled on to my side in the crash. I thrashed about in the darkness trying to work myself free and push aside the packs. They were sodden with water and weighed a ton, and there seemed no end to them.

At last I broke free and swam upwards, trying to picture in my mind where the entrance hatch would be. With everything turned upside down and only a faint emergency light to guide me it was next to impossible to orient myself. And I was running out of air fast.

Swimming was a huge effort. My body felt heavy and clumsy in its waterlogged clothes. I didn't want to inflate my life vest in case it pinned me up against the floor, unable to reach the hatch. Pain started in my chest and spread from my lungs to my head. I made myself ignore it as best I could, and concentrated on swimming towards the glow of the lamp.

I could sense other members of the crew blundering about in the water around me, and I tried to remember the lectures they had given us on underwater survival. The instinct not to breathe in water means that carbon dioxide builds up in the blood until it causes loss of consciousness. The average person can hold out for approximately ninety seconds before they pass out and take an involuntary gasp of water. Snorklers regularly hyperventilate before going under, taking lots of deep breaths to saturate the blood with oxygen. They can hold out for two minutes or more. Professional free divers can last underwater for as much as four-and-a-half minutes.

In the end, though, physiology takes over. I could sense darkness closing in on me, a sign my brain was suffering from acute oxygen deprivation. Without fresh oxygen in the blood the heart begins to beat erratically and finally shuts down. Blood pools in the brain – but you aren't dead yet. The brain can hold out a long while on residual oxygen. People have actually been pulled out from under ice fifty minutes after their hearts have shut down, and been revived without brain damage. The colder the water the longer you can live.

They tell you these things to keep you from panicking. If you understand the risks you can assess them properly. Now I knew that as long as I could get through the hatch and not get dragged down to the sea bed by the weight of four tons of aircraft, I had a good chance of being picked up. So I tried to ignore the dark mist closing in on the edges of my consciousness and flailed on. And all the time I could feel the pressure in my ears growing, as the fuselage sank deeper and deeper.

A minute is a long time when you're down in the darkness without air. And it must have been all of a minute before my hands first felt the edge of the hatchway. By now I was completely disoriented; I had no idea which way up the aircraft was. It might have been sinking on its back, or it might have tumbled in the water and now be plunging nose first.

On my first attempt to pull myself through I got a kick in the face from someone else who had made it out and was striking out for the surface. Strangely this gave me confidence; if he could do it I could too. I was entering a strange, dreamy state of accepting what was happening to me. Somewhere in my head I knew this was another of the symptoms of oxygen deprivation, but it didn't seem important. I pulled myself through the hatch and saw a patch of light overhead. Now I remembered my life vest again. I gave the tag a pull and began to float upwards. I wasn't going to fight any more. I was simply going to let myself be drawn towards the light.

I stopped with a jerk. Something was pulling me back, holding me down. I realised it was my leg; my left boot was caught in the slide of the door. Desperately I twisted and tugged, struggling to free myself, but my strength was ebbing away. I tried to work my foot out of the boot, but it was laced up too tight. Stupid, my brain was telling me – stupid to lose your life because of a well-laced boot.

If this is dying, I thought, it's not as hard as I'd imagined it would be. All I had to do was stop struggling and let it take over. It was simple, really. And just as I decided to give myself up, I felt another hand on my leg. Someone else was coming through the hatch after me and realised what had happened. His hand reached down, caught a hold of my foot and jerked it round, and I felt myself float free. The buoyancy of my life vest took over, and rushed me up towards the light.

My head broke the surface suddenly, and with it the instinct for survival reasserted itself. I dragged in deep breaths. Nothing in my life had ever felt so good. The darkness cleared from my brain. I could make out a ship in the distance. It looked to my eyes like half a mile away, but perhaps in reality it was only a few hundred yards. The water was quite rough, but my life vest was supporting me. I looked round for the others, especially

42

for whoever it was had saved my life. I could see heads bobbing among the waves, but it was too dark to make out faces. I was worried about Andy. Surely he would have made it. I had got so used to thinking of him as indestructible.

There was a noise overhead and a searchlight beam cut through the dying daylight, dazzling my eyes. One of the ships nearby must have put a helicopter up the instant the accident occurred. The winchman must have missed me in the waves because he shifted the beam and I saw him drop down into the water a dozen yards away and return with a dripping figure.

I pulled my knees up to my chest to conserve body warmth and checked my light was showing; I didn't want them to miss me.

By the time my turn finally came I was so numb I could hardly think straight. They winched me up into the helicopter and someone wrapped me in a thermal blanket. It wasn't till we reached the ship that I recovered enough to take in what was happening.

I became aware of Andy, standing over me asking if I was OK. He told me they were two bodies down and still looking. We were lucky that the Sea King's tail had broken off on impact, freeing everyone in the rear. According to eyewitnesses the cause of the crash was a sea bird ingested by the engine air intake.

The missing men must have been unable to free themselves. One of them was the pilot, the other was Nick. As soon as I heard this news something inside me told me it was Nick's hand that had pulled my foot free.

43

And if I hadn't blocked the exit hatch, he might have survived too.

As soon as we had kitted ourselves out again, the survivors mustered in the Portakabin. Major Clayton stood up and spoke briefly. This had been a bad start but the mission was going ahead. It was not in the tradition of the Regiment to quit. Nevertheless, anyone who wanted to pull out could do so. There were no takers. I glanced at Andy and his face was expressionless. I knew, though, that he would go on doing what he could to look after me. He was a stubborn bastard, and so was I. It ran in the family.

We replaced our kit from the stocks aboard and drew fresh weapons from the armoury. When the replacement Sea King arrived we flew out to the carrier, this time without incident. I couldn't stop thinking about Nick, though, and what his family would have to go through.

SIX

The carrier steamed through the night at high speed without radar. She would close to within 250 miles of the enemy coast, and the helicopter would fly a low-level, circuitous route south to the extreme tip of the continent and Tierra del Fuego. We would then turn north and fly for fifty miles over Chilean territory before making the final course change and head east, crossing the border into Argentina to approach Rio Grande from the north-west. With six men aboard and all their equipment, plus three crew, the helicopter would have only sufficient range to reach the target, land us, then fly as close as possible to the task force before ditching. We were operating on very fine margins.

All night long we plunged on through heavy seas with only the frigate *Gazelle* for company. The ships were darkened, not a light showing. Down below on *Invincible* engineers were stripping all surplus equipment from one of her Sea Kings and installing huge bladder tanks in the cabin to give extra range. Anything that was not vital was ripped out, partly to save weight and also because the aircraft would not be returning.

The skipper of the aircraft was around twenty-six and

bespectacled; he looked more like an accountant than a pilot. He was already angry at the amount of ammunition and stores we were bringing. With all the weight there were serious doubts we would even make the coast, let alone the border, eighty miles inland. We were so overladen we would have to do a rolling take-off, running the helicopter up the flight deck to generate sufficient speed for lift, like a conventional fixed-wing aircraft. If it failed we would plunge over the end of the deck into the sea and this time go down like a stone. Twice in twelve hours, we thought. Terrific.

We tried to catch some sleep while the ship crashed on across the ocean in the darkness. No one spoke about the crash earlier, but some of the team had the idea that the mission was jinxed. Taffy was still doing his doom-ster bit. According to him, the mission was all a waste of time and lives, the main assault would never go in. 'An entire squadron, fifty guys in two Hercules? It's too big a risk. The Regiment couldn't take that kind of loss.' Whenever he spoke like this, Doug would needle him for being gutless and the two of them would keep it up till I was tired of the sound of them.

Most of us figured that even if the main attack didn't go in we could still do a useful job lying up by the airfield and reporting sorties as they left. Our warning would give the defending fighters time to get into position.

I lay in the half-light of the lower flight deck with the sounds of the ship all around, thinking about Nick and how he had saved my life. What could I say to his wife?

Andy was a few feet away. Thinking about Jemma and his kids most likely. Hard to imagine going into battle knowing people depended on you. I wished I hadn't had that row with him earlier, and determined to say something before we lifted off. I knew why he was taking care of me. If the positions were reversed I'd probably have acted the same way.

I thought about the girl again, wondering what had happened to her. If she had escaped drowning it would only be for a prison cell aboard another ship. She must have thought she was finished, locked in that cell when the bombs struck. I wondered if she felt she owed me one for pulling her out. Probably not. To her I was just another enemy.

I had finally managed to get an hour or so of sleep. Then at midnight Andy came round checking we all had our kit as we were helping each other with our bergens. He and Tom were carrying the biggest loads. Andy because he had the GPMG – the general-purpose machine-gun. Taffy would be his number two with Guy, the Rupert, as back-up. Tom was our Stinger expert; in addition to the launcher, he had four missiles strapped to his pack. Tom was hugely strong and never minded how much weight was laid on him. Doug was our comms man and carried the satcom pack.

Guy gave us a little pep talk, saying that the Argy bombers were knocking hell out of the task force and this was a real chance to make a difference, perhaps bring the war to a speedy conclusion, and we climbed aboard the helicopter. It was a hell of a crush inside, among the gurgling fuel tanks, squatting on top of our gear because they'd ripped out the seating, and I could sense that everyone felt nervous as the engines started.

I had done rolling take-offs before, and they're hairy enough on land. On a ship, where you know you're going to run out of space and drop off the end of the flight deck into the deep dark unknown, it's a pisser.

As we stepped off the helicopter gave a terrific lurch and we clutched the straps. The engines were roaring deafeningly, straining under the effort as they fought for altitude. An overheated gearbox or a snapped drive shaft, I thought, and we'd be fucked.

But very slowly we gained height, clawing our way up to 2000 feet, then set a course to the west. At the same time *Invincible* was turning away from us, steaming at full speed back the way she had come, anxious to put a good distance between her and the coast before dawn. At first light she would launch a strike by two of her Harrier jump jets against Port Stanley. This would have the double effect of damaging the airfield there – with luck taking out some enemy planes – and making the Argentines believe that the carrier was patrolling off that sector.

Andy was either on the headset to the pilot, or up checking the map with the navigator, Guy looking over his shoulder. Time passed slowly. Some of us snatched a couple of hours more sleep. Doug was his usual annoying self, needling people, trying to pick a quarrel. He kept talking even when no one could hear what he was saying. I tried to doze, but once an action is under way I find it difficult to switch off. I ran through my kit in my mind, going over where everything was stowed. In an emergency my life might depend on knowing exactly where an item was and being able to lay my hand on it quickly and without fumbling.

My L42 sniper rifle was between my knees. It was a bolt-action weapon based on the Lee-Enfield .303 calibre rifle used in the Second World War, but converted to 7.62 calibre and fitted with a new, heavy barrel and a Schmidt & Bender 6 × 42 telescopic sight. It was very much the product of an earlier generation, but it was a rugged and serviceable sniping rifle capable, in the right hands, of giving excellent first-shot results at ranges in excess of 800 metres. The ammunition consisted of special Green Spot high-accuracy rounds that I'd individually selected. The gun had a new ten-round box magazine to accommodate rimless ammunition, and the forestock had been cut back over the barrel. The butt had an added cheek-rest, and alterations had been made to the trigger mechanism to give a lighter firing pressure. Barrel and stock were wrapped with camouflage scrim, and I'd added some more over the scope sight.

Once in position we would infiltrate the outskirts of the base and establish an observation post from which to spy out enemy positions. In particular we would have to locate and identify the revetments where the bombers and their missiles were stored. When and if the main assault came in, it would fall to me to take out the anti-aircraft gunners before they had a chance to man their weapons, then to pick off the pilots running for their aircraft.

As soon as the Hercules touched down and lowered their ramps for the Land Rovers to roar out, my task would switch to harassing fire, targeting officers attempting to organise resistance, disrupting enemy efforts to organise a defence, spreading chaos and alarm and maximising the potential of the attacking force. When the battle was over, on the way out I would loiter with the rearguard, picking off the point men of an advance, taking out machine-guns or other weapons, and making troops reluctant to leave the protection of armoured vehicles. A lot was going to depend on me.

Like the rest of the team I was a fully trained signaller. We also numbered among us two medics and two demolitions experts. SAS teams are always multi-skilled.

In addition to me as sniper, we had Andy's 7.62 general-purpose machine-gun. The GPMG – known to us as the 'gimpy' or more simply as 'the gun' – was a superb weapon, belt fed, firing 750 rounds a minute to 1000 metres, giving the squad terrific firepower in an emergency. In fact it was so good the Argies were using it too. To keep the gimpy supplied, each member of the squad carried a couple of 200-round belts slung around his neck. All apart from me carried the 203 M16 and 40mm grenade launcher combo, and every one of us took a 9mm Browning semi-automatic as a firearm of last resort, plus a black-bladed fighting knife, which doubled as an all-purpose tool.

Fifteen minutes out from the coast, the pilot gave us

a shout through the headsets. 'Wake up, you people back there. This is where it starts to get hairy.'

'Fuck him,' mouthed Doug.

We dropped down to low level and were soon skimming the wave tops in the darkness. This was very demanding flying; an instant of misjudgement could have plunged us all into the sea. It was terrifically hot inside the cabin and the turbulence made us all nauseous. I put my head between my hands and stared at the floor and tried to think about something else. Everyone else was doing the same.

Taffy was the first one to go. He just opened his mouth and let everything out. He was sitting right opposite me and the moment I heard him and caught a whiff of his vomit, it was enough to set me off. I coughed up my guts between my feet, trying to keep it away from the bergens. There was a narrow trough running the length of the cabin deck, and with every pitch of the aircraft a greasy tide of vomit lurched from end to end. Very soon the entire squad was joining in, puking away like a bunch of kids at a school treat. It was a relief when Andy told us we'd reached Chilean airspace and could relax a little.

For thirty minutes we headed across Tierra del Fuego, then turned north, flying just inside the border. The Chileans were supposed to be friendly, but it was always possible they might fire on an unidentified aircraft at night. We flew over isolated clusters of lights and occasional tongues of flame that Guy told us were gas jets being flared off from oilfields. When we passed

Vicuan and drew level with Rio Grande, the pilot announced that we were heading into enemy territory.

Around twenty miles from the coast, the pilot came over the intercom again. He sounded tense. 'Range to drop zone, sixteen miles.'

'Shit!' came the co-pilot's voice at the same moment. 'That's a search radar just swept over us.'

'Lock on?'

'Negative – so far.'

We could hear the clicking of the threat-warning receiver up in the cockpit as the beam from the Argentine missile battery passed overhead. 'Get down!' I wanted to shout. But the pilot needed no urging. We dropped as low as we dared, feeling our way between the hills. Everyone was tense. This was the point of maximum danger. If an enemy night fighter or missile battery locked on to us we wouldn't stand a chance.

We crouched, sweating in the gloom of the cabin, and suddenly the clicking turned to a continuous high-pitched whine.

'Lock on! Lock on!' came the cry from the flight deck.

'Shit! Shit! Shit!' the pilot screamed. Somewhere out there in the darkness an X-band fire control radar had fixed on our return signal. I could imagine the launch crews going through their countdown procedure. Within thirty seconds a SAM could be blasting towards us.

We felt the helicopter jink violently to starboard – the pilot was turning away from the signal, trying to put distance between us. There was a snapping of switches as the navigator engaged the ECM jammers. Please God, I prayed, let us be outside missile range. Seconds ticked by. Everyone was sweating as we waited for the radar operator to call out that a missile was tracking us. I lifted the edge of a blackout blind. The sky outside was pitch black. No sign of a missile. We were moving parallel with the coast. It was just possible the radar had mistaken us for an Argentine machine on patrol.

After another two or three minutes the pilot came on the air again. 'I can see flares!'

'What direction, for Christ's sake?' Andy shouted back.

'South, about five clicks . . . They're gone now. No, there's another. They know we're here. What d'you want to do?' He sounded close to panic.

Guy came back and spoke to Andy. Had the mission been compromised or not?

'We have to abort now, damn it!' the pilot was shouting. 'If the Argies reckon we're out here they'll scramble fighters to shoot us down.'

Andy told Guy, 'I reckon the pilot's shitting his pants at the thought of ditching in the sea.'

This was true, but I didn't blame the crew for wanting a way out from what would be almost certain death. If we aborted now they probably had just enough fuel to fly to neutral Chile, land the helicopter and turn themselves in.

'We've come this far,' Andy said. 'I'm not bottling out without taking a crack at the mission.'

The seconds were ticking by. We were eating into precious fuel. Guy was hesitating – in two minds over whether to abort or continue. If he delayed much longer we wouldn't have any choice.

Exasperated, Andy pushed past him to the hatch and swung himself up on to the flight deck. 'Listen, you gutless bastards,' we heard him shout. 'Get us back to the drop point. After that you can do what you like.'

We listened anxiously to the radar operator, but the signal to the south had faded out. There were no more flares. It must have been a nervous sentry on the base.

Andy crouched by the navigator, plotting a course to the landing point. We planned to set down near an isolated estancia three kilometres to the west of the air base. It was only a couple of minutes away, so everyone started getting their gear together.

'OK, this is it,' the pilot shouted into the headsets. 'Touch down in one minute. I'll give you exactly thirty seconds to get your gear out before I lift off again.'

SEVEN

It was 5.05am and still pitch dark as we settled in to land. The helicopter touched down in a cloud of dust. Taffy was first out, followed by Tom and then me. We spread out in a rapid circle around the aircraft, covering all the arcs, weapons at the ready. Taffy made a sweep with his night-vision goggles. 'All clear,' he announced. We were in the centre of a shallow bowl surrounded by steep hills. There appeared to be no trees, only tussock grass and some kind of prickly bush. There was a dusting of snow on the ground. After the aircraft it was bitterly cold. My nausea vanished as I filled my lungs with fresh air.

We began rapidly passing out the bergens while the Sea King sat there, motors running and rotors spinning, ready to lift off at a moment's notice. It was vital to get the helicopter unloaded and safely away before its presence was detected.

'Get a fucking move on, can't you?' Doug hissed at me as I fumbled a pack.

'Up yours,' I told him, heaving the 50lb bergen on to Taffy. After the anxieties of the trip it was a relief to have our feet on the ground and be active. The mission was on schedule and we were confident we could pull it off. Our map would guide us to the edge of the airbase. We would set ourselves up an OP and be ready to play our part when D Squadron hit the place in two or three days' time.

We were just removing the last of our kit when a blaze of light filled the sky to the east of us, the direction of the airbase. Another flare. Instantly we froze, expecting shots from the darkness. Had we walked into a trap? Was it the signal for an attack?

The Sea King pilot didn't hesitate a second. He yanked on the collective lever and pulled maximum power. The helicopter rocketed up into the air with the navigator clinging on to the open hatch. Doug, who was nearest, was knocked off his feet by the rotor wash. He jumped up swearing. 'Bloody gutless crabs!' Actually they were Navy aircrew but to Doug they were still fliers.

From the sound of the engines they were heading back westwards. They had decided to try to make for the Chilean border.

As officer, Guy had to make a quick decision. The helicopter was less than a mile away, still within radio range. Should he summon it back to evacuate us, aborting the mission? This was the last chance. Was he going to bug out for Chile or were we going to grit our teeth and stay? Not for the first time, I felt glad I wasn't an officer. Sometimes it calls for more courage to call a mission off than it does to stay.

Andy began arguing fiercely. 'These are raw troops,'

he was saying, punching his fist into his palm. 'Conscripts. They get jumpy at night and fire at shadows. They set off flares to chase away the dark, like frightened kids. They are no threat to us.'

Guy was unhappy. 'They picked us up on radar. They got a lock on for God's sake. They must be aware there was a helicopter out here. They've tracked it across the border on their screens, seen it land. They'll search until they find us.'

I was not so sure of that. The SAS were trained in concealment. We could go to ground like crabs in a whore's bush.

'If they do take us it'll blow the main operation wide open,' said Guy.

'Without us on the ground the assault would have to be aborted anyway,' Andy answered back. 'It would be suicide for them to go in blind. They know that.'

We peered into the darkness with the night-vision goggles. After the blasting noise we had all been subjected to in the helicopter it seemed astonishingly quiet. I was aware of the wind and the rustle of the grass. It was bitterly cold too.

If we had been spotted the patrols would be already setting out; there was no time to hang about, it was stay or go.

As if determined to make up our minds for us, another flare arched up, much closer this time, bathing the sky in a lurid glow.

It was enough for Guy. 'Doug, get on the radio. Contact the helicopter and have them return to pull us out.' To Andy he said, 'I'm sorry, it's no use. We have to abort.'

Doug whipped out the VHF band 320 radio with its V-shaped aerial and started transmitting. According to the mission plan the helicopter was supposed to remain on station for fifteen minutes after dropping us off, ready to return for extraction or repositioning if we should need it. Doug tried two different frequencies before turning back to Guy.

'Can't raise them on the comms!'

'Keep trying,' Guy told him. 'They may be shadowed by the hills.' If the helicopter was hugging the ground to avoid radar it might well be out of radio reach.

'Bloody Argies,' Taffy swore. 'Bloody Navy. Fuck the lot of them. All this way for nothing.'

All of us felt a bitter disappointment. The mission had failed before it had started. No one, though, questioned Guy's decision.

Doug flung the transmitter down. 'Fuck all!'

'Try the satcom,' Andy told him. 'Send the abort code. Say we need extraction and we've lost contact with the helicopter.'

'Maybe they'll change their minds and send in another Sea King to lift us out,' suggested Tom as Doug snapped shut the 320 set and unfurled the satcom dish. This transmitter was more risky because the satellite communications system made a bigger splash-out, and its transmission was easier to detect, but it was imperative that we let Hereford know as soon as possible that the mission had aborted. The coded message was recorded and sent in a high-speed burst. It took just seconds for a transmission to be made once a connection had been established.

Doug dispatched the message and got a bald acknowledgement back. It would take Hereford a few hours to figure out an extraction. The probability was that we would have to leg it for the border. In the meantime we had to operate on the assumption that the Argies had heard the helicopter land and were searching for us. That meant finding a safe hiding place to lie up until nightfall.

'Right,' Andy ordered. 'Shoulder packs and move out. Hard routine.' Hard routine meant no fires – so no hot food, nothing to eat or drink in fact but a mouthful of water from our canteens and some chocolate to keep us going.

Andy and Guy studied the map. The shortest route to the border was due west, but the country was mountainous and cut by rivers. We would do better to take the longer route across the pampas to the north.

'It's about forty miles,' Guy said. 'If we follow the line of the main coast road, travelling by night it should take us four days, a week at the outside.'

That didn't sound too bad. The road looked pretty straight on the map with only one village which we could bypass. Otherwise all we would have to watch out for were a few isolated estancias.

We set off in single file, Taffy leading. It was his job to scout out the route ahead and see we didn't walk blindly into a trap. It was almost 5.30 and still dark, so we had to use the night-vision scope. It was imperative that we find an isolated spot to hole up in before daylight. The country was flat and bare with thick spiky grass and shrubby trees and bushes, mostly bent double by the wind. There was no sign of human habitation or animal life except for the occasional bird that flew up as we neared. I walked with my rifle cocked and cradled in my arms, head moving from side to side as I swept the ground ahead. This was my first major mission in enemy territory and I was anxious to acquit myself well.

We had been trudging for about an hour when we reached the highway. It was a gravel road, unfenced but flat and straight, running almost due north. By chance – it seemed like a quiet road – the lights of a heavy truck came grinding down towards us but we lay flat in the grass and it went past in a cloud of dust without seeing us. Then we jogged across while Andy stood guard and dived into cover on the far side.

We were in open country now, a succession of shallow ridges covered with heather and tundra-like grasses. There were traces of snow about, but not enough to leave a trail. We tabbed on for another thirty minutes till Andy found a shallow depression on a rise from which we could watch the road about a thousand metres away. It was sheltered from the wind and there were some scrappy bushes to give cover. He examined the land on every side with care through binoculars before giving it the OK.

'This'll do,' he said finally, unslinging his pack. 'It

doesn't look like anyone comes here. Doug, you take the first watch with me. The rest of you into your bivvy bags. Snap to it.'

He wanted us under cover while there was still some darkness remaining. I shed my pack and pulled out my light camo net. I knew exactly where it was stowed. I could find any item of kit blindfold at night. Using my field knife, I worked a rough scrape big enough to take my body. It took some doing; the vegetation was incredibly tough. I spread out the net and plaited it with grass. Swiftly I pegged it down around the scrape and wriggled underneath with my rifle.

I pulled my bergen in after, working myself further in under the netting until everything was out of sight. It had taken me less than a minute and I would be completely invisible from the air. The others had done the same. On a flat grass plain an entire section of men had vanished into the ground.

Hidden under the net, I extracted my bivvy bag, crawled inside and zipped it up. Now I was warm and sheltered from the cold and wet. I could lie here all day if necessary.

Dawn came, creeping slowly over the flat landscape, revealing saw-toothed mountains to the south-west. Soon the first alarm came – a light plane passing overhead half a mile away to the south. It was flying low and we hoped it was a rancher's private aircraft. In this remote land, with few roads and some ranches extending over hundreds of thousands of acres, aircraft were essential vehicles. We watched it pass away in the direction of the border. The sun was over the horizon now, but obscured by dull cloud.

Moments later, Taffy reported vehicles approaching from the south-east at high speed.

'Firing positions!' Andy called. In seconds we were out of our hides, packs closed, our weapons cocked, crouching at the edge of the rise, ready to move out at the run.

The trucks drew level with our LUP and continued without pause, trailed by clouds of spiralling dust. We counted six four-tonners, ten to twelve men apiece, probably with a weapons platoon among them. Evidently the helicopter *had* been detected. Their job, if they didn't run down their quarry on the road, would be to set up a patrol line ahead of us. The main force would follow behind like beaters driving us on to the guns.

Most soldiers are unwilling to dismount from vehicles unless they have a positive sighting of the enemy. Our tactics would be to stay where we were and wait till nightfall. Then we would tab out and work our way around any roadblock. Only very experienced troops can handle night operations. What worried us was the aeroplane. The country we were in was featureless, a succession of shallow hills covered with long grass. It was easy to move across but it gave little cover. If we were to move an observer in an aircraft could spot us miles away, even at night.

Leaving Andy and Taffy on watch again, we crawled back inside our hides. After two hours Taffy would come back and one of us would take his place. Another two hours and it would be Andy's turn to rest. Before long it came on to sleet. The cold ate into my bones as I lay there unable to move. Through the holes in the camo netting I could periodically make out the plane in the distance. It was working back and forth along our track, flying north and south in long slow loops at an altitude of around 1000 feet. They were obviously searching for us and had guessed that we would be making for the border. I wasn't particularly worried at the thought – escape and evasion was a major part of our training. There was nothing we didn't know about hiding up or slipping past cordons. Come nightfall, I was confident, we would find a way through. The majority of Argy troops were barely trained conscripts; they'd be no match for our skills.

It seemed like an age before the sound of the plane's engine finally faded away to the west. Even then we didn't move – Andy wasn't taking any chances. The plane was still around and we were better off staying where we were for the present. It is the hardest thing in the world to lie still and wait. We could do it though; we could wait all day if necessary.

The sleet fell, but still we lay in our grass hides. My thoughts wandered about in a vain attempt to keep my mind off the cold and damp. Other fellows I know count to a million. Some claim to run blue movies in their heads. The day seemed endless, but Andy knew we were better off lying up like this than running around in the open.

It was late afternoon, and the winter sun was below the horizon when I heard Andy's voice calling us. I was so stiff my body could hardly move; every muscle in my limbs ached. I ripped off my canopy and struggled out, pulled on my pack and slung my rifle, ready for action. Without a word we formed up in open order and started moving again, as if nothing had happened.

Doug got the satcom set out and we made contact with Hereford again. This time there was a response: the abort was confirmed. There were no recriminations; they would come later at the debriefing. We were to tab out northwards as planned. The agent would rendezvous with us in a day or two at a spot to be arranged and lead us to an unguarded crossing. Nothing was said about a helicopter extraction.

We ate a bar of chocolate each and drank a little water, then Andy led us back down to the highway.

EIGHT

We were chilled, stiff and hungry, but it was a great relief to be out and moving about after the endless hours lying still. We marched rapidly, revelling in the open air. The wind was biting but the sleeting rain had eased off. Our boots crunched on the frosted ground. We walked like automatons, leaning forward to balance the weight of our packs, eyes constantly checking the sector that was ours to watch, covering each other's arcs. The secret of survival is to see the enemy before he sees you.

We walked parallel with the road, about twenty metres out. It gave us a useful navigational aid and we would have plenty of warning from the headlights of vehicles approaching. Andy was leading this time; he had the night-vision scope and the GPMG carried on a sling around his neck. We were ready to react to any threat. All it would take was one shout: 'Contact!'

As the night wore on we grew more confident. We were covering ground at a steady pace of between two and three kilometres per hour. Our only problem was with the compasses – they were designed for use in the northern hemisphere and were prone to erratic readings this far south. We had to keep stopping to identify features, which wasn't easy in an essentially flat land-scape, but night travel was something we had practised a lot and were good at. In this country with few obstacles it was relatively easy. Occasionally we struck patches of bog and marsh, but in general it was all good firm grass.

The downside was the weather, which was deteriorating again. Before very long it was sleeting a blizzard, an unremitting blast of freezing cold that must have come straight from the Antarctic ice cap. It sliced through our wet clothes. There was nothing to do but clear it out of your mind and carry on. I tried to empty my head of everything except putting the next foot on the ground in front of me. The Japanese have a saying, 'Step by step, walk the thousand-mile road.' I practised repeating it to myself over and over, slipping into a hypnotic rhythm as we tramped on and on across the pampas.

The sleet stung my eyes and my rifle weighed like lead in my arms. Of course Andy was carrying the gun, and I kept telling myself it was worse for him. The GPMG weighs over thirty pounds, three times the weight of my rifle. Andy always was a tough bastard, but I wasn't going to let myself be beaten by him. If he could keep going without complaining, so could I.

I thought about the girl on the ship again. The image of her naked under interrogation was burned into my mind. Then I reran the helicopter crash in the sea, replaying it in my head like an endless loop. The sensation of drowning, the moment I felt Nick's hand release my trapped foot.

Whenever truck lights showed up in the distance we flung ourselves flat until the headlight beams had passed. Vehicles were scarce, though; most drivers had the sense to keep off the road in the hours of darkness in winter.

Andy set a good pace. When his eyes tired he handed over scout position to another of us. We changed over every thirty minutes or so – any longer and our eyes became exhausted staring through the scope. There's no depth perception in the green-tinted field of view, which makes it hard to judge distance.

For hour after hour we stumbled along, bent double under the load of our huge bergens, picking our way by the dim shape of the man in front. Several times we encountered bridges but they were unguarded and we crossed them on the road, keeping in the tracks of vehicles to disguise our own. Occasionally we saw the lights of homesteads in the distance, but they were well back from the road and caused us no anxiety.

At around four o'clock, after about ten miles, Tom, the lead scout at the time, halted suddenly and held out his hand. We all stopped, crouching low, weapons ready.

Was it a patrol or what? Andy went forward to confer. After a minute he came back. 'It's a village,' he whispered. 'Half a dozen shacks beside a crossroads. We're practically on top of it.'

This was serious. We couldn't risk walking through for fear of arousing dogs. The only way round was to cut across country, making a wide circle.

'We'll double back a quarter of a mile and head west,'

Andy ordered. He took the lead and we set off. The
wind was in our faces now, and once we turned away
from the road the going became much harder. It was all
up and down, shallow rises followed by wide gullies that
were confusing and made it hard to keep a bearing.

I was walking behind Andy when I heard him curse.
At the same moment my right foot plunged through a
layer of ice into deep mud. We had walked into a half-
frozen swamp in the darkness. It was too deep to wade
through; there was nothing for it but to feel our way
around.

'Back and turn south,' Andy ordered.

We turned into the wind again, ducking our heads
against the driving sleet. 'Give me the Beacons any
time,' Taffy grunted.

'You've gone soft,' said Doug.

'Quiet, both of you!' snapped Andy.

We moved south a hundred yards before turning
cautiously west again. This time the going was firmer,
consisting of tussock grass, but slow to move over. After
about half an hour of this Andy judged it safe to head
north. We plodded on till at last we struck a smaller road
running east–west. This must lead to the village again, we
figured. We crossed over, trusting to the sleet to obliterate
our tracks before morning, and circled round to pick up
the highway again half a mile from the far side of the
village. The detour had taken us an hour and a half.

But it was a relief to be following the highway again.
'We'll crack on now,' Andy said and he set a pace of
around three kilometres per hour. It was gruelling going

with our heavy packs bouncing on our shoulders, but we kept our spirits up with the thought that we were covering ground to our destination. Traffic on the road seemed to have thinned out and we went for an hour at a time without having to duck for cover.

We kept going in this way throughout the night with just two fifteen-minute stops. By the time dawn finally broke we were tuckered out, but we had covered a good fifteen miles and were well satisfied. At this rate we would make the border in another two days, a good forty-eight hours less than Guy had originally estimated.

We found a place to lie up and made contact again with Hereford over the satellite set. Hereford gave us coordinates for a rendezvous with the agent. It was the site of a cave in a prominent rock formation at a crossroads some five miles short of the border.

Then we crawled into our bivvy bags and tried to sleep in spite of the cold. During the day there were more convoys of troops on the road passing in both directions, but no foot patrols, which was a relief. We heard the plane again: it seemed to be searching the ground in our rear still, so we judged we were moving ahead of any cordons.

The next twenty-four hours were a repeat of the first, lying up during daylight and marching through the night, the same wind howling across the unrelenting tundra. The march followed the previous pattern − a mix of following the road and detouring around unmarked hamlets, only there were more of these and it took us longer to cover the ground. By dawn we had covered another eleven miles and were more than half-way to the rendezvous point. The effort had left us drained, our feet were sore from pounding on the iron-hard ground, and we were tired and edgy as we prepared the lying-up point.

'One more slog should see us to the border,' said Guy. From now on though, he warned, we'd have to proceed carefully as it was likely that the border zone would be patrolled.

'Doug, you take first watch,' Andy ordered as we spread out our bivvies.

'Shit, how come it's always me has to stand first watch freezing my balls off?' Doug grumbled. 'Why doesn't Mark do a stint for a change – or are you going easy on him in this too?'

'He'll take his turn when the time comes along with the rest of us. Who he is doesn't matter a damn,' Andy responded.

'Oh yeah?' Doug sneered. 'So how come he's only been scout once all night? You know fucking well you always put him in the middle of the line where he can't get hurt. Fucking baby brother.'

Andy's face darkened. 'Shut the fuck up!' he snapped. 'If you're knackered, say so and someone else can stand first watch.'

It was just the way to needle Doug and his temper flared instantly. 'Don't come the tough guy with me. I'll fucking drop you any time!'

Guy intervened hastily. 'Knock it off, the pair of you. I'll take the first watch and leave it at that.'

Andy turned away and Doug subsided, growling. I climbed into my bivvy bag seething with anger. Not at Doug, because he had a point – I hadn't been given my fair share of scout duty. That was Andy's fault. He was up to his old trick, trying to protect me again. The others resented it, and so did I.

We had been down this road before. Though Andy had resisted me joining the army and tried his hardest to prevent me joining the SAS, he had been proud when I was finally badged. The real trouble began when we were sent to Northern Ireland.

I had done the NI course at Llangwern Army Training Area in Wales, where you'd spend four months learning the tradecraft necessary for undercover operations in the Province, including skills like lock-picking and covert photography as well as the surveillance and combat driving techniques, such as drills for approaching a hostile VCP, J-turns and ramming. We had received instruction on the operational structure of the Provisional IRA; we'd learned about booby traps, counter-sniping and urban area fighting. After that we'd exercised field scenarios, setting up OPs and ambushing terrorists. These would be followed by realistic debriefings, to the extent of mock court inquiries into how the terrorists had died.

On completing the LATA course I'd been assigned to Andy's troop. This was unusual, though not unheard of. There were other examples of brothers working together in the Regiment, but now I was fully operational Andy's attitude towards my protection became obsessive. I rapidly realised that he must have engineered my assignment so he was able to keep a close eye on me.

Our first major operation together involved an ambush. A surveillance aircraft had spotted two figures behaving suspiciously near a road in South Armagh – bandit country.

RUC and army intelligence suspected an attempt to place a roadside bomb in a stream culvert, a well-established PIRA tactic. If so, the terrorists would most likely return at nightfall to detonate it, taking out a passing patrol. We were ordered to check it out and apprehend the bombers before they could act.

The orders reached us at four in the afternoon. There was very little time for preparation. A couple of RUC liaison officers briefed us on a large-scale map. The Land Rovers of the patrol were due to pass the site around midnight, so it was likely the bombers would loiter in the area until they received the go signal from one of the dickers – part-time scouts – twenty minutes or so back along the route. They would then creep out to the firing position in time to trigger the ambush.

In order to bring the bombers on, it was necessary to have the patrol keep to its designated schedule. We couldn't let the regular unit take the risk so they were replaced with an SAS team in two armoured Land Rovers – in the dark the dickers wouldn't be able to tell the difference. Three pairs were detailed for the ambush: a hit team, consisting of Andy and an old hand named Lewis, whose job it would be to nail the bombers; and two back-up teams in case the bombers managed to evade their fire. I was detailed to ride one of the Land Rovers. The moment we heard over the radio that the trap had sprung we would debus to prevent the bombers escaping over the road. At the last minute, however, Andy ordered Lewis to swap roles with me, saying he wanted me to have experience on the killer group.

We moved in just as dusk was falling. A vehicle dropped us off two miles from the target point and we tabbed it across country by a route carefully designed to avoid detection. The land was all narrow fields intersected by thick hedges – ideal for ambush. It was another bitterly cold night with a freezing wind and bursts of drenching rain. We made a lying-up point about 500 yards from the stream, and Andy and I crawled forward on our bellies to reach the culvert.

Andy had a small torch with black tape over the lens, leaving just a tiny hole for the bulb to shine. The culvert was just wide enough to crawl through and running a foot deep with water. We approached it tensely. If there was a bomb and the IRA were watching they would detonate it without hesitation. Taking out a couple of SAS troops would be reckoned a big coup.

Andy stuck his head inside the mouth of the culvert, shining his torch carefully. PIRA bombs routinely contained anti-handling devices, some sensitive enough to be set off by a torch beam touching a light-sensitive cell. He emerged again and tapped my shoulder, indicating that I should take a look. I took the torch and squirmed carefully inside. The water was freezing cold and running so deep there was hardly any room to breathe. Working my way forward I suddenly saw the bomb and my heart rate leapt.

It looked enormous. Wedged across the culvert, slightly over to the far side, was what looked like a large metal pipe. PIRA bomb-makers generally favoured old steel milk churns as containers, but on this occasion they appeared to have gone to the trouble of welding up a section of wide steel tubing. This bomb looked as if it contained enough high explosive to rip open the roadway and hurl a Land Rover into the neighbouring field.

Bastards, I thought.

I tried to memorise a description of the container and its position to give to the technical people.

Squirming back outside again, I found Andy feeling around with his fingers at the mouth of the culvert, trying to locate the command wires. There would be a pair of these running out to a firing point two or three hundred yards away. The firing team would carry a battery pack with them. A touch of the bare ends of the wires to the terminals and *bang!*

It took Andy some time to locate the wires leading to the firing position, buried in the bed of the stream. The bombers had run the wire up the stream in a waterproof covering to keep it hidden from view. We now saw that the stream fed in through a rough pasture to a gap in a dilapidated stone wall at the far end, which was surmounted by a thick hedge. Standing in the hedge, the look-out would have a clear view of the patrol as it approached. And the bombers could duck down after detonation and run, out of sight behind the wall and out through a gate into another lane at the bottom of a neighbouring field.

Andy set out the ambush quickly. One team was placed to cover the gate and cut off the bombers' escape. The second pair he stationed out on the far wing, in case one of the players broke the other way. He and I took cover behind some tussocks some thirty metres back from the wall. The grass gave good cover without being obvious.

We worked our way as deep as we could into the ground, getting our heads well down. We were carrying Heckler & Koch G3 7.62mm assault rifles, as issued to the West German Bundeswehr. As a weapon it is a whole generation ahead of the standard SLR carried by the green army. It is deadly accurate and packs a heck of a punch, and unlike the SLR it can be fired on full automatic. There are few moving parts so stripping and maintenance are simple. We were using the LMG version with a bipod and a twenty-round box magazine.

Fixed to the top of my G3, where the telescopic sight would go, was a kite sight. About the size and shape of a pint glass, the kite sight was an image intensifier that magnified ambient light to show an image so distinct, it was like looking at a green TV screen. Through it, the gap in the wall showed up clear and sharp.

Having got ourselves comfortable, Andy and I settled down to wait. It was eight o'clock. The patrol wasn't due till midnight, so we guessed it would be at least a couple of hours before the players showed up. We couldn't be sure though, so it was essential to keep dead still and silent.

The night was very dark, rain fell intermittently and we were both wet through and frozen from playing in the stream. From time to time I flicked on my kite sight, checking the gap in the wall.

We each carried a radio with an earpiece and throat mike, plus a transmit button clipped to the smock. If it was dangerous to speak, Control could question us over the earpieces and we could reply in button clicks – one click for no, two for yes.

Andy bleeped his radio to alert the command vehicle a couple of miles down the road. Control responded immediately.

Two hours slid slowly by. Our guys would be in the Land Rovers by now, trundling through the darkness towards the culvert, knowing that if we buggered this up they could all be blown to pieces.

An hour later we were still lying in the grass. I was starting to worry. Had we got it wrong? Had the wires been a dummy, laid to deceive us, while the bombers sneaked into another firing position on the other side of the road? No, they wouldn't risk an attack knowing that the SAS were in the area. This had to be the firing point. Had we been spotted by a dicker on the way in? That was possible. Or a dicker might have clicked the command vehicle or one of our OPs further back, or spotted the QRF – the quick reaction force, a regular army team standing by to cordon off the area the moment the balloon goes up.

Operations like this were complex; a hundred things could go wrong.

Twice Control came on the air with information that someone had been seen moving in the area, but each time it was a false alarm. Then, at a quarter to midnight, the radio bleeped again. 'Alpha Charlie. Three patrol Charlies mobile, direction target.'

We stared into the darkness. Somewhere out there the three Land Rovers containing the patrol were moving down the road towards the culvert. No lights yet, but it wouldn't be long now. We waited, but still there was no sign of movement by the gap in the wall. By now we should have been hearing from our own observers covering the approaches to the target, warning us that the players were moving into position.

'Looks like this one went tits up on us,' Andy muttered.

If the bombers didn't show, we'd have to let the patrol pass and remain on station all night and through into the next on the off chance the bombers might return.

Suddenly I picked up the dim glow of sidelights on the road. I nudged Andy and he bleeped Control. 'Eyeball patrol Charlies.'

I switched on my kite sight again. It was trained directly on the gap, and everything immediately leapt into sharp focus. I was getting really worried now. If the players *were* there they could take out the Land Rovers in the next couple of minutes. I heard Control come over the air again, asking if we had any eyeball on the terrorists. Andy answered with a single click of his button. Negative.

The sidelights of the convoy were moving up the road. The lead vehicle was no more than five hundred yards from the culvert. Another thirty seconds and it would be on top of the bomb. Four hundred yards . . . three hundred . . . I checked the kite sight again – and suddenly my pulse hammered. Rising above the rim of the hole in the wall was the outline of a head. It was turned towards the road and as I looked another one came up to join it.

The terrorists *were* here. With a shock the appalling truth jolted home. We had expected the bombers to come up the same way we had, from the rear along the lane and through the gate. Instead they had crept along the bottom of the wall till they reached the gap and pulled the wires through to connect them up. They had no idea we were here, and any second now they would touch the contacts and blow our boys to hell.

I whacked Andy's arm and in the same moment snapped the safety on the G3 to auto. My sight was centred on the right-hand head. According to the rules of engagement I should shout a warning but there wasn't time for any of that crap. I let go with three short bursts. Almost at the same time Andy opened up beside me. Both heads dropped down out of sight. At the same instant a titanic explosion split the night.

They said afterwards that there had been more than

thirty pounds of Semtex inside the bomb. It erupted with a thunderclap of sound and a brilliant strobe of light that momentarily whitened out my kite sight.

Andy and I were already jumping up and sprinting for the wall, firing as we ran. There were flames burning on the roadway, lighting up the scene. I jumped through the gap in the hedge and landed on something soft. A man was lying curled up in the stream, unmoving. I spun right, my weapon up, searching for a target. There was no one else in sight. I heard Andy fire two quick bursts behind me and swung around in time to see a dark figure drop to the ground twenty yards along the hedge to the left. Andy fired another burst into the body to make sure, waited a few seconds, and then called in over the radio to confirm the killings.

I was staring at the culvert. The roadway was shattered from side to side. The bomb had dug out a crater twenty feet across. The lead Land Rover was halted a dozen yards from the lip. The occupants must have had the fright of their lives. The bombers must have been holding the wires over the terminals when we opened fire, the shock causing them to touch off the detonator. Another second and they would have taken the patrol with them. We had brought it off, but only just and at the risk of several lives.

No one in any of the vehicles was hurt, and we had killed two terrorists. The only casualty was the road surface. It was an excellent result for the team.

Andy subsequently received a medal. I told him I was applying for a transfer to a different squadron, and we had a stand-up row, one of many. Then Andy was posted on a course for a year – but at the time war broke out in the South Atlantic we were back together again.

And now the same problem was starting over. The fact was, Andy didn't trust me to take care of myself.

NINE

On the third night out from Rio Grande the weather was worse than ever. The sleet was blowing from the south so we had it at our backs and our bergens kept the worst of it out of our faces, but it was miserable walking even so. There were drainage ditches along the sides of the road in places. They seemed to have been dug quite at random and were effectively camouflaged by vegetation so as often as not the first warning we had was when someone fell into one.

At about midnight again, Taffy, who was scouting ahead, reported he was in a deep marsh. We couldn't find a way around and were forced to walk on the road. Each time we tried to strike off to the side we found ourselves sinking into mud again. This went on for four or five miles.

Eventually we came to an iron bridge spanning a wide river. 'Tom, take the scope and check it out,' Andy ordered as we hovered near the southern end.

Tom slipped away into the darkness. For a big man he was light on his feet. Ten minutes later he was back. 'The bridge is clear but there's a building at the far end. I could see a light in an upstairs window.'

'Any vehicles, military trucks?'

'I didn't see any but they could be parked out back.'

Andy took the scope and studied the river below. It was wide and fast flowing and it looked deep. There was no way it could be crossed except by the bridge. We took turns looking at the building. It was close to the far end – a two-storey construction with outbuildings. It looked like a farmhouse.

'Bet there's a fucking dog in there,' Taffy said.

'No takers,' I answered. Almost any place this remote would keep at least one guard dog. It would hear us go past and give tongue. Chances were the owners had already been warned to be on the look-out for a party of British soldiers. If they had a phone or a radio they could bring a search party down on our heels.

'If there is a dog it's downwind of us; it can probably smell us already,' Guy chipped in.

'So why isn't the fucker barking?' Doug wanted to know.

'We're not on its territory yet,' Taffy told him. Taffy had been a dog handler before he joined the Regiment. 'Step off on to the other side of the bridge and it'll be a different story.'

'So what do we do?' I asked Andy.

'We wait.'

'For what, a miracle?' said Doug. 'Piss this for a laugh. I'm sick of freezing my bollocks off.' He slapped the butt of his 203. 'I say we make a dash for it across the bridge, kick in the door and let 'em have it.' He was in earnest. Doug wasn't the kind of man to let a family of Argentine farmers stand between him and escape.

'These are civilians,' Taffy said.

'They're fucking Argies, man. They'll set the army on to us, you fucking puke.'

'We could tie them up,' I suggested. 'Cut the phone wires, smash the radio if they have one.'

'And suppose they have a gun?' Doug countered. 'This is the outback, not bloody England.'

'There could be soldiers in there for that matter,' I said.

Andy was peering through the night scope again. 'I can't see if there's a barrier or not.'

A pole barrier to halt traffic would be a certain indicator of a military control post. And this would be an ideal place on a wide river with no other crossing point for miles.

'It's too risky,' Andy said. 'We'll have to swim it.'

I had been afraid he would say that – but he was right, there was no other way.

'Fuck it!' Doug spat. 'Fucking weather, fucking country, fucking Argies. Fuck the lot of them.'

We moved off the bridge and tabbed along the riverbank till we found a bend out of sight and earshot. The banks were firm here where the water had drained out, but the river was flowing fast. It was about twenty metres across and the edges were encrusted with ice. We checked the far bank with the night scope in case the Argies had a patrol out, but it was deserted.

'Right, everyone strip off,' Andy ordered.

We peeled off our clothes, bagged them and stuffed them in our bergens, taking off our socks but replacing our boots in case we had to leg it suddenly. We put our waterproof outer jacket and pants back on to cover our white skins against being seen. It kept the wind out some – not much, but some. Then we tied the bergens together to make a raft.

'Wrap them in the ponchos first,' Andy said. 'It makes more buoyancy and keeps them drier. Taff, see if you can find some bits of wood and grass to stuff in to help.'

Shivering, we tied the weapons on to the raft and carried it down to the water's edge. The ice splintered under our boots. The river was flowing fast underneath. The raft floated well with plenty of air trapped inside the bergens and the ponchos. Andy had chosen a point where the bend in the river meant the current should carry us across to the far side. There were no rocks that we could make out to impede our swim. With one hand on the raft each, we pushed off.

God, it was cold! The freezing water crushed my chest in an iron vice, squeezing the air out from my lungs. I was scared I was going to have a heart attack. It was so cold I couldn't breathe. Desperately I kicked out as hard as I could, clutching on to the poncho for dear life and paddling with my free hand. I had done this before a couple of times in Germany and in Norway on exercise, but never in water so fast-moving and cold. I could feel the current rushing us along at a terrific speed. If it didn't sweep us against the far shore we would be done for. Waves, dark and heavy, were breaking over our heads. No way could we survive this cold for more than a few minutes. I thought of the helicopter again. This was worse. My whole body was completely numb. It was all I could do to keep my legs moving. If I stopped I knew I'd freeze up and drown.

We seemed to have been in the water for ever and still I couldn't see the far bank. I couldn't see anything at all except tossing black waves smashing against me in the darkness. I felt a sudden panic. How long had we been in the river? I pictured ourselves being carried past our landing point and swept downstream under the bridge.

Just when I was beginning to think we couldn't survive much longer in this freezing water, I felt the motion of the raft alter. Tom, in front of me, had ceased to splash with his free arm and was plunging forward with great lunging movements. All at once I felt firm ground under my boots. Mud and stones. We were nearing the far side. Relief coursed through me. My chest was still in agony, my breath coming in painful gasps, but at least we were making it across. Still kicking and paddling frantically we pushed on, even as the current towed us sideways. Another minute or two and we were able to stand up to our waists, dragging at the raft. The wind shrieked at our wet waterproofs as we struggled to pull the heavy bergens up out of the water.

'Guy, take a weapon. Go up and clear the bank,' Andy ordered. Guy untied a 203 from the pile on top of the raft and clambered up the bank.

'All clear,' he called back after a few seconds. 'There's a hollow up here with shelter.'

Slipping and stumbling in the biting wind, we dragged the raft of bergens clear. The bank this side was steep and we had a hell of a job getting it up, till Tom hauled himself out of the water and, wedging his legs in the mud, jerked it out as if performing a snatch with weights in the gym. My hands were too numb to untie the knots that bound the packs together, but I had looped my fighting knife around my neck and I used it to cut the cords. Swiftly we sorted out our kit and tore open the bags with our dry gear. It was vital to get ourselves sorted out quickly and be ready to face the enemy.

My pack had remained almost completely dry, thank God. I shook out my waterproofs and the water spun off them. Just standing in the bitter wind dried us off fast. It was a huge relief to pull on our clothes again. We doubled on the spot, working our arms to restore the circulation. As soon as we were ready Andy called Guy back to change too.

'Chocolate each,' he said.

I gulped down a whole bar to give me warmth and energy. I don't think I've ever been so cold. Then we helped each other on with our bergens, took up our weapons and started back for the road. We walked fast, burning energy to put warmth back into our bodies. Within a few minutes we were feeling human again.

'Jesus, I hope we don't have any more of those,' Taffy grunted.

'You've gone soft,' Doug taunted him. 'Remember in Norway when we had to swim that lake?'

'Aye, but that was still water. That last bugger was like Niagara fucking Falls.'

We tabbed on for the next five hours taking only a single break of fifteen minutes, and by five o'clock reckoned we were within a couple of miles of the crossroads where the cave was. We found a shallow depression that was sheltered from the worst of the wind. We daren't risk a fire but we had some more chocolate and a drink of water. We were all tired but the knowledge that we were nearing the end of our long march raised everyone's mood. Even Taffy and Doug were reluctantly cheerful. We had made it this far without being detected, and were confident that if necessary we would find the border on our own somehow.

Doug set up the satcom to report back to the UK. We told Hereford we were close to the rendezvous point now. If the agent wasn't there to meet us we would strike out for the border on our own. Andy reckoned it was only a matter of time before the Argentines picked up our trail, so to remain any longer in the border zone – which was bound to be heavily patrolled – was inviting capture.

We finished our hasty meal and broke camp half an hour later. As always we took care to erase all traces of our presence. The longer it took the enemy to find our trail the more lead we would have. There was not the slightest doubt they would be searching for us again at first light.

The wind was fierce still, blowing fine snow, but that suited us. The snow would be in the enemies' eyes and the driving flakes would screen our approach as well as muffling any sound. Even better, the steady fall would rapidly cover our tracks, making us harder to spot from the air.

We tabbed off, setting a good pace. Visibility was lousy, but the grass was more or less flat. The map showed a river running parallel to us about five miles distant, intersecting the border at right angles. The probability was that if the Argies were in the area they would use that to anchor the right flank of a cordon. If I were their commander I would throw out a light screen to act as a trip-wire, with the main body of troops held back in reserve. Orders would be given for the first section to make contact and pin us down while radioing for reinforcements. With plenty of trucks available, they could quickly rush up additional men and weapons to encircle us. We could also expect assault by helicopter-borne infantry. That was why it was important to take advantage of the poor weather.

The enemy didn't hold all the cards, though. Distances in this remote land were huge. There were few roads or towns, and it would take an army to seal the border properly. Trucks were slow across country and the weather would affect the soldiers' morale. The temptation to stay in cover out of the wind would be strong. We were experienced and heavily armed, whereas they would have a high proportion of ill-trained conscripts who had probably never been under fire before. So the screen would be thinly held and composed of low-grade troops. With luck, and our concealment skills, we should be able to slip through the gaps into friendly territory.

We were following a compass heading to the San Sebastian crossroads. Sheltering in the cave there was too fucking good to think about. The snow blew against my forage cap and seeped up my wrists. The heavy pack made it hard to look up. In this sort of work, you got used to walking with your neck cricked. The rifle felt heavy again, but I told myself we had only four more hours to go to the border, and I concentrated on walking in the footsteps of the man in front. Walking and waiting, waiting and walking, that's what soldiering is about.

We had trudged for a good hour in silence, and somewhere above the snow and wind the night was ebbing from the sky. Objects were becoming faintly visible and it made the going that much easier. Snow still blew about, and on the ground was a couple of inches deep. Any deeper and it would slow us down, but it would hide us all the same. Our tracks filled as fast as we made them, and the snow stuck to our backs and shoulders making us hard to spot. Only the wind was constant. I tried to decide whether this was worse than some of the exercises I had been on in Scotland and the Beacons. Not a lot in it, probably.

Andy was carrying the GPMG again. Earlier he had swapped with Taffy, taking the Welshman's 203 to give himself a change. The 203 is a development of the M16,

the standard American assault rifle designed by the
legendary Eugene Stoner to take the 5.56 Fireball
cartridge, and produced by Colt. The M16 was in use in
all branches of the American services, and with its high-
velocity bullet is effective at most combat ranges. The
SAS like it because it is three pounds lighter than the
SLR, and weight counts on special operations. In the
early days there were concerns that the rifle lacked
power; the impact of the smaller bullet was significantly
less than the SLR's formidable 7.62 slug. However, the
Fireball made up for this by its tendency to tumble on
impact, causing massive wounds with severe shock
effect. When linked to the 40mm grenade launcher it
made a truly formidable weapon.

I wondered if the main mission was still on. Probably
not. It was hard to imagine how two Hercules could
make an approach unseen when we had failed using a
single helicopter. Certainly the Argentines appeared to
be on their guard. Their response to our arrival had
been swift. An SAS assault force could expect to take
severe casualties, particularly without us on the ground
to prepare the way for them. We all felt badly about this,
but it looked as though the critics were right – the
mission was too risky.

The snow was beginning to ease up when Andy
called a halt to check the map. We had tabbed for two
hours without a break, and reckoned we were now
close to the crossroads. From here on in we could
expect to encounter enemy forces. We would have to
travel slowly, keeping a careful lookout, and be

prepared to detour around them. This was the usual SAS practice. Only rarely do special forces units attempt to fight their way through enemy lines. In any prolonged engagement, the enemy can call up reinforcements to swamp our superior training.

We had hardly got the map unfolded though when Tom, who had been detailed to stand watch, called out that he had a contact. An Argentine patrol a dozen strong was heading towards us, about two hundred yards off.

The situation was critical. The snow had stopped falling and our tracks would be visible. The best course was probably to stay where we were, huddle down into the snow and hope to escape detection. If that failed, we would have no choice but to take them out.

TEN

I crawled up the slope with my rifle at the ready. If it came to a firefight it would be my job to take out the radioman, followed by the officer and the man carrying the light machine-gun. Without communications, leadership or firepower a small unit will rapidly lose cohesion and break up in retreat. The best thing would be to try to take them from behind and make them flee westwards, leaving the road to the border clear for us.

Andy moved quickly to the flank with the GPMG, ready to enfilade the enemy line. Other members of the squad tossed down the ammunition belts they were carrying in a heap nearby in case they were needed. Guy was Andy's Number Two. A machine-gun always has two men, one to fire and the other to feed the belt and to spot. The rest of the team were readying their 203s. In the event we were detected, the response would be a shattering burst of fire that would cut down every member of the opposing squad before they had time to react.

For several long minutes we watched the patrol moving across the pampas. I counted twelve of them in a straggling line all looking towards their front and chattering among themselves with no proper discipline at all. As they neared, they bore away to the right till it was evident they would pass us by a good hundred yards. It appeared as though they were patrolling more or less at random in the hope of picking up our tracks. We had had a lucky escape.

We waited until they were out of sight before moving on again. As soon as we could, we picked up their line of march and followed it, back tracking in their footsteps. As well as disguising our trail, this would steer us clear of any mines that might have been laid across our path.

We travelled in single file. Andy couldn't take point himself because he was carrying the gun. So he put Taffy out front, with Doug at Number Two. We walked cautiously, knowing that enemy troops were close by. My weapon didn't feel heavy at all now, just reassuringly deadly. My eyes moved constantly, searching the ground away to my right. We were still in grassland, passing through the remains of a small wood, its low trees bent almost double by the relentless Patagonian wind.

All at once there was a burst of firing ahead and Taffy threw himself on his face. Instantly I leapt several paces to my right, dropping to one knee, rifle at the ready, searching for a target. We had made a contact. All the other members of the team were fanning out left and right into an arrowhead formation, ten yards between us each, that brought the maximum firepower to bear ahead. Taffy cracked off a grenade round from his 203 and followed it up with a magazine from the rifle. Tom was firing too. I stood up to see over the rise, searching for a target. Taffy turned and came doubling back, his pack bobbing up and down. The others were firing to cover his withdrawal. I saw a helmet moving among the grass a hundred yards beyond him and ripped off two shots in quick succession. The helmet dropped back. 'A hit,' I thought dispassionately. I was too pumped up with adrenalin to exult or regret.

Doug and Tom were doubling back now, the rest of us giving covering fire to protect their retreat. The arrowhead was reforming itself as a line abreast, still firing at any enemy that presented itself. I saw Doug curve his arm back in a throwing motion and smoke burst in front of him as a white phosphorous grenade exploded, obscuring the scene. We began dropping back in threes, sprinting five metres and falling to one knee to cover the others. I loosed off a couple more rounds, reloaded, turned and doubled past them to the rear. My bergen thumped on my shoulders; running with 120lbs of kit was a strain. I made fifteen metres, turned to face the front again and dropped to one knee. At the same time the other half of the section came running past me again. I could hear the hammer of the GPMG as Andy blazed away. We were dropping back in three-metre bounds, firing and dropping back again. Shots whistled overhead but the firing was wild. Nothing came near us.

We kept it up for about 500 metres till our lungs were bursting with the effort. At last though the firing died away. The enemy had had enough and broken contact. 'Break right!' Andy called and we reformed, tabbing off at ninety degrees towards the west in single file again.

Andy called a momentary halt to check there were no injuries. Everyone called out his ammunition state and injuries. Luckily no one had been hurt. That done, we set off immediately at a fast pace. 'They'll all be after us now,' Taffy grunted. It was vital to put as much distance as possible between ourselves and the enemy. My back ached from the weight of my pack. I'd have given anything to be able to ditch it but in this weather nobody survives long without a sleeping bag and warm clothing.

When we had made about a mile, Andy called a change of direction and we cut off back towards the crossroads again. Then Guy passed the word that we had run into a platoon-sized formation. 'Twelve to fourteen men with FN Brownings. Most probably local conscripts.' We tabbed on for another mile at a fast pace across the featureless landscape, hoping to throw off any pursuit. Then Andy called a respite and broke out the satcom dish again. It was vital we reported the contact. A weak sun was showing through the overcast behind us. Doug sent a burst message reporting contact with the enemy; there wasn't time to listen for a reply. There was nothing that Hereford could do for us right now anyway. It was a simple question of tabbing on and trying to work our way around any enemy formations in our path.

Andy came down the line checking everyone's packs,

seeing how we were off for ammunition. 'You OK?' he asked me.

'Why wouldn't I be?' I said. I told him I had fired four rounds and dropped at least one of the opposition . . . I thought, but there wasn't time to be positive. He seemed pleased. Other members of the team had scored too. The reckoning was three or four enemy dead. After a blooding like that they would think twice before engaging us again.

I was thinking I'd been lucky to get out of that alive, because those rounds had been coming in bloody close. This was my first proper battlefield engagement, and I reckoned I had acquitted myself well. The same went for Doug. We were now both fully paid-up members of the Regiment.

'Just as well you were here,' Andy said. It was as near as he could get to an apology.

I didn't say anything, and he passed on down the line.

'Thanks,' I called out after him. Andy didn't hear, and I didn't repeat it. Afterwards I wished I had.

We headed due west. The country here became very flat. About half a mile off we made out a low ridge. That would be where the cave was. We walked over stony ground, covered with loose gravel and lumps of jagged flint. Spiky grasses and low thorn were the only vegetation and there were occasional deep patches where snow had been piled up by the wind. From what they had told us at the pre-mission briefing this was an indication we were in the immediate area of the border.

It was easier walking and we made good time, but the lack of cover was worrying.

We reached the crossroads – two gravel tracks in the wilderness running away into the distance. There was no sign of anyone. The rock outcrop was about a quarter of a mile off, with the cave at one end.

We covered the last stretch in just fifteen minutes. Doug was on point, but at the cave entrance he drew up sharp and made a gagging sound. Sheep carcases were dumped all over the cave floor. They must have gone in there for shelter and died of starvation or cold. The stink was disgusting, so we moved back on to the plain to wait in the fresh air.

Then we heard the sound of the plane again.

'Take cover!' I heard Andy shout. Sod this, I thought wearily as I pulled out my camo net again. The ground was hard as iron. On this barren plain I figured we'd stick out like turds on an ice rink. The plane was flying due south, following the line of the border. We were that close. Just as we were thinking it had passed over and missed us we heard a change in the engine note. 'Bastard's seen us and he's coming back,' Taffy growled. I squirmed into the ground and tried to lie as flat as possible. It's a horrible feeling being hunted from the air. There's no escape from the all-seeing eye.

The plane was circling round, picking up speed. Guy was close by me. I heard him calling to Andy, discussing what to do. They agreed it was no use sticking where we were while the plane vectored ground units on to us. Now we had been spotted our best chance lay in making a break for the border and to hell with cover.

We jumped up and pulled on our packs. We could see the plane swooping towards us in a shallow dive. 'Shit, he's going to strafe us!' I shouted, unslinging my rifle. There wasn't a prayer of bringing down an aircraft with a single-shot weapon, but the gesture would make me feel better.

Tom, our Stinger man, was crouched on the ground with the tube to his shoulder. I could see the plane clearly now. It was a twin-engine Pucara ground attack equipped with air-to-surface rockets. A salvo of those landing among us could wipe out half the unit. The pilot was readying up for his attack. He must have reckoned us for a soft target, I thought. He'd let us have it with the rockets and bombs, then come back for a second pass to finish us off with his guns. With luck he hadn't realised we had a missile launcher.

The other guys were readying their weapons like me. Aircraft had in the past been destroyed by small-arms fire, but it was a remote chance. They say the only way is to wait till the plane is overhead and then fire directly upwards.

I saw Tom press the eyepiece of the missile launcher to his face and heard the whine of the generator as he switched on the battery and lined the target up on the graticules. The missile's maximum altitude was around 3000 feet, and it performed better against an approaching target. We all waited as the plane grew larger, urging

Tom silently to hurry up and press the tit. He was carrying three rockets with him but at this rate there wouldn't be time for a second shot.

Everything happened very quickly.

The pilot must have seen the plume from the launcher as Tom let fly, because he jerked the plane's nose up in a frantic scramble for height. He must have triggered his rockets automatically at the same instant, because the front of the plane was suddenly obscured by a burst of smoke. It was just as well for us he did pull up, because the salvo screamed over our heads as we threw ourselves to the ground, and exploded yards behind us, showering us all with rocks and dirt. I was smothered in a cloud of dust and gravel and for a moment I thought the plane had crashed on us. By the time we picked ourselves up we could see it staggering away towards the south-east, flying very low and trailing smoke from the port engine. The Stinger's proximity fuse had exploded the warhead right under the wing, peppering the fuselage and nacelle with shrapnel fragments.

'Got the fucker!' Tom was shouting exultantly. There was no time to waste, though. This plane would have sent out a distress message including our position, and the enemy would be massing for an attack. The patrol we had surprised earlier must still be in the vicinity, and now they would know where we were. And there would be others, some of them ahead of us. It was vital to get moving.

Andy gave the order to ditch our bergens. There was

no way we could cover the terrain fast enough with all that weight on our backs. If we reached the border we could find shelter in the nearest town.

The ground was too hard to bury them so we chucked them into the cave, as far back as we could, reckoning no Argie would be mad enough to hunt through the decomposing sheep. With only our weapons and the satcom unit we set off at a rapid pace.

It was such a relief to have shed the weight that I felt light-hearted as we jogged on across the plain. The stony desert gave way to grass again which was easier and the light powdering of snow crunched under our feet. Overhead, the sky was dark with the threat of further falls to come.

We reached a small river which we forded at a narrow spot without difficulty, though the water was waist-deep and freezing cold like before. The ever-present wind played on our backs as we hiked up the slope on the other side. In the far distance was a line of jagged mountain peaks. If our map was correct we were very close now.

Reaching the top of the slope, we saw the line of the road less than a mile away. A civilian truck was moving slowly along it towards the west. The first sign of normal life we had seen all day.

The ground beyond the river was steeper, bisected by small streams and, where there was shelter from the wind, clumps of trees and shrubs. In spring or summer it would have been attractive. As it was, we at least had some cover for a change. Andy was still carrying his

GPMG and he took point position to lead the way on this final stretch. He was trying to keep the road in sight as a guide.

We came to a fair-sized lake, fringed with marsh and rushes, and tabbed round it till we encountered a gravel track leading in the general direction we wanted to go. There were signs of sheep here and a few birds, but no other wildlife. The whole land was eerily quiet save for the occasional hum of a vehicle on the road. We paused a moment to catch our breath. After a minute I looked back and saw something moving along the gully we had just come from. Signing to Doug to cover me, I dropped back to take a closer look.

Whatever it was moved very cautiously, keeping in the rushes. I squatted under a bush, the L42 at the ready. If there was any doubt I would shoot first and no questions. The shape edged closer. It was a figure in camouflage carrying a long weapon. Too close for comfort. If I took out this one, his buddies would slow down a while. I raised the rifle and centred the cross hairs. Fifty metres, an easy shot.

My finger was tightening on the trigger when he moved out from behind some grass. In the circle of the sight I saw he was wearing civvies under his camo jacket. Shit, I thought. Now what?

'Hey, you!' I called out. 'Halt!'

He spun around, the hunting rifle in his hands training towards me – a tall, sunburnt man, bearded, with harsh, gaunt features, what I could see of them. His face was taut with suspicion. For a moment I actually had the impression he was about to fire, then he lowered the barrel.

'*Tienne una habitacion?*' he called out in Spanish. 'Have you a room?'

With a shock I realised this must be the agent sent to meet us. I tried to make my brain work. There was supposed to be a response to the codeword recognition system but for the life of me I couldn't recall it.

He must have understood my confusion because he added, 'SAS? My name is Seb.'

'Jesus,' I whispered, 'I almost shot you.'

Slowly, he relaxed and stood up. He was a big man, dressed like a hunter, and swarthy, his wrists and the backs of his hands matted with dark hair. He looked like someone who spent much of his life outdoors, a man who could take care of himself. His expression was closed and hard. A loner, I thought.

'I did not see you properly for a moment,' he confessed, lowering the rifle and coming over to join me. 'I thought you were an Argentine soldier. I'm sorry I couldn't reach the rendezvous; the roads were crawling with soldiers. I managed to work my way round and pick up your trail.'

Doug moved up to join us. 'Welcome, friend,' he said drily. 'We missed you at the rendezvous.' Doug mistrusted spooks.

Seb shook his head as if he had no time for pleasantries. 'The Argentines know you shot down a plane. There's a patrol right behind me. Fifteen men with a light mortar.'

ELEVEN

Seb didn't need to say more. A platoon of men with a mortar could sit out of range of our weapons and blow us to pieces. Then they could pick off the survivors at will. The three of us scrambled back to the others. We had two options: to lay an ambush and take them out or to quicken our pace and try to lose them. Ambush would've been the preferred option, but with the possibility of other patrols in the vicinity it was too risky. We could delay them a bit, though. Tom and Taffy, our demolitions experts, rigged up a couple of grenades on trip-wires across the path – it took them no more than a minute – then we moved out at a run.

We jogged on in single file, Taffy leading this time, Seb following to give directions and myself bringing up the rear. I had been worried about whether he could keep up but Seb ran easily. He wore hiking boots and carried a hunter's light knapsack. He steered us unhesitatingly through a confusing tangle of small intersecting valleys. It was a relief to feel we were in safe hands. We splashed across a small river that chattered over its rocky bed, and Seb paused to check out the country beyond.

We had come out on to open ground again. In front of us stretched undulating ridges of pampas with tall grasses waving in the wind. Silently Seb pointed to a line of fence posts marching across the horizon half a mile off.

'The border?' Guy asked after a moment.

Seb nodded.

'Is it guarded?'

He shook his head. 'Not here. Further up where the road crosses the frontier there is a customs post.'

I turned around to scan back the way we had come with the scope sight on my rifle. It looked as though we had shaken off the pursuit. Then abruptly I spied a cautious movement among the trees along the stream, about 500 metres off, long gunshot range. 'Andy,' I called softly, 'that patrol is moving along our trail. They'll be up with us in the next ten minutes.'

'Do not shoot,' Seb whispered. 'If you do they will claim hot pursuit and follow you across the border into Chile.'

'Will they respect the frontier line otherwise, do you think?' Guy asked.

'They have instructions not to cross unless fired upon,' Seb answered soberly. 'If you six will go straight on over now, I will try to delay the patrol.'

'How will you do that on your own?' Andy wanted to know.

'I will tell them that I saw your party, numbering twelve or fifteen men, heavily armed, heading north-west towards the border,' he said simply. 'These are conscripts, not regular troops. They will not hurry to catch you up if they think you are so many.'

We looked at the border, half a mile off, and back in the direction of the pursuing enemy. 'You sure you wouldn't rather come with us?' Guy asked him. 'You're taking a risk going back.'

'I know what I am doing, trust me,' Seb told him. He shook hands briefly with the six of us. 'Now go quickly,' he said. 'Five hundred metres beyond the fence posts you will come to a track leading south-west. Follow that for two miles and you reach a village. There you can get transport to San Sebastian.'

With a quick wave of the hand he strode away into the bush, vanishing rapidly among the trees. I felt an obscure sense of loss at his going, this stranger who had risked his life to help us and was now putting himself on the line for us again.

'Come on,' Andy said. 'Let's do as the man said.'

We tabbed forward at a rapid pace, bending low to keep from being spotted. Luckily the tall grass provided plenty of cover. It took us only ten minutes to reach the fence. There was no wire, just a line of weathered posts set at twenty-yard intervals running straight across the pampas and disappearing into the distance. As we passed through I felt a huge sense of achievement. We had made it. The mission had been a failure, but that was not our fault. We had tramped forty miles across enemy territory in wartime, evading capture for four days. We had fought a successful contact engagement and shot down an enemy aircraft sent to strafe us. Truly I had been blooded in combat.

A few hundred yards on, we came across the track Seb had described. Andy ordered a halt to get the satcom out. The rest of us stood guard while Doug checked in with Hereford, letting them know of our safe arrival on Chilean territory. It led in the right direction and we followed it cautiously in single file, still keeping our eyes peeled and our weapons at the ready. Any soldiers we ran into now would probably be Chilean and friendly but even so we were careful. I thought about Seb and wondered how he was doing. He was a brave man.

We had covered about a quarter of a mile when I heard a sudden shout from Tom in the lead, followed by a burst of machine-gun fire from a low ridge ahead. My heart leapt into my mouth. Shit. Seb was wrong – the Argies weren't respecting the frontier. They had guessed our route and laid a trap for us on Chilean soil. We had run straight into a well-laid ambush.

There was no hesitation now and no question of breaking contact or withdrawing. With another patrol on our heels our only chance was to fight our way through. The unit went into action as smoothly as a machine. The GPMG team moved out fifteen metres to the flanks and opened a storm of covering fire. Tom and Doug were hurling smoke and firing grenades from their 203s, laying down an accurate barrage upon the enemy who were shooting back from the small ridge to our front. Taffy and I moved up at the run, opening up with our own weapons, leap-frogging our buddies, while the machine-gun kept the enemy's heads down as we advanced. Five metres on and we flung ourselves down to take up firing positions from which to cover the next wave as they came running through. More smoke was thrown, and 40mm grenade rounds thudded against the enemy line as the machine-gun hammered away.

Everything was happening by the book. We were working by standard operating procedures just as we had been trained, and it gave me a degree of confidence.

The firing was very heavy though, zipping over our heads and cutting up the turf around us. Some of those rounds were coming from behind and I thought, shit, those bastards in the other patrol we saw are moving up to take us from the rear. We were in a bad situation, outnumbered more than three to one and pinned down with enemy forces preparing to surround us.

The shooting grew more intense still. Through the gunfire I could hear orders being yelled. They must think they had got us cold. Andy was still rattling away with the GPMG, firing back at the enemy machine-gun. I saw Guy swing round, assessing the situation rapidly. We were in a bad spot; it was urgent that we break out somehow before the enemy overwhelmed us with sheer numbers.

Guy came to a decision and jumped up. 'Come on!' he shouted. 'We've got to push through. Follow me!' And leaving Andy with the GPMG, he grabbed his 203 and charged ahead straight for the ridge, yelling at full pitch.

For fuck's sake, no! I thought, but I knew Guy was right. We were pinned down and it was crucial that we somehow gain momentum, otherwise we were knackered. It took a brave man to show that kind of leadership.

'He's doing it, follow him!' I shouted to the others, springing to my feet and running after him. Tom and Doug had jumped up too and were tearing forward. I triggered my grenade launcher, saw a round go arching into the rolling smoke, and heard the crash of the explosion. Taffy was with us now and we were all firing as we ran.

Tracer from the GPMG swept the ridge like a storm. I saw Guy turn for a moment to urge the rest of us on. In the same instant a bullet hit him. It spun him round like a toy and he pitched on to his side on the ground at the foot of the ridge. 'Man down!' I shouted and sprinted over. Guy was lying hunched up with his knees against his chest. The front of his camo jacket was soaked with blood. There was so much of it everywhere it was impossible to see where he had been hit. His eyes were dull with pain and terror. I snatched the field dressing pack from his harness. At first I thought it was a chest wound, then I saw the huge hole in his throat. Snipers are trained to go for a throat shot and with good reason. There's almost no way to stem the blood flow. I grabbed the sides of the wound, attempting to hold them together while warm blood spurted through my fingers. 'Taffy!' I shouted. 'Man down, for Christ's sake!'

Doug and Tom took up positions a couple of metres in front of us, putting down sustained fire from their weapons. Taffy doubled over. He and I grabbed Guy by his harness and dragged him into the shelter of a nearby hollow. Doug and Tom moved across, continuing to cover us. Taffy ripped open the dressing pack and stuffed a big cotton wool pad into the wound. It turned red instantly and went sloppy to the touch. Guy's carotid artery was ripped to fragments. The blood was emptying out of him in a flood we couldn't stop. His breathing had stopped and his eyes had rolled up. He was in shock, dying in front of us. The gush of blood ceased as the internal pressure fell and the heart ran ragged for a few seconds, then seized.

'Fluids!' I screamed to Taffy. 'Get fluids into him.'

Taffy was fumbling with the plasma bottle filled with colourless, coagulable liquid that will bulk out the remaining blood in the veins and keep the heart beating. You insert it through a vein with a catheter. We had practiced this dozens of times on the first aid course. Seal off a wound and replace the fluids and the victim will survive till he gets to hospital – that's what they taught us. Except that Guy's wound was too huge to seal, and all the plasma in the unit wouldn't replace the blood he had lost.

But I couldn't get my head around that. I kept shouting at Taffy to set up the plasma tube.

'Mark,' Taffy yelled at me. 'Mark, for God's sake. It's no use. He's gone.'

'Fuck you!' I shouted. 'Just try!'

A rocket came whizzing overhead and smashed into the ground close to us, bursting in an explosion of fiery fragments. More shooting erupted. The second enemy patrol must have been closing on us. Seb must have failed in his effort to head them off. We were caught between two pincers.

The GPMG fell silent suddenly. That couldn't be a stoppage too – the gunner must be hit. Shit, that was Andy's gun!

The attack was faltering. With Guy down and our heavy firepower out, the enemy to the front had a chance to regroup. Another anti-tank rocket came whizzing over, and the blast knocked me sideways away from Guy's dead body. Grenade fragments zipped and pinged off the ground around me. I picked myself up. Blood was welling from cuts on my hands. There was no time to think about Guy or Andy. Up on the ridge, twenty metres away, the enemy machine-gun chattered from a sandbagged emplacement. At all costs we had to regain the momentum. Andy wasn't here; it was up to me to give a lead now. The vital thing was to take out the GPMG that was pinning us down so we could break through the enemy line between us and freedom.

'Smoke!' I yelled. 'Now let's get the bastards!' I dumped my rifle and grabbed Guy's 203. It would be more use in this kind of battle. A phosphorous grenade exploded just below the ridge. Another followed and the smoke blew back into the machine-gunner's eyes. I loosed off bursts in his direction, crawling across the two dozen yards of dead ground below the ridge, zigzagging to throw off the gunner's aim. Taffy, Doug and Tom, the only others left on their feet, were crawling after me, covering me with bursts from their weapons. We had momentum going again now.

Smoke and fumes tore at my lungs and eyes. All I could see was the flame from the gun, stabbing out through the belching whiteness. I reached the ridge and flung myself flat. Taking an HE grenade from my pouch, I pulled out the pin and posted it over the sandbags into the emplacement. I saw the handle fly off and a second later came the hollow boom of the explosion. The machine-gun stuttered to a halt and someone close by began screaming loudly.

Before the smoke from the blast had time to clear, I jumped over the sandbags into the gun position. I landed on something soft though there was no time to see what. I squeezed off half the mag to my left, swung around and squirted another burst to the right-hand side. The weapon let out three or four rounds then jammed. Shit!

The enemy machine-gun lay abandoned, a dead man slumped over it. Amid the smoke dim forms were clambering out of the hollow, running away. A burst of automatic fire sprayed overhead and I ducked down hurriedly. There was another gun lying at my feet – an FN with a bayonet fixed. The Argies were using the same weapons as our regular guys. I snatched it up and tried to fire it. Empty. 'Fuck!' I shouted.

Panicking and still holding the FN, I scrambled my way to the rear of the dip. It was piled with junk, weapons, ammunition boxes and a couple of bodies. Another shot whined past me, and then I saw the solitary Argentine, a terrified young conscript. He was shaking with fear so much that he could hardly hold the gun. I had no ammunition. The only thing for it was to go for him with the bayonet.

They teach you this kind of fighting at training school but no one takes it seriously. No one imagines they are going to have to stab somebody in the belly with a pike – which is what it amounts to – in a modern war. You go through the motions, running up to the stuffed figure and jabbing at it, competing to see who can scream the loudest. Afterwards everyone has a good laugh.

It's different in real life. For a start this guy wasn't standing up ready to receive the point of the bayonet in his belly the way all armies practise. He was squatting curled up on a level with my knees with his back against the rear of the trench. He held a loaded FN in his hand and if I stopped for long enough to let him get his wits about him he would blow me away with a single burst at point-blank range.

So, springing towards him, I whacked him in the chest with the point. The boy screamed and writhed. I pulled it out and stabbed him again. Still he wriggled and cried. I was sweating and cursing. He slid forward and the next thrust struck him in the head. The point of the bayonet went into his cheek and he shrieked, a high-pitched squeal like a pig. But he still kept a hold of the rifle. I couldn't work out what had gone wrong. According to the training he should now be dead. I pulled the bayonet out again and gave it another go. This time I stabbed him in the shoulder, just nicking him. Now he seemed to find the trigger of his weapon, and he let off a burst that sliced through the sleeve of my coat. I jabbed at him again with all my strength; he flinched away as he saw me coming, and the point went into his ear. It sank deep horribly easily with a crunching sound. I pulled it out again and torrents of blood squirted from the wound. It ran over his tunic and legs, soaking them. The boy gave a convulsive shudder and went floppy as if his strings had been cut. The gun fell from his grasp and slithered down into the crimson pool at the bottom of the trench.

I stared down at his torn and bloodied face. Both the other kills I had made had been clean. I hadn't even been close to the victims. But this was butchery.

The rest of the team were charging past me, blazing away at the fleeing Argentines who had no fight left in them now the trench had been taken. All they wanted to do was get back across the border to safety. A few shots were still coming our way from the platoon behind us. I ran back to the machine-gun and pushed aside the gunner I had killed. It was a 7.62 American M60, a reliable weapon we often trained with. There was half a belt still left in the feed and more ammo in a box nearby. I recocked and started spraying the ground behind us with short bursts. The Argies on that side weren't using their mortar; I guessed they couldn't for fear of hitting their own people.

The others came running back. Doug was holding his

left arm. He had stopped a round in the last minute of the action, but he could still fight.

When the belt on the machine-gun ran out, I dug another out from the box and fed it in.

Soon the firing from the other side diminished and stopped. The Argies there were falling back too.

And then I remembered Andy. I had been so caught up in the momentum of battle I had forgotten all about him.

I left the gun and scrambled back down the ridge into the long grass. Taffy and Tom were clustered around the GPMG, and I could tell from the way they were moving that it was bad. They had a poncho stretcher out and were rolling someone into it. No one was holding a plasma drip or working on his breathing, and the figure on the stretcher was inert – a dead person, a battle casualty. I knew it instantly. And Andy was nowhere to be seen. It had to be him.

As I came running down, Taffy stopped me. 'Mark, I'm sorry. We did everything we could. It was a head shot. He never had a chance.'

Tom was kneeling by the body, arranging a camo net over Andy's face. Another sniper round, I thought sickeningly. It must have hit him in the back of the head and taken off half his face. They didn't want me to see.

I knelt and took one of Andy's hands in mine. It was all I could do. The tears were streaming down my face and I couldn't find words. He had tried hard to keep me safe. We had rowed about it, because I couldn't get my head around the fact that to him I was always the little brother. Now he was gone.

Tom stood up. He had picked up the GPMG and slung it around his neck. 'We can't stay out here,' he said grimly. 'The Argies may regroup.'

I slung my rifle and took one side of Andy's poncho. I was damned if I was going to leave him here. Taffy was fixing a dressing on Doug's arm.

Together we started to carry Andy out. There weren't enough of us to carry Guy as well. We would have to leave him where he lay and come back for him.

On the way up the ridge we passed the hollow where I had killed the boy. I felt cold and drained of all feeling.

We saw nothing else of the enemy. We reached the village, and two hours later found ourselves in a small Chilean town. Hereford had been to work and the military attaché from the British embassy was waiting for us with transport. He took charge of everything and saw to the recovery of Guy's body.

I slept most of the next day, which was just as well. Then I tried to find out if Seb had got away or been caught, but they don't tell you things like that.

The Chileans were decent. They kept the press off us. The Argies imposed a complete blackout on news of the battle in their media too. I guess they were embarrassed that a bunch of half a dozen SAS on foot could fight their way fifty miles across the country and not be stopped.

After two days' rest we were flown up to Santiago and repatriated to the UK on a civilian flight.

Andy's and Guy's bodies were brought back for burial with military honours. I stood with Jemma and Andy's two little girls at the funeral, and the experience was almost as bad as seeing him dead.

The projected SAS assault on Rio Grande never went ahead. Argentine air attacks continued, and by the end of the fighting hardly a single British ship of the task force remained undamaged. The Argentine navy and air force lost over a hundred aircraft.

TWELVE

The news broadcast from London was short and to the point: 'The political situation in Argentina has deteriorated further in recent days, and the danger of a takeover by nationalist elements in the armed forces grows. However, any threat to the Falkland Islands has been discounted.'

There were no medals for the Rio Grande mission, not for the living nor the dead. It seemed that Whitehall and Buenos Aires both wanted it buried. The only memorial was a painting that a war artist completed privately for the Regiment of the 'Battle of the Border', as it was known. The picture now hangs in the mess at Hereford. It shows the charge on the ridge held by the enemy with Guy, the lieutenant, being hit. Andy is still alive at that moment, visible firing his machine gun. It's a picture I like a lot because it represents my last memory of him. He went down fighting, which is how he would have wanted it.

I spent the next two decades in the Regiment. I fought terrorists in Ireland and drug lords in Colombia. There were wars in Iraq and Afghanistan and clandestine operations that I still can't talk about in other parts of the world. I married and divorced, saw my nieces, Andy's girls, grow up into fine young women.

It was twenty years before I returned to the South Atlantic.

This time I was thirty-nine, and a senior NCO with the mountain troop of D Squadron. There was an SAS exercise planned that included a night landing on South Georgia, and it was my troop that had been picked. We flew into Mount Pleasant, the big new airbase outside Port Stanley, on an RAF Hercules from Ascension Island. Ascension is near the equator, and the twelve-hour flight to the Falklands was only possible with midair refuelling. We had a special forces crew, and the flight was part of their training package.

There were six of us making the trip. Major Jock Duggan, the Rupert commanding the expedition, was one of those small men who take on any challenge for the heck of it. He was a passionate outdoorsman and explorer, who had climbed Everest and trekked across the southern ice cap. Like me, he was approaching forty and had pretty much reached the end of the line as far as special operations were concerned. The two of us had been planning the South Georgia trip for a year. It was to be a last great yomp, a final test, measuring ourselves against the very worst that nature could throw at us.

South Georgia is a dependency of the Falkland Islands, separated from Stanley by 800 miles of hostile ocean. A bleak, glacier-encrusted island, riven with steep fjords, it resembles Antarctica more than South America. In 1982, an SAS patrol had been dispatched to

South Georgia to expel a group of Argentines who had established a base on the island at the outset of the Falklands War. Set down high on the Fortuna glacier in atrocious weather, the advance party had struggled to drag their equipment through a nightmare landscape of savage crevasses, beset by continuous whiteouts and wind strengths exceeding 100 knots. After five hours, in which they progressed just 500 metres, a decision was taken to withdraw the patrol – a rare case of the SAS admitting defeat. Two helicopters sent in to recover the patrol crashed on the glacier, and it was only heroic flying by the pilot of a third that completed the rescue. Since then South Georgia has come to be regarded as the ultimate test in human endurance.

With us in the party was Juan Dimitrikov, an American on secondment from the US Delta Force. A great, smiling bear of a man, Juan had been a close friend of mine ever since we fought together on a mission against the drug lords in Central America. Juan had trained extensively in Greenland and the Canadian Shield and was an expert in Arctic medicine. We counted ourselves fortunate to have him along.

The rest of the six-man team consisted of Nobby Clark, a cockney always ready with a joke or a bit of crack; my troop sergeant Kiwi Dave, from New Zealand, who stood six foot six in his socks, and was immensely strong and reliable; and Josh Brown, son of my old friend Nick, who'd died in the helicopter crash in the Falklands. Josh was now a twenty-something trooper who had only recently passed selection into the

Regiment. I had chosen him for the trip at his own request. Although there had never been any proof, I was certain that his father had saved my life in the crash during the war, and I wanted to do what I could to further the boy's career. He was a bright lad, already qualified in Spanish, and would probably make officer before very long. All together we made good mates and a well-balanced team.

'Christ Almighty!' Nobby exclaimed as we clambered out of the aircraft, dizzy from the ear-shattering noise of the trip. It was his first visit here. 'Where is everybody?'

I saw what he meant. Mount Pleasant was enormous – and empty. There were only a handful of aircraft stationed here: four Tornados, about the same number of helicopters and a couple of VC10 tankers. The vast runway looked as if it was built to handle an armada of aircraft – as indeed it was. In an emergency the revetments and hangars would accommodate scores of fighters and strike planes flown out from England, and the runway would take the heavy transporters flying in reinforcements for the garrison.

A couple of RAF trucks trundled out to pick us up. We unloaded our bergens and Lacon boxes full of weapons and ammunition and other equipment from the plane, checked all the items off on the manifest to make sure nothing was missing, and slung them in the back of the truck for the trip up to the barracks.

It was strange to be back again among the low, treeless hills and the settlements with their tin roofs. Ironically the Argentine invasion of twenty years before had sparked off an economic boom in the islands. Cruise liners disgorged 40,000 tourists a year on shore excursions to Stanley. Now, alongside the timber and corrugated-iron cottages, there were expanding suburbs of new semi-detached homes for contract workers. But the streets were still full of Land Rovers and the weather remained the same: ceaseless, freezing wind and a dusting of snow on the heather and gorse.

The emptiness of the islands this time round came as a shock. When I had been here last, San Carlos Water was filled with shipping and 3000 men had been camping out on Sussex Mountains. Now there were many civilians but hardly any military to be seen. The current garrison for the islands consisted of a reinforced company from the Royal Green Jackets and a token force from the RAF regiment guarding the airfield – a total of no more than 500 men and women, of whom 150 were combat troops.

Our schedule called for us to spend a couple of weeks getting acclimatised to the South Atlantic winter before setting off for South Georgia. Major Jock and I immediately instituted a punishing regime of route marches and cliff-climbing exercises. In the evenings, apart from watching videos of films we had seen before, there wasn't a whole lot to do except party. A submarine was paying a visit to Port Stanley – HMS *Superb*, one of the big hunter-killer nukes – and we took to joining up with her crew.

'Jesus, Mark,' Juan said after our first night in the mess, during which we had witnessed a submariner take in a gallon of beer via a stirrup pump. 'Your sailors are something else.'

'I guess when you've spent three months underwater in a steel tube you have just two things on your mind,' I agreed, 'to get pissed and to shag everything that moves.'

All the different service messes were part of the same complex. We were bunking with the Green Jackets in the army section, which was joined to the RAF and naval messes by miles of internal corridors. The barracks were designed to hold several thousand in the event of some future conflict, and covered an acre – with the effect that it was easy to become lost. Late-night muggings were not uncommon, and we were warned not to walk the passages alone after dark. This of course was an affront to the manhood of any SAS trooper, and when we were bored we would roam the uninhabited regions in the hope of starting a fight. The only excitement we had, though, was when two MPs jumped on Dave, our giant New Zealander, mistaking him for a sneak thief, and they landed up in the base hospital with a fractured skull apiece.

There was television beamed out from England via satellite, and we avidly watched the world news. In Argentina the left-wing government in power had run into difficulties: a nationalisation programme that had seized heavy industry and large farms had failed to stimulate the economy. A slump had turned into a recession, complete with mass layoffs and queues at soup kitchens. Bank defaults were adding to the chaos. As always in South America, extremist factions were exploiting the situation and right- and left-wing groups were battling one another in the streets. On the screen we saw pictures of tanks defending government buildings against stone-throwing crowds.

One night after we had been on the Falklands for about a week, I went down to the sergeant's mess. Jock was in there because he'd got bored drinking with his fellow officers. It was a submariner's birthday, and his buddies were mixing champagne and Guinness in a bucket and passing it round. There were a few women, too – sergeant signallers who seemed to be having a ball with so much male attention.

One of the girls was a blonde, my height, with a ponytail and a pert little body. Her name was Jenny and she looked about twenty-four. She wore dark ski pants and a pale embroidered sweater that showed off her figure. She kept darting me little sideways glances and tossing her hair about.

Jock noticed. 'You're in there.'

'She must go for older blokes.'

She was talking to a couple of matelots I knew, so I wandered over to join them and introduced myself. 'Hi, I'm Mark from Hereford.'

'Jenny,' she grinned, holding out a hand. Her accent puzzled me – was it laced with London estuary? I was surprised when she told me she was an islander and had been here during the war.

'I don't remember much. I was only four at the time. We were living at San Carlos. Planes and loud bangs and lots of soldiers. My mum saw it all. She helped arrest an Argentine spy.'

Her words jolted me. 'A spy?'

She grinned. It was obviously one of her party pieces. 'A woman spy. Off the container ship *Northland*.'

'The *Northland*. That was one that was bombed.' I had sudden images of the gaping deck, flames pouring up. And the naked girl below.

She must have spotted my look of recognition because she nodded. 'The spy was on board when it happened. They caught her but then the ship was hit and she ran up on deck and jumped into a lifeboat.'

'What happened to her?'

'She got ashore. Our house was in San Carlos settlement, close to the beach. Mum saw someone sneaking into a shed and thought it was a squaddy on the scrounge. She went to look, found this girl hiding under a trailer and handed her over to the soldiers, who took her away.'

'Who was she?'

'Some Argentine who'd stowed away on the ship in England. One of our lads found her down in the hold with a radio transmitter and pulled her out.'

It was strange hearing myself talked about like a character from history. Which in a sense I was. It made me feel old. I wondered what the girl would look like now. Would I recognise her if we met again?

We talked a bit more. I asked Jenny what made her join the forces. Was it the war?

She shook her head. 'Only way of getting out of this

fucking hole – except now they've sent me back again.'

I couldn't resist changing the subject back. 'What did your mother think about her, about the spy?'

Jenny glanced at me as if I'd said something stupid. 'Said she was guiding in the planes that bombed our ships. A lot of lads got killed that night. Why? Does it turn you on – a female spy?'

'I was on the *Northland* too.'

She was drinking rum and coke. I bought her another at the bar and a pint for myself with a whisky chaser. 'You're wasting your time with Jenny,' one of the submariners at the bar told me. 'Strictly officers only.' Jock caught my eye and winked. I wanted to talk to the girl some more but the racket of the drinking games in the mess made it hard to hold a conversation.

'You married?' she asked. I thought the enquiry hadn't come out quite as casually as she would've liked.

'Divorced,' I said, trying not to smile.

'Same here.'

She didn't look old enough, but the services are like that. Relationships are hard to keep together. Your mates are the only constant.

'So, did you come with anyone?' If there was going to be a fight, I'd like to know who with.

She jerked her head towards one of the other girls, who was holding her sides laughing at something a matelot was saying into her neck. 'My friend's dating one of the *Superb* lads. We came over for the party.'

'I'm only here a few days.'

'I know. You're one of the SAS troop. I've been sending signals about you people all day.'

An hour later I was on my sixth pint. She had been keeping pace. The bar was filling up and the atmosphere was growing more boisterous. A bunch of lads had got up an impromptu game of indoor rugby at one end of the room – grunts versus matelots and crabs. Juan was leading one of the teams. The air was blue with smoke and a raucous crowd was egging on the players to greater excess.

'I sleep somewhere round here,' I told her. 'But if I drink any more I won't be able to find my way back.'

'I'd better come along in case you get lost,' she said. 'You know it's not safe to walk the corridors alone at night.' It was the first time she'd shown a hint of humour. She was slow to come round, and I liked that.

The cubicle I had been assigned had posters on the wall left by some other occupant and exuded the temporary feel of barracks blocks the world over. Jenny tied a T-shirt round the lamp to soften the light as we undressed each other slowly. Beneath her bra her breasts were small and high and delicate, and she shivered when I touched them. I thought of how the girl aboard the *Northland* had shivered from the cold twenty years before.

This one was a good girl though, warm and soft with a throaty chuckle that escaped when she was aroused, which made me laugh. We made love slowly at first, then with increasing urgency.

After the second time we fell asleep in each other's

arms. When I woke it was seven in the morning and still dark. She was gathering her clothes quietly.

'I'll walk you back to your quarters,' I said.

'I'll be quite safe. It's only men who get attacked round here.' She leaned down to kiss me. 'By the way,' she said, 'her name was Concha.'

'Who are you talking about?'

'The spy. The one you caught on the *Northland*. Mum told me they found out her name. Don't ask me how. It was Concha. That means shell in Spanish.'

I shook myself fully awake. 'How did you know?'

She chuckled again. 'I told you, I've been reading all the signals about you.'

And she was gone.

I lay awake for some time thinking about Jenny's words and about the girl on the boat. Now I had a name for her, the spy seemed real again.

But when I finally fell asleep it wasn't her I dreamed about. Or Andy. It was the face of the man I'd bayoneted in the Battle of the Border.

THIRTEEN

'No need to ask if you scored last night,' Juan said next morning in the mess as I downed a hearty breakfast.

I grinned. To pull a girl in Stanley, especially a sharp looker like Jenny, was a real achievement. No wonder the submariners were looking pissed off at me.

'How did your game end?' I asked Juan in turn.

He let out a deep American rumble of laughter. 'Boy, you missed a show there. It was a gas. One of the guys decided to break up the scrum by diving in off the piano – only he missed, hit the floor and fractured his collar bone. He just gulped a glass of scotch and kept on playing.'

'So did you win?'

'Well, I was the only guy still standing upright at the end.'

Easy to see why everyone liked Juan.

I felt a hand fall on my shoulder and looked up. It was Major Jock. He looked serious. 'We need to talk, Mark,' he said.

I followed him to the secure briefing room set aside for our use. It had a high-security lock on the door, and when there were no SAS on station the key was kept in the custody of the garrison commander. There was a military policeman on guard outside. He stood aside to let us in

Inside I saw Nobby seated at the desk, pencilling in the decode of a message that had just come in over the secure fax machine. The message was headed 'SAS EYES ONLY' in big letters. I noted the reaction on Nobby's face as he scanned the text. 'Read this, boss.' He thrust the flimsy paper at Jock.

Jock studied the message. I saw his jaw tighten and he flung it over to me without a word.

'They're cancelling the exercise?' I said in dismay.

'Read on,' Jock said.

I scanned the message. With immediate effect the exercise was cancelled. We were ordered to draw up a plan to land our party on the Argentine coast in the vicinity of Rio Grande and secretly reconnoitre the airbase there to discover what preparations the Argentine military were undertaking.

'Jesus,' I muttered. 'They're not serious. Do they think there's going to be a war?'

Jock shrugged and sighed. 'What you and I think isn't important. Mutual mistrust is all it takes to start a war.'

'The Argentines wouldn't be such fools, surely?'

'Whitehall doesn't want to take chances. How d'you feel about going back?' Jock was familiar with my past, including the expedition that had resulted in my brother's death.

It was my turn to shrug. In this job you do what

you're told. 'I never even got to see the base. Let's hope the Argies won't be so alert this time.'

Our minds were racing ahead, thinking and planning. We had on the boat all the kit necessary for a prolonged recon op. Weapons we could obtain from the stores here. There was enough material in the depot to fight an all-out war.

'Maps,' I said. 'We need maps and decent satellite photographs before we start to plan properly.'

Jock agreed. 'I already thought of that. Complete sets of the latest intelligence data and mapping software is being flown out by fast jet tonight.' His eyes were glinting with excitement now. This was a last chance of action for the pair of us. I was feeling the same way.

I asked Jock how close he thought *Superb* would drop us in. She was a hunter-killer submarine rather than one of the huge fleet ballistic missile Trident class, but she was still 4500 tons displacement, the same as a Type 22 frigate; the Navy wouldn't want to risk her close inshore.

Jock reckoned we'd have to count on at least three miles' ride in by Gemini inflatables. 'If the Argentine navy detects a British submarine that close to the coast, they'll do their best to sink it,' he said.

There was a silence in the cabin as we speculated on the possible consequences of the destruction of a British nuclear sub at the hands of the Argentines. The hard-liners would have their war then.

'This is crazy,' I said. '*Superb* has Tomahawk missiles. Why doesn't she lie off out of range and blast the airfield to hell?'

'Because they can't risk doing that until they know for sure the bombers are going to be used. We supply the proof. It's that simple.'

'Shit. They can't be serious?'

'They're deadly serious,' Jock said. 'Apparently the Firm believes a military coup is imminent in Buenos Aires. They want us over there to watch the base. *Superb* will take us in, and we'll do the job.'

'When?' I asked.

We drove down to the harbour together to discuss the details of the insertion with the submarine's skipper. It was snowing again outside – it snows for eight months of the year down in the Falklands. HMS *Superb* was moored against the mole. Submarines look black and sinister out of the water, nuclear subs especially so. There is something evil about the way their deadly weapons are all concealed. There was around 200 feet of her hull length showing above the water, with probably half as much again beneath, and her conning tower stood up from the middle like a two-storey block.

The quayside was empty. A grizzled chief petty officer and a rating with an SA80 combat rifle stood guard at the foot of the gangway. The CPO checked our warrant cards and went back below to confirm that we were allowed aboard. The rating stayed on the gangway with the rifle across his chest. The Navy doesn't take any chances with its subs.

Finally the CPO came back with the officer of the

watch to conduct us inside. We entered through a hatch at the base of the conning tower – what Juan would call the sail – and down a ladder to the main deck. The big nukes are huge inside, with multiple decks and crews of a hundred and more.

The commander was waiting for us in the operations centre. He was a short, fit man with hard grey eyes, and his manner was brisk. Commanders of nuclear subs are God Almighty on their boats, and with good reason. He couldn't talk openly in front of me, because operational details about the boat could only be revealed to an officer, so I waited outside his cabin while he told Jock who would tell me later. Jock had no inhibitions where rank was concerned.

The gist of his report, when he came out, was that the skipper was deeply unhappy about the prospect of risking his precious submarine anywhere near a foreign coast. It would take a direct order to make him do so, and even then ten miles was as close as he could go. Jock and I tried to imagine doing ten miles of open sea in a Gemini.

Jock was more worried about getting out again. The usual procedure would be to hide the boats so we could use them to ride out and rendezvous with the sub again. We would fix a spot with GPS and pass on our co-ordinates for the RV. If the Navy thought that too risky, an alternative was to have them send a helicopter in through Chile to exfiltrate us. 'Otherwise, in an emergency,' he told me, 'we can hijack a truck and drive like hell for the border.'

I chewed my lip. I had had experience of trying to make that border against opposition.

Back at the barracks, Jock called a full briefing for the whole team. Juan, Josh, Nobby and Kiwi Dave gathered round the table with us. The other four were as surprised as I had been, but equally eager to go for it. Juan was especially keen to play his part in a genuine SAS mission. There was a brief discussion of the deteriorating political situation in Argentina. 'What it comes down to,' Jock said finally, 'is that the militarists among the Argentines are on top again, and the bastards are crazy enough to start something.'

Jock and I took an inventory of the weapons and equipment we had brought with us, trying to figure out what else we needed to take. We had all our winter warfare kit as well as stores to keep us supplied for a fortnight and our own satcom set. For personal weapons most of us carried the C-5, the Canadian built version of the 203 'over-and-under' 5.56mm assault rifle with a 40mm grenade launcher attachment. It's a well-made system, light but extremely robust. As a sniper, my own weapon was now the Accuracy International rifle, firing a 7.62mm cartridge. This was a superb weapon capable of achieving a first-round hit at over 600 metres, and a big improvement on the old L42 of two decades before. What we lacked, though, was ammunition and the heavier weapons – GPMGs and anti-armour and anti-aircraft missiles.

'We'll have to break into the war stocks,' Jock said.

The garrison on the islands maintained huge amounts of equipment, including arms and ammunition for use in case of hostilities. In the event of a threatened invasion all they needed to do was fly in the bodies – the guys would pick up their kit at Stanley and be ready to fight. The SAS maintains war stocks of weapons and equipment at strategic locations around the world. The Falklands is one of these points. These stocks are held separately from the general armouries and can only be accessed by the SAS as needed.

We piled into the Land Rover they had given us and drove over to the armoury compound. Jock saw the quartermaster-sergeant on duty and obtained from him the key to our war stock building. We followed the QMS through the gate to the inner compound. The truck drove down long lines of warehouse sheds and dome-shaped magazines. There were hangars full of vehicles, ACVs and light tanks, trucks and jeeps, artillery pieces and missile launchers. It was eerie to see all this equipment needing the soldiers to man it, waiting for a war that might just come again.

Finally we drove through into a separate fenced-off area, with its own armoury shed and low-roofed ammunition bunker. We dismounted, and Jock unfastened the lock.

Inside, I switched on the lights and whistled. A real treasure house. There was enough weaponry to outfit a couple of squadrons for any conceivable mission. There were racks of the superb American 81mm mortar, LAW anti-armour missiles and 7.62 calibre GPMGs.

Row upon row of C-5s and Heckler & Koch G3 assault rifles along with MP5s, the sub-machine-gun version. The regular stores would be full of the standard SA80 rifle as issued to the average grunt and useless from day one. It couldn't be fired by left-handers, of which there are any number in the military. In tough conditions – and of course most combat takes place in less than ideal conditions – the SA80 was prone to jamming. The army had spent a fortune trying to rectify its faults, without success. In my view it would have been cheaper to ditch the lot and re-equip the entire force with C-5s. The civil servants in the MOD and Treasury don't understand that the rifle is a soldier's single most important item. If it's no good, he has no faith in the rest of his kit.

'Hurry up!' Jock said. 'No time for gawping.'

Quickly we started helping ourselves to what we needed. Big Kiwi Dave chose his favourite weapon, the GPMG, for firepower support. This was the same weapon we had carried in Argentina twenty years before, still used by the British army, as well as by the Israeli forces and a host of other countries, including Argentina itself. Extremely sturdy, it can stand rough treatment in the field and will work for long periods without maintenance.

I was looking for belt ammunition and 40mm grenade rounds for our C-5s. Jock wanted explosive charges in case we were called upon to destroy the bombers in their revetments. Juan selected an American LAW launcher to deal with any Argentine armour we might come up against, and I took a couple of Starstreak anti-air missiles, remembering how we had defended ourselves against air attack the last time.

The Starstreak is a hyper-velocity missile carrying three dart-like projectiles specifically designed to combat high-performance, low-flying aircraft and helicopters. Each dart has a chemical and kinetic energy penetrating shell, and the missile has a single-shot-to-kill probability in excess of 95 per cent.

We were like kids in a toyshop, all picking out the bits of kit we fancied. Josh turned up a Spyglass thermal imaging sight. It had a nifty laser rangefinder which would be useful for plotting the layout of the base from a hide.

'Fucking hell, look at this!' Nobby Clark was chuckling over a 51mm light mortar, a platoon-level indirect-fire weapon that could be carried and fired by one man and could lob a 1kg bomb almost a kilometre. It had a useful short-range insert that enabled it to be used in close-quarter battle situations with accuracy. 'With a couple of these buggers we could take out every bastard bomber on the base if it comes to a war.'

'Yeah – well let's hope it doesn't,' I said.

The QMS stood by, looking amazed as we fetched out brand new flak jackets, medical packs, wire cutters and third-generation night sights costing £5000 a pop. We also needed survival suits for the boat ride. We scribbled them all down on the requisition sheet and Jock signed it happily.

In the afternoon I took the team on a run to blow the

cobwebs away. Nothing too punishing, just a twelve-mile trot up the hills and back to get the blood circulating. There was no point anyone breaking an ankle at this stage. Afterwards I had a shower and was catching a few minutes' kip in preparation for a reunion with Jenny in the bar later, when there came a tap at the door. It was Jock. Juan was with him. The looks on their faces told me something was wrong.

I let them inside and Juan sat heavily on the bed. All the bounce was gone out of him. Wordlessly Jock handed me another signal flimsy. It was short and to the point. Attached Master Sergeant (US), Juan Dimitrikov was ordered to return to the UK by first available transport. His replacement was flying out tonight.

'The bastards!' I exclaimed furiously. 'They can't do this to us. Juan is all trained up. It'll hammer the troop's morale!'

'Easy, Mark,' Jock said.

But I wouldn't give up. 'It's crazy. Juan is a Spanish speaker. He can pass for an Argentine. It makes no sense at all.'

'Josh has Spanish too.'

'Josh can get by, but no one would take him for a South American. Juan here is fucking bilingual.'

Jock didn't answer. He felt the same way, I knew, but the decision had been made back in England. We could say all we liked and it wouldn't do any good. That's what was making me so mad.

'You can't blame them,' Jock said when I had calmed down. 'This operation is near enough the edge as it is.

If we get taken and it comes out there's an American involved, the shit will really fly.'

'I could exchange IDs with one of your squaddies,' Juan suggested hopefully. 'Then no one would know.'

But we were pissing in the wind and he knew it. Jock tried to soften the blow. 'There's no one in the Regiment we'd rather take with us than you, Juan. I want you to know that. You'll be a real loss to the team.'

Juan screwed up his face. He was an emotional guy. More than any of us he had been looking forward to taking part in a piece of real action after all the training. It was true what Jock had said – Juan was hugely popular in the Regiment. He had taken to the training like a natural; no test was too tough for him. He was a crack shot and skilled with weapons of all kinds, particularly missiles, and on this mission his language skills would have been vital. We would be very hard put indeed to replace him.

'To hell with it,' Juan said resignedly. 'Let's go out and get pissed.'

We went back to the mess, where Jenny and a friend were waiting at the bar. We teamed the friend up with Juan, and paired off.

Over beers I told Jenny that this was my last mission with the Regiment. In September I would be leaving the army and going back to civvy street.

'What will you do then?' she asked.

'On the outside? God knows – go into the security business, I suppose. Bodyguarding and the like. It's well paid.'

'I want to get out too,' she said. She meant away from the Falklands – she was ticking off the days till she could return to the UK. 'A whole fucking year,' she said. 'Another whole year of my youth spent down here on the arse-end of the world.' We were both smiling.

She wanted a life, any life, and I was looking to start afresh. Was it just coincidence that had placed us together? It all seemed so natural. I imagined settling down with Jenny in a farmhouse in Fife. Maybe civilian life wouldn't be so bad.

I woke in my room to a thunderous noise. Someone was banging on the door of my cubicle. A familiar voice: 'Mark, you sheep-shagging bastard! Drop your cock and grab your kit, we're sailing at eight hundred. Assemble out the front in thirty minutes.'

I leapt out of bed and unlocked the door. In the passage stood Doug Hatton, veteran of the Rio Grande trek twenty years before. He was a troop sergeant now.

'Christ, where'd you spring from?' I said, rubbing the sleep from my eyes. Last I'd heard, he was in Norway.

His eyes lit up lecherously as he looked past me to Jenny's form under the sheets. 'How's about you and me have a quickie while he takes a shower, love?'

'Fuck off, Doug,' I snapped. 'What are you doing here?'

He grinned. He knew I never liked him. 'Flew in last night. Replacement for the Yank. Ain't you glad to see me?'

I slammed the door in his face. 'Give her this one

from me, mate!' he yelled back and hooted. Fuck, I thought. This was all I needed. It was bad enough losing a bloke like Juan. Having him replaced by a nutter like Doug made me want to bang my head against the wall.

I turned back to look at Jenny. She was pulling on her T-shirt.

'Last night,' I said, 'you knew we were leaving today.'

She put a finger to my mouth. 'There was a signal yesterday evening putting *Superb* on standby. Confirmation must have just come through.'

I was moving about the room mechanically. She didn't ask when she would see me again. She knew the score. She slipped on her knickers and buttoned up her skirt. With a deft movement of the fingers she made a ponytail and pushed it through an elastic band.

She was almost ready to go. A low-maintenance woman. I liked that.

We went to the door together. 'I know a little,' she said, 'about where you're going. Take care of yourself. Some of us might miss you if you didn't come back.' Her lips tightened.

'This is peacetime,' I reminded her. 'I'll be back.'

'For you it's never peace, is it?'

FOURTEEN

HMS *Superb*'s surface route followed the usual track taken by other naval vessels leaving Port Stanley. After exiting the port, she steered north-east on the surface as though clearing the islands for Ascension. To cover our departure, two of the garrison's four Tornado fighters flew a sortie, making sure no Argentine reconnaissance aircraft were in the vicinity.

Air movements around the islands were monitored by radar sites on mountains ringing Stanley. From these, operators could watch planes taking off from Rio Grande, 300 miles away on Tierra del Fuego, and from other bases along the coast. As the two Tornados became airborne they reported in to Mount Kent and turned west to check if any fishing craft or other small vessels were in the vicinity.

It was a grey and gusty day with white caps riding up from the south. Modern submarines, even ones as big as *Superb*, do not handle well on the surface, and the rolling motion after we left sheltered water was unpleasant.

The planes were still flying protective cover overhead, watched by the radars. Jock and I went on to

141

the bridge to play at seadogs with the skipper in the cold and spray. Nobby and Josh were aft in the ops room where the radio operators were listening in to the pilots' commentary. Doug was getting in a kip after his long flight last night, and Kiwi was stripping down the GPMG. We had been allocated a secure cabin for our kit on the upper deck, and we pretty much had the freedom of the ship with the exception of the code room.

One of the operators turned to the officer of the watch. 'Sir, I can't make it out. I think one of the guys is in some kind of trouble.'

They patched the radio link through to the bridge and we listened to the transmissions. The two pilots were talking between themselves, breaking off occasionally to speak to the controller at Mount Pleasant. It wasn't easy to hear what was going on because the transmissions were fragmented, but the concern in the voice of one of the fliers was apparent.

'He reckons his mate's been taken sick, I think, sir,' the operator said.

We heard Mount Pleasant asking if the patrol was returning to base. 'Affirmative,' came the response from the other pilot, the one who was OK. 'Turning two-four-zero inbound at one-five thousand.' Then we heard him say something to the one in trouble that I couldn't quite catch but sounded like, 'Follow me. I'll see you home.'

There were further exchanges between the planes and Mount Pleasant and between the pilots. The planes had evidently come round on to a new course and were returning to base. From what the pilot in the lead plane was saying it seemed his partner had been taken ill suddenly. Both planes descended to 10,000 feet about twenty miles out, and we heard them confirm they were descending into their approach pattern.

The lead pilot was encouraging his pal to hang in there. 'Just another few minutes, Paddy, and you'll be OK.'

'What's the matter with him, do you think?' Jock whispered.

I shook my head. It sounded serious, but it couldn't be a heart attack, surely. These guys were young and fit.

Then we listened to the air-sea rescue crew becoming airborne, and minutes later heard them clatter overhead on their way to take up station. Mount Pleasant reported the base on full emergency station with fire tenders and ambulances standing by and a doctor in readiness.

Then another report came in that was just as disturbing. In the control room of one of the radar stations on the hills, an operator at one of the screens had suddenly clutched at his stomach, doubling up in convulsions. As his colleagues had clustered round, he'd pushed his chair back and scrambled to his feet, chest heaving, and vomited explosively across the floor.

Out on the submarine's sail, we had visual sighting of the returning planes descending from the south-west. One of them was wobbling badly, weaving around the sky as if the pilot was having trouble holding it steady.

Our radio operator reported hearing gagging sounds from the sick pilot, as if he were choking or having difficulty breathing.

Mount Pleasant control came on speaking urgently to the stricken plane, warning the pilot that he was dipping below his safe angle of descent.

Abruptly the airwaves filled with transmission noise. Mount Kent, Mount Pleasant and the other pilot were all talking at once. The radar screens at both facilities had lost the second plane's trace. The healthy pilot was screaming to his buddy, 'Pull out! Pull out, for God's sake!' From where we were we could no longer see the planes through the haze. I heard someone below shout up, 'He's going down!' The sound of aircraft engines was increasingly loud – the dreadful noise of a plane diving, a long sickening wail that ended suddenly.

The silence told us all we needed to know. Moments later came the shocked voice of the first pilot: 'Alpha two-zero flown into the sea.'

We altered course towards the scene of the crash, but we were too far away to be of any help.

The Sea Kings were on the scene within half a minute. The plane had broken up on impact and there was very little wreckage. If there was an attempt to eject it had been too late.

'Poor bastard,' Jock said. We all felt sickened. The guy had gone out to fly us cover, and now he was dead. It was an ominous start to the mission.

In sombre mood, the captain ordered the tanks filled and we slid down to periscope depth. A short while later we reached deep water and descended to 100 metres cruise depth as we swung on to our new course towards Tierra del Fuego.

Steaming at twenty-plus knots, it would take us around sixteen hours to reach our drop-off point. After two hours elapsed, the skipper streamed an aerial and took a radio message confirming that salmonella had struck at the airbase. A second pilot had reported symptoms, and all flying was now prohibited. Medical facilities were on full alert and the hospital was being cleared to receive casualties.

The bug seemed to have struck at the airbase first, and by midday there was hardly a person left unaffected. The staff at the hospital were run off their feet. The infection was extremely virulent, inducing stomach cramps and projectile vomiting. At one point there were over fifty patients on intravenous drips. Standard antibiotics seemed to bring limited relief, and further supplies were being rushed over from England. The garrison commander put in a request for replacement pilots and reinforcements, which was denied on the grounds that there was no point flying in replacements until the source of the infection had been traced, though medical help was promised.

One problem was the huge distances involved. The Falklands are over 8000 miles from the British Isles. A radio blackout on the epidemic was being enforced until such time as it was brought under control. Whitehall did not want it known in Buenos Aires that the islands were virtually defenceless all of a sudden. So it was necessary that all assistance be routed via Ascension Island in the South Atlantic instead of by the civilian route through Montevideo or Rio de Janeiro. This involved fifteen-hour flights supported by half a dozen tanker aircraft, an amazingly complex procedure even in normal circumstances. With Mount Pleasant's own tankers grounded for fear of another accident, a mercy flight of doctors, nursing staff and more potent drugs would take at least twenty-four hours to set up.

Food poisoning aboard a submarine is every naval officer's nightmare. There were the inevitable jokes about the filthy habits and hygiene standards of the Falkland Islanders, but we were all bloody glad that the sub's food had come out from England.

By noon we learned that the bug had spread to the army garrison as well. I thought of my poor Jenny with her head stuck down a lavatory bowl.

Shortly after midday there came a knock on the door of the cabin we had been allocated aft of the ops room on the main deck. Kiwi opened up and the ship's medical officer entered with an orderly bearing paper cups and a water container.

'What's this?' Jock demanded.

'Captain's orders,' the MO told him. 'All personnel to receive broad-spectrum antibiotics as a precaution against salmonella poisoning – though the amount you people have probably been drinking no bugs would stand a chance in your stomachs.' He started to pass out packets of bloody great capsules. 'Take two now and two four times a day for the next six days.'

'Fucking hell,' Nobby said, looking at them. 'These aren't for humans!'

'Get 'em down, you great twat,' I told him. 'I'm not sharing a hide with you crapping yourself all night.'

A little later the sub's captain sent for Jock and made it clear that if salmonella struck aboard he would abort the mission immediately. He was not risking his ship inshore with a crew down with sickness.

Because there are just sixteen nuclear subs to command, an RN submarine commander is a very rare beast indeed. No other western nation is more exacting in its selection process for these officers. This results in extremely determined and aggressive skippers, willing to take risks when necessary. The question today – assuming his crew remained fit – was just how close in he was prepared to take us.

In part the answer would depend on the weather. The forecast for the next twenty-four hours indicated heavy seas and force-seven gales. High seas would make it harder to pick up a sub's conning tower on radar and hamper any sonar listening devices. Nuclear submarines are not silent machines; the pumps that circulate coolant around the reactor core give out a steady sound recognisable to a trained operator on another sub. In shallow water too, cavitation noise from the screw becomes a problem. Heavy waves would blanket these factors to some extent but they would also greatly complicate the process of launching the Gemini boats.

The fifty-metre-depth line ran approximately ten miles out from the shore. Fifty metres was the absolute minimum as far as *Superb* was concerned, so ten miles was as close in as we could go. The plan was for us to loiter out beyond the 200-metre line till dusk, then make a high-speed run in, float off the boats at around midnight, and dash out again at thirty knots to reach deep water by daylight.

The truth was that this was a mission ideally suited to a small diesel-powered boat, drawing much less water, that could slip in close to the coast using her battery-powered electric motors and remain almost undetectable. The same submersible could lie offshore until our mission was completed, then slide in again to take us off. But due to cutbacks in the defence budget, the Royal Navy had done away with its fleet of conventional boats, leaving it dependent on big noisy nukes.

The Argentine navy was known to possess two ultra-quiet German diesel submarines. If one of these came after *Superb* in inshore waters it would be at a considerable advantage. It would be able to hear the big ship coming and lurk invisibly in the shallows, while manoeuvring silently into a firing position. The first we would probably know would be the alarm cry, 'Torpedo in the water!' And a torpedo fired by a diesel electric was every bit as deadly as one fired by a nuke.

No doubt there were plenty in the Argentine navy who still carried a grudge against the British for the sinking of the cruiser *Belgrano* during the Falklands campaign, and no doubt either that some of them would leap at the opportunity to nail a Royal Navy submarine close inshore.

So all day we loitered at around a hundred metres depth, streaming a massive array sonar from our stern, alert for any indication of hostile warships. Our listening devices could pick up moving vessels a hundred miles off. Mostly it was fishing boats and inshore traffic, occasionally bigger ships heading up for Drake Passage into the Pacific.

We passed our time in the cabin, organising our kit and making it watertight. Nuclear subs are huge, but they cram a lot in. The passageway floors were stacked with crates of tinned food, so we had to watch our heads wherever we went. Our cabin was small for six men and all their equipment, and the crew got used to stepping over some trooper lying out on the deck checking the sights of a GPMG, or seeing us casually handling missiles capable of blowing a hole in the hull.

The day passed slowly underwater. Some of the guys snatched a bit of kip while they could. Jock and I spent a lot of time studying charts and maps. The plan was that on going ashore we would meet up with a guide, a UK national attached to one of the oil companies prospecting in the region. He would take us to a safe lying-up point. A lot was going to depend on his reliability.

Meantime, Doug had woken up and was back to his old trick of needling other members of the team. First he had a go at me about Jenny.

'So what was she like, Mark? Gagging for it, was she?'

It made me mad to listen to him harping on about Jenny like she was some scrubber, but I'd learned that it made his day if he got a response, so I held my tongue.

Then he tried it on with Kiwi. 'Reckon Stanley must be like home to you. All them farmers screwing their frigging sisters and mothers. Just like back in New Zealand, eh?'

But Kiwi just laughed amiably. 'Yep,' he said, 'that's farmers.' Doug left it at that. Maybe he knew that Kiwi might thump him one.

So it was Josh's turn.

I guess he thought that because he was a new boy, Josh was fair game. As troop sergeant, Doug had authority over him that he proceeded to use mercilessly. He kept inventing little tasks for him. 'Fetch me out the night sight, I want to check the batteries,' he'd say. Josh would jump up and dig out the night sight and bring it over. 'No, I didn't mean that, I meant the Spyglass.' So Josh would go back to the mound of equipment and fetch that out. Then Doug would want something else. Or he would send Josh down to the ops room to synchronise his watch. This went on and on through the afternoon.

Like a lot of younger guys fresh out of training, Josh had all his kit together, everything in its right pouch. I remembered being like that, checking my kit over and over again when we'd flown out to the last mission.

Josh's face fell when casualties were mentioned. 'So where does the rescue come from if we're compromised?' he asked at one point.

'There isn't going to be any rescue, you prick,' Doug jeered. 'If we're busted we fight our way out on foot. Same as we did last time, eh, Mark?'

'That's about the size of it,' I acknowledged.

'Well, if you guys can handle it, I guess I can,' Josh said.

'The fuck you can! When we were slogging it across the pampas you hadn't even made it to primary school. College boys like you don't know they're born. You only passed selection because they needed to get the fucking numbers up. I know that 'cause your instructor asked me to keep an eye on you.'

'Jesus, Doug, when are you going to give it a rest?' Nobby said wearily.

But Doug wouldn't give up. The numbers game by which SAS selection standards were being lowered was his pet hate. He went on needling Josh for his perceived lack of soldiering skills. And when he got bored of that, he started to get personal. 'You got a sister, ain't you? What's her name then?'

'My sister's called Judy.'

'Judy, eh? You think she'd go for me then?'

Josh shrugged unhappily.

Doug didn't let up. 'You going to introduce us then, when we're back in the UK?'

'Leave it out, Doug,' I said.

'Ha, what's this, the big brother act again? Just like you and Andy?'

The mention of my brother's name sent a hot wave of anger through me. I jumped up. 'Leave his name out of this!'

Doug thrust his face in mine. 'Not so easy without him to back you up, is it?' He was swaying about on the balls of his feet as he always did when he was about to swing a punch. He was a dirty fighter, fast on his feet and hard as nails. I could put him down, but if I didn't get the first punch in, he'd do some damage.

Luckily, at that moment Jock came in. 'What gives?' he snapped, seeing the pair of us squaring up to one another. 'We're on a mission, for Christ's sake!'

Doug snorted and turned away. I sat down again, the anger still burning in my gut.

'What was all that about?' Josh muttered.

'Nothing,' I told him. 'We go back a long way, that's all.'

At a prearranged time just before five in the afternoon we came up to communications depth to receive messages from our trailed antenna. There were further reports about the salmonella outbreak, which had spread into the civilian population at Port Stanley, and advice on treatment. We discussed the possibility that it might be some kind of biological attack by the Argentines, targeted against the RAF. Jock agreed with me that, without fighter protection, the islands were left wide open.

Josh wondered how a bacterial agent might be introduced. 'What do they do? Drop it in the water supply?'

'Doubtful,' Jock said. He expected that public water supplies, even in Stanley, were filtered and chlorinated and treated with ultra-violet specifically to protect against hazards like salmonella. 'Besides, the quantities are too great. To contaminate the drinking supply you'd need a road-tanker load of the bugs.' Agents and materials needed to be prepared and handled correctly. He thought it likely that any salmonella would have to have been introduced directly into food, probably via the RAF mess. If it had been in today's breakfast, that would explain why we were OK – we'd left before eating.

I was thinking that it must have been a highly potent strain, whatever it was, if a pilot could be feeling well enough to take off and yet half an hour later be too sick to land his plane.

I wondered how much Jock and the skipper really knew about the background to the current crisis. The government in London must have been very nervous to risk a nuclear submarine close inshore, and to authorise inserting an armed party into a country we were not officially at war with. I thought about my glib words to Jenny, that this was peacetime. For how much longer?

Around five-thirty we abandoned our holding pattern and headed westwards under cover of darkness. It had been a very long day. An hour later, our speed dropped to ten knots as we approached the 100-metre line. The commander explained that we were entering an undersea canyon, as much as five miles across and 500 feet deep at the entrance, that had been gouged during the last ice age. It wound back to within a few miles of the coast and would provide us with deeper water during the approach to our destination. Over the past two decades, British submarines had surveyed scores of similar natural features in the region, charting their twists and turns in the knowledge that, in war, possession of such undersea maps could mean the difference between destruction and survival.

The submarine's active and passive sonars, coupled with the echo-sounding fathometer and inertial navigation system, enabled her to plot a course accurate to within a metre. It was an eerie sensation even so, sliding along in the black water, 200 metres below the surface, knowing that sheer walls of rock loomed over the vessel on either side, and that the smallest miscalculation in handling could result in a catastrophic collision.

The atmosphere became noticeably more intense as the minutes ticked off. In spite of the air-conditioning our cabin smelt stale with the tang of cleaning oil from the weapons. With every mile that passed the depth above our tower lessened and the canyon narrowed. If we did detect an enemy we would have to come up to fifty metres in order to turn. We were like a big fish swimming up a tunnel. We had just thirty metres of water under our keel, and the upwards-looking high-frequency under-ice sonar registered the same to the surface.

An hour from our drop-off point we had begun donning our black emergency survival suits and packing our kit into dry bags, when there was an alert. The sonar teams had picked up a ship's screws ten miles dead ahead. High-speed turbines: very probably a patrol vessel. Immediately the skipper ordered Dead Slow and we settled gently towards the sea bed. We couldn't actually touch bottom without risking damage to our sonar dome but we rested about ten metres up and sat silent, hoping that the shallow-water clutter of the waves overhead would smother the sounds of our reactor pumps. Every small sound in the boat seemed suddenly magnified.

'Contact bearing 040 degrees. Course 190. Speed eighteen knots. Range 20,000 decreasing.'

The enemy vessel was on our starboard bow headed towards us. At this rate she would acquire us within fifteen minutes. Given current weather conditions we could probably outrun her given enough start, but then her sonar would certainly pick up the sound of our engines. It would mean breaking cover. On the other hand if we stayed where we were much longer we risked a torpedo.

'Range 18,000 metres decreasing,' the sonar operator called. 'Speed seventeen knots.' The ship's speed was dropping. It might be slowing down to turn away; alternatively it might have guessed there was a big sub out ahead and reduced speed to improve the capability of its own passive sonar.

'Like a man picking his way through a forest at night, who stops to listen,' the skipper murmured to Jock. His coolness astonished me.

Three minutes of silence, then, 'Range 16,400. Speed fifteen knots. Now bearing 045 degrees,' came the operator's voice. The vessel was a little over eight miles off, slowing further and turning away from us, but not by much. She might be questing about, trying to locate us. We would know if her sonar started pinging us.

Another man on the sonar watch sang out. 'Sonar trace conforms to signature of Foxtrot Alpha 3.' The atmosphere of intense concentration among the crew continued unchanged.

'Argentine naval rescue craft,' the skipper explained for our benefit. 'Built by our own Vosper-Thorneycroft for the Dutch navy and sold by them to Argentina. Dual-use capability – that's to say, sonar-equipped for inshore ASW. We've tracked her before. Probably out after a fishing boat in trouble. Let's hope she wraps it up smartly.'

An air-sea rescue boat could be a threat to us if it came close enough, though, and this one was fitted out for anti-submarine warfare. And if there was a rescue launch out, there was a possibility that it was backed up by a helicopter overhead. Even if that weren't the case, it would be a simple matter for her to fix us with her sonar while radioing Rio Grande for aircraft with depth charges and torpedoes.

And then abruptly, without warning, somewhere in the boat an alarm pealed.

FIFTEEN

The noise was so loud we almost leapt out of our skins. It seemed incredible that it would not be audible out on the patrol boat.

'Bridge,' the captain snapped into a microphone. 'What's the problem?'

'Forward turbine room reports smoke, sir. Lots of it.'

'Shut watertight doors. Fire party close up.'

'Aye, aye, sir. Shutting all watertight doors and hatches. Fire party close up,' the officer of the watch repeated.

All of us on the team had been through this drill before in the course of exercises. Fire is a constant and deadly hazard underwater. Modern subs are stuffed full of electric cabling and plastic insulation that if heated can generate deadly toxic fumes.

Heavy steel hatches slammed shut, clunking home like safe doors, isolating the upper deck from the bridge area. A seaman appeared in the door and tossed smoke masks into our laps and told us to be ready to put them on if ordered.

We were trapped in a narrow undersea canyon in shallow water on a hostile coast with a patrol vessel bearing down on us, and now the boat was on fire. In short, the situation was fucked up. I was willing to bet, though, that the captain would be as calm and collected as if he were tied to a pier at Devonport dock. He couldn't fight the fire personally; other people would do that. They were well trained and could be relied upon to do their job in a speedy and efficient manner.

In the event of a fire, then the water- and smoketight doors would confine it to a single compartment on the lower deck. Water sprays would dowse the flames, while a fire party equipped with breathing equipment and extinguishers tackled the source of the blaze. If necessary, and should the flames prove too fierce, then the captain would give the order 'Execute CO2 drench' to flood the compartment with carbon dioxide gas, stifling the oxygen from the fire. It would be bad news for anyone in the compartment without breathing equipment, but that was why he was commanding a nuclear submarine and why the men trusted him – because he had the guts to do it.

The alarm was still shrilling. Why didn't someone switch the bastard thing off? There was a pounding on the locked hatch in the passage; a brief exchange over the intercom and the hatch was opened to allow a party of seamen through with tools and extinguishers. They went aft through the bridge area and clattered down the ladder to help fight the flames on the lower deck. Briefly through the open hatch I saw the operations centre functioning as before. The sonar operators' attention would still be fixed on their job of tracking the patrol vessel.

Josh glanced at me, a bit pale. If there's one thing we hate in the SAS it's having to sit on our hands in a crisis. 'What d'you reckon?' he said. 'An overheated bearing?'

'More likely an electrical fault,' Jock told him casually. 'A bundle of wires heat up, reach flashpoint and bing! Smoke alarm.'

'Yeah, that's what I figured,' said Josh.

I smiled inwardly. He reminded me of myself at his age – fresh-faced, eager, but a bit apprehensive. This was his first time on a real combat mission. Now things were starting to go wrong he was trying to keep the nervousness out of his voice. I wanted to reassure him, then I remembered how angry it used to make me when Andy tried to do the same to me all those years ago. I was beginning to understand what it meant to feel like an older brother.

The alarm bell cut out suddenly. Over the intercom we could hear the operators calling down the range to the patrol boat. The distance was opening up again as the boat turned. Had it overrun the mouth of the canyon and put its helm over to circle round and pick up the scent again? I tried to picture where the forward turbine room was in relation to the reactor. I've never trusted that radioactive stuff. They had given us little radiation badges to wear, but all they did was measure the size of the dose that killed you. Interesting to the scientists, but not a fuck of a lot of help otherwise.

'If that fire spreads to the reactor room then we're in

mega-trouble,' Nobby observed, as if reading my thoughts.

'Us and all this end of South America,' said Doug.

Surely someone would be able to shut down the reactor before we all blew up or melted or whatever it was a runaway nuclear reactor did. But if we did manage a controlled shut-down, that would still leave us lying on the bottom of the canyon without power. At a rough estimate we currently had just under 200 feet of water over our heads.

Departing a submarine via the escape hatch is something I have had to do as part of my SAS training. It is not a method recommended for the claustrophobic. There are two escape hatches, one either end of the boat. In our case we would have to use the forward hatch located in the torpedo storage area. It consists of a steel tube just wide enough for one man to crawl up into, with a watertight hatch at each end. You open the bottom hatch and climb in with an emergency air breathing set. The lower hatch is then closed and the tube flooded. It's pitch black inside, and the experience is like being buried alive and drowned simultaneously. If all goes well the pressure within the tube equals the water pressure outside and the top hatch can be opened. You climb out, pull the inflation cord on your life jacket and swim up to the surface.

That's the theory. There are a number of things that can fuck up, most of which involve getting stuck in the tube and running out of air. The procedure is so dangerous even submariners rarely practise it. It's better than drowning or suffocating in a disabled submarine – but not much.

Even if we made it to the surface, it wasn't as though our troubles would be over. We were still ten miles out from the shore at night in near-polar waters, without boats in a force-seven gale. Our survival suits would give us only limited warmth. I envisaged the winds blowing our bodies ashore after we had died of hypothermia.

I was wondering if the fire was accidental. If the salmonella outbreak at Stanley could be part of a biological attack, then it would certainly be one hell of a coincidence for the one submarine present at the time to catch fire. On the other hand, why plant an incendiary when a high explosive would do the job better? None of it made sense.

We went back to our cabin. There was nothing we could do to help and we'd only get in the way. Nobby Clark cracked a joke about being roasted or boiled. Jock grinned at him and went on studying his map. Kiwi was reading a paperback; he seemed completely unconcerned. The rest of us lay on our bunks or fiddled with our equipment.

There was the ominous thud of a small explosion from somewhere down below.

'Air bottle going up,' said Doug.

'Steam pipe fracture more like,' said someone else.

The alarm bell resumed and was joined by another with an alternating note. The Argies would have to be deaf not to hear the racket. Jock yawned with elaborate unconcern and looked at his watch. 'Seven o'clock. Another two hours to go. Well, I hope the Navy get things under control in time for us to go ashore on schedule.'

The hatch outside was unlatched again and more people could be heard coming through. A waft of smoke reached us. Doug said that this showed they had the fire under control and were reopening the hatches. 'Or else,' Nobby suggested brightly, 'the back end of the boat is burning and the matelots are jumping ship.'

The bells and sirens continued to sound intermittently. We could hear equipment being dragged about and sailors shouting to one another. There was no sign of panic that I could make out. Kiwi laid down his book and glanced across at Jock, one eyebrow raised. I saw Jock shake his head slightly. All we could do was wait.

The door to the passage opened and a young officer stuck his head in. 'Don't want to cause alarm, but the captain just wanted to check that you chaps are all familiar with our escape drill.'

'You mean underwater escape?' Jock said. 'Everyone here has done the course. Some of us,' he nodded in the direction of Doug and myself, 'have more experience than others.'

'Excellent. If it does become necessary, your departure station will be in the torpedo room forward. Just a precaution, you understand, so you know where to go if you have to.' He cast an eye at our bergens. 'I should try to take as little as possible if I were you.'

I told myself that this was just procedure. If the situation got that bad we would still have residual power left in the stand-by batteries sufficient to blow the tanks and bring us to the surface. But that would effectively mean surrendering the ship to the Argentines. The captain would rather die.

It was getting hotter in the cabin and the air quality was noticeably deteriorating. The captain must have switched off the air conditioners to prevent smoke from circulating through the rest of the boat. On a submarine fumes can kill quickly. Battery compartments and electrical wiring release toxic vapours when they burn and portable oxygen sets provide only a few minutes' breathable air.

Nobby cracked open the door to our cabin. 'What's happening, mate?' he called cheerily to a seaman. 'Are we sunk yet?'

'Nah,' came the reply. 'Just the fucking engineers set their grots alight.' The fire, the matelot told us, had begun in a storeroom on the engine deck, next to the turbines. Lagging on a lubricant feed pipe had suddenly caught ablaze. No one knew how it happened. There was no flame source nearby. Equally inexplicably the sprinklers in the compartment failed to function. Flames spread through air vents into the turbine room. Huge volumes of smoke made it difficult to isolate the source of the blaze. At one point the heat was so intense it had cracked a steam pipe. Fortunately a courageous rating turned off the valve before major damage was done. At one point it had looked as if the blaze might go critical.

Luckily the rear bulkheads held and sprinklers in neighbouring compartments kept the heat down and prevented a flashover.

The lights went out, leaving only an orange emergency bulb in the ceiling. From time to time the hatch nearby would clang open, letting in fresh draughts of smoke. We could hear more feet on the ladders, calls over the intercom for a medical team, and the sounds of an injured man being removed to the sick bay.

Meanwhile we still had the patrol vessel to worry about. We had heard over the intercom that the sonar trace was continuing on the same heading. The range was now down to 8000 yards, four nautical miles – but after an anxious few minutes it started to open up again. Evidently while the soot-blackened fire parties fought to bring the blaze under control, the sonar operators had continued calmly at their posts, listening to the engine sounds and computing the track.

If the patrol boat was conducting her own sonar search, she *must* have picked us up by now. We were making enough noise to be heard at twice the range. Maybe the walls of the canyon were confusing the return signal. Or maybe she was hanging back, waiting for an armed helicopter to join the hunt. If we came to periscope depth and stuck up an air mast for ventilation they would spot it on radar.

I was sweating in my survival suit but couldn't take it off. I might need it in a hurry. The lights came back on, which cheered us, but although someone had restored the circuits the ventilation stayed shut down. After a while the air quality became even worse as the hatches below were opened up again. But it was a sign the flames must be finally out. A nauseating cocktail of fumes eddied through the boat until the captain at last gave the order for the air conditioning to be switched on to scrub the atmosphere.

Nobby went out to see what was happening. The submarine was in a filthy state. The lower deck was running with water and foam and powder residue. There were ash and smoke stains on bulkheads and overhead panels. Half a dozen men had been injured, two with serious burns. We had full power available on the turbines again so if necessary we could come up to periscope depth, find room to turn around and make a run for the open sea. At least we weren't going to be frazzled by radiation or poisoned by smoke or drowned!

The launch didn't come any nearer, though. A few minutes later sonar announced that she had broken off the search and was heading away south along the shore in the direction of Rio Grande. Either she had found what she was looking for or else had given up.

Even so the skipper didn't move. For the next two hours we stayed just where we were. His patience was immense. He set his men to work cleaning up the ship, and while they did he waited. For us it was intensely frustrating. All we could do was wait, with nothing to do but speculate over whether the mission was blown. Doug, of course, took out his boredom on the rest of us. Even Kiwi got scratchy, telling him to button his mouth before he got it shut for him permanently.

At nine-thirty – half an hour after our planned drop-off time – with no sound detected by the sonar, the skipper ordered the tanks blown gently to bring us up to periscope depth. Briefly we stuck an ESM aerial up to check for radar emissions. If there was a helicopter up there still searching we wanted to know about it.

A few minutes later a message came down for Jock saying he was wanted in the operations centre. He was gone some minutes. When he returned he was grim. He shut the door of the cabin.

'This is the position,' he said. 'The patrol boat has gone. The fire is out. The skipper says his people can't be certain but it looks very like sabotage. An incendiary device inserted behind the lagging of a pipe in the machinery area. Nothing else could explain a fire of such intensity at that location.' Every inch of the sub was being searched now for further firebombs, he added.

'How does the captain think it was brought aboard, this device?' I asked.

'During replenishment back in the UK most probably. There aren't many other moments when an outsider gets access to a sub. That's a matter for the security people. It was probably just luck that it detonated when it did. The point is the damage is serious but not critical. The reactor is unaffected but power is reduced. We can still make it back to the Falklands.'

'And the mission?' Doug said. 'Do we abort?'

'That's up to us. We are a mile from the drop-off

point now. The captain is prepared to surface to let us off but he says he can't promise to remain on station indefinitely to bring us out again. The possibility of damage to the steam plant means he must return home for repairs. He can't hang about here waiting for us. If we choose to go ahead, we'll be on our own. No back-up, no exfiltration.'

I looked at Doug. 'In short, it means a walk-out like last time.'

We could talk and vote on this but it was Jock's decision. The SAS is more democratic than most units in the army but at the end of the day it is a fighting force. We obey orders. If the damage to the submarine was deliberate, that made it all the more urgent to put a recon party ashore to find out what the Argentines were preparing.

SIXTEEN

I could hear compressed air hissing into the tanks, indicating that *Superb*'s black conning tower was rising out of the waves. The submarine continued to surface, pumping water ballast out. A seaman opened a hatch in the base of the tower and clipped it back, and a sudden draught of cold air struck my face. The sub's casing diver stepped out on to the deck and beckoned to me to follow. He wore a dry suit with a tiny LED torch strapped to his head with a red filter so as not to destroy our night vision. It was his job to prepare the Gemini inflatables for release and guide us into them.

The lighting was almost invisible a few metres away. With all the spray and water in the air we were pretty much undetectable. Our sonar wasn't picking up any noise, but there could be a boat lurking out there with its engines off. We didn't dare turn on our radars for a sweep for fear of alerting the Argentines. That was why the captain was keen to float us off quickly and get the hell out of here.

I trod out carefully on to the casing. Waves were slapping up against the submarine's smooth hull, flinging up sheets of spray that drenched us instantly. It felt bloody freezing and I was thankful for my survival suit. The crew had rigged rails to help us, with safety lines clipped to stanchions in case anyone fell overboard. The lines were a mixed blessing: if, say, a helicopter materialised out of the night, then the sub would have to crash dive, and anyone who didn't have time to cast off his line would be dragged down with it.

The two Gemini boats were stored in wells in the submarine's deck casing, their engines encased in dry-bags. The engines were silenced – the exhausts ran out underwater – which reduced speed but cut noise by a hell of a lot. Running silent we could sneak up on a beach at night and not be heard by anyone a hundred yards off.

It was a complex procedure extracting the boats from the deck wells in the darkness. The casing diver opened the gas-bottles that automatically inflated the air cells, then stripped the dry-bags from the engines, fitted them on and screwed them down. Next our kit was loaded in and strapped down, with important items like guns and paddles secured by lines. Then the boats were slid off one at a time and the engines started. An officer leant down to give us a last-minute weather report. Sea conditions were deteriorating. The sooner we got started the better. Jock was checking the GPS heading. On a night with no stars and heavy seas it was vital to get properly orientated at the start. In this case we were being advised to offset to the north by a few degrees to avoid finding ourselves carried down into Rio Grande by wind and currents.

It was lucky we had Kiwi on the team. His parent unit was the Royal Marines and he had originally qualified with their Special Boat Service. The SBS train off the west coast of Scotland in all weathers, practising exit and recovery from submarines in deep water or parachuting with canoes into open sea and paddling in to the shore. They think nothing of thirty-mile non-stop paddles. Tonight's operation would be a piece of cake to Kiwi. The incredible thing about him was that he'd been the runt of the litter; he had three brothers all bigger than him. What a family. Dave was twenty-four and the nicest guy you could meet. Was it the Maori blood in him that made him simply indestructible?

The GPS fix put us about eleven miles out. GPS has made life a lot easier for special forces – it showed us our position down to the nearest metre. The captain had brought us closer in than he had promised, which was decent of him. That meant a total distance to the shore of around thirteen miles, allowing for tide effect. I doubted we'd be able to average more than about eight knots, so we could reckon on being in the water for an hour and a half to two hours. We were aiming for a landfall in a sheltered lagoon protected by a sand bar across the entrance. From there, if all went according to plan, we would strike inland to rendezvous with the agent sent to meet us about three kilometres behind the beach.

It was a chilly few minutes, getting ourselves sorted out, making sure our weapons were secure. The waves slamming against the sub's hull were kicking us up and down through four and five metres. Josh clambered into the lead boat with me and Kiwi. Nobby Clark and Doug were following behind with Jock. Finally we got the signal from Jock in the second boat to say they were all set. I had a torch with a green filter and flashed back acknowledgement, then cast off the warp holding us to *Superb*'s side. Kiwi let the engine have some juice and we pulled out from the lee of the hull into open water. We were on our way.

It was a wild trip. We were riding waves the size of houses. The official definition of force seven on the Beaufort scale is for wind speeds up to thirty-four knots, with heaped seas and white foam from breaking waves blowing in streaks. Four metres is the average wave height. The extreme peaks can spike the graph at anything from fifty to a hundred per cent higher. In fact, wave-height depends on the fetch – that is, the distance over which the wind has travelled. Distances in the South Atlantic are vast. Antarctic storms can generate swells that measure half a mile or more between crests and reach thirty knots. They hit the Falkland Islands as breakers fifteen metres high.

The skipper had told us that he would wait at the departure point for two hours exactly. If we got into trouble on the run-in and had to abort before reaching shore, then we could turn around and signal for him to pick us up. It was immediately evident however that putting about in these seas was a complete impossibility. If we turned broadside on to one of these waves, we would broach and be flipped end-over-end, buried and broken. We had no choice but to keep on going.

We were all wearing heavy-duty survival gear. And we were frozen. The cold numbed my limbs so it was all I could do to hang on in the boat. Josh was a hooded silhouette barely discernible across the thwart in the darkness and spray. I was thankful we had an SBS man along. Kiwi was gripping the tiller bar and peering through the spray into the waves. God knows how he could see in the darkness, but he steered us effortlessly up the rollers and down the other side. The only way you get through the SBS selection course is if you enjoy this kind of life. Kiwi had told me that the RAF helicopter rescue hate the SBS, because they are always getting called out by civilians who've seen some mad swimmers miles out at sea in a storm – and when they get there it's the SBS who wave them away and carry on happily with their exercise.

The SBS are responsible for the protection of oil platforms in British waters. Not a single UK rig has ever been attacked by terrorists, which is a testimony to their fearsome reputation. Nowadays they work closely with the SAS, and there is no finer body of men.

We'd been running twenty-five minutes. The cold was numbing even through my survival suit, and the waves caused a constant jarring. I tried to concentrate on our various exit options. Walking out had been tried the last time and was not the ideal option, as we had learned to our cost. The best bet seemed to be to have a helicopter slip in over the border under the radar net and pick us up. Maybe with all the oil exploration going on in the area it was unlikely that a single chopper flight would excite too much attention, and with luck by the time they scrambled an aircraft to investigate we would be back over the border into Chile. It would only be a short flight and the six of us could pack in tight. Our equipment might have to be ditched, but that's a penalty of clandestine ops.

Then I thought about the landing. Waiting for us at the RV point inland was supposed to be a British guide who would lead us to the base. I wasn't too happy about relying on local help – it's too easily infiltrated by the other side. Jock seemed content, though.

Rio Grande intrigued me. Last time the mission had been called off at the start and we never got near the air base. It would be interesting to see what the defences were like. What would London's response be if we did find evidence of an invasion being planned? A strike by Tornados was one option but would be tantamount to a declaration of war and the Americans might exercise a veto. The same went for a Tomahawk missile attack. Which left assault by special forces as the only viable alternative. It could be a rerun of the Falklands campaign of twenty years before.

I uncovered the luminous dial of my watch; we had been travelling for forty minutes. That put us half-way to the coast. The waves were getting shorter and steeper which was an indication of shelving water. Somewhere up ahead of us the rollers would be breaking along the surf line, dumping their energy in one final explosive burst. I could sense Kiwi peering ahead to try and spot any patches of whiteness.

A larger-than-usual wave surged underneath us. It was so steep it felt like riding the side of a mountain – the dark slope loomed over us and for several seconds I thought we would topple back and slide under. Then at the last moment we topped out and burst through the crest. I caught a brief glimpse of lights scattered in the darkness ahead. That was the shore, less than a mile away at a rough estimate. The lights were grouped over to the south, which was where Rio Grande ought to lie. We were coming in dead on target.

At about 600 metres we had to slow for our run-in. Although it was after midnight there was still the possibility of some vessel creeping along the shore making a night run into Rio Grande, or even of guard boats patrolling the coast. Our muffled engines would be inaudible except at very close range, and we were so low in the water we would be hard to spot. We were aiming for a point about five miles up the coast from the mouth of the river, where a sand bar broke the force of the waves. According to the chart, there was a narrow gap allowing access to a shallow lagoon behind with a shoreline of sand dunes backed by scrub – ideal for concealing the boats.

We began crabbing up the shoreline towards our objective. It was slow going because we were moving against the current. As we drew nearer we made out the sand bar as a line of broken water about half a mile off shore. The entrance was intermittently visible as a dark gap, two-thirds of the way along. Huge waves were pounding the breach here, and shooting the gap was going to be exciting.

We were about 400 metres off when Jock's boat flashed a covered light at us to signal that it was in difficulties. We drew alongside and Jock shouted that their engine was playing up. There was a brief discussion, and it was decided to tow the other craft in behind our boat. We wallowed uncomfortably in the heavy seas for several minutes while towlines were exchanged and made fast. To lighten the disabled boat, we transferred Nobby Clark across into our craft, leaving only Jock and Doug behind. It was exhausting work, having to seize moments between huge waves then cling on while the sea swept over us, but finally we got Nobby aboard. Jock and Doug would do the best they could to steer with paddles, while we towed them into the lagoon.

As soon as we had tethered the boats we set off again, with our craft straining beneath the increased load. As we neared the narrow entrance to the lagoon the battering from the rollers breaking across the sand bar increased. Our boat was tossed about like a chip of wood. Josh and Nobby and I clung on for our lives. The engine was roaring; the prop shaft and exhaust exposed as they bucked and rolled in the boiling surf.

And then I saw it – away to the south, a fast-moving shadow that momentarily obscured the lights dotting the blackness in the direction of Rio Grande. It was moving fast against the wind, and heading in our direction. I caught a momentary gleam of metal and glass and yelled to Kiwi, 'Helicopter!'

He snatched his attention from the waves to follow my pointing arm. It was flying without lights, which could mean only that this was a military machine. Skimming the coast, it would pick us up for certain if we entered the lagoon.

Kiwi pulled the tiller bar over, and his huge hands fumbled for the controls as he cut the engine, killing the give-away wake we were trailing. All four of us cowered down in the lead boat, keeping our faces hidden. Jock and Doug were doing the same. Without engine or paddles we were at the mercy of the sea. At any moment we could be swept against the sand bar and smashed to pieces by the pounding surf. Water hammered us with brutal force. We were caught up in a maelstrom, struggling to maintain our grip on the boats. I fought to keep my head clear but there was so much spray and water in the air it was next to impossible to breathe. I couldn't see where the helicopter was any longer, but for the moment my only concern was to hang on.

Then I lifted my head for an instant to snatch a look upward. The helicopter's silhouette was hovering over the lagoon. Had it spotted us?

There was no time to think about that. Another series of rollers crashed down on us. Something heavy struck me in the back, knocking the remaining breath from my body and catapulting me over the side. Dragged down by the weight of my equipment I was whirled away into the sea. Kicking out frantically, I fought my way back again, thankful for my life vest as

I clawed for the side of the boat. My first breath was a gulp of spume that set me retching, but I managed to get an arm on to one of the sponsons and clung on with all my strength. A moment later a huge hand came out of the darkness and grabbed me by my harness and hauled me bodily aboard. Kiwi must have seen me go and pulled me out.

There wasn't time to thank him, though. The second Gemini had flipped and was floating upside-down in the water, still secured to us by the towline. One of the occupants – I couldn't see which – was clinging on to the upturned hull. Grabbing the towrope, I pulled the boat in towards us so we could help.

Josh and Kiwi had the paddles out and were digging in like maniacs, trying to get us under way, while Nobby baled. Our only chance now was to get through the gap in the sand bar before we were broken up – and to hell with the helicopter. It was that or drowning for all of us.

I reached down to help the person in the water and saw that it was Doug. I heaved him spluttering inboard and he shook himself like a rat. That left Jock. I scanned the surface quickly but couldn't spot him; in these conditions visibility is measured in inches. Jock had his survival suit and life vest; we just had to hope he'd found something to cling on to.

Doug and I grabbed two more paddles and started stroking away with the rest of them. The boat was awash and sluggish with the weight of the five of us aboard – as well as a hull full of water – but with the other boat floating bottom up there was less drag on the stern.

As we neared the gap in the sandbank the turbulence became worse than ever as the current took us. Huge volumes of water were being forced through the opening. Breakers burst around us in explosions of white foam, and it was impossible even to see our own hands. We could only hope that the current would take us through.

We felt the boats spin around as if we were entering a violent rapid, then shoot forward at great speed. We were rushed towards the opening in a torrent of broken water, seas foaming and leaping around us; waves swept the inflatable from end to end, surging above our heads. All we could do was gulp breaths when we had a chance, and keep paddling frantically.

And then, suddenly, the turbulence abated, and we found ourselves wallowing in sheltered water. The swell inside the lagoon still heaved to the rhythm of the breakers pounding the sandbank in our rear, but after what we had endured at the entrance it was a blessed calm.

The shore in front of us was fringed with a pale beach, and the dunes behind it showed faintly through the darkness. There were no pinpricks of light showing, no signs of habitation. I glanced up, searching the sky for a sight of the helicopter. Nothing. It must have moved away, either up the coast or inland.

We were still some 200 yards from the beach, but the wind was pushing us in towards the land. There was no time to lose – this was the moment of maximum danger. It was vital to get the boats ashore and under cover before we were spotted.

I reached behind me and gave the towrope a yank, intending to pull the second boat alongside, but the cord was loose in my hand. I pulled some more but there was no resistance: the fastening had broken, and there was no sign of the second Gemini, and no sign of Jock.

SEVENTEEN

I took charge. We had to get ashore. If the landing had been compromised, this was the point at which searchlights would stab out from the beach, followed by shouts of alarm and gunfire.

I felt under my life vest for my night sight. Holding up the eyepiece I made a slow sweep of the lagoon, praying for a glimpse of the other boat.

'Can you see it?' Josh called.

'Keep your voice down,' I snapped. With the wind blowing onshore we were close enough to the beach to be overheard.

There was so much spray I couldn't be sure what I was seeing. I took another careful sweep, concentrating on the opening we had come through, looking for the upturned hull bobbing in the surf. Jock could have righted the boat, maybe even restarted the engine.

Kiwi backed his oar, spinning our boat around and heading back the way we had come. Doug and the others did their best to help, but the strength of the waves pushing through the gap made the task almost impossible. Water came foaming over the bow, filling the boat, forcing us backward. Three times we tried to get close to the gap, and three times we were beaten back.

Kiwi put his mouth to my ear. 'Shall I start the engine?'

I wanted to say yes, but we were less than 200 yards from the land. Our own boat was heavily laden, and a rescue attempt would be putting five lives at risk for a slender chance of success. Even with the engine I doubted whether we would make it through, and if we did there was no guarantee we would find Jock or get back again ourselves. It would mean the end of the mission.

I took one last look at the line of boiling surf, and made up my mind. 'No,' I said.

I knew I was condemning Jock, if he was still out there, to almost certain death. His life vest was a roll-down, activated by a pull-tab – if he had been knocked unconscious it wouldn't save him.

'No, there's nothing more we can do.' I took another deep breath. 'Steer for the shore.'

'Aye, aye,' Kiwi responded. He put the boat around. None of the others spoke. It was a terrible moment. Jock was liked as well as respected.

First Andy, and now Jock.

But there was no point dwelling on it. We had come here to do a job and I was determined to see it through. 'Paddle easy,' I told the others in an undertone.

Using careful strokes to avoid a telltale wake, we closed in on the beach. I crouched low in the bow with the night sight, scanning the shore and dunes, alert for any sign of an ambush. Unless someone up there had night-vision equipment we would be all but invisible against the darkness of the ocean – until we reached the sand.

The instant we felt the keel ground, Nobby and Doug sprang out. Their packs were lost with the missing boats, but they still had their personal weapons slung over their backs and secured by lanyard, as well as their night-vision goggles. They splashed forward through the shallows, charging up the beach into the dunes, guns at the ready, poised to give us cover.

As soon as they were in place Kiwi, Josh and I leapt out of the boat and, seizing the grab handles, rushed it forward up the beach, dragging it with all our strength towards the cover of a dark gully. We were gasping for breath and sweating in our thick suits by the time we made it, but the relief of being on solid ground was enormous. Out of the wind it felt strangely calm and silent after the battering we had taken at sea.

Nobby came running back to meet us. 'All clear. No sign of a reception party yet.'

'Take Kiwi with you and get back to the beach. Each of you scout the waterline for ten minutes in opposite directions to see if you find Jock or the boat, then come back here.'

'Understood.' The two of them ripped off their survival suits and doubled away into the dark in the direction of the beach.

I turned to Josh. 'We need to bury the bastard boat. Start digging while I contact Hereford.'

I found the communications pack, extracted the satcom, connected the co-ax leads and set it up. I composed a brief message to the effect that we had made an unopposed landing 23.30 local time, but had lost one Gemini with the boss aboard. I gave our present position from the GPS and said we were about to attempt a rendezvous with the guide.

Josh was at work unstrapping the bergens and other equipment from the boat. Then he depressed a valve in each side to deflate it. The hull was formed of rigid panels, and Josh removed them with a practised hand. The whole boat then folded up into a compact package two metres long.

I closed up the satcom, grabbed a collapsible shovel, and started to dig. Josh pitched in with me, chucking out spadefuls of wet sand. Together we excavated a pit about two metres square – it took about fifteen minutes to get it deep enough. We slid the hull with its collapsed sponsons into the trench. The outboard engine went on top, sealed inside a waterproof bag. The fuel tank followed, then the oars. Finally we flung in all the survival suits and scooped the sand back in, packing it down hard and raking over the surface to disguise our handiwork. I took a GPS fix to be certain of finding the spot again. With the wind that was blowing, any traces would be wiped out by dawn.

Nobby and Kiwi returned, shaking their heads. 'Nothing doing,' Kiwi reported. 'We covered the beach for half a mile in both directions – nothing doing.'

There was still a chance that Jock might have

survived. He might have been washed up further along the coast. If so he would do like us: get away from the beach as quickly as possible and lie up under cover. Then he would try to re-establish contact using his personal radio. We needed to be ready to come to his assistance.

We were silent for a moment. 'Now what?' said Nobby. 'A nice jaunt in the countryside?'

'Knock it off,' I hissed. I was in no mood for jokes. The coast was evidently kept under aerial surveillance and it was probably patrolled as well. It was essential we got clear without delay. 'We'll move inland a couple of kilometres and establish an LUP. You, Kiwi and Doug will remain there to make a report over the satcom while Josh comes with me to keep the rendezvous with the agent.'

I half expected Doug to protest against this out of sheer bloody-mindedness and to show he wasn't going to accept orders from me – but he just grunted his agreement. I knew he didn't much take to the idea of keeping the rendezvous on a strange continent with an unknown agent. I didn't blame him. I wasn't looking forward to it either, but it wasn't a task I could delegate to anyone else.

We checked around to make sure we hadn't forgotten anything. Doug and Nobby had lost their bergens in Jock's boat.

'We'll return at first light to look for Jock,' I told the others. 'With luck the boat will wash up somewhere along the shore and we can collect the packs too. If not we'll just have to share.' Sharing bivvy bags was possible since two guys would always be on watch, but the lack of spare clothing and medical packs was a serious loss. The Starstreak missiles had been stowed aboard the missing boat as well, so our anti-aircraft capability was lost. Fortunately communications packs had been duplicated for each boat.

We shared out the bergens and other equipment. At least the loads were lighter now. I took a reading on my hand-held GPS and checked our position on the map. It was almost midnight and we were approximately ten kilometres from the airbase. Our rendezvous point with the agent was three kilometres south-west, by the ruined stone chimney of an abandoned estancia. As far as I could tell there was no other human habitation in the area.

I led the way up the gully. Almost immediately we found a path threading back through the dunes. This made me nervous because it showed that the beach was used, and I was more determined than ever to get away. We made a stiff climb for ten minutes, then we came out on to flat ground covered with thick grass and heather. I heard Doug curse in an undertone as we started to pick our way through.

Through the night sights the landscape stood out in tones of eerie green. The gale was blowing at our backs now – the unremitting wind of the pampas. I was transported back twenty years, stumbling through the night across the endless plain. I half expected Andy to loom out of the darkness, checking to see we were all

OK, and the thought was oddly comforting. I decided that if I was in any doubt, I only had to ask myself what my brother would have done.

We plodded on. The ground underfoot was hard as iron, and punctuated by outcrops of stone that we had to detour. A thick layer of cloud obscured the moon. There was no wildlife, no trees and the landscape seemed utterly deserted. We walked in silence, broken only by occasional warnings, passed back by whoever was acting scout, as the ground changed. All the weariness had left me, and my senses were keyed up as I experienced the tension of active duty.

After half an hour or so it came on to snow – a light dusting that wasn't uncomfortable but degraded the performance of the night sights and slowed our progress. I was aiming for a low hill that stood around two-and-a-half kilometres inland, a vantage point from which to cover surrounding country, giving us the opportunity to leg it if necessary. It was just after midnight; there were still eight hours of darkness left.

My pack sat comfortably on my shoulders. The long journey in the Gemini, constantly battered by heavy seas, had been draining, but the hike was doing us good, blowing the cobwebs out. With luck, if we could keep our rendezvous with the agent sent to meet us, he would guide us in to a point from which we could survey the base while darkness still remained.

It was one o'clock by the time we reached the hill. I sent Kiwi and Josh on ahead and kept the other two back with me while they checked it out – the summit was just the place a patrol might have chosen for a look-out point. After a while Josh came back to report that it was all clear, and we moved in to establish a base for ourselves.

'OK,' I said, 'Josh, you come with me. Doug, you're in charge of the LUP. Keep a listening watch on the radio for any message from Jock. If you don't hear from us by dawn you're to assume that we have been taken and break for the border with Chile.'

'Yeah, I'll know the fucking way an' all,' he grunted.

Josh and I shed our packs and set off with only our personal weapons and harness equipment. We had ground to cover covertly, so it was better to travel light. Also, if we failed to make it back, Doug and Nobby would need our bergens to survive on the journey across the pampas to Chile.

Aided by our night sights we moved swiftly downhill in the direction of the ruined estancia. The nearer we got to the RV point the slower we had to go as the danger increased. The plan was to approach cautiously till we were within three or four hundred metres, then check for signs of enemy special forces lying in ambush.

We stopped for a nav check. 'You okay?' I asked Josh.

'Yes, course.'

Snow was still falling intermittently, and the cold intensified as we crept towards our objective. About an hour from leaving the LUP, we entered a thick bed of dried reeds that rustled furiously in the wind. I was pausing to check my bearings when Josh touched my arm silently and pointed ahead. I raised my night sight and there, outlined against the sky, I saw the tip of a broken stone chimney. It looked to be about half a kilometre from us.

Carefully we backed out from the reeds and surveyed the land. The reed beds appeared to extend in a broad triangle to the south-east of the remains of the farmhouse and were bounded on the north by a stream. The house itself stood in a small dell, giving shelter from the wind, with a few stunted trees nearby. Otherwise it was all open grassland. I tried to imagine what I would do if I were planning an ambush. The best tactics, I decided, would be to hold one's forces back to the north and east and wait for the target to approach. They could spring the trap as soon as we got in among the buildings, opening up on us from two sides to catch us in a crossfire, while the stream and reed beds would hinder our escape.

I signed to Josh that I wanted to circle around the lip of the dell to check if anyone was lying up there with a GPMG targeted on the RV point. At a rough estimate the dell was some 600 metres across, meaning we had a distance of about two kilometres to traverse before we would know for sure whether there were troops up there waiting to ambush us.

We started off anticlockwise, moving past the reed beds and across the stream. It was not deep, but it made up for that by being agonisingly cold. We crossed it in absolute silence, without a splash or a clink of stone, crouching low, moving on all fours like animals through the water and into the grasses on the far bank. An ambush party would most likely lie up on the reverse slope with a couple of look-outs forward. At every step we scanned the skyline with our night sights, looking to catch a glimpse of a head lifted above the grass, a rifle barrel carelessly handled, anything that would give away the presence of a chilled soldier tired of waiting.

The wind was now blowing towards us, and we kept our ears alert for the slightest sound. We had to assume the enemy was here. There is no other way to handle a situation like this. So we crawled through the long grass, telling ourselves that somewhere up above us in the waving blackness a platoon of Argentine marines crouched with GPMGs poised to let rip at the first sound – an enemy as tough and ruthless as ourselves, prepared to wait all night if necessary for a kill.

An hour later we had made about a mile, and we came to a halt. I was leading, and as I stretched out my hand in front of me my fingers touched a strand of wire. My pulse gave a sudden jump. Had I touched the trip-wire of an Argentine anti-personnel mine placed on a tripod a couple of metres ahead, ready to sweep the grass with a deadly hail of ball bearings? The Argies loved mines. The Falklands were lousy with ones they'd left behind. Or was it an alarm wire that would send phosphorous illumination rockets blazing into the sky and bring down crashing mortar rounds about our heads? I waited tensely but nothing happened, and I began to breathe again. Withdrawing my hand and parting the grass carefully, I saw that I had run up against a sagging barbed wire fence abutting an overgrown track.

I squirmed around on my stomach to warn Josh. For all we knew there might be a sniper lying up the slope with one hand on the wire waiting for the tug that would tell him someone was trying to slide through. We found a point where the wire was broken, checked that no one had stuck a mine in the gap, and wriggled through.

The track leading down to the estancia was deeply rutted. It looked to have been used by vehicles within the past few days, whether going or coming there was no way of telling, but there was fresh snow in the tyre marks. We crossed over, dragging some grass behind us to hide our footprints, and dived into cover again on the other side.

It was 3.00am by the time we arrived back at the reed beds. We had found no indication of an ambush, but there still remained the possibility that the Argentines might have opted for the simple tactic of holing up in the ruined barns and were waiting for us to show. The only way to find out was for one of us to go in. And that person had to be me.

In sign language I indicated to Josh that I was going in to the chimney and he was to follow and cover me over the last stage. In single file we crawled to the edge of the farmyard. From here it was apparent that the place had been deserted for a long time. There was no roof to the main house and most of the walls were tumbled down. We waited a long time in perfect stillness.

Nothing moved. Then I edged forward into the shadow of a collapsed shed and pushed my head through the undergrowth on the far side. I was now looking directly at the stump of the massive main chimney of the original house. Parked right up against it, in the centre of what must once have been the main living room, was a four-wheel-drive utility vehicle.

I trained the night sight on it. The vehicle was facing towards us and there was a man in the driver's seat. I could make out his head leaning back. He wasn't moving. Maybe he had fallen asleep. I swept the scope round the yard. There was no sign of other life in the vicinity. From my harness I extracted my GPS unit and pressed the button for my position. The coordinates exactly matched the RV point we had been given at the briefing.

It was now or never. If there were Argentines lying in wait among the ruined barns I would find out about it in another minute. Signing to Josh to cover me, I rose to a crouch and picked my way around the edge of the yard, my rifle at the ready. It must have been all of thirty yards to the far side and it seemed like the longest walk of my life. At every step I expected a bullet to take me.

A dozen yards from the line of crushed rubble that had once been the front wall of the house, I halted and rose to my full height. I wanted the agent, if it was him, to be able to see me clearly. For several seconds I stood there unmoving in the silence of the deserted estancia. Nothing in the car stirred. Maybe the guy was asleep.

Maybe it was a dummy made to look like a man and the ambush party was playing a game . . .

There was a metallic click and I stiffened. Slowly, very slowly the driver's door opened. '*Buenos noces, señor,*' said a quiet voice. 'Are you lost?'

My mouth was so dry I could hardly speak. '*Buenos noces,*' I replied. 'I am looking for a place to sleep.'

'I know of a place. Are you alone?'

'No, there are others with me.'

The car door opened further. 'I am coming out,' the man called softly. 'I am unarmed.'

I covered him even so as he emerged into the yard. He was a bearlike man in civilian clothes, his face shadowed in the moonless dark. He wore a long sheepskin coat against the cold and he held his arms in front of him so I could see he was not carrying a weapon. He was taking no chances. He must have known there were guns trained on him but he didn't seem nervous. He had made all the responses correctly. He was in the right place. He had to be our man.

I moved in closer, being careful not to block Josh's line of fire. 'We are SAS.'

He nodded. 'I have come to meet you.' His voice was low and even, remarkably composed, a Spanish accent overlaying the English. 'My name,' he added, 'is Seb.'

EIGHTEEN

Seb! At the sound of the name a flood of images rushed through my mind: our first encounter twenty years ago in the valley near the border, when the two of us had almost shot one another; Seb's offer to lead the pursuit away from our trail, and the final ambush when Andy was killed. It had never occurred to me that Seb would still be active.

Seb seemed equally surprised to learn I had been on the earlier mission. Our meeting on that occasion had been so brief that he had scarcely had time to register faces.

I filled him in on the loss of the boat with Jock aboard, and he grew serious. 'That is bad,' he said. 'The prevailing winds on this part of the coast mean that any drifting object will wash ashore at some point. If the authorities are presented with an inflatable boat containing military equipment they will draw the obvious conclusion that a clandestine landing has been attempted – and the airbase is the only logical target.'

'There's a chance the major may have reached land somewhere alive, but his radio isn't working. We've searched the beach along the lagoon, without result.'

'I will send people out to scour the shore as soon as dawn breaks. They are Yaga indians, a despised minority in these parts who can be trusted not to talk. If they find your major they will bring him to me; if there is only a body they will bury it on the beach.'

I radioed in to Doug a pre-arranged code to summon the other three to join us at the RV point, and we settled down to wait in the shelter of Seb's Toyota. As he lit a cigarette, I made out his face for the first time, bearded as before, harsher and more gaunt than I remembered. I dare say the same was true of mine. The intervening years had been hard for both of us.

We talked of the previous mission.

'After we parted, I made contact with the pursuing patrol,' he told us. 'They accepted my story and moved off towards the south as I hoped. Very soon afterwards though there came the sound of heavy firing and I heard later that you had run into an ambush.'

I told Seb how the Argentines had laid a trap for us on the other side of the border. I described the battle and how Andy and Guy had died.

'I am sorry,' he said. 'If I had come with you the odds would have been better.'

'You did everything you could,' I told him. 'You risked your life to try to draw the other patrol off.'

'I was born not far from this estancia. As a boy I learned to know this sector of the coast well. Not till I was twelve did we move to the Falklands.'

'Then you came back?'

'Yes, my mother was Spanish, from an Argentine family. She felt trapped on the islands.'

'How long ago was that?' I asked him.

'Thirty years near enough. There was no work on the Falklands except sheep or fishing. Here I am a geologist. I do consultancy work for the oil companies.' He shrugged. 'It's a useful cover.'

Doug and the others made good time even though they were burdened with packs, and were with us in not much over an hour. I went out to meet them. I wanted to break the news of Seb's return to Doug personally.

In the intervening hours Doug had been brooding on our current position and now he was tired and edgy. 'They sent who?' he said incredulously when I gave him the news. 'Seb? But that's the bastard who steered us straight into a fucking ambush, man! If he's not working for the Argies, then he's fucking useless.'

'He did his best to save our lives, for God's sake. He's come out here to meet us. He has a vehicle and says he can take us to a place where we can lie up in safety, close to the airbase.'

'How do we know we can trust the bugger?'

'We don't have any choice, dammit. He's all the help we've got. We have to trust him.'

Doug curled his lip. 'You trust him if you want. So far as I'm concerned he's an Argy.'

In the end Doug consented to meet Seb and he shook hands with ill grace. I could see that his hostility was being picked up by Nobby and Kiwi, who were becoming suspicious in their turn. If Seb noticed this attitude he did not let it show. At his direction we stowed our kit in his Land Cruiser and climbed aboard ourselves. The snow was getting thicker now, driving in from the sea. Seb told us to take off our ponchos and put on some civilian coats he had brought along so that we would not seem obviously like soldiers to a passing vehicle. When we were all safe aboard he spread a rug over our kit to conceal it.

He kept his lights off as we bumped along the farm track, explaining that he did not want to attract the attention of any vehicle passing on the main road. I offered him my night-vision goggles, but he declined. He seemed to have eyes like a cat, for he never once missed the way. He said the estancia was one of many abandoned when the bottom fell out of the sheep market two decades ago.

I asked what he made of the political situation here now. Was there a strong likelihood of war?

'I will tell you,' he said. 'These people are desperate. The economy has broken down. There are no jobs, there is no money. The banks have shut up. Ordinary people's savings have been wiped out. All that is left are debts. We are reduced to a barter economy. Even the foreign oil companies cannot get currency to pay their workers.

'People have lost their jobs, their pensions; they have lost faith in the government, lost faith in each other. They live day by day with no idea how they will feed their families. New administrations are formed and fall within hours. There are strikes and demonstrations every day. The people are desperate.'

'Desperate enough to go to war?'

Seb lifted his eyes from the track a moment to look at me in the darkness. 'Understand this, my friend – among all the quarrels and political divisions that are tearing this unhappy people apart, one topic only unites them. Socialists, communists, Peronists, right wing, left wing, from the gutter to the mansion, there is one common cause: the Malvinas – a belief that the islands are rightfully Argentina's and should be returned. The militarists have taken over power; they will snatch at anything that will bring the country behind them again. Some of them believe that if they could pull off a great coup, somehow seize the islands and hold them, it would act as a catalyst, healing the nation's wounds.'

'Have they forgotten what happened last time?'

Seb glanced back towards the track, twisting the wheel gently as we ground forward up the snow-covered surface. 'You forget, this is South America, where memories are short and passions hot. Anything is possible.'

We reached the blacktop road and turned south. Seb switched on the headlamps. The beams shone on the driving snow and the screen wipers worked steadily.

'There is another thing you should know,' he said after a while. 'Tierra del Fuego is the territory of the Argentine Third Marine Division, officered by fanatical supporters of the military coup. The division fought fiercely in the Malvinas war. It has re-equipped with modern arms and there are many in its ranks who would leap at the chance of a second invasion.'

We drove on along the highway. I assumed it was the same road Doug and I had followed on our epic trek twenty years before. Then, though, it had been composed entirely of gravel. Now it was half and half – one lane was made up with tarmac, and a gravel bed ran alongside.

We had covered three or four miles when suddenly, about two hundred yards ahead of us, the lights of a vehicle clicked on.

Seb let out a curse. He slowed and dropped a gear to bring the revs up. 'All of you, quickly, get down below the seats and cover yourselves.' The guys in the rear squirmed down under the rugs Seb had provided, and I curled myself up in the footwell. The lights evidently belonged to a big truck, because we pulled over on to the gravel to get by.

'Military?' I said to Seb.

He nodded. 'Almost all traffic is army. No one else can afford the gasoline. I use this vehicle to drive survey parties for an oil company. It provides useful cover.'

My rifle was stowed in the back. I drew my automatic pistol from its holster. It was a Sig-Sauer P228, designed in Switzerland and made in West Germany, and probably the finest weapon of its kind ever produced. It could be chambered for 9mm parabellum, 0.45 automatic Colt or .357 magnum, and was the pistol of choice for the US Secret Service as well as the SAS. My particular model carried nine 9mm rounds plus one ready in the breach.

I could hear the boys in the back releasing safety

catches and slotting rounds into their grenade launchers. Doug was swearing in a monotonous undertone, as he often did before going into action. 'Fucking Argies, fucking country, fuck the lot of them!'

Seb kept the Toyota moving at a steady, slow pace on the gravel surface. If the truck flagged us down or tried to pull across us, our best bet was probably to use our manoeuvrability to pull a J-turn and hare off back the way we had come, trusting our greater speed to outrun them. If for any reason that was not possible and we were forced to stop, we would burst out from the doors either side, firing as we ran. I would let the others go first; my pistol was chicken-feed beside the massive firepower of their C-5s firing on full auto. A single salvo of grenades from four weapons would take out the truck and all its occupants. Chances were there would be no more than ten men facing us; I was confident we could cut them down before they realised what had hit them.

If that happened, though, there could be no question of continuing with the mission. It would be a case of high-tailing it for the border with all possible speed before the inevitable helicopters had a chance to get on our track.

The truck stayed where it was while we ground slowly towards it. A hundred and fifty yards now. Was it a regular roadblock with orders to stop and search suspicious-looking vehicles on the roads at night, or was it hunting us?

Seb spoke. 'It's a checkpoint to catch smugglers from over the border.' His voice was flat, without emotion.

He reached down into the glove pocket and took out a big automatic. It looked like a Colt or Browning High Power. He thrust it into his waistband without taking his foot off the accelerator. The distance between the headlamps was under a hundred yards. 'With luck they will not bother us. If they wave us down I will get out and speak to them. Do not move unless I call to you to join me, then come out shooting.'

'Don't worry about us, mate,' Doug growled. 'We've done this before.'

One time in Ireland he and I had run into a paramilitary roadblock manned by the Continuity IRA. The usual trick when encountering one of these was to spin out and disappear. On this occasion things had happened too fast – we came around a corner and there was a farm trailer backed across the road, and four guys in balaclavas manning it with AK47s. Doug hadn't hesitated. He'd put the car into a broadside skid that sent it sliding towards them at fifty knots. I would never forget the expression of the nearest player as two tons of vehicle came slicing down on him, catching him by the knees and pitching him over the bonnet. A second later I was debussing, rolling out of my door and laying down bursts of fire from my HK53 as I hit the ground. I dropped two guys and the last one had just time to throw up his hands and shout, 'Don't shoot!' Result: two players dead, one maimed, and a prisoner so shit scared he'd wet himself. Only one of them even got a shot off. Doug was a good soldier even if he was a prat.

While all this was running through my head we were closing on the truck. It was now only about thirty yards off. There was a ditch running along the side of the road. If it came to a fight, when we had killed the soldiers we could throw the bodies in there and take off in the truck.

The lights of the truck were muted by the falling snow. 'A five-tonner, canvas topped, maybe half a dozen men with light automatic weapons,' Seb called out softly. 'They will not be expecting to meet resistance.' He was keeping well over to the right-hand side of the highway and the gravel rattled against the underside of the Toyota. As we drew close, the driver of the opposing vehicle suddenly let out a double toot-toot on his horn that made me jump.

'Steady,' Seb said between his teeth. 'It is only a greeting. They recognised the vehicle. I am known on this road.' He pumped his own horn twice and next moment we were back in the darkness, moving past the truck's length with snow spraying up against our sides. Even if they had wanted to, no one could have seen how many of us there were inside.

'Sometimes they stop cars to demand bribes from drivers,' Seb said as we slowly relaxed. 'Tonight we were lucky the weather is bad. The soldiers wanted to stay under cover.'

I snapped the safety back on the Sig and restored it to its holster. Behind, Doug and the others were picking themselves up from the floor.

Seb turned on the radio. A girl's voice came on,

crooning in Spanish, a sad song. I asked Seb about the security around the airbase at Rio Grande.

'In recent days security on the military sector has been tightened considerably and is now very intense indeed. All vehicles have to show passes at the gates and there are regular patrols of the perimeter fences.' He shook his head. 'I do not know why London has sent you in to do this when I could have given them all the information they needed.'

'Maybe they'll want us to take these planes out,' said Doug.

Seb drew on his cigarette, dragging the smoke deep down into his lungs before he replied. 'Madness,' he said finally. 'What are they trying to do, hand the Argentines an excuse for war?'

'We just obey orders,' I said.

Seb let out a mirthless laugh. 'It is OK for you boys. You will do your job and get out. I have to live here.'

I told him about the salmonella outbreak in Port Stanley, and the Tornado crash we had witnessed. Seb let out a low whistle. 'We have heard nothing of this. They must have imposed a blackout on the news leaving the islands. You think these incidents are connected to the current crisis?'

'I'll tell you what I reckon,' I said. 'I think the epidemic has got worse. So bad maybe that most of the garrison is down and that includes the remaining pilots. The only way replacements can be flown in from the UK is by using the refuelling tankers at Mount Pleasant. With those out of action the islands are cut off. I think

London is terrified that if the Argies learn how bad the situation is they might be tempted to seize the opportunity to invade. How quickly could the marines here act, do you think?'

Seb shook his head. 'This is winter time, there is no shipping down here to transport large numbers of troops. They would have to come from further north, on the mainland.'

'What about transport aircraft?'

'None that I have seen. Rio Grande is a bomber base. Always has been.'

Seb was straining to see the road ahead as if searching for a marker. Whatever it was he must have seen it, for he slowed the Toyota and cut the headlights again. 'We are near the airfield now.'

Another minute and we were bumping along a disused track with thick undergrowth either side. Seb stopped the vehicle. 'We are less than half a mile from the airfield,' he said. 'From here on we proceed by foot.'

It was half-past four – four hours to set up the lying-up point before first light.

NINETEEN

Before we set off for the base, Seb produced a detailed map. We squeezed round to study it in the light of a small torch.

'We came in along the main highway here,' Seb indicated. 'And we turned off down this track, like so. We are now at this point on the north side of the field,' he tapped the map. 'The entire airfield is protected by a high wire fence. The military and civilian sectors lie on opposite sides of the single, shared runway. A secondary inside fence topped with razor wire prevents access to the military side with its hangars and revetments. The space between is patrolled, and there are also minefields covering access routes from the sea.'

A couple of the lads chuckled but I was impressed. Seb had done a thorough job. The map was beautifully marked out with the minefields indicated by rows of little crosses. 'How accurate is the position of these fields?' I asked him.

'They are taken off a map issued to officers on the base,' Seb answered. 'Even so, you will need to exercise great care. Some of the minefields may be dummies, others left over from the earlier hostilities may be unmarked. The route I will show you is safe. I have watched soldiers moving along it.'

'You're coming in with us this time?' Doug inquired sarcastically. He was letting him know he still wasn't trusted, but Seb didn't rise to the bait.

'I will guide you as far as the inner fence and leave you there. I suggest you set up your observation point as close to the fence as possible. You should have a clear view of all the activity on the base from there. The guards patrol round the inside of the fence. In general they avoid the zone between the fences for fear of mines. So you should be undisturbed.'

'Do the patrols have dogs?' Kiwi asked.

'I have not noticed any, and I think they would be little use in the winter. Be warned, though, the guards are all drawn from the Third Marine Division. Whatever your general opinion of Argentine troops may be, do not underestimate these. They are highly motivated and well disciplined. Expect patrols to be vigilant and to pursue intruders aggressively.'

I studied the layout thoughtfully. He was right. The zone between the fences would be a good place to lie up. Fear of mines would deter pursuit and the undisturbed vegetation would provide good cover. It was a question of locating a good spot from which to observe the runway. We would also need to survey a quick escape route in case we had to exit in a hurry.

We established communication procedures. Seb gave me a cellphone I could use if we needed help or evacuation. We would use agreed code words in

Spanish to convey messages. 'I have been instructed that when the mission is complete I am to drive you to the border, where a helicopter from the Chilean side will rendezvous for a pick-up.'

Doug grunted at that. No more border crossings and ambushes on this trip. And no more yomping out across the freezing pampas either.

We also agreed a fallback assembly point two kilometres north of the base, to meet at if we had to abandon the LUP, and an emergency rendezvous point we called the War RV; on the edge of town for use in the event anyone became separated. Seb wanted to know how we would transmit reports back to the UK. 'I recommend great care. Restrict communications to urgent messages only,' he said. 'The territory is considered a frontier zone and the authorities monitor all transmissions very closely. They can home in on you within seconds.'

I shrugged. We had our own rules for transmitting messages and they were none of his business. Our orders called for us to check in with a status report twice daily. We also had to report any contact with the enemy or significant intelligence on the target. As soon as we reached the airfield and established our LUP, I would set up the 320 set and inform Hereford that we were in position to begin observations.

With Seb's help we disembarked from the Toyota and shouldered our bergens and weapons. Doug and Nobby had no packs, so we loaded them up with the heavy weapons, including the GPMG, and the satcom set. We were all now wearing winter white camouflage smocks and trousers. One side was all white for use in the arctic; the other was a mix of white slashed with black for use where there was a tree line. Tonight we were wearing all white. Seb carried no weapon but he brought along a set of long-handled bolt cutters. 'For the gate,' he explained grimly.

Then we set off. I went in front with Seb. The night-vision scope made the track easy to follow. All of us were vigilant in case someone was following. Seb evidently found our operations procedures strange, but said nothing and tagged along.

Nothing happened to raise an alarm, and after about an hour we came over a low rise and saw the lights of the airfield shimmering through the falling snow. After a few more minutes the outer wire fence loomed up. The track running outside it looked to be in regular use. 'How often do they patrol this?' I asked Seb.

'The outer fence is checked at dawn and dusk, but the inner fence is patrolled at two-hourly intervals around the clock. A Jeep with a driver and observer. They look mainly for holes in the fence.'

I glanced at my watch, and reckoned we had three-and-a-half hours till dawn. The falling snow would obliterate any traces of our passage well before the next patrol showed up.

The track led down to a set of double gates, firmly padlocked. Seb applied his bolt cutters to the hasp and together we heaved on the handles. It took our combined strengths to shear through the toughened steel. Seb slipped the lock off and pushed the gate open enough to let us through.

'This is as far as I go. You are on your own now. Watch for mines and remember the patrols. At first light I will check the beach for any sighting of your comrade and contact you over the cellphone.'

He closed the gate behind us and padlocked it shut with a fresh lock. He handed me a spare brass key with a plastic tag. 'This exit is rarely used. Anyone trying to get through will assume the keys have become mixed up.'

I pocketed the key and nodded. 'Thanks for your help.'

'I will call you,' he said and vanished away into the snow.

I turned to study the situation. The two fences were approximately a hundred metres apart. On the plan the strip between where we were standing was shown as being sown with anti-personnel mines and the area was thickly overgrown. Just to make the point, there were signs fixed to the wire with a skull and crossbones.

'Bloody typical of the Argies,' Doug grunted. I agreed with him. If they were going to have a mine barrier, they should have done it the East German way – spray the ground with weed killer and rake it over regularly, then there's no vegetation to hide behind and any tracks show up.

The map showed that the mines were clustered in the centre, leaving pathways along the fences where repair parties could work in safety. If we crawled along the edge of the inside fence until we reached a spot from where we could observe the runway, we should be okay.

As I looked, details of the airfield started to become clearer. According to the map it was about two miles long by a mile wide. The fence here ran parallel to the main runway, which was laid out east to west. The military sector – where we were – lay to the north of the runway and the civilian side to the south. The military installations were grouped in two sections; what looked like the control tower and mess blocks could be made out almost directly opposite where we had come in. A little further on and closer to the edge of the field stood the dark silhouettes of aircraft revetments and hangars. Seb had done a good job of leading us to the target.

On the far side of the inner fence a road ran around the airfield perimeter, presumably the one used by the patrols. We had no means of knowing when the next patrol would be round. Hopefully, though, any check in the current weather conditions would be cursory.

'Doug, take Kiwi with you and do a recce,' I told him. 'Keep close up to the inner fence to avoid mines. See if you can find a spot where there's a good view of the landing strip and all the main buildings.'

My intention, if we weren't all blown up in the process, was to establish the LUP not far from the gate in case we needed to get out in a hurry, then set up an observation point about a hundred metres further in, from where we would monitor activity on the base.

Two of us would man the OP around the clock on two-hour shifts, while the others rested up.

'Got it,' Doug said. He handed Nobby the GPMG, which he had been carrying to give Kiwi a break, and took Nobby's rifle. There was a narrow path, presumably used by fatigue crews carrying out routine maintenance. The pair of them dropped on to their bellies and crawled off into the darkness.

Nobby, Josh and I crouched down out of the wind to wait in the darkness. I set Josh to watching the gate and the way we had come, in case a vehicle on the road noticed the Toyota tracks before they were covered by snow and decided to follow them down, while Nobby and I scanned the airfield before us. The wind was blowing gusts of snow in from the sea, at times obscuring the control tower completely. At other times we could make out the gleam of headlamps moving between buildings, which may or may not have been patrols.

On the apron in front of the tower half a dozen aircraft were drawn up. As far as I could make out at this distance through the night-vision scope, they were jet trainers and ground attack machines. I had spent some time studying an Argentine aircraft recognition manual, and had a pretty fair idea of what planes to expect. Presumably the bombers were all safely snugged down in their revetments.

'No runway lights,' Nobby muttered. It was true. The approach lights looked to be switched off too. Evidently no aircraft movements were anticipated in the near future. The tower still appeared to be manned, though – but that would be standard procedure at all times.

There was a scuffling in the grass and Doug reappeared. 'I found a good place about 300 metres up,' he reported. 'There's what looks like an old light array or windsock post located between the fences – a fucking great wooden thing set in a concrete base. It looks unused now and all grown over with gorse and crap, but I reckon there can't be any mines there and the five of us could hide up behind the concrete. Beyond that the path goes on the same and you come to a drainage channel running out from the base. I reckon we could use that as a means of entry.'

He led the way back along the inside of the fence, the rest of us following in single file. We moved on our bellies at a crawl, trusting our winter whites to camouflage us against the snow-covered undergrowth behind. It was cold going, but better than standing waiting and shivering. The grass under the wire had grown long over the years and, provided we kept low enough, we were effectively crawling along a narrow trench between areas of vegetation.

The spot Doug had chosen was just as he had described – a concrete platform set back twenty-five metres from the inner fence, surrounded and over-grown by heather and gorse. As Doug said, it was a safe bet that no mines had been set in the immediate vicinity in case access was needed. Even so it was worth taking precautions.

'I'll go first,' I announced to the others, telling them to stay well back. Facing outwards from the fence, I extracted my combat knife, parted the tough stems of gorse and pushed the blade into the ground ahead of me. The earth was hard and tangled with roots, but there was no obstruction that I could feel. I drew the knife out and moved it over to the side a few inches. Modern anti-personnel mines are no bigger than a saucer, but they contain enough explosive to blow your legs off. I slid the knife in again, and this time the tip came up against something strong. From the slight scraping sound it made I was fairly certain it was only a stone, and a couple more prods with the knife a little further over met no resistance so I judged it safe to ease forward on my elbows a few inches.

Again I repeated the process, starting at my right and working across methodically. Minelayers almost always work to a pattern – so many mines to cover a given patch of ground. Mines achieve their effect by fear; once a platoon has seen one of their number blown up, they become very reluctant to move until engineers come up with detecting equipment. There's no sense in sowing the damn things too close. The idea is that you don't find out about a minefield until you're in the middle of it.

It was a slow business, but we still had a few hours before dawn and it was better than someone losing a foot through being in too much of a hurry. I got into a routine of feeling ahead and inching forward, ignoring the cold and numbness in my fingers, concentrating only on the sensation at the tip of the knife as it slid under the topsoil. I tried to remember all the training courses I had attended in mine and demolition clearance. Sometimes, I knew, minelayers would plant a few mines out of pattern to deceive the clearance team – but this was airfield defence and I figured they wouldn't bother with tricks.

Within a few minutes I was hidden from view under a canopy of gorse. It was hard stuff to work in, but it kept the wind off and provided cover from any observer. As far as I could, I tried to bend the stems aside rather than cut them and run the risk of chucks carrying away in the wind. Swath by swath I edged onward, scanning a track as far as I could reach either side of me. I was three metres short of the concrete plinth when the knife blade slid a fraction deeper than before and I felt the tip skim the edge of a curved shape. Instantly my heart-rate leapt. Carefully I withdrew the blade a fraction and probed to left and right. Each time the point connected with the same smooth surface. It felt exactly like the hard ceramic shell of a modern anti-personnel device. Shit, I thought. Whoever laid this was smart enough to guess an intruder might make for the plinth as being a safe spot and planted a mine to catch him. Bastard.

I lay still a minute, wondering what to do. The obvious course was to back off and try somewhere else to hide up. That wasn't going to be so easy though. This was our best chance. If the minelayers had been as thorough as this there would be precious few other options. In all probability we would find ourselves reduced to using the pathway and trusting our camouflage nets to cover us.

On the other hand I was close up to the plinth now. If this was a mine there was a strong possibility it was the only one. Maybe the layers had one too many in the batch and had stuck it in here without thinking.

'Doug,' I called behind me.

'What's up?' he whispered back.

'I think I've found one!'

'Fuck!' There was a moment's pause, then, 'What you going to do?' he asked.

'Christ knows. Lift the bastard thing I suppose.'

'You want help?'

'No, just tell everyone to keep well back. And hunt around in case there are any others back there I missed.'

Most mines require a certain minimum pressure to set them off, generally around five kilograms – otherwise they could be detonated by every passing rabbit. So you have a bit of leeway to play with. Not much, but some. Generally, so long as you are careful, it's a fairly straightforward matter to dispose of them. I set to, scraping away the soil and working as gently as if I were a palaeontologist uncovering a piece of a dinosaur. It didn't help that the ground was frozen hard and I had to prise the earth away in lumps. Behind me I could hear the rest of the team prodding away to either side to locate the edges of the minefield.

After ten minutes' cautious digging and scraping I had the top of the thing uncovered. I started excavating away around the edges, trying to get the blade of the knife underneath. There was a danger it was fitted with an anti-handling device, but they take time to rig up and are dangerous to set — they're just not practical when you're laying hundreds of the fuckers. In spite of the cold my hands were clammy and beads of sweat were trickling down my face into my eyes.

'How's it going?' Doug called softly.

'Nearly got it,' I told him. 'Just a little bit longer.' I glanced at my watch. It had taken us an hour and a half to get twenty-five metres.

'We can't find anything back here. Looks like yours is the only one.'

That wasn't a lot of comfort. If this thing went off it would take my hands and probably my head with it. Everything considered, it would be better all round if it took my head. At least it would be a quick way to go. I scraped some more earth away from around the back of the mine and prepared to lift it.

At that moment there came a warning hiss from Doug behind me. 'Lights! Shit, there's a patrol heading this way!'

TWENTY

Every muscle in my body went tense instantly. We were lying out in the open in single file. The wind was driving snow in great gusts and we were clad in winter whites with hoods pulled over our heads, but if a torch beam were played in our direction we'd be picked out for sure.

I didn't dare look round in case my face showed up. 'How far off?' I called softly.

'Four hundred metres,' Doug whispered back. 'Coming alongside the nearest hangar now. Estimate another four or five minutes till they reach us.'

Fuck, I told myself angrily. There was only one thing I could think of to do – continue. I slid the blade of the knife underneath the base of the mine and levered slowly upwards. After a brief resistance the black ceramic casing freed itself from the surrounding earth and came smoothly out. I picked it up gingerly and laid it as far away to one side as I could reach. Taking up the knife again, I started to probe the short strip of ground remaining between me and the edge of the concrete plinth. I thought it unlikely there would be another mine placed so close to the previous one but it was necessary to make sure.

I kept at it while behind me, Doug relayed a soft-voiced commentary from the others on the patrol's progress. 'Heading down towards the gate we came in by . . . turning right . . . coming in our direction . . .'

I felt a gentle clink as the tip of the blade touched the concrete foundation of the plinth base, and a wave of relief swept through me. 'All clear,' I whispered to Doug. 'Make sure you keep in my track.' I wriggled forward, forcing the remaining stalks of the gorse apart with my bare hands. The ground cover arched over the concrete slab, forming a natural cavern some two feet high. I scrambled on to the plinth. Doug followed, with Josh behind him; Kiwi and Nobby brought up the rear. Carefully, so as not to betray our presence, we pulled the gorse stalks down behind us. With luck, anyone seeing our tracks would reckon it was only a fox or some other wild animal.

'Here they come,' muttered Doug.

'Keep still,' I growled.

The long beams of the headlights came into sight, probing through the snow. The driver was moving cautiously, probably more on account of the atrocious weather conditions than because they were searching for anyone. It was some kind of military four-wheel-drive with a spotlight mounted on the roof, but the beam was trained ahead on the track rather than swinging to each side. It drew level and ground on past us, the red tail-lights disappearing into the murk.

Heaving sighs of relief, we took stock. The concrete slab was around three metres square with two massive wooden posts rising from it. The surface was cushioned with a thick layer of moss and dead leaves. Gorse and grass had grown up on all sides so thick that it was almost impossible to see out or be seen from inside.

'Jesus, but I hate fucking mines,' Nobby said under his breath with feeling as he wiped snow from his eyes. 'Give me a clean bullet any day.'

'You'll get one if you don't shut up talking.' I hate idle chatter on a mission. Andy never used to allow it, and I tried to follow his example. 'Three of us can kip down here while the other keeps watch out the front,' I went on. 'We'll take turns, an hour each. Josh, you stand first watch with me. Take the Spyglass with you.'

'Gotcha, boss.' Josh squirmed back along the tunnel, clutching the handheld thermal–imaging observation sight. Mounted on a tripod, it combined with a laser rangefinder and was designed to let mortar teams direct fire accurately day and night in all conditions.

Kiwi and Nobby were clearing space for the bivvy bags and laying out equipment. 'Doug, make a sitrep,' I told him. 'Use the patrol set, not the satcom.' The 320 patrol set was a VHF radio that communicated with the guard net at Hereford. Messages could be passed but it could take as much as twelve hours to get a reply back, depending what was going on at the other end. But the unit had a much smaller splash–out than the satcom, and was less likely to be detected. I didn't want to run any more risks than we had to. 'Inform Hereford we are in position on the target with no air movement observable as of current time and date. Then you can all three get your heads down. I'll send Josh back in an hour and Nobby can relieve him.'

Josh and I wriggled our way up the tunnel through the undergrowth till we reached the path along the fence. For some minutes we occupied ourselves constructing a hide around the entrance and camouflaging all traces of our presence. Luckily for us the falling snow was rapidly obliterating any tracks we had left.

We set up the Spyglass on its tripod, and with the help of the rangefinder I measured distances to points of interest. The tower was 900 metres off – long rifle shot – with the main runway beyond. The same distance again beyond that, shrouded from view by falling snow, were the buildings of the small civilian terminal. On this side of the tower we could make out some humped shapes, presumably the revetments housing the bombers. Nearby were the main hangars, their massive roofs blanketed with snow. Closer, only about 200 metres away, were some half-buried structures that I took to be fuel bunkers with pipes running in a ditch back towards the apron. Snow was piling up on the lip of the ditch and the pipes stood out in a dark line. I reckoned it was the same drainage channel that Doug had spotted on his recce.

There were lights burning in the tower. Otherwise, aside from the single patrol that had just passed us, there was no sign of life. It looked as though the whole base was shut down for the night.

I rubbed my hands to warm my numbed fingers. It was getting on for seven when I checked the time. 'Your watch is about up,' I told Josh. 'Better get back up the tunnel and send Nobby down to take over.'

Josh didn't answer straight away. After a moment he said, 'I think I can see lights over on the runway.'

He moved away from the Spyglass to let me take a look and I lowered my head to the eyepiece. He was right. Intermittently through the snow I could make out the glimmer of green and white lights twinkling along the strip.

'I'd have sworn they weren't there five minutes ago,' Josh said.

I trained the Spyglass on the tower and buildings nearby. It was hard to be certain but it looked to me as though there were more lights showing over there too.

'Let's wait a bit longer and see if anything happens,' Josh said. 'Maybe they're expecting something.'

'Either that or they're getting ready to send a flight off,' I agreed. It was more likely an arrival expected; we would have noticed more activity on the apron otherwise.

We listened for any sound of a plane overhead, but there was too much wind to hear anything. After a wait of some minutes, headlights could be seen in the distance moving off down the runway. 'Fire tender,' Josh reckoned.

We kept the Spyglass focused on the end of the runway, taking turns to watch. Even so we almost missed the plane. It was flying without lights, and slipped in almost soundlessly through the driving snow to touch down at the eastern end of the base. It was only the sight of the fire tender chasing down the runway that alerted us. Josh was at the eyepiece and he let out a quiet yelp of triumph. 'Got it! There, look! Just turning on to the taxiway. You can see it when the fuselage blocks out the lights on the ground.'

He passed me the sight and a moment later I had it too. 'Looks big – a bomber? No, a transport more likely.'

'I thought Seb said there were no transports down here?'

'He meant not permanently based here. They must have to fly in stores sometimes.'

We watched as the plane taxied off the runway on to the apron on the military side. As it did so the runway lights clicked off as someone turned a switch. 'Saving power, do you suppose?' said Josh.

'Perhaps. More likely they don't want to draw attention to what's going on.'

We continued observing. The arrival aircraft came to a halt in front of the tower. Looking through the sight I made out figures moving around on the ground with hand torches and vehicles circling.

After a few minutes the aircraft started rolling again, but this time it was preceded by a vehicle. 'What do you make of that?' I asked Josh.

Josh took a quick squint through the sight. 'Tow truck,' he said. 'They must be bringing it in to shelter.'

Together we watched the truck move nearer, dragging its huge tow. From one giant hangar a sudden shaft of yellow light spilled out on to the snow-covered apron and grew rapidly larger. 'They're opening the doors,' I said. 'They must be going to bring the plane inside.'

'Bloody big whatever it is,' Josh whispered back.

Excitedly we waited as the truck and aircraft approached the patch of light. Identification was going to be difficult because of the distance and because the hangar was between the aircraft and us. As the convoy rolled towards the light it vanished from view. Peering through the flying snowflakes I made out a swept-back T-tail but no markings that I could distinguish.

'A civilian airliner?' I hazarded. 'A 747?'

Josh shook his head. 'No windows that I could see. More like a freighter being brought inside to offload.'

That made sense. The question was, what cargo was it carrying? Were the Argentines flying in consignments of missiles? That would explain the night flight and secrecy. On the other hand it was equally possible that it was an ordinary freight delivery. With weather like this it was hardly surprising that the ground crews elected to unload under cover.

Josh rubbed his hands to warm his fingers. 'I wish we could get inside that hangar and take a look.'

I was thinking the same, but there was almost a kilometre of open ground between us and the hangar. The fuel bunkers were quite close, though – if we could somehow make it across to them it might be possible to crawl along the pipeline ditch until we were within reach of the hangars.

It was time to change over the watch. I sent Josh back up the tunnel to get some rest. Nobby appeared to take over. 'Doug's having some problems with the radio. Can't establish comms.'

'What's the trouble?'

'He can't seem to get a message received back. He's tried tweaking the aerials but all he gets is static.'

Fuck, I thought wearily. It seemed that however sophisticated communications systems became they remained a pain in the arse. Leaving Nobby on watch, I crawled back up to see how Doug was doing.

Up on the plinth, Kiwi was asleep in his bivvy. He had an amazing facility of being able to switch off and sleep whenever he wanted. Josh had climbed into the warm bag just vacated by Nobby. Doug had the 320 set out with the aerials stretched up in a Y shape. He was staring at the LCD message screen and swearing under his breath. He had been sweating away at it for an hour in the freezing cold.

'Nobby says we're not getting an answer.'

'Stupid fucking thing,' Doug grumbled. 'All I get is a bunch of fucking static. There's no way of telling if the message has gone through or not.'

'Maybe the net is down for some reason.'

'Yeah, and maybe this pissing set is bust for all we know.' He glanced up at me. 'You want me to try with the satcom?'

I shook my head. 'No, it's too risky. We'll wait and try again in the morning.'

'Aye, well good luck to you then,' Doug said, and scrambled into his bivvy.

I wasn't too concerned. It was common not to get an acknowledgement on the first attempt. Atmospheric conditions, pressure of traffic at the other end – there could be any number of reasons why Hereford was not responding. Anyway, we had nothing urgent to report so far. They knew we were on the ground, that was enough. If the 320 set was damaged and not transmitting at all, then in an emergency we would just have to get through on the satcom and hope we weren't picked up.

I was more concerned that if the set was damaged Jock might not be able to get through to us. He would be left on his own with no choice but to bug out for Chile.

I left the 320 set up, and was scribbling down a note of what we had seen to go into the operational log later, when there was a warning hiss from behind and Nobby came squirming up the tunnel from the OP.

'Mark,' he called. 'The landing lights are back on. Looks like the Argies are expecting another flight.'

I forgot about the log and hurried back down to join him. The wind had eased off a trifle and there was less snow blowing. Consequently we could make out the runway lights quite distinctly.

'Why do they turn them off and on each time?' Nobby wondered aloud. 'They must be trying to hide something.'

We waited in the cold, rubbing our hands to keep the blood flowing in our fingers. Just as before, we saw the headlights of the fire truck as it took up position at the end of the runway.

This time I heard it, faint but distinct, the roar of aircraft engines coming in over the sea.

The procedure was exactly the same as before. The aircraft taxied to the apron underneath the tower and was then towed out to one of the enormous hangars on this side of the runway.

'I'll tell you one thing,' Nobby said, peering through the sight. 'That's one big fucker of an aeroplane. Those hangars must be a good five storeys high and a hundred metres long.'

I was wishing we could see more. To identify the type of aircraft that were being flown in under such secrecy was important. Maybe daylight would give us a better view of what was going on. But in winter in these high latitudes, dawn was not due for another hour with fifty minutes of twilight after that.

The thought gave me an idea. I checked my watch, and a plan began to take shape inside my head.

TWENTY-ONE

Leaving the LUP behind us, Josh and I wormed our way eastwards along the fence path on our stomachs, heading in the direction of the fuel bunkers. According to Doug the drainage ditch from the refuelling area ran out under the fences approximately 200 metres away. My plan was for the pair of us to enter the ditch and crawl along it till we got to within twenty metres of the hangars.

'We've more than an hour till dawn and weather conditions should continue to screen us for some while afterwards,' I had told the others when outlining what I proposed. 'The rest of you will wait behind and cover our retreat if necessary.'

'Taking a fucking risk, aren't you?' Doug had said. 'The mission briefing was to observe and report. They didn't say anything about breaking into hangars.'

'Something is going on, and unless we find out what it is we may not be in time to warn Hereford.'

To cover myself I had prepared a situation report for Doug to send to Hereford, outlining my intentions. I also left him the cellphone. I would take one of the UHF handsets with me and give him a regular update on our progress. If for some reason we lost contact and failed to return by an hour past dawn, his orders were to call Seb and arrange an immediate pull-out.

The UHF sets were a little larger than a cellphone and provided limited-range two-way communication. The handsets operated on clear voice with a built-in scrambler system to ensure security. Prior to setting out I had refreshed the encryption system from a handheld computer that was a part of the comms package.

'If we meet opposition we'll attempt to deal with it silently,' I instructed Josh. 'We'll take side-arms – knives and pistols – but at all costs avoid shooting. We don't want to bring the entire base down about our ears.'

Wearing our webbing and snowsuits, we crawled along the fence path till we reached the ditch Doug had found. It ran under the inner fence and beneath the roadway beyond in a culvert, emerging on the far side in a steep-sided trench that was half blocked by driven snow. Stepping warily for fear of mines, we slithered down into the ditch and crawled headfirst into the mouth of the culvert. It was a precast concrete pipe with several inches of ice in the bottom. From the stink I gathered it was also an overflow from the base septic tanks.

I unclipped my webbing and pushed it ahead of me into the dark mouth of the drain along with my pistol. 'It's a hell of a tight fit but I think we can manage it,' I called back to Josh. I inched my way forward, sliding on the surface of the ice, the concrete roof of the pipe scraping my head.

'Jesus,' I heard Josh mutter. 'Talk about a rat hole. Bet you the Argies have put a grille across.'

He was right. Half a metre from the entrance my groping fingers encountered three stout bars mounted vertically across our path. 'Saw,' I said to Josh, who was carrying the tools. 'Keep watch outside while I deal with this.'

Josh stayed squatting in the stream while I sawed away at the bars with the diamond-tipped blade that we carried. It was slow going because I had to lie on my side and the narrowness of the pipe meant I could only move my elbow a short distance. The noise it made was terrible, but I trusted the wind to drown out any sounds. I was set for a long job, but was thankful to find that the contractor had skimped, installing hollow tube bars instead of the solid steel the contract would have specified. It took me no more than ten minutes to cut through the bottoms of two bars close to the ice level and bend them up against the roof so that there was just space enough to slide underneath.

The second stroke of luck was finding that the drainage pipe ran on for a considerable way under the patrol road and beyond into the heart of the airfield. This was a big bonus because it lessened the chances of our being spotted; the downside was that it meant a long crawl down a stinking dark drain with no certainty we would find an exit.

'They must have dug the ditch, put in the drain, then run the fuel pipes along the top all in the same trench,' I said to Josh.

'Why not bury the fuel pipes too?'

'Easier to spot leaks if they're on the surface, I guess.'

Crawling into the darkness of the tunnel was one of the toughest things I've had to do. Ever since the helicopter crash in the sea during the Falklands War I'd had a horror of being trapped underwater, and it was the same with confined spaces underground. The pipe was only just wide enough to squeeze through and we had to pull ourselves along on our elbows, pushing with our feet. We had no way of telling if there would be a way out, and all the time we had to fight down the fear of getting stuck. If the drain narrowed at any point or the water got deeper, there was no space to turn around; we would have to crawl out backwards. The prospect made my stomach knot.

I forced myself to make my mind a blank and concentrate totally on moving up the pipe. Push and heave, push and heave. At least we were well concealed and out of the dreadful wind.

We moved in darkness, feeling our way with our hands, pushing our kit in front of us. I had an infra-red torch which in conjunction with the night sights would have made everything as bright as day, but I didn't use it in case the Argies had a PIR sensor monitoring the pipe. The stink was awful and there was a strong smell of aviation fuel. After a few yards the ice became a thin crust that gave beneath our weight, and soon we were soaking in raw sewage. I scraped my hand along the roof constantly to check for a manhole to the surface – all I got though were the joints of the pipe sections. Several times we encountered smaller drains discharging their contents into the main duct, but fortunately there wasn't a lot of water coming down because of the freezing cold.

At one point I came to a halt. 'What's the matter?' I heard Josh gasp from behind.

'I'm not sure. I'm stuck against something,' I called back, fumbling about with my hands. 'There seems to be a blockage.' I inched myself up, feeling the slimy walls for an obstruction. 'It feels like cement has squeezed through the joint between two sections and formed a big lump in the roof. I think we can get under though.'

The cement hung down from the roof like stalactite, barring our path. Using my knife, I broke off bits until there was room for us to squeeze through, just. It meant immersing our heads in the stinking flow but it had to be done.

'Boy, the guys are going to be pleased to see us when we get back,' said Josh.

We pushed on. At a rough guess we had travelled around two hundred metres. Surely even the Argies must build inspection chambers into their drains, I kept telling myself. If we became trapped down here, how long before the others came to look for us? Would the radio work this far underground if we called for help? If it did would they be able to get us out?

After what felt like an age the darkness up ahead seemed to diminish slightly. Not so much light as a hint of grey in the blackness. The effect was so faint at first I convinced myself my eyes were playing tricks. Gradually, as we drew nearer, it resolved itself into a crescent of pale gloom seeping down from overhead.

Urgently we heaved ourselves towards it, terrified we would find a barred grille or a hatch too small to escape through.

With a final spurt I dragged my stinking body up to the gap, my lungs revelling in the fresh air filtering down. Snow was piled on the floor of the pipe, and I seized a handful to wipe the filth from my face. Reaching up I found a square manhole with a cracked lid that was partly dislodged.

'How is it? Can we get out?' Josh's voice came urgently from behind. He could see nothing and had to rely on bulletins from me for encouragement.

'Some kind of access hatch,' I whispered back. 'I'm going to stick my head out to take a look and see.'

Squirming round on to my back in the water, I fished out my pistol, pushed up cautiously on the broken halves of the lid and slid them apart. Snow cascaded down through the hole on to my face. When I pulled myself upright the sides of the trench were level with my head so I could crane my neck to see over the edge. The blizzard was turning to sleet, driving across the bleak airfield like the surface of a glacier. I made a slow and cautious sweep round with the night-vision goggles – I could pick out the two big hangars, and there were lights burning nearby, but no sentries that I could see. On a night like this they would be sheltering inside if they had any sense at all.

I dropped down again to confer with Josh. 'We're on the edge of the concrete taxiways round the revetment area. No Argies I could see.'

'So do we go on or take to the surface?'

I hesitated. I'd have given a lot to get away from the claustrophobia of the drain. It looked to me as though a quick dash of 200 metres would take us to our objective. Surely no one would spot us in this weather? Reluctantly I put the temptation aside. It was taking an unnecessary risk. 'We need to get nearer in,' I told him. 'There must be another access hatch among the revetments. Let's press on.'

Josh made no protest. He was a good lad. And the fact we had found one manhole was a big boost to our morale. I jerked the pieces of the concrete lid back into place. In the confined pipe it sounded like the lid going down on a tomb. I wriggled round on to my stomach again and we crawled on. This time it was worse because we were running deeper underground.

The drain seemed endless. Quite possibly it ran right under the apron and on to the runway. Twice we came to narrow sections where we could only squeeze through with difficulty. I was trying to keep some idea of how far we were going, counting each jerk forward as about four inches, making three to the foot. The stink was worse than ever. I just hoped it wasn't all going to end in some massive tank of filth. I had to keep checking the roof with my fingers in case we missed the next hatch. At what I reckoned was 150 metres I called out to Josh that I was halting for a rest.

'I don't know how much further we can go on.'

'No sign of a manhole?'

'Nothing. And the water's getting deeper.'

Josh let out a chuckle. 'Yeah, I noticed that. Some Argy air force colonel taking a shit. You want to go back?'

I dreaded the thought of trying to squeeze backwards down the pipe. I was tempted to use the torch to look ahead but it would risk giving ourselves away. 'No,' I told him. 'We'll keep on for a bit.'

Elbows, feet; elbows, feet; we heaved ourselves along, pushing our weapons and kit before us. Then I heard something. 'Listen.'

A low rumbling sound had become audible. We lay still in the darkness as it grew steadily closer, filling the pipe, setting the concrete vibrating. 'Must be a truck,' Josh said. 'Maybe it's the patrol going round again.'

The sound drew nearer. Dust and droplets of moisture rained down from the roof. Suddenly my straining eyes caught a gleam of light that filled the drain in front of us, a light that persisted for several moments then abruptly cut out. The noise passed us without stopping, continuing along the line of the drain for a while, then turning off towards the north. The booming sound diminished and finally faded out completely.

'Those were headlights. The next manhole must be very close.'

'Not close enough for me,' Josh panted.

Encouraged, we redoubled our efforts to reach the hatch, forcing ourselves to ignore the stinking flow rising around us. By now, I judged, we had put ourselves well inside the aircraft revetments. With luck we should have only a short distance to cover to the main hangars.

At last my groping fingers met the manhole rim. The ground level was higher here and there was a short access shaft to the surface. As before, I cocked the Sig before edging the lid up to peer out. A blast of freezing wind burned my throat but after the foetid air of the drain I breathed in thankfully. Once again I made a careful 360-degree survey. No one about, no sign of life. We had surfaced right in the middle of the dispersal area, next to what looked like a refuelling point and fire-fighting station. Not far away a single floodlight illuminated a twin-storey building with big roller doors firmly closed, which presumably housed the fire trucks we had seen earlier. Twenty-five metres beyond, the massive bulk of one of the main hangars loomed like a cliff.

'All clear,' I whispered down to Josh. 'Quick, hand out the kit.'

He passed up the weapons and webbing and levered himself out after me. We slid the lid back in place and scuffed snow around the rim to make it look as if it had never been opened. The sleet was interspersed with a freezing rain. With luck it would hide our tracks before the patrol came round again. Without pausing, we sprinted for the side of the fire station and crouched in its shadow. In the whirling night our camouflage whites made us invisible at twenty yards, the dark pattern of our webbing melding into the blackness.

I put my mouth to Josh's ear to make myself heard

above the wind. 'We'll move round the back. Walk together normally as if we're a couple of Argy marines. And don't shoot unless we have to,' I reminded him.

The chances of being spotted in this weather were remote and anyone who did would think twice before venturing out into the cold to investigate. We would do far better acting naturally than sprinting from cover to cover like intruders. Shouldering our webbing, we ducked against the wind. If we were seen, with luck we would be taken for members of the garrison.

Trying our best to look purposeful, we walked around the rear of the fire station. There was a light showing from a second-floor window that looked to open on a stairway, but no other sign of life. The hangar we were aiming for opened out on to a vast concrete apron. Parked outside it were several heavy vehicles, their cabs blanketed with snow, and the main doors were firmly shut. The guards, if there were any, must be inside.

We turned to our left and passed along the side wall, looking for an entry point, a window or hatch that would give us a glimpse of the interior. I put the length at about 325 metres. One hell of a building. The walls towered up at least seventy feet by my estimate. Obviously it had been constructed with ultra-large aircraft in mind. We found several doors, but all were firmly locked and bolted – security in this sector was efficient. Attempting to saw our way in would take too long, and it would leave evidence of forced entry.

We reached the end of the building and turned right

along the rear wall. Our night sights revealed more equipment parked up here, including bomb cradles and missile trolleys for arming the bombers in the revetments. I made a mental note to mark them on the plan when we got back. The vehicles and trailers gave us some cover and we crouched down by the wheel of a big hydraulic loader, looking for a means of ingress. Josh grabbed my arm and pointed. He had spotted a service ladder giving access to the roof. It terminated a good ten feet above the ground. That was no problem.

I nodded and we darted across. Josh positioned himself beneath the end of the ladder and made a stirrup with his locked hands. I put my left foot in and jumped as he heaved me up. The bottom rung of the ladder was shrouded in snow but I got a good grip and hauled myself up hand over hand. As soon as I was secure I extracted a length of rope from my webbing and clipped the end to one of the rungs. Josh swarmed up and in a moment the two of us were on the ladder and mounting to the roof.

We climbed steadily. The rungs were caked with ice and the wind tore at us constantly. I was hopeful that the noise of constant buffeting by the gusts would cover any sounds. On the roof we found a walkway, running right around the hangar. I guessed it was all part of a fire-escape route. The roof was laid out in a series of long ridges with valleys in between, all choked with snow.

We were now invisible from below, and I figured this had to be as good a time as any to call in and check with Doug's team. I pressed the talk button on the UHF handset. Immediately Nobby's voice came over the earpiece, responding.

'We're on the hangar roof,' I said. 'No problems so far. The drain runs all the way through into the refuelling area. It's a tight fit. One motorised patrol heard fifteen minutes ago. Propose making CTR of hangar now.'

'All clear this end,' Nobby answered back. 'One set of lights moving near where you are. Must be the same lot you heard.'

'Any response from Hereford yet?'

'Negative. Nothing so far.'

'Roger. Wait out.' I clicked off the talk button.

'Look for a door,' I said to Josh. 'There has to be one somewhere up here.'

We crawled along the walkway, hanging on to the waist-high safety rail. Up here we were exposed to the full force of the storm, and the strength of the gusts was incredible. It was like being on the side of a mountain. The roof was slippery with ice and in places the snow had drifted above the height of our knees. A steady rain was now falling, making the surface underfoot extremely treacherous. Our hands were numbed with the cold in spite of our gloves, and it took all our strength just to hang on. The wind tore at us, sometimes pinning us against the roof, then switching in an instant to suck us out towards the edge. Several times I thought I was going to lose my footing and slide off. With a drop of about twenty-five metres it would have meant certain death.

At one point Josh stopped.

'What's the matter?'

'I thought I heard someone moving.'

We both stood still, straining to catch a sound in the wind. 'I didn't hear anything,' I said. 'Let's get this over.'

We worked our way around the hangar till at last we came to a hatch set into the end of one of the roof peaks. There was no window, just a low metal door that opened outwards. It was half blocked by snow that the wind had piled up against it, which was now rapidly melting because of the rain.

'Careful,' I said. 'It's slippery.' I tried the handle; it was locked on the inside.

'Fuck,' Josh shouted into the wind. 'Now what? Bust it down?'

'Quiet. We don't know what's inside, for Christ's sake.'

I used the infra-red torch to check around the edge for any wires or other indications the door was alarmed. All seemed clear. Assuming this was a fire escape, the Argies would most likely be relying on the perimeter defences for security. The hinges were on the inside so they couldn't be unscrewed. It would have to be brute force or nothing. I took out my knife and scraped some of the crusted snow away from the doorjamb. The lock didn't appear particularly strong. It had been designed more to be weatherproof than as a security measure. My saw would cut through the bolt but it would take too long. I forced the blade of the knife into the crack in the jamb and thrust my weight against it. The thin sheet steel of the frame bent but the lock held.

'What about the lights inside?' Josh whispered. 'If we open the door won't they see us from the ground?'

I paused a moment. 'The lights will all be directed downward into the hangar and this door faces outward towards the fence. We'll chance it.' We had come all this way, crawling through a load of crap, and I wasn't going back without seeing inside the hangar.

I wedged the knife in deeper and levered hard. There was a snap and the bolt popped out. We held our breath for a few seconds, listening for any sounds of alarm. I had my foot wedged against the door to stop it blowing open in the wind.

'Take your cammies off,' I said, struggling out of my whites.

'I'm going to have a leak too.'

'Good idea.' It might be the last chance we would have for a while. We unzipped and peed into the pile of melting snow by the door. Then I zipped up again, cracked open the door a fraction and peered into the hangar.

TWENTY-TWO

I blinked. I was looking at a scene of incandescent brightness. I had pushed up my night-vision goggles, and after the pitch-blackness of the night outside the glare was dazzling.

The hangar was immense. From outside it had been hard to get a true impression of its real size. We were at the south-east corner and from where we were perched the vast space ran away before our eyes like the Houston Astrodome. The inner walls were painted black or maybe a dark green, I couldn't tell. There must have been at least two hundred great arc lights slung from the gantries running across beneath us. Their blinding glare bounced off the plane and the concrete floor, and the heat thrown back by the reflectors was so immense it was like staring into the sun.

The hangar was huge, but the plane was more awe-inspiring still. I'd seen these big cargo freighters before, even flown on an American Lockheed C-5 Galaxy, but this was the first time I'd seen a plane like this inside a building. The great tail was towards us with its high T-fin practically touching the light arrays. The rear ramp was down and we could glimpse the entrance to a cavernous interior that gaped open like a railroad tunnel. The wings sprouted straight from the plane's back, with the enormous fuselage and the four giant engines slung beneath. The whole effect was of colossal power and strength, and yet with surprising grace in the angle of the swept-back wing and tail surfaces and in the upward-turned winglets protruding from the wing tips.

'Jesus,' I heard Josh whisper behind me, 'a Globemaster.'

The name seemed to sum up the massive power and capacity of the beast. This was the next-generation cargo airlifter developed for the US Air Force's Air Mobility Command. Although smaller than the Lockheed C-5, I knew the Globemaster's hold was spacious enough to accommodate the sort of heavy armoured vehicles that even the massive Galaxy would baulk at.

'The RAF just leased some of those beauties,' Josh breathed. 'Word is they can stick an entire Tornado fighter inside one and fly it 5000 miles at 400 knots, then land on an unimproved airfield less than a thousand metres long.'

'The question is,' I said, 'how in hell did the Argies get hold of one and what are they going to do with it?'

'With two of them, you mean,' Josh reminded me. 'That was its twin brother that went into the hangar next door.'

I had pulled the door shut after us. We were crouched on a narrow platform close to the outside wall. Around us were the steel beams and trusses that held up the roof. Below were the lighting arrays and steel joists carrying cranes for lifting heavy equipment. From where we were it was a thirty-metre direct drop to the concrete floor. I held on tight to the platform railing, felt for the UHF handset and pressed the transmit button.

The response was a burst of static in my earpiece.

'Nobby,' I said quietly. 'Can you hear me? Bleep for yes.' More static. I listened for a moment, then shut the set up. It was no use. Maybe some equipment in use down below was interfering with the signal. Or possibly the entire building was hardened against leakage of radio transmissions. Either way we were on our own for the present.

From the platform a spindly ladder led down to a catwalk that looked to run clear across the hangar at main roof level. From that another ladder led down to a similar one serving the lighting gantries at a level three metres above the tops of the main doors. So long as no one climbed up into the roof space, we were completely shielded from view by the glare of the lights.

A heavy electric motor whined into life somewhere down below and a tow cart came into view pulling a two-storey steel gantry. There were other gantries already in position by the tail and next to the wings. A couple of dozen men in white overalls were clambering about the aircraft. Some were servicing the engines while others worked away with long-handled brushes, swabbing down the aluminium skin. Others seemed to be scrubbing away at the camouflage paint job on the hull. They were jabbering away among themselves, clattering equipment and generally creating sufficient noise to cover up any sounds we might have made breaking in. Even if they hadn't been, the drumming of rain on the roof and the booming of the wind gave us all the cover we needed.

'What are they doing?' Josh whispered.

'Drying the aircraft off and repainting it, I think.'

'In the middle of the night?'

It seemed strange to me too, but there had to be a reason. I guessed an Argentine air force commander wouldn't worry about turning his men out in the middle of the night to get a plane prepared. I was more concerned over why the Argentines thought they needed a pair of heavy lifters like the one below us.

The mission was starting to make sense. Suppose someone in the MOD or the Foreign Office had got wind of the imminent arrival of the Globemasters? The acquisition of airlift capacity on such a scale might change the balance of power in the South Atlantic. With these planes the Argentines could fly in reinforcements from the mainland in large numbers. A single Globemaster could embark over two hundred fully armed paratroops.

But that didn't make sense. If the Argies needed to ferry troops around they had the use of the state airline's fleet of passenger aircraft – take a jumbo jet out of service, pack it full of grunts and fly it down to Rio Grande where the runway was easily long enough. No, there had to be another reason.

An electric polisher started up below. Someone kicked over a tray of tools and the sound echoed off the hangar walls. 'I want to get closer,' I said, still speaking in a whisper, though at fifty metres' distance with a dozen power tools in operation there was no danger of being overheard. 'If we could climb down a level we'd have a less obstructed view.'

Josh pointed down the ladder to the catwalk below us and gave me a questioning look. I hesitated. It looked horribly exposed. Then I reflected that was because we were looking down upon it. The catwalk ran above the level of the lighting; from the floor of the hangar it would be invisible. And even if someone did look up and catch the dim shadow of a person moving up there, chances were he would take us for maintenance workers going about their business.

Silently we climbed down the ladder to the next level. No one would pick us out against the dark back-drop of the hangar wall. We reached the catwalk and I put a tentative foot on it. 'Fuck!' I said, drawing back.

There was no need to explain. The catwalk was swaying alarmingly. It was suspended on guy wires from the overhead beams and moored at intervals to cross members. The slightest weight set it bouncing and snaking like an Andean rope bridge. Any attempt to cross it would draw the attention of the whole workforce.

'We do this, we'll be spotted before we've gone a dozen steps,' Josh said.

We scanned the roof together. 'It looks like the team

on the starboard side of the aircraft are ahead of the portside lot in whatever it is they're doing,' I told Josh. 'If we can find a way to crawl around the tail we could get a better look.'

'What about the beam above?'

I followed the direction he was looking. The hangar was constructed on a steel skeleton plated over with metal sheeting to form the exterior skin. Massive columns rose from concrete foundations and were joined by horizontal members running the width of the building. One of these ran three metres above where we were crouched, providing anchorage points for the guy wires from which the catwalk was slung. At intervals it was joined by cross beams and trusses supporting the roof peaks, making a complex web of steel designed to resist the incredible winds prevailing in this part of the world.

'If we could crawl out and wedge ourselves in where two of those trusses meet we'd be in clover,' Josh said.

I looked down. It was a hell of a drop. The beam was around ten inches across. If we could sit on that and pull ourselves along we could cross out to the centre of the hangar and look down on to the other side of the plane. It was a long run but no worse than some of the assault courses we'd had to face in our time.

'Come on then, let's get stuck in.'

We crossed one at a time to minimise the risk of being spotted. I went first. I settled myself on the beam and locked my legs underneath. It had a convenient lip either side I could grip on to and pull myself along. The outer leg of the first truss was about forty metres along, slanting upwards away from me into one of the roof peaks. I would have to work my way past it somehow. The temptation to look down again was strong but I forced myself to keep my eyes level and concentrate on moving. It felt horribly exposed away from the side of the hangar and I had to keep reminding myself that anyone looking up would see only a glare of lights.

As a kid I'd hated heights, but I've always approached any fear head on, so I took up rock climbing. Eventually I became a mountaineer and even climbed K2 in the Himalayas with Jock, which many in the business rate a harder climb than Everest. I learned to trust my ability to support myself with my own body strength and to break up an ascent into a series of steps.

The truss, when I reached it, was easier to negotiate than I had feared. A crossbeam joined two horizontals at this point and I was able to grip the truss and clamber round to the other side. There was one nerve-jangling point, at which I had to stand on the beam twenty-five metres up and turn myself round in order to face the front again. The smooth surface of the steel made it hard to find a grip, and I was conscious of a hollow sensation in my legs. Relax, I told myself firmly. You know how to do this. I wrapped an arm around the beam, turned around and lowered myself till I was sitting sideways on the beam with an arm still around the upright. Then I swung a leg across and I was settled.

At the fourth truss I waited for Josh to catch up with me. We were now directly over the aircraft, with the huge tail-fin almost beneath us. Josh reached me and heaved himself alongside on the crossbar. Together we spent a long time staring down at the technicians working below.

'What does that new paint job remind you of?' Josh whispered after a while.

'RAF European winter overall?'

'That's what it looks like to me too.'

The plane had originally been a mix of sandy hues, suggesting an origin from one of the Gulf states, perhaps even Saudi. I watched a man with a long brush smoothing grey paint against a pattern of darker blue. If the plane was to be based down in the South Atlantic it was natural the Argies would want to change. Many nations used similar camo schemes; there was nothing especially sinister about what was happening, except perhaps the haste with which it was being carried out.

'Let's edge out a bit further and see if we can spot the insignia to tell us which unit it belongs to now.'

I had to force myself to lead the way this time. The further out we went, the longer the distance to get back. A cold sweat was pouring off my body and my hands were slippery with moisture. I tried not to think about how easy it would be to slip sideways off the beam. I pictured myself hanging on with my fingers, arms at full stretch, and the sickening moments before my hold slipped and I crashed down to the concrete below. Perhaps if I were lucky I would break my fall on one of the lighting arrays.

Josh seemed unaffected. He shuffled along behind me as if he was enjoying it.

We did two more trusses before I called a halt again. It was now possible to see the starboard side of the plane clearly. The Argentines were using big electric fan heaters to dry the fresh paint, and the draughts of warm air and fumes wafted up to where we squatted on the beams. I watched a man on a high gantry stencilling some kind of insignia on to the side of the tail-fin. It was evidently an important job because there was an officer with him, supervising.

The painter put the finishing touches to the task and removed the stencil. He and the officer stepped back a pace to observe his handiwork. I could see their hands gripping the safety rail of the gantry behind them. The job was evidently important because the two men spent a while discussing it, pointing out details to one another. Finally, at the officer's direction, the painter took up his brush again and added more colour to the central section.

The vertical angle of the fin made it hard to distinguish the design. I leaned out to get a better view but the swept-back T-section of the upper tail obscured my vision. 'Josh,' I said softly – the gantry where the men were standing was only some ten metres below us and we could be overheard now. 'Josh, see if you can crawl out along that crossbeam and get a squint of that insignia.'

'Sure thing.' Like an acrobat he swung himself round the base of the truss to drop down on to the beam. Then cautiously he began to crawl outwards in the direction of the door. The plane had been towed in at a slight angle, and by getting further out he should be able to see the device on the tail-fin clearly. As he got into position I saw him peer downward, his brow furrowed as he tried to make out the design.

The painter was still stooped at his work and the officer was consulting a ring binder with photographs of aircraft identification marks, the kind of thing all services keep around for information on their own aircraft and those of other nations. All of us on the mission had studied similar recognition shots of Argy planes before setting out.

The painter finished what he was doing and stepped back again. He was quite young and, unusually for a South American, he was fair-haired. I saw Josh's face clear momentarily as he got an unobstructed view of the fin at last. Then abruptly he stiffened. He stared again, long and hard. I saw his lips move as he memorised the markings. Then very carefully he began to work his way backwards along the crossbeam towards where I was waiting.

As he reached the upright I stretched out a hand to help him back on to the main beam again. He turned to face me and his eyes were shining with excitement.

'Well?' I whispered impatiently. 'Mickey Mouse Airlines?'

'You're not going to believe this, but it was an RAF red, white and blue roundel on top of the badge of the 30th Air Transport Squadron from Lyneham.'

I stared at him blankly for a moment. He wasn't kidding either. This was far too serious for that. I looked down at the Globemaster, gleaming under the lights with the aircrews swarming over it. It was impossible to believe, and yet . . .

Suddenly everything became horribly clear. I knew now why the aircraft had been brought in under cover of darkness and why they were being prepared and repainted with such desperate haste.

And in the same moment I realised that our mission had now become one of frantic urgency. It was vital we got out and contacted the rest of the team.

TWENTY-THREE

The Argy plan was plain. Somehow they had succeeded in getting their hands on a pair of Globemasters, planes exactly similar to those now used by the RAF to fly reinforcements into the Falklands. All they had to do was paint the aircraft in RAF colours, give them English-speaking pilots and pack them full of troops, and fly them into Mount Pleasant as if they were a routine flight staging out of Ascension Island.

'It's madness, but it might just work,' I told Josh. 'And like Seb said, the Argies are crazy enough to try anything. If those planes can land four or five hundred troops on the tarmac without warning, our guys wouldn't stand a chance.'

Josh agreed. 'What does the garrison have – a single company group, a handful of RAF Regiment guarding the airfield? Two hundred combat troops if they're lucky. Less than that, probably. If the Argies timed it right, say for a Sunday morning when half the garrison are dead drunk, they could take over without firing a shot.'

'Even if they only managed to seize the airfield they could fly in reinforcements at their leisure. And with a modern airfield in their hands they could stage their own strike bombers out of the Falklands and prevent our ships ever getting close.'

Josh thought a bit more. 'It's a huge risk they're taking, even so. The Tornados at Mount Pleasant intercept and escort all arrivals at least a hundred miles out.'

'Assuming the pilots are fit to fly,' I reminded him grimly. 'And right now there are only three Tornados left on the islands.' We were both silent for a moment, both thinking of the salmonella that had struck the garrison the day we left.

'Everything begins to fall into place,' Josh said. 'What about the radar sites though? NATO aircraft carry transponders identifying them as friend or foe. If the Falklands radar don't get the proper signal won't they smell a rat?'

'Maybe the Argies have acquired transponders too, I don't know. What I am sure of though is that no British fighter is going to shoot down one of these planes if it's wearing friendly colours.'

Josh fell silent. Deep down we were both convinced. It was so much in the Argentine character – the bold, defiant gesture, the daring surprise blow that would turn the tables on a more powerful enemy.

I pictured in my mind the planes landing at Mount Pleasant, taxiing to the control tower, the ramps dropping and the sudden storming out of hundreds of crack marines. I imagined the seizing of the tower and missile defences, and the rapid deployment against the mess blocks and armoury. They could bring their own combat vehicles with them on the planes. I could picture the wild scenes as Argentine marines careered across the airbase, shooting at anything that moved. It would be a replay of the assault we had planned against Rio Grande all those years ago, except with a better chance of success.

'If it doesn't succeed what have they lost? A couple of planes that probably don't belong to them anyway and 400 men. If it works they hold the Malvinas for ever. Come on,' I told him. 'This is no time for arguing. We need to get back to the others and send a warning to Hereford before the bastards get the drop on the garrison.'

As we edged our way back along the beams, Josh leading this time, I felt elated. My decision to penetrate the hangar had been vindicated. There was no other way we could have unearthed what was being planned. The Argentines would keep the planes inside the hangar until the very last minute, in all probability loading the troops on under cover as well. The planes would have taken off, heading north to circle round out of radar range, and approaching the Falklands from the course the RAF flights usually used.

It was imperative to get a message back to Hereford that the Globemasters must be turned back. Even if there were no Tornado pilots fit to fly it would still be possible to block the runway at Mount Pleasant and prevent planes from landing. Once the Argentines realised we were aware of their plans they would be forced to abort the mission. The Globemasters would return to wherever they had come from and the crisis would be over.

I checked my watch again. Half-past seven, and the base would soon be coming to life. We had to get clear rapidly and reach the cover of the drain again without being spotted. Once we were underground we would be safe. Before that, though, we would have to radio Doug and instruct him to send a message back to Hereford.

We were making good progress when disaster struck. Josh was about forty metres ahead of me, and had begun to negotiate the last truss; we were both of us well practised in the procedure now and it was giving us no trouble. He gripped the upright nearest him and was drawing himself straight when suddenly from the other side a figure jumped out.

It was the last thing either of us was expecting. He must have been standing to the rear side of the beam keeping dead still, and the gloom of the roof space had hidden him from us till the last moment. All I saw was a thin, narrow-faced man in his twenties, in civilian clothes and trainers. At the sight of us he went scuttling away to our right, along the transverse beam that led to the neighbouring horizontal. He moved with incredible agility, crouching over the beam like a jockey, with the soles of his shoes on the lower rim and scrabbling along as if he were running on all fours.

I was so shocked all I could do was stare. He reached the next beam, swung himself on to it like a monkey and went skittering back, parallel to the direction we had just come. My first thought was that he was part of the hangar workforce, a maintenance man of some kind who had been spooked by our appearance. I couldn't imagine what else he could be doing up here. His panic at the sight of us was understandable. In full battle dress with camo stained faces we must have presented an alarming picture. Shit, I thought. Any second now he'll give tongue and bring the whole place about our ears.

All our plans were up for grabs again now. There was just a chance if we made a run for it that we could make it on to the roof and from there down to the ground before the people inside got themselves organised. I figured we could probably handle the technicians I had seen around the plane. Marines, though, were a different proposition.

There was a gasp ahead. I swung back and my heart went into instant overdrive. Josh had fallen. He must have been thrown off balance by the sudden appearance of the man, made a grab for one of the uprights and slipped as he did so. Now he was dangling from the main beam by one hand, his left, hanging over a sheer drop to the concrete below. His face was contorted with effort, his fingers straining as he struggled to draw himself up one-armed and get a grip with his other hand on the beam. He was trying not to swing his legs or make any sudden movement for fear of breaking the hold he had and dropping to his death.

It was a single-handed pull-up, about the stiffest test in gym repertoire. Everyone in the Regiment was expected to be able to do it, but unlike a gym here there was no nice rubber-gripped bar, and Josh was wearing full kit with webbing. I was about forty metres behind him. I launched myself forward, but I knew it was hopeless; I wasn't going to be able to get to him in time. If he couldn't get a hold with his other hand and somehow haul himself up, he would lose what grip he had before I could reach him.

Josh didn't make a sound. He didn't look at me or call for help. He didn't have the concentration to spare. All his strength and will-power were bent on hauling himself back on to the beam. I almost heard the muscles in his left shoulder creak as his biceps tautened, lifting him upwards. Sweat was running down his face and his teeth were clenched as if they were going to break. He was holding his legs and torso stiff and straight to minimise the risk of swinging and dislodging himself.

Josh never lost his cool, not for a second. Every muscle in his body was rigid and tense as slowly, agonisingly, he inched himself up. He knew that if he snatched at the beam with a sudden effort, there was a chance of grabbing a hold with his right hand, though he could just as easily lose his grip with both hands and fall back. It had to be done steadily or not at all.

The temptation was to reach up by the shortest and most direct route, straight overhead to where his left hand was gripping the steel. But the best way would be to pass his right hand underneath the joist and get a grip on the far side. Then he would be able to swing his legs up and lock his ankles around the beam to take some of the weight. From that position he could haul himself right-side-up again, or at least wait for me to reach him. It meant, though, a longer stretch, and securing a handhold that was beyond his range of vision. He would have to manage by touch alone. And he would only get one attempt.

I was ten metres away, working my way along the bar, trying desperately to hurry and at the same time conscious that any shaking of the bar on my part would probably break his grip and hasten the end. The best I could do was to get as close as I could and pray he could hang on. It crossed my mind to shout down to the Argentines below. There wasn't time to get a ladder or bring up one of the gantries – they wouldn't have reached anyway – but it might be possible to rig some kind of tarpaulin to catch him. I knew in my heart though that it was hopeless.

I watched as his head tilted back to balance as his right fingers found the far side of the beam and inched their way up. His eyes were closed, his breath coming in short gasps. Beads of sweat burst from his skin, staining his clothes. His fingers touched the lip of the beam. Now they had to reach round and up. Another inch would do it. I saw his fingers claw their way on to the upper surface of the beam. Every fibre in my body was screaming for him to make it. 'Only a little more!' I wanted to shout to him. 'Just one more effort and you'll do it, by God!'

Josh seemed frozen under the beam. His head was almost level with the underside. He needed only an inch more to get a purchase with his other hand. His left arm was quivering under the strain of holding the position. I heard him draw in his breath through his teeth for one convulsive final effort. His right hand twitched and abruptly jerked upward. The top two joints slid over and clamped convulsively against the smooth steel. The muscles of the arm tensed. He was facing me now and I heard a long gasp of relief break from his lips.

The sweat was pouring off me in rivers. Josh wasn't safe yet, but he had a good chance. Even if he was too exhausted to bring his legs up, he could probably hang on long enough for me to reach him. I can bench-press two hundred pounds, and I knew that if I could only get to him I could haul him back to safety. I flung myself across the remaining five metres, no longer having to worry about vibration shaking him loose. All that mattered now was to reach him with all possible speed. Any moment I was expecting the guy who had seen us to shout down to the fellows on the ground that there were intruders in the hangar. It seemed impossible to me that everyone else could be unaware of the drama being enacted above their heads.

I needn't have worried though. Josh caught my eye and managed a grin, as if to say, 'You didn't think I could do it, did you?' Tightening the grip of his hands, he tensed his stomach muscles and bent his legs upwards towards me as smoothly as if he were putting on a display. He brought them up either side of the beam, crossed them at the ankles and locked them in position. Then, and only then, did he relax.

Josh permitted himself just a quarter of a minute's rest before reaching across the beam with his right hand to grip the other edge. With a smooth flip he brought the weight of his body round and a moment later he was pulling himself back up on top of the beam. He sat there, shoulders bowed, getting his breath back till I came up to him.

I didn't say anything, just patted him on the shoulder. That minute would be a defining moment in his existence. His life had been on the line, with only him to save it. He hadn't panicked or cried out for help. He had saved himself and saved the mission too. He had proved himself a true soldier.

I could guess he was still shaky after his escape but we couldn't afford to lose time. The man we had surprised hadn't given us away yet; maybe he was waiting till he got back down among his friends. Either way we had been compromised and it was vital we got away with all possible speed. Josh knew that as well as I did. We set off together, working our way across towards the side of the hangar as fast as we could.

We were negotiating the last truss when a sudden clamour of shouts from the floor of the hangar made us freeze in our tracks.

TWENTY-FOUR

The noise of shouting increased. We heard running feet and any second expected torch beams to flash upon us. Then there came the sound of a crash from the middle of the hangar, followed by the bang of a small explosion. Glancing back, I saw the figure of the stranger clinging to one of the lighting arrays three metres below us, giving vent to high pitched shrieks of terror. He had slipped from a beam he had been crawling on and fallen ten feet. The popping sound we had heard must have been one of the arc lamps bursting. All hell was breaking loose – but at least to us it was a diversion.

There was a screech of rending metal and a frightful scream. The light array snapped apart and with a desperate cry the clutching figure pitched downward. I turned away before the thud of the impact as his body hit the concrete floor twenty-five metres below. Poor bastard.

We had no time to stay and watch. We had to get out fast. Josh scrambled forward and slid across the last beam to the end of the hangar. A minute later I was next to him. Out on the floor we glimpsed Argentines running around hunting for ladders and shining torches upward.

It would be only a matter of moments before they started climbing into the roof space.

We mounted the ladder, making for the door we had come in by. Although by now there was a great deal of noise we dared not move too rapidly for fear of attracting attention. All it would take was one sharp-eyed person to swing a torch beam our way and we would be done for. If we could only reach the outside undetected I was confident we could make the fire-escape ladder and get down to the ground again before a search got organised.

My heart was in my mouth with every step but our luck held. We climbed back up to the roof door and Josh pushed it open. Freezing air blasted through the gap bringing a shower of rain with it. Hastily we scrambled through and I pushed it shut behind us, searching around for something to wedge it fast.

'Who the hell was that?' Josh was demanding. 'The fucker near on killed me.'

I used the haft of my knife to bend the metal of the doorframe back into position. It might disguise the route we had taken for a minute or two. 'I'm almost sure he came down through here by the same way we did.'

I pushed Josh towards the rear of the building and punched the talk button on the UHF set.

'Is that you Nobby?' The howling wind and rain made it hard to hear even with the earphone. 'Listen carefully,' I told him. 'I want you to get this message off to Hereford right away, understood? The aircraft in the hangar is a C-17 Globemaster being painted up in RAF colours and squadron markings. Repeat, RAF colours and squadron markings. Second hangar believed to contain similar aircraft. Transmit that immediately, OK?'

'Roger. Anything else?'

'Yes,' I told him. 'We've been compromised. Use the mobile phone to send the codeword to Seb requesting a rendezvous for a pull-out. Tell Doug to have the team packed up and ready to move out by the time we return.'

'You need any help?' Nobby asked.

'Negative. We should be able to make it to the drain. Then we'll be under cover.'

The last thing I wanted was to bring a rescue party blundering about the airfield in the dark.

We made our way back along the roof to the ladder, expecting to hear pursuit at our backs. The conditions were ferocious – violent gusts tore at us constantly. The rain had washed away most of the snow and the roof surface was treacherous with melting slush. Hanging on to the safety rail we struggled on, slipping and sliding till we reached the ladder. Before we could start the descent, though, my earpiece clicked. I felt for the handset and depressed the button. 'Nobby?'

'Mark, bad news. Convoy of six plus vehicles heading your direction from south-west travelling fast. ETA your location two to three minutes.'

From his vantage point out by the fence, Nobby had spotted headlights moving across the apron. Shit, I thought. The guy we had bumped into must have been brought down and told what he had seen; with the result that an alarm call had been put out for the guard. By the sound of it they weren't pissing about either. Six vehicles could mean anything from twenty men to more than sixty. They'd sent a fucking army out to fetch us in.

'Roger Bravo Two. We'll stay put and keep our heads down.'

'Josh,' I called up quietly. 'Back up on to the roof again and get under cover. Looks like we'll have company very soon.'

Going back was a desperate step. We were effectively putting ourselves into a trap. Once the Argies pinpointed us they could surround the hangar and shoot us off the roof like rats. On the other hand, to be spotted out in the open meant certain capture. There was no way we could hope to reach the drain manhole inside two minutes. The only hope was to lie low and pray.

Luckily we were still at the top of the ladder. Josh swung back under the safety rail and I followed. 'Follow me. We'll work our way along one of the valleys towards the front and lie flat,' I said. 'There's a chance they won't spot us unless they carry out a thorough search.'

I was counting on the fact that nobody had put a light on us yet. I picked my way forward along a valley between two peaks of the roof trying to make as little noise as possible, till I reached the front of the building – the further away from the ladder the better, and I wanted to catch a glimpse of what was happening. Small chinks of light escaped around the edges of the great doors, showing that the interior was lit up. I threw myself flat, pulled my cap low and risked a quick squint over the edge.

I could make out the approaching column clearly now, moving at a rapid pace past the fuel depot towards the hangars. The lead vehicle was a 4x4 of some kind with a canvas top. Three more similar followed. Bringing up the rear and dwarfing the others was a pair of massive machines. I could hear the clatter of tracks and, as they swung round to draw abreast of the hangar, the ominous armoured turrets of two American infantry fighting vehicles were outlined against the glow of headlamps. M2 Bradleys with 30mm cannons and co-axial chain-guns, I thought, identifying the silhouettes, and my heart sank. A brush with one of those beauties was to be avoided. Even with an anti-tank missile I would think twice before taking one of them on.

The stench of diesel fumes wafted up as the column slowed to a halt. The next moment there was a rumbling sound below and a shaft of light spilled out on to the apron. The main doors were opening. Evidently they intended searching the building from the inside. I tried to snatch a glance at the trucks to see how many troops were aboard but the tail-flaps were all lashed down against the rain. Two of the Jeeps drove in, while the rest of them waited outside with the Bradleys, their engines idling.

I tried to figure out the intentions of the officer in charge. Standard operating procedure for a suspected infiltration would be to surround the building and send in search parties from both sides to flush out the intruders. The Argentine commander was doing it by the book. He was posting a cordon outside to catch anyone trying to escape, and at the same time probably sending a squad to the rear to cover the ladder while others of his men climbed up inside to the roof. The IFVs were on hand to provide heavy back-up and run down any leakers who managed to escape the search parties.

From down below came shouts of NCOs bellowing at their men. It looked like they were going about it in a professional manner, and I didn't rate our chances highly. A couple of guys walking down each valley would soon flush us out, and up here we had nowhere to run. If I had been on my own I might have made for the ladder and tried to get down it before the lower party was in place, but with two of us the odds were we would be cut down by machine-gun fire before we had made a dozen yards.

I wondered if there was some way of busting inside, fusing the lights and setting the place on fire – with the hope of escaping in the confusion. It was a thin chance, but all I could think of. At the very least it could set all the Argentines shooting at each other. And anything was better than lying here waiting to be caught.

I was about to go back and tell Josh when I glanced down again and something struck me. It was impossible to see the hangar doors because they were right underneath me, and the roof had a slight overhang to keep the rain off the rollers. The rollers ran in guide rails, the tops of which formed a ledge about three feet below where I was lying – a narrow shelf about eighteen inches wide below the line of the roof. If Josh and I could somehow crawl down there and lie out, we would be invisible to anyone searching the roof. Even spotlights from the ground would not pick us out.

We would have to act fast, though. At any moment now troops would appear on the roof and we would be lost.

I crawled back to where Josh was crouched and told him my idea. 'I know I can do it, but it's quite a drop. Are you up for it?'

'Hell, anything's better than giving in to the Argies. I can manage it if you can.'

Already we could hear booted feet clanging on metal stairs inside the hangar. We scrambled forward quickly. 'If you hang on to a stanchion and lower yourself down, I'll keep a grip on your webbing,' I told him.

Josh didn't hesitate a moment. He wrapped one arm around the safety rail and lowered himself down, legs first, while I supported him until he was lying face down on the ledge. It was wide enough to hold a man – just. Luckily there were brackets every few metres, supporting the roof overhang. Josh latched on to one of these. 'Okay,' he whispered. 'I'm fine. You can let go.'

Now it was my turn. I moved along a little and slid under the rail. There was no one to hold me – but then I hadn't nearly lost my life a few minutes ago. Holding on to the rail like grim death, I reached down and fumbled in the dark for a bracket. It felt horribly insubstantial. I tried not to look down at the IFVs and the figures of the soldiers moving about. Tensing my stomach muscles, I bent my legs down until my boots touched the ledge, and drew myself down on to it. There was a film of slush on the surface of the ledge and it felt slippery.

Right, I thought. Now comes the bad moment when I have to make myself let go of the rail. Sweat broke out on my body and my hands started to shake. My right hand was gripping the roof stanchion so tightly it seemed to have developed a will of its own.

Jesus, I told myself, pull yourself together man! Josh managed it and he's already had one bad fright tonight. The ledge is perfectly wide enough. All you have to do is relax and lie still. But my right hand wasn't listening. Fear was keeping it closed tight.

There was a bang overhead as a door opened and a bunch of men came pouring out on to the roof at the rear. Flashlight beams jinked across the valleys. In a few seconds they would spot me. I felt that age was catching up with me and I was losing my nerve.

Take charge! I told myself. Breathe deeply and slowly. The only thing that is going to kill you now is fear. I forced my legs to straighten out on the ledge and increased my grip on the bracket with my left hand. I pulled myself in against the side of the hangar as close as I could. Then, one finger at a time, I willed my right hand to relax.

A torch beam flashed across the rail overhead. There

was a hoarse shout. With a sudden effort I tore my hand away and dropped down into the cover of the recess below. Had I left it too late? I could hear feet thumping along the roof directly overhead. Droplets of water cascaded over the edge. The Argentines were shouting to each other with the heady excitement of troops on the chase. More voices were shouting from below. Had they seen us? I kept my face turned into the side of the hangar. If they found me they would have to drag me out. I'd never be able to move from here. I had to fight down a mad urge to let go and roll out from the ledge and end it all. Calm down, I said to myself. If you think this is tough, try and imagine how much worse it would be getting captured and interrogated.

There were more orders shouted above; it sounded like an officer was organising some sort of systematic search. They appeared to be starting at the rear and working forward in a line, coordinating over the roof peaks by voice command. This was the really dangerous bit. Someone with a bit more sense than the others might take it into his head to check over the edge of the roof and, looking down, spot the ledge.

In the meantime more troops were moving about on the ground below. They must have finished searching the inside of the hangar. I reminded myself that Josh and I would be invisible from down below, lost in the patch of shadow above the roller track.

The team on the roof was getting nearer, working its way steadily forward along the valleys. I tried not to picture what it would be like if we had remained where we were, listening to the searchers approaching, expecting any moment to feel a bayonet thrust between the shoulder blades. There was a sudden cry as one soldier lost his footing and landed on his back with a thud.

It was at that moment that another sound caught my attention – a quick scuffle overhead, quite close, or so it seemed to me. Light steps moving hurriedly across the roof, as if a person who had been hiding at the end of a peak had made a wild break for the edge.

The sound came nearer, and I caught a quick glimpse out of the corner of my eye of a dark shadow moving against the sky. I shifted my head a fraction and saw a small, solid body in the act of flinging itself under the rail and sliding down as we had done, to conceal itself on the ledge beside us. A second later a small hand reached out to close around the same steel bracket that I was holding.

Out of the darkness came a whisper. '*Por favor,*' it begged, '*por favor, socorro.*'

A woman's voice.

TWENTY-FIVE

The marines carried out two thorough sweeps of the roof before giving up and retreating from the vile weather. A few torch beams jinked above our heads, but luckily for us no one seemed anxious to hang out over the edge and peer downwards on to the ledge.

After they had gone the roof fell silent. The rain continued to pour down but we were sheltered from the worst effects by the overhang. It was only when the wind blew horizontally that we got really wet. From the sounds below I judged that a search of the surrounding area was in progress. The troops were being deployed in a wide sweep of the neighbouring premises – evidently without success, because after about twenty minutes we heard whistles being blown summoning them back. Boots clattered on the concrete apron. Radios crackled and NCOs' shouts split the air, as they mustered their formations and chivvied their men aboard the vehicles. I risked a quick glance down and saw the body of the man who had fallen from the hangar roof being dragged out and thrown into the back of a truck.

At last, to our relief, we heard motors being restarted and the column began to move out. The hangar doors were shut again, and everything went quiet. At least we could be certain we hadn't been seen – or they would have kept going till they found us.

We stayed where we were, not moving. It was on the cards that a party had been left behind to watch and wait for anyone who had been hiding to emerge, thinking the coast was clear. I twisted my wrist till I could squint at the face of my watch – 7.45am. People would be starting the morning shift even though daylight wasn't due just yet. We couldn't afford to wait around much longer. It was imperative that we left the roof soon and made it to the cover of the drain or we would be trapped here.

I could feel the woman's hands still gripping the bracket alongside mine. Who the fuck was she, and what was she doing here? Was she connected with the guy we had surprised inside? It seemed likely. The search of the roof could have been simply a routine precaution after he had been killed. But what business were he and the woman engaged on? Were they thieves trying to make off with valuable equipment? Judging by Seb's tales the economic situation in the country was desperate enough to make that a possibility. Or were they part of some other intelligence outfit trying to gather information in the way we were?

Either way I felt pissed off. We had come here to do a job; we had virtually pulled it off and were set to go home and now these two had fucked everything up.

Well, it was just something that we would have to deal with. The most important task now was to get off the roof without being noticed. Gently I moved my hands out from under the woman's. 'I am going up on top to see what is happening,' I whispered, speaking slowly so as to make myself clear. 'You stay here. If it is safe I will come back and help you out. OK?' It was important to establish control of her. I figured she might be capable of getting back on to the roof on her own and I didn't want her running off.

There was a moment of hesitation, then a single, breathed response in English. 'Yes.'

Holding tightly on to the bracket, I reached up and felt for a stanchion supporting the safety rail. I got a grip on it and swung myself back up on to the roof again.

Jesus, it was a relief to be off that ledge. I crawled along until I located Josh and helped him up. 'We've got company,' I said, and told him what had happened.

'A woman? Christ, where the fuck did she spring from?'

'I don't know yet. We'll have to find out, but for the moment we're stuck with her. Let's get her up and back to the LUP before we hear what she has to say for herself. First, though, we'd better check the roof in case they left an ambush.'

Swiftly and silently we fanned out across the roof along the gullies between the peaks, using our night-vision goggles to check the shadows for lurking snipers. There was no sign of anyone. The weather was worse than ever and gale-force gusts blasted the rain straight into our faces. At least it would give us cover when it came to crossing the open ground to the drain entrance.

As soon as we were satisfied the roof was clear I blipped my UHF handset again and reported in to Nobby. There was no time for a long conversation; I simply informed him that we had evaded capture and were now coming in.

'Right,' I told Josh, stowing away the transmitter. 'Let's get the girl out.'

She had obeyed my orders and was lying where I'd left her, good as gold. I reached down, took her by the arm and hauled her up bodily. She weighed not much more than 120 pounds fully clothed, and I judged her height to be around five foot six. It was impossible to make out her features; all I could tell was that her hair was shoulder-length and dark. She wore dark pants and a parka that looked too big for her with the hood pulled up. Younger than me, I guessed, but a woman, all the same, not a girl.

'You got a name?' I asked her when we had got her back from the edge.

She hesitated as the rain ran down her face and plastered her hair against her chin. 'Tell me yours first,' she said.

I nodded at Josh. 'He calls me Boss, I call him Boy.'

She was silent a moment, then with a shrug she said, 'You can call me Dona.'

Dona I knew meant woman; it would do for the present. 'OK,' I told her. 'How many more of you are there?'

'I don't know what you mean.'

'There was a man inside the hangar. He fell from the roof and was killed. We saw the marines drag his body away. Was he with you?'

'He was a friend, yes.'

'So what were the two of you doing here?'

She shook her head. 'That is our business.'

'Answer the question.'

Again there was a moment's hesitation. Her shoulders stiffened. 'I make a deal. Get me out of here and I will tell you.'

Josh and I exchanged glances. It was clear she had recognised us as British soldiers.

I looked at her, wondering what to do with her. We couldn't let her go, that much was clear. I put my hand on my knife.

Josh saw me. 'She's a civilian, Mark. We can't do it.'

'It's either that or take her with us.'

'If we get her back to the LUP we could find out more from her.'

I shrugged and took her arm.

She shook me off. 'What are you doing with me?'

'You're in luck. We're going to have to take you with us.'

We returned to the escape ladder. Josh and I spent a couple of minutes scanning the ground below with our night-vision goggles while the girl watched us with impassive hostility. I kept a hold on her arm. It must have been clear to her that her best chance of getting clear was to do what we said, but she didn't like it. If an opportunity presented itself for bunking off I was sure she would take it.

As soon as we were satisfied that there were no guards hanging around the bottom waiting for us, I sent Josh down the ladder. He went down rapidly and silently, sliding with his boots to the side and controlling his descent with his gloved hands. With practice it's possible to drop down very fast in this manner. He reached the bottom and crouched, ready to respond to any threat. Then he raised an arm to signal that all was clear.

'You next,' I told the girl.

I made to help her on to the ladder but she rejected my offer with an angry gesture. 'I can manage,' she snapped. 'I climbed up.'

Jesus, I thought to myself.

I let her start down while I kept watch from the vantage of the roof and Josh remained at the base of the ladder ready to receive her. There were lights coming on around the base now as the shifts changed over and the morning duty teams checked in. In a way this might work to our advantage, I thought, as it might be more natural to see people moving about.

The woman took some time to get down but eventually I got a second thumbs-up from Josh, and I took my place on the ladder. I went down the same way as Josh, in a controlled fall. It was a quieter as well as a quicker way of descending.

'Head for the manhole?' Josh queried.

I looked around carefully. Already there were more

lights showing as the base came to life. I shook my head. 'No,' I said. 'Not the one by the fuel depot. Too much activity in that direction now. It only takes one person coming on shift early to spot us. We'll head out for the first manhole we came to on the way in.'

I took out my GPS receiver and checked the bearing. On the way in I had taken a fix just in case, and now it helpfully gave me a direction and distance. All we had to do was follow the heading. We grabbed one of the woman's arms each and set off at a trot before she could protest.

We passed a couple of revetments where aircraft were bedded down snugly behind massive blast walls. None of them was armed as far as I could see; no missiles were slung under the wings. Nearby were anti-aircraft emplacements protecting the airfield, their radar dishes pointed silently at the sky. But the warheads of the rockets were shrouded in weatherproof covers, the crews nowhere to be seen. Evidently there was no anticipation of a sudden attack. Maybe we were on a wild goose chase after all.

Out here on the edge of the runway we could look across to the civilian side. There were lights showing over there and we could dimly make out the shapes of two small airliners by the terminal. A convoy of vehicles began moving out across the main runway. 'Snow clearance team,' Josh said under his breath. 'Must be expecting another flight soon.' It was now getting on for eight o'clock and I was anxious to be out of here.

We overshot the manhole and had to double back a

few metres to find it. I got the lid up and dropped down into the inspection chamber. I was relieved to note that there was the same level of water in the drain – with all the rain coming down I had been worried it might have filled up. 'You lead this time,' I told Josh, climbing out again. 'I'll push the woman in ahead of me.'

Josh stripped off his webbing and dived into the drain without hesitating. He was proving to be a good lad and I was very glad I'd brought him along. I turned to the woman. I was worried that she might baulk at entering the stinking dark tunnel or throw some kind of a panic attack, which we certainly couldn't afford. If that happened I'd just have to clip her one behind the ear and drag her unconscious up the tunnel behind me.

'We came in this way,' I told her. 'It's dirty but quite possible.'

She shrugged in a fatalistic, Latin way. 'If you can do it I can. I am much smaller,' she said.

I took her arms and lowered her carefully down into the hole. She bent down and wriggled her way inside after Josh. I followed, pulling the lid of the manhole back into position after us. Just before I got down on my belly I made one final call on the UHF handset.

'Nobby,' I said. 'We're off the hangar and in the drain. Expect two of us plus one prisoner.'

Then I set off.

Before long I discovered that I had been wrong in thinking the water level wasn't rising. Quite soon we found ourselves crawling with it up to our chests. It made the going much harder and more exhausting, because we had to hold our heads up all the time. There was also the very real possibility that it might rise further and drown us like the proverbial rats. But we were committed now, and the only thing for it was to press on as fast as we could.

Josh had clearly grasped this and he set a rapid pace. The woman slithered along behind him. Like she said, it was easier for her because she was of a slighter build. In fact I was hard pressed to keep up. We passed the two narrow points that I remembered from the way in, and at last Josh called back that he had reached the bars at the far end.

'The water's deep here. We'll have to duck under to get through.'

This was just what we needed. Maybe, though, the water would wash some of the stinking muck off us, which would be a good thing. I could hear the water churning in the tunnel ahead. I guessed the ditch outside had become charged with water which was now backing up fast. Luckily there was only about two metres to go before the open air.

I explained this to the woman. 'Take a deep breath and pull yourself through past the bars. Keep swimming till you meet Josh. He'll drag you out.'

'I can do it,' she said tersely. I heard her gulp air, then she was gone. Whoever she was, she certainly had guts.

The water was rising fast. My big anxiety was that something would happen to her and she'd get stuck, blocking the passage. I couldn't afford to wait long either way to find out. I gave her a minute, then, with the water rising around my nostrils, I took a deep breath and dived.

The water was cold against my face and thick with filth. I kept my mouth and nose shut, feeling with my hands for the bars in front of me. The gap was tight, but we had squeezed through on the way in. Water was bubbling past my ears, flowing back into the tunnel at a fast rate. I found the gap and pushed my webbing with my pistol and delicate equipment like the night-vision goggles in a sealed bag through ahead of me. Being underwater had once been something that didn't bother me. Diving through a flooded conduit was a standard part of every training assault course, and I had been good at it. The helicopter crash back in the Falklands had changed that. When my hands touched the bars, I rolled over on my back and started to pull myself through. All was going fine till I was about half-way and suddenly I found I was stuck. I couldn't go any further. Fuck, I thought. I'd snagged on something. I knew it wasn't either of the main bars because I was holding on to them to pull myself through. So it had to be one of the sawn-off stumps that had caught. I tried to reach underneath to free myself but there wasn't room. I wriggled and squirmed to work myself loose, but still I couldn't get away.

By now I was starting to run low on air. Shades of going down in that Sea King began to close in, but I forced myself to ignore them. I relaxed my legs, took a firm grip with my hands and pushed myself back up the tunnel. I had to push myself a good few metres with my nose bumping against the roof before I found a pocket of air again. There was no time to waste. If I didn't get a move on I wouldn't have enough puff left to reach the bars again, let alone pull myself through. I took a couple of deep breaths, filling my lungs, and submerged again.

This time I went in on my front. Pushing myself along with my feet as fast as I could, I felt for the ends of the bars on the floor of the tunnel and covered them with my hands as I slithered past. I kept on pushing, felt my arse scrape under the roof bars and prayed that there was nothing else to catch. Something bumped up against my nose in front. It was my dry bag with my kit inside. I shoved it ahead up the tunnel. Another couple of metres should see me clear.

Next moment I felt a hand grasp my arm and start to draw me clear. I burst out from the water gasping. It was great to be in fresh air again. I turned to thank Josh, then I realised it wasn't he who had helped me out.

'Nobby!' I exclaimed, surprised. 'What the fuck are you doing out here?'

Nobby's voice was sharp with anxiety. 'Boss,' he said, 'we've got trouble.'

TWENTY-SIX

'Have the dawn patrols been round yet?' I asked Nobby as we set out.

'No, but we figure any time soon. There's a lot of activity.'

I pushed the woman up the track beside the fence in front of me. Nobby was leading, with Josh following and me and the prisoner bringing up the rear. We were crawling on our bellies. I had explained to her about the minefield and she had replied scornfully that she already knew. It was still dark but lights were showing across the airfield, and Nobby said an aircraft had just taken off from the civilian side.

We were drawing close to the LUP. I told the woman to wait with me a moment while I sent Nobby on ahead to warn whoever was on observation stag that we were bringing in a prisoner. It was Kiwi. The sight of his massive silhouette was reassuring; so was the calm with which he greeted us. 'Doug's in the back. Trouble with the comms.'

Whatever the problem was I didn't want to discuss our plans and difficulties in front of the woman. I sent her up to the LUP with the other two and told them to

281

keep her there and send Doug down to me at the fence. Inside a minute he came crawling back through the bush.

'Mark,' he snapped, and that was a sure sign of trouble – he hardly ever used my first name. 'Fuck, are we in trouble. I still can't contact Hereford. The fucking satcom's given up on us.'

My heart sank. First the 320 set, now the satcom. 'What's happened?' I was thinking it couldn't be water in the electronics; the set was packed in a sealed box. 'It was working all right when we landed.'

'The fucking connector leads are missing, that's what,' Doug snarled. He was very angry. I was appalled. The leads connecting the transmitter to the aerial were a vital part of the kit.

'But you took spares?'

Doug gestured furiously. 'Of course there was fucking spares! I always pack spares! They were both together in a pocket in the sat pack. The fuckers must have dropped out somewhere.'

I didn't ask if he had searched the area we were in. He must have discovered the loss almost immediately and been searching frantically for them all the while Josh and I were out on the airfield.

'We had the leads on the beach. Did you check again when we left the Toyota?'

'Fuck you! I checked we had the pack. I didn't open up to see if the cables were there. It was too fucking dark to see.'

I was trying to control my anger too. It had dawned

on me that if the cables weren't here then the best bet was that they had been left behind on the beach when we sent a landing sitrep to Hereford – in which case the loss was down to me. Doug was angry with me, not himself.

'I swear I put the cables back inside.' The truth was that I couldn't remember. There had been so many things to think about back on the beach. Jock was missing and I had to take charge. It would have been all too easy to pack the set up and leave the cables behind on the sand. 'We checked the whole site before pulling out,' I said lamely. 'Besides, I only used one set.'

'Well they're both gone now,' Doug said savagely. He took a deep breath. 'So what do we do? Give up and go home?'

The sneer in his voice made me blaze with anger. He was suggesting that we had to abort and all because of my negligence. And I wasn't having any of it. 'The fuck we do,' I told him. 'Did you try to raise Seb on the cellphone?'

'Yes. No response. All we got was an answer service.'

'It's almost morning – we'll get a call back soon. The satcom set uses standard sockets, and oil company geologists use satellite phones all the time. He can find us cables to fit.'

I was still kicking myself for my stupidity. I thought it likely that Seb would be able to fix us up, but it would take time – and time was something that we didn't have. The Argies were working round the clock to have those planes readied. They must have been planning to have the work completed by tomorrow at the latest. It made me mad at myself. Andy would never have let this happen.

Five minutes later we were moving out up the path towards the gates. I had had to take a decision fast. Dawn was approaching and the patrols would be coming round soon. If we were to get away it had to be now before daylight trapped us in situ. And above all it was vital to establish contact with Seb and arrange for an urgent message to be passed through to Hereford.

The gear was all together. It was simply a matter of cut and run. Before we pulled out, we scoured the plinth and path, removing every trace of our presence. I even replaced the mine that I had lifted, thinking that it might keep the Argies busy removing it.

The woman looked shaken by our weapons and the speed and silence with which we moved. She did not protest when I pointed her down the track after the others.

Rain was still falling as we reached the gates and the first hint of light was creeping into the sky. Not dawn yet, but a darkness that was easier to see in. While the others crouched at the side in the bushes, weapons at the ready, I approached the gate. Into the lock I inserted the brass key with the plastic tab that Seb had given me and twisted it. Nothing happened. I tried again, still no joy. I tugged at the hasp but it remained locked. I tried putting the key in the other way, pulling it a short way out. Nothing worked. Still it wouldn't turn.

'Bugger it,' I muttered under my breath and, taking a grip with both hands on the key, I twisted it with all my strength. There was a metallic snap and the key broke off at the lock. Shit!

I went back to the others and told them what had happened. 'The fucker jammed in the lock. All this snow and rain must've rusted it up. Now it's busted.'

'You fat-handed twat,' Doug snarled in a whisper. 'Can't even work a key. Now what?'

I looked at the gate. It was strung with barbed wire across the top. Kiwi followed my gaze. 'No sweat, boss,' he said.

We ran back to the gate. I took off my pack and slung my weapon over my shoulder. Kiwi made a stirrup for my foot and heaved me up effortlessly. I gripped the bar at the top of the gate and pulled myself upright, holding on to the barbed wire with my gloved hands. I hooked one leg over to get a firm stance and Kiwi passed up the pack. I heaved it over and dropped it down on the ground on the far side. I swung my other leg across, let go and jumped down. I was back outside the base. 'Easy,' I whispered.

Josh came next, then Doug. As soon as they were down they took up positions with their weapons covering the tracks in both directions. Kiwi seized the woman and boosted her up on his shoulders till she was level with the top of the gate. She picked her way neatly over, gripping the wire between the barbs with her slim fingers. I reached up to help her down but she motioned me curtly out of the way and jumped. She landed lightly as a cat. I laid my hand on her shoulder just in case she had any ideas about taking off now she was outside. She shook herself away angrily, but made no attempt to escape.

That left only Kiwi and Nobby, the biggest and the smallest of the team. This time Kiwi went first. Nobby made a step for the huge New Zealander and in a second he was up on top of the gate. Nobby handed up both their packs and Kiwi threw them over. He took a strap from his pocket and lowered the end to Nobby, who wound it round his wrist and gripped tightly. With a grunt Kiwi heaved him up beside him on the gate. The two of them climbed over and jumped down one after another. As they did so there came an urgent hiss from Doug up the track. 'Vehicle approaching.'

'Take cover!' I rapped instantly, grabbing the woman by the hand. Seizing our bergens, we ran for the bush on the far side of the track, threw ourselves flat and began wriggling in underneath as fast as we could go. I pushed her in front of me, whispering at her to keep her head down. She didn't seem to need telling though. She was crawling along on her belly like a pro. Maybe she had been trained – that was something else to bear in mind when we had a moment to question her.

The noise of the approaching vehicles was loud behind us now. This must be the dawn patrol Seb had warned us about. It was fortunate that the rain had washed away the snow and we weren't leaving any tracks.

We were around thirty yards into the bush and our

cammies would give us good cover at this range. Even the woman's dark clothing would be hard to spot.

Headlamps swept among the scrub overhead and halted. The engine note died to an idle and there was a shouted order. We all tensed. Had we been spotted? I heard the sound of a man jumping down, probably from a Jeep. There was a rattle from the gates. Checking the lock, I thought. Seb had been right when he said the marines here were well disciplined. There was a call in Spanish followed by the sound of the man returning. Evidently everything was in order. The engine picked up again, there was a clash of gears, and the headlights moved on past us down the track.

Before we moved off I checked my GPS. We still hadn't managed to contact Seb but we had agreed an RV point in a clearing about two kilometres due north. There was an old stone sheep-creep there, apparently, which would provide some sort of cover for us to lie up in during daylight. He had given me a grid reference which I had entered into the GPS memory. All I had to do was call it up to get a bearing.

We moved out quickly, Kiwi leading this time. We had less than an hour of darkness left and a good way to hike. Even if we kept on going through the twilight of half dawn we would be pressed to make the RV point before sun-up. Whether or not we could keep going would depend on the terrain. The one thing we couldn't do was risk being spotted. A lot depended on the rain keeping up and forcing people indoors.

I worried that the woman wouldn't be able to keep

up, but she seemed fit and accustomed to walking and at least she wasn't carrying a bergen. It occurred to me to ask her what she knew of the country round here, but I decided against it. I wanted to keep her under our control at all times, and it was necessary for her to be convinced we knew exactly what we were doing.

Shortly after leaving the airfield we were back in the pampas again. There were few trees, and the rain had left many deep pools into which we plunged constantly.

We were headed north, parallel with the coast. The main road was away to our left a couple of kilometres. That was the direction in which there was most likely to be human activity, and we kept well clear.

We constantly checked behind us, but detected nothing and pressed on.

The sky was definitely lightening towards the east now, and we still had over two kilometres to go.

It wasn't long before Kiwi signalled us to halt. I went forward and found we had almost blundered on to a small house, almost a shack, built into the side of a slope. It looked like the sort of place a shepherd might hole up in, almost certainly with a pack of dogs at his command. We backed carefully away and circled round downwind to the west, giving the place a 500-metre berth.

At one point Nobby, who had taken over the scout position, spotted car headlights in the distance. The main road was less than a kilometre away. I checked the GPS and changed course towards the east again. The trouble with this coastal strip was that it was hemmed in between road and sea with little room to manoeuvre.

Soon afterwards we made a second break and dogleg: we cut back across our own track and halted for a moment to check for followers. We were about to move off again when Josh said, 'Wait.'

Everyone dropped flat, safety catches snicking off. I glanced at Josh. He signalled to me that he had glimpsed one figure back down the track in the direction we had been coming from. Grey streaks of dawn were now lightening the sky and the landscape was taking on a ghostly appearance as objects emerged mistily from the darkness. The rain had eased off and the wind was dropping. The temperature was hovering near freezing, though – a raw, damp cold that penetrated my clothes and set me shivering.

We waited in the wet grass for ten minutes as water dripped from the bushes, but nothing happened. Eventually I signed to Josh to go forward and investigate, with Doug to cover him. They crawled away into the misty gloom while the rest of us waited, weapons cocked, ready to come to their aid. Visibility had increased till it was just possible to make out faces in the murk. Finally my earpiece gave a click. 'Fuck all here,' came Doug's voice, irritated and abrasive. 'Reckon your kid brother has been jumping at shadows.'

'Are you certain?' I responded. Doug was a good soldier – fast, aggressive and courageous in action, but he lacked patience.

'You questioning my judgement?' he snapped back, his short fuse igniting in a trice. 'You don't trust me, is that it? You think this jerk knows more soldiering than I do.'

I was tired. 'Fuck off, Doug,' I told him. 'I asked if you're certain we aren't being stalked. If you're happy, fine. Come on back and bring Josh with you.'

Doug emerged from the bush with a crestfallen Josh following. He was sure he had seen something among the gorse and even reckoned he had found a footprint but Doug remained dismissive. 'It was one of the chick's,' he sneered. 'Though what we've brought her along for I dunno – unless it's to have some fun while we're waiting at the RV.'

Even if the woman's English wasn't good enough to follow this exchange, Doug's leer made its sentiment plain. She shot him a look of contempt and spat. 'English soldier. *Bastardo!*'

'Drop it,' I told them. 'We've got to get moving. I'll lead. Josh, you look after her. Kiwi, you take the rear slot and keep your eyes skinned.'

I cracked on, setting as fast a pace as I could. I was desperately anxious to reach the RV point before daylight made it too dangerous to move. If there was anyone behind us then perhaps we could leave them behind. The only pursuit we really had to fear would be by vehicles.

Or from the air.

Less than half an hour later, just as it was nearing 8.15am, we heard the thud of helicopters approaching from our rear.

TWENTY-SEVEN

'Take cover!' I shouted, flinging myself down into the wet grass. Dawn was breaking slowly, drawing a thick mist out of the ground which covered the country in a dense cloud. The sun was coming up, a weak, wintry orb with no warmth to it. Beads of moisture clung to our clothes and weapons. We could see only a distance of a few metres. All sounds were muffled, and we lay in a nebulous, white world.

I pulled my camo net over me and lay flat. The machines clattered overhead at speed, invisible in the low overcast as we burrowed blindly into the grass like animals. Heavy-duty troop carriers, I judged by the engine note. Something like the American Black Hawk or our own Puma, each carrying a stick of twelve to fifteen fully armed troops. Enough to give us a headache. It sounded like they were flying high and heading north. Maybe they were trying to spot us through patches in the mist, or perhaps it was just a routine patrol. There was no way of telling.

As soon as they had gone I held a quick briefing. According to the GPS we now had less than 1000 metres to go to the RV point. 'While the fog holds we'll risk it and push on,' I told the others. There was no dissent, even from Doug. We were all anxious to reach a place where we could lie up.

I made another attempt to contact Seb, but he still wasn't answering. I was getting pissed off. First his key didn't work, and now he wasn't picking up his messages. That was the trouble working with intelligence types; they were unaccountable. We needed him to arrange our route over the border, and to take over the woman if possible.

Five hundred metres from the RV we executed another ambush check to the rear. The sun was coming up fast now, and starting to burn off the mist. We only had another few minutes in which to establish ourselves in a fresh LUP for the day. According to the GPS the sheep-hide we were supposed to rendezvous at lay just over the neighbouring ridge. We halted under some stunted trees in a small gully, and I sent Doug forward to scout the route. He had hardly gone when there was an urgent message from Josh to the rear.

'Four men moving up the trail in our direction. Armed.'

'Ambush positions!' I snapped to the others, grabbing the woman as I spoke. Instantly we dispersed ourselves in a ring facing back the way we had come. Kiwi had the big GPMG deployed to enfilade the gap in the gorse through which the enemy would approach, the rest of us had rounds chambered. 'Doug, watch our front!' I said into the radio.

'Roger,' was his reply.

'Stay under cover everyone. Don't shoot unless they fire first.' A battle now, so close to the RV point in breaking daylight, would be disastrous.

Josh came scuttling back to join us. I pushed the woman down into the grass beside me. 'If shooting starts, keep your head down and play dead,' I hissed. 'Don't look up and don't run. Understand?'

She nodded. Her face was pale. It was the first time I had been able to take a really good look at her in the light. A strong face, fine featured, very dark eyes smudged with tiredness, and older than I'd first guessed.

She clutched my arm. 'These men, they may be friends of mine.'

I stared at her, trying to work out whether I was imagining that I'd seen her before. Before I could think any further the first of the group stepped out from a bank of gorse into the gully. He was a young man, in his mid-twenties at a guess, thin and drawn looking. He was dressed like a hunter in khaki trousers and a loose-fitting camo jacket, and he carried a hunting rifle with a telescopic sight on a sling over his shoulder. The man who followed him was older; he wore a woollen hat pulled down over his ears, and carried a pump-action shotgun with a bandolier of cartridges across his chest. Behind them were two more men, also civilians by the look of them, armed in the same way with sporting weapons.

They moved cautiously in our direction. I had already figured that whoever they were, the best thing would be to let them pass, hoping they didn't spot us. If we could avoid a contact we would save ourselves a lot of grief.

The woman, however, had other ideas. Ignoring my orders she jumped up. 'Julian!' she screamed.

Instantly the men swung to face her. The man with the shotgun had his weapon up. He was three metres away. If he fired at that range he would cut us both in half. I rose slowly to my feet. My rifle was centred on his chest and my finger was on the trigger. The rest of the team rose from their positions to cover me. I saw the newcomers' eyes widen as they took in the grenade launchers and the yawning muzzle of the GPMG clutched in Kiwi's great paws.

For a long moment we stared, guns trained on each other. Alerted by the scream, Doug came running back along the gully. He took in the scene in a glance and dropped to one knee, his rifle pointed at the guy with the shotgun.

'Doug,' I told him. 'Cut round the rear and check there aren't any more behind.'

'Gotcha, boss.' He jumped up and took off, skirting the group and keeping his weapon trained on them all the time.

The leader of the Argentines seemed to come out of shock. He shouted something in Spanish at the woman. Then the others started calling out too.

The situation was rapidly slipping out of control. The four men were in a highly nervous state. The one in front was unslinging his rifle and yelling to the woman, and the other men were waving their guns in my direction. Any moment now someone was going to let off a shot and we'd have a load of corpses on our hands.

'Tell them to put down their guns!' I shouted to the woman.

'It is OK,' she yelled back. 'They are my friends. They mean no harm.'

'Fuck that! Tell them to throw down their weapons or we'll shoot!'

She could see from my manner I wasn't kidding. One look at Kiwi and the others must have confirmed it. But her friends were growing increasingly agitated. They had seen Doug move in behind them and knew their escape was cut off, and they were all shouting.

'Josh!' I shouted. 'Tell the bastards to throw down their weapons or we'll drop them!'

Josh stepped forward. 'Put down the guns! Now, or we will shoot!' he said in Spanish.

The men gaped at him. Either they hadn't understood his accent or were astonished at being addressed in their own language. The woman stepped forward, repeating what Josh had just said. She spoke quietly but firmly, adding something that sounded like 'English soldiers'.

English soldiers – the four clearly got that much. They gaped at us blankly, and we stood our ground. They were bunched together with their guns held defensively in front of them. I studied them carefully. Educated men by the looks of them, ranging in age from early twenties to fifty. They were confused and frightened and there was a woman at stake. They might do anything.

'Put down the guns,' the woman said, speaking in English for our benefit this time. 'I am OK. They have not hurt me. They helped me escape from the base.'

There was a long pause. The young man she had called Julian spoke to the others, evidently translating what she had just said. None of us made any move. 'Please, Julian,' the woman said quietly. 'Please, no shooting for my sake.'

Slowly, reluctantly, the young man lowered his rifle to point at the ground. After a moment his companions followed suit.

'Nobby,' I said, 'get the weapons.'

Nobby went forward. Firmly but not roughly he took the guns off them and moved away out of the line of fire. The men stood with their hands by their sides. They looked angry still, as if they had been forced into something shameful. The woman spoke softly to them in Spanish. She turned to me. 'What are you going to do with us?'

'Let you all go as soon as we can,' I told her. 'We are on our way out of here and the last thing we need is a lot of prisoners.'

'Then why not let us go now?' demanded the young man whose name was Julian. 'With her too,' he added fiercely.

'First tell me what you are all doing,' I replied.

He looked at the woman. I caught her shaking her head in a quick negative. 'That is our business,' he said sullenly. 'We are Argentinians. This is our country.'

'You are fighting the marines. We are against them

296

too,' added one of the older men, who looked like a doctor or a lawyer in his forties, and who evidently also had some English. It sounded as though they were part of some kind of resistance group. There had been nothing said in our briefings about any such organisation, though I knew that there was a great deal of opposition to the government. That didn't necessarily make them pro-British, though.

'You cannot take us with you. Let us go, all of us. Her included,' Julian said reasonably. 'We will promise not to tell the military you are here.'

'We'll fucking shoot you too and all,' growled Doug. He hated foreigners on principle.

Our problem was this: we now had five prisoners who needed at least three of us to watch them. That left barely enough to do a proper recon of the RV point. If we were attacked we would have to leave the prisoners and leg it. I decided to hand them over to Seb to deal with.

We threw their weapons into a patch of bog. They were unhappy about it; a couple of the guns looked valuable. We didn't need them though – they were so much extra weight to carry. We had to crack on now. I was worried these people might be followed and be leading the military on to us. All in all, the sooner we handed them over to Seb the better.

I crawled up to the top of the ridge with Doug for a squint at the RV. Three hundred metres away across open grass, a cluster of broken stone sheds huddled under another low rise. Seb had told us it was once a refuge where shepherds brought their sheep on harsh nights. Now the bottom had long since dropped out of the sheep market and such buildings were gone to ruin. I studied the place through my binoculars. No sign of activity or human occupation.

I took a 360-degree check around. The area seemed long abandoned; there was no sign of any activity. The mist was lifting away fast and patches of grey sky were showing through. 'If we don't get a move on soon we'll never make it across with this lot without being spotted,' Doug said. I agreed. Once among the buildings we could hunker down with the prisoners out of sight and await Seb.

'Let's do it,' I said.

I sent Kiwi and Nobby on ahead to scout the buildings. Together with Josh, Doug and I prodded the reluctant prisoners to their feet. 'Hurry it up,' I snapped. Any moment, I thought, the bloody helicopters will come back.

Kiwi came on the radio. 'Looks all clear up here.'

'Right,' I said to the others, 'get 'em moving.'

With our packs bumping on our shoulders, we ran the prisoners across the grass and up the slope. We were about fifty metres from the buildings when I heard the sound I dreaded.

'Helicopters!' I shouted. 'Everybody down!' I grabbed the nearest Argentine and hurled him bodily to the ground.

The engine noise swelled and grew louder and nearer, coming directly for us. It was plain that we had been seen. We would have to make a fight for it. Our anti-aircraft missiles had been lost on the boat but we still had our personal weapons. Rolling over, I raised my rifle.

A burst of automatic fire crackled overhead. Bullets zipped and pinged all around our position. More guns opened up from the flanks. The fire was coming from both sides and ahead. From behind the tops of the buildings and from the flanks to either side the helmeted heads of combat troops were aiming heavy calibre weapons at us. I estimated a company of infantry with light automatic weapons, firing from fifty to a hundred metres' range. Now the helicopters were sweeping in beneath the overcast, stooping low for the kill. A machine-gun mounted in the side hatch of the lead aircraft winked at us like a red eye, and more bullets thudded into the ground nearby. The troops must have been lying in wait on the other side of the hill. They had called in the air power the moment they saw us start to move. We had walked straight into an ambush. Perhaps the prisoners had led them to us.

'Pull back!' I shouted, but before we could move, from the direction of the road came a rumble of diesel engines. A troop of infantry fighting vehicles had broken cover and was closing in, the muzzles of their cannons swivelling towards us. Any moment now we would have 30mm shells bursting around our ears. A patch of gorse burst into flames as incendiary bullets zipped through. We were pinned down and surrounded, under attack from air and ground.

Josh was carrying the light anti-armour weapon, a 94mm anti-tank missile in a single-shot tube capable of taking out a main battle tank at 500 metres. Ignoring the bullets whipping past, he ripped the launcher off his back, snapped the tube out to its full extent and crouched, aiming at the nearest IFV. A huge smoke plume belched from the rear of the tube and there was a swoosh as the missile ignited. The rocket scorched across the ground, arrowing towards the lead vehicle. It impacted against the offside track near the front with a boom that echoed across the clearing. The vehicle swung round and stopped, rocking on its tracks, smoke pouring from its engine compartment.

The turrets of the two other machines barked angrily. Shells smacked into the earth among us, exploding with showers of dirt. Splinters of steel sang viciously overhead and the air was filled with the stench of cordite.

'Fucking great shot,' Doug was yelling. But next moment there came an ominous double thud and the whine of 81mm mortar bombs descending. More explosions fountained up as bombs and shells searched the hillside.

We had shot off our only missile, and the enemy had us at their mercy. They could sit back and blast us to pieces at their leisure.

The marines had been waiting. We had fallen into the hands of the enemy.

TWENTY-EIGHT

The shelling stopped. The machine-gun fire slackened off. An officer's voice crackled over a loud-hailer. 'British soldiers. Put down your guns and raise your hands. If you attempt to escape you will be shot.'

The guys were looking at me for guidance.

'Sod the bastards. Let's make a run for it,' Doug growled. 'Some of us should make it.'

I looked around. The prisoners had scattered and were lying shaking on the ground. They seemed unhurt. The Argy armour had paused on the track leading down from the road, and squads of infantry were dismounting to move across country and surround us from the rear. The helicopters were beating the air overhead. 'No,' I told Doug. 'Sorry, but it's a bust.'

'Fuck them!' Doug snarled. 'The fuck I'm going to surrender to fucking Argy cunts!' He jumped up, clutching his C-5, and instantly a machine-gun opened up from one of the vehicles, sending a stream of tracer winging towards him. The rounds, clearly visible, seemed to start slowly then speed up with a sudden rush as they got closer. The stream of bullets reached Doug, there was a terrific smacking sound, and he was knocked flying off his feet and on to his back.

He lay there, seemingly stunned. 'Doug!' I shouted. I crawled over to him, keeping my head against the ground as more rounds went screaming overhead like angry wasps. There was blood on his hands and face but I couldn't see exactly where he had been hit. I ripped open his jacket to check for chest wounds, but couldn't see any. His rifle was lying nearby, almost split in two across the middle. It looked as though Doug's gun had taken the main impact.

The voice with the loud-hailer was shouting something else about resistance being futile. I was in agreement with him.

Kiwi crawled over as Doug gave a grunt and stirred. 'How bad is he?'

'OK by the looks of him,' I replied. 'He was fucking lucky. Those marines aren't pissing about. If we give them any trouble they'll let us have it.'

'Looks like we're in the shit then.'

' 'Fraid so,' I said. 'Better tell the boys to do as they say. We don't want anyone else hurt.'

I was ripping open Doug's medical pack as I spoke. His injuries were just scratches, splinter wounds where the bullet that hit his gun had shattered. Like I'd said, he had been very lucky. An inch either way and the slug would have gone clean through his body.

He groaned and rolled over, rubbing his head. 'Jesus,' he coughed, squinting at me. 'Am I hit?'

'Not as badly as you should've been,' I told him.

'Next time, keep your stupid head down.' Now I knew he was OK I felt a sudden burst of comradeship for him. Doug and I had had our differences and he was a difficult bastard to live with at times but we had been through a lot together.

'Here they come, boss,' Kiwi called. 'Better throw down the weapons and show our hands.'

I saw the woman nearby and she was looking scared. I wondered what the Argies had in mind for her, and resolved to make it clear that she and her friends had been our prisoners. I would say we had stumbled across them in the woods and leave them to invent their own story.

All I could think was that I had blown the mission and got the lads caught. I felt gutted. The worst of it was that thanks to the communications failure we hadn't been able to contact Hereford, and now there was no way of warning them of the Argy plan for invading the Falklands.

Argentine marines were moving down the slope fifty metres away, weapons at the ready, to take our surrender. Doug reached into his pack for the satcom set. Slung over his shoulder was a Claymore bag with an anti-personnel mine in it. He stuffed the satcom set inside and the 320 VHF set with it. All the encryption gear went in too, along with the codes. I added the maps I was carrying, the GPS and my UHF handset – no sense in making the Argies a present of them. Doug set the timer to fifteen seconds, closed the canvas flap and fastened it down. I could see his lips move as he counted off the seconds. Then, lofting the bag briefly, he flung it away from him down the hill. There was a loud explosion as it hit the ground, and a pall of smoke rose into the air. Bits of debris rattled down on top of us.

There were shouts of anger from the marines, and a volley of shots cracked over our heads.

Doug grinned.

Then I remembered the cellphone Seb had given me. If the Argentines found that it would be a dead give-away. They would work me over until I gave them the name of our contact out here. I slipped it out from my pocket and prised it apart with my knife. Then I snapped the SIM card and broke the circuit board apart so that they couldn't be used again. I shoved the bits into a hole in the ground and pressed some mud down over them. With luck they would never be found.

The marines came doubling up now. They pushed us roughly down on the ground again, kicking our legs apart and forcing us to put our hands behind our necks. They patted us down, searching for weapons and equipment. They took away my pistol and fighting knife. They made us strip to our vests one by one to check our clothes for anything we might have tried to conceal. My watch was taken and the dog tags ripped from my neck.

The Argies were in a state of high excitement, whooping and laughing as they squabbled over our possessions. They evidently considered they had won a great battle and everyone wanted a souvenir.

'SAS?' they kept jeering. 'SAS?' They evidently knew

who we were, and were over the moon about their cleverness in catching us. There seemed to be the best part of a company of them, fifty at least – so we had been outnumbered by a good ten to one. This made me feel better.

When the searching was complete our hands were tied behind our backs with plasticuffs and we were placed face-down on the ground. The civilians were subjected to the same treatment; we heard them protesting their innocence to the officers, but with no effect. They were cuffed too and thrown down with us. Some of the men were slapped around roughly in the process – evidently the marines had no love for dissidents.

There was a long wait then, of an hour or more. From the little we could see, it appeared the Argies were conducting a fingertip search of the ground, looking for any fragments of our comms gear and encryption equipment. I doubted if they would have much luck – a Claymore mine packs a pretty big punch.

My real fear was that they would turn up the remains of the cellphone, in which case I was in for a rough time. I figured I could handle that if I had to, at least hold out long enough for Seb to get clear. In a small community like Rio Grande, news of the capture of five SAS troops would spread rapidly, and a man like Seb would have his escape plans prepared in advance.

They made us all sit up and identify which was our equipment and our individual weapons. I couldn't make out what this was for apart from a bit of general intelligence. The officer in command, a major who spoke some English, tried his hand at a spot of questioning, but we had all done the interrogation courses at Hereford and pretended we didn't understand him.

This pissed them off, so they brought the woman out.

They stood her up in front of us, and though she was doing her best to be brave about it one of her legs was shaking uncontrollably. She was Argentinian, and she knew what was coming all right. The major took his time, letting the fear get to work. He was a small man, olive-skinned with very white teeth, broad in the shoulders and smartly turned out – a typical officer, in fact. He said in English his name was Oliveras. He explained how he understood that we couldn't talk, that we were forbidden to give more than our names and numbers, all that crap. It was a pity, he said, because in the absence of help from us he would be forced to make his own deductions.

'We know you have been on the base at Rio Grande,' he smiled. 'Oh yes, we know all that. We know you were in the hangar and this woman was with you. If you will not tell us how you entered the hangar and what you saw, then we shall have to conclude that it was this woman and her friends who helped you. Which makes her a traitor. And that is a very serious matter, oh yes.'

He paused to let us think about the seriousness of it, and lit a cigarette. 'I wonder,' he went on, 'have any of you ever witnessed the interrogation of a woman?'

There were sniggers from the men, who obviously

felt they were in for a good show. The woman stared straight ahead stonily, but her leg was still shivering. The young boy, Julian, was looking white in the face. The major drew on his cigarette, then said something in Spanish to the woman. She replied in a harsh, clipped tone, from which every emotion had been ironed out. Pleading would do no good with this man; her fate depended on whether or not we were prepared to let her be tortured.

'So it is down to you English,' the major said evenly. 'You brave SAS will decide if this woman is to suffer and how much.' He signed to two of his men standing behind the prisoner, and they seized hold of her by the arms. She stiffened but did not struggle. It would have been pointless anyway, they were huge men and she was slight.

The major unzipped her parka and pulled it down from her shoulders. He did it deftly and his movements, the way he touched her, were obscene. He was demonstrating his complete dominance. I can touch her any way I like, he was indicating to us. Underneath the coat she wore a black shirt and a grey turtleneck sweater. Reaching behind her neck, Oliveras grasped her hair tightly with his right hand. It was black hair and springy with a wave in it, and he wound a bunch tightly in his hand to get a good purchase.

From where I was sitting to one side, I could see the tears coming into her eyes as he jerked at her head. 'Still,' he commanded. He drew on his cigarette until the end glowed red, then took it in his free hand. 'Do not struggle. One touch of the tip on your eye and – phut – you are blind.'

He tightened his grip on her hair. As the glowing cigarette end approached her face, she fought to turn away but he held her firm. He was a strong man. The marines either side had her pinned between them. Oliveras brought the cigarette closer. There was a sharp intake of breath from the woman and her body went rigid, but no scream came.

After what seemed an endless moment the major stepped back. An ugly red burn sat at the corner of her left eye, no more than a centimetre from the eyeball itself.

Oliveras turned his flashing smile on me. 'So, you are the senior man in this band of pirates. Are you going to tell us what you saw in the hangar, or must I put the next cigarette in the eye itself?'

I had already realised that this was a man for whom the act of inflicting pain on a woman was an active pleasure. He was going to hurt her whether we answered him or not. Once he had finished with her it would be our turn, probably beginning with me. There was nothing to be gained by helping him along. I shook my head. 'I have nothing to say.'

Oliveras shrugged. He produced a gold lighter, and with deliberate carelessness selected a fresh cigarette from his pack. 'Imagine,' he said holding it up. 'This red tip is the last thing she will ever see. Red fire, and then . . . darkness.' He gripped the woman's hair again. She fought against him with all her strength this time, twisting her head from side to side. Oliveras laughed and jabbed at her face with little stabbing motions. 'There and there. Ah, so near that time. You make it worse for yourself when you struggle.'

My stomach knotted. The guy was sick and there was nothing any of us could do about it. The woman was going to lose one eye at least. It was just a question of how long Oliveras wanted to prolong the agony.

'Are you ready, Concha?' he grinned as if addressing an old friend.

I gaped. How did he know her name? Of course, he was an intelligence officer stationed down here. As dissidents, the faces and details of all her group would be familiar to him. The marines must have tracked them from the vicinity of the base to lay the ambush. They evidently figured we were working together.

And then, suddenly I saw it. It must have been the way the woman was standing, her arms behind her, fear and courage mingled in her face, that same face that had hurled defiance at her enemies two decades ago in another war.

Concha, Oliveras had called her. The name Jenny had told me the spy on the *Northland* had given. Suddenly I saw her as she'd appeared to me some twenty years before – naked, outstretched and lashed to ringbolts in the ship's bulkhead while smoke from the Argentine bombs billowed through the deck. The girl spy who had come nearer than anyone to taking out the British fleet. I had been walking beside her all this time in the darkness and I hadn't guessed.

So, she *had* escaped from the ship. I had only seen her for a few minutes on board in the gloom below deck; and last night it had been dark – it was hardly surprising that I hadn't recognised her. She would have been young then – eighteen, perhaps. I remembered how we had fought in the back of the truck, how I had forced her down and pulled her sweater up to check she was a girl. Now she must be in her late thirties; she looked younger.

Back on the march I had almost guessed – but the light had been poor and I'd had too much to think about. Now I was certain. It was as if I were back on the *Northland* once more with the bombs falling and my brother Andy shouting at me to get a move on.

But how was this possible? Then she had been an Argentine patriot, a heroine of the war on their side. If anyone could be expected to back the attack on Port Stanley it would be her. And yet now here she was being tortured by her own people! None of it made sense.

I was still trying to take all this in when there was an interruption – a truck came lurching down the track from the road. A marine NCO came up and said something in Spanish to Oliveras, who glanced up at the truck and scowled. He gave an order and turned back to us.

'It seems transport has arrived to take you back to Rio Grande. We shall have to terminate our little experiment, but only for the present, you understand? We shall resume the investigation in due course.' He patted

Concha tenderly on the cheek and turned away.

At gunpoint we were prodded towards the truck and helped aboard. Once inside the rear we were handcuffed back-to-back in pairs, with steel cuffs this time in addition to the plastic ties already binding our wrists. Concha and I were the last to be put aboard. Her head was drooping and she was evidently in pain. Had she recognised me? Probably not – I would have been just one face among her English captors. And I'd changed too.

As soon as we'd climbed aboard Major Oliveras called a halt. Pointing at Concha and me, he rapped out an order and the guards pulled us out again. We were put into the back of Oliveras' personal Jeep, handcuffed together like the others. Evidently the major had not finished with us yet.

The other truck set off, accompanied by a marine escort in a second vehicle. Oliveras had a few words with his junior officers, slapping their backs in high good humour. Capturing us was apparently a real coup for him. After a few minutes he climbed into the front seat beside the driver. '*Vamos,*' he said, then leaned over into the back and grinned at us. In his hand he held a .45 automatic. 'Just in case,' he said, his teeth gleaming.

We bumped along the track till we reached the road and turned south. This was the road we had travelled on last night with Seb. I struggled to remain upright while supporting Concha as the vehicle lurched across the potholes.

Oliveras was chatting away in Spanish – telling

Concha, I imagined, of the treats he had in store for her. The burn by her left eye was deep into the flesh and looked horribly painful.

I was still trying to figure out her part in all this. Julian and her friends had implied that they were a group opposed to the military. It occurred to me that Seb might know. The overriding urgency at the moment was somehow to get a message through to him, warn him of the Argentine plan, but I couldn't think how that was going to be possible. We hadn't even been interrogated yet, and I couldn't see Major Oliveras permitting us any kind of consular access until after the attack on the Falklands had gone ahead.

We jolted along for some minutes. It had come on to rain again. I was sitting behind the driver where Oliveras could cover me with the gun. The other truck had a good start and was lost in a cloud of dust. In the side mirror I could glimpse the road behind – the rest of the task force had not yet begun to pull out. We had the road to ourselves.

Looking ahead I could see that the land fell away to the left. A bridge was coming up on a bend; the road crossed a fair-sized river that ran in a steep ravine between thick stands of pine trees. Oliveras was telling the driver to hurry up – evidently he was impatient to get back to work – but the road approaching the bridge was badly worn. We were travelling at around fifty-five kilometres per hour.

It was now or never. I had to act before the driver took his boot off the accelerator to stand on the brake.

I brought my knees up sharply to my chest and rammed the soles of my boots into the back of his seat with every bit of strength I had. The seat support snapped and the back part smashed forward, pinning the driver against the wheel. He could only scream as the Jeep crashed through the safety railing at the foot of the bridge and pitched over the edge into the ravine.

TWENTY-NINE

The Jeep was skidding down the steep slope in virtual free-fall. The rear end was toppling outward; at any moment it would crash over on to its back. None of us was wearing a seatbelt and we were being hurled about inside the cab, bouncing off the seats and against the roof. Major Oliveras was clinging on to the dashboard and trying at the same time to get a shot off at me with his pistol. I was hampered by being handcuffed to Concha who had fallen forward on her face. I managed to free my left leg and launched a kick which by luck caught Oliveras under the chin, knocking his head back against the door pillar.

From then on everything became a blur. The drop was much worse than I'd guessed, and the Jeep pitched over on to its near side. Stones and gravel showered inside as the windows shattered. I fell into the rear foot-well, dragging Concha down on top of me. The Jeep rolled again, tumbling over on to its roof. We hit a large rock, bounced and hit the ground again with a bone-jarring crash. The driver was still screaming, or maybe it was Oliveras this time. The roof buckled and the interior filled with sand and dust so we could hardly breathe. I prayed it wasn't smoke. All we needed was a ruptured fuel tank spraying vaporised gasoline across a hot engine and we would end up in a fireball.

Dimly through the flying dust I was aware that one of the doors had been torn off. We seemed to be sliding backwards down a steep drop on one side again now, and I could feel the roof pressing down on us. There was another spine-breaking crash as we hit another rock and slewed round to roll again. The world was spinning; there was mud in my mouth and on my clothes. I could hear Concha gasping as the bumps knocked the breath out of her body. I was trying to hold us both wedged in between the seats. In car accidents it is the ones who are thrown clear who die.

The car seemed to roll over and over; I didn't think we could endure much more of it. Surely we must have reached the bottom of the ravine by now? Then I remembered the river – Christ, suppose we roll into mid-stream and sink? We'd never manage to get out with the cuffs on and the roof squashed in.

I didn't know where Oliveras and the driver were, but I couldn't hear them screaming any more.

And then, suddenly, it all stopped. The jarring and crashing ceased, and in its place there was a blessed stillness. My ears were still ringing but we were no longer being tumbled about and hammered from all sides. The interior of the Jeep was so full of dust that I couldn't see anything at all, just greyness in front of my eyes like smoke. The stuff caught in my throat, making me choke as I struggled to right myself.

The Jeep was lying right side up, tilting over to the near side, and my head was facing downward. I was squashed hard down between the seats, which had collapsed on to us, and Concha seemed to be lying inert across me. I tested my limbs, and as far as I could tell nothing was broken, though my head was splitting where I had banged it against something. It seemed a miracle I could still be alive.

I called out to Concha and got a moan back. Evidently she was more or less conscious. Carefully I started to heave myself free, pushing up with my elbows till I was crouching on my knees. She was half lying on the back seat with the roof pressing down on her. I bent my legs up and kicked at the door above me. To my relief it swung open with a scraping sound.

'Concha!' I called. 'Can you hear me? We have to get out of here.'

I got another groan in answer but I felt her stir. At least she was responding. 'Are you hurt?' I called.

There was silence for a moment, then she spoke in a weak voice, choking on the dust. 'I don't think so.'

That at any rate was a miracle and I felt encouraged. 'We're going to have to get out of here. The Jeep could catch fire. The door is open – see if you can't wriggle your legs out.'

I felt her squirm on top of me, trying to get clear. 'I think my legs are in the door,' she said eventually, sounding a little stronger.

My hands were still handcuffed behind my back to hers. The only way I could move was by twisting my shoulders, working them against the seats, and kicking with my legs. After considerable effort I managed to get my knees out. That gave me more of a grip. I was able to kneel down outside and, by lifting Concha with my arms, work her out through the door.

She subsided into a sitting position behind me. 'We need to stand up,' I told her. 'Push against me with your back.' I had practised this on escape-and-evasion exercises, but she had never done it before and it was difficult for her. Nonetheless, somehow we tottered to our feet.

The Jeep had ended up at the bottom of the ravine, under the bridge and just a few metres from the bank of the river. We had come nearer to falling in and drowning than I liked to think. The front of the car was badly smashed in and the driver appeared to be dead. The door on the other side had been torn off, and there was no sign of Oliveras.

'Come over this way,' I said to Concha. There was a piece of torn metal sticking out from the crumpled side of the Jeep. Rain was still falling steadily but we hardly noticed. By squeezing ourselves alongside and manoeuvring our locked hands, I got myself into a position where I could saw at the plasticuffs on my wrists. The metal was jagged and cut into my skin, but it was razor sharp and in a couple of minutes I had one hand free. The other was still shackled to Concha.

'Now your turn,' I told her. This was easier because I could use my free hand to help. I hardly cut her at all, and soon we each had a hand free.

She looked at the metal cuff that still joined our two wrists. 'What about these?'

I looked around inside the wrecked Jeep. I had hoped to find an axe or saw but I could see no tools that might hack through a steel chain.

'Come on,' I told her, dragging her up the slope.

'Where are we going?'

'To find Major Oliveras. Now hurry.' It was just possible that Oliveras might have a key on him. I also had hopes of finding his pistol. With a weapon we might hold up a car and get a ride out of the country. The border was only an hour away.

We scrambled up the face of the ravine, clawing at the loose shale with our hands. We found Oliveras twenty-five metres up. He was not a pretty sight. He had been flung out of the Jeep and fallen a long way. His neck was broken, and I wondered if I had done that when I kicked him. If so, no regrets. I checked his pockets swiftly. There was the lighter, which I took, but no pistol – it must have fallen out somewhere – and no key to the handcuffs.

'We need to get out of here. That convoy will be coming across the bridge.'

'I need a drink,' she said.

'Later,' I told her. 'Unless you want to face your interrogators again.'

Pulling her after me, I set off westwards along the riverbank. If we could reach the fir trees we would at least be out of sight.

The wreck had rolled in under the bridge; it might

not be seen by following vehicles, in which case it was possible that Oliveras' disappearance might escape notice for some little while. Then they would have to search the road to find the Jeep. All that might take hours if we were lucky.

We had only gone a few paces when Concha let out a cry and pointed. She had spotted Oliveras' pistol lying in the dirt. This was a piece of luck. I stuffed it in my waistband and immediately felt better. At least now we had a weapon.

After ten minutes of hard scrambling we were inside the belt of trees. They were tall and gloomy, great timbers stretching to the sky, covering scant undergrowth. Our feet crunched on a carpet of pine cones and broken twigs. Occasionally we had to clamber over rows of trunks felled by the wind. There was no animal life, and we moved in silence broken only by the noise of our own footfalls and the sighing of the branches overhead.

We had been walking silently for around twenty minutes when we came to a stream running down towards the river, and stopped to drink and wash the dirt from our faces. It was icy cold but it washed the dust from our throats. I wiped some over my face and head and felt better.

I was trying to formulate a plan. In case of just this sort of emergency we had agreed with Seb a special rendezvous point, the RV, by the ruins of an old copper mine close to the railroad, about two kilometres north-east of the town. Anyone becoming lost or separated during the mission was supposed to make for this RV and wait there. Seb would check the place every day between six and seven pm.

Concha guessed I was deciding what to do. 'I have friends still in the area,' she suggested. 'They would help us perhaps.'

I thought about it and shook my head – I didn't want to trust anyone I didn't know. If we could only reach the RV we would find food there and perhaps shelter. Assuming Seb was still able to move around freely, I was sure he would keep the rendezvous.

It was around ten o'clock in the morning – there were at least six hours to go till dusk. The army would undoubtedly be out searching for us before long, and they had the advantages of helicopters and vehicles – at the first sighting a stick of airborne commandos would be dropped in to round us up. At all costs, therefore, we had to stay out of sight. If I had been on my own I would have struck out for the border and trusted to my survival training to get me through, but shackled to this woman that was impossible.

I wasn't sure how far I could trust her anyway. However badly the marines had treated her, she plainly had no great love for the British. If she knew I was trying to frustrate an invasion of the Falklands she might try to turn me in along with herself.

Again I thought about running for the border. That was what the Argies would expect me to do, so it would be better to take the opposite direction – back south, across the river and towards the town. If I could keep the rendezvous with Seb he should be able to get a message out to the islands warning them of the invasion plan.

I dragged Concha down the hill, back towards the river. We needed to find a way across. I searched along the bank until we came to a narrow bend, where I weighed the situation up. The river was about ten metres wide, fast flowing but not too deep. We could wade it, I decided.

'Collect sticks,' I told her. 'Hurry.'

'Sticks? What for? Are you going to make a fire?'

'No, a raft,' I said. 'We're going to swim the river.'

She gaped at me, then her gaze swung back to the water, racing between the high banks. 'You are crazy. No one could get across there. We will drown.'

'Not with me along you won't, girlie.'

She glared at me, white with anger. 'I am not your girlie,' she said. 'And I tell you we will drown.'

Ignoring her, I went about gathering a bundle of dry wood and lashing the pieces together as best I could with bits of ivy and bark. When I judged I had enough, I marched Concha down to the bank. I sat her down, undid my boots and started peeling off my trousers. She stared at me, bug-eyed.

'Get your kit off,' I told her.

'What?'

'Get undressed. We'll wrap up our clothes tight to keep the water out and put them on top of the raft.'

A look of horror came over her face. 'Take off my clothes? You are not serious!'

The water looked very cold and dangerous; I didn't blame her for being scared, but I hadn't time to argue. 'Hurry,' I told her. 'Otherwise you won't have anything dry to put on when you reach the other side and you'll catch pneumonia.'

'And if I refuse?' she said stiffly.

'If you refuse, I put you on the raft and carry you over. You'll get twice as wet and a lot madder – but like it or not you are going across. We don't have time to fuck about.'

She stared at me for a long moment. She must have seen I was deadly serious because finally she took a deep breath and sat down to unbuckle her boots. 'This is how I am going to die – naked, drowned by a crude idiot of an English,' she said bitterly. I liked the crude bit. It showed that I was getting to her.

It was impossible to undress completely linked together with handcuffs. The best we could do was to strip off our bottom halves and tug our jackets, shirts and underclothes down on to our shackled arms.

Naked, she was no longer the skinny teenager of the war years, but her figure had a litheness that would have taken my breath away if I hadn't been too intent on what we were doing. I shooed the image out of my head and concentrated on the task in hand.

I told her to put her boots back on to protect her feet from the stones in the river. I pulled my own kit off, and we wrapped the garments as well as we could, given that we couldn't get them over the handcuffs. Then we put everything on top of the raft.

'Just walk into the water steadily,' I told her. 'Don't fight the current. It will carry us across further down. If you get out of your depth, kick with your legs. Keep your head, hold on to me and I'll get us across.'

She glanced down ruefully at the handcuffs linking us. 'I have no choice,' she said through chattering teeth.

Side by side we walked out into the river. It was bad, much worse than I had thought. Well before we reached the middle of the channel the water was up to my neck. It was freezing too – I felt as if I had stepped into a solid block of ice and the cramp in my chest was terrifying. I remembered the time twenty years before when Andy had made us swim a river in the middle of the night. That had been rougher, but I had been part of a team then.

Concha was out of her depth already, paddling with her feet like a dog. The current was sweeping us along it in midstream, and I prayed a helicopter wasn't going to choose this moment to over-fly us. The other bank still seemed as far away as ever.

My feet were only just touching the bottom; this must have been the deepest part of the channel. Waves were swirling down on us, and I did my best to shield Concha with my body from the worst of them.

Just when I was beginning to think we would never make it, the riverbed began to shelve again – we were nearing the far side. 'Only a little further,' I gasped.

But just then something huge and heavy struck me in the back. I lost my footing and the water closed over my head. Instinctively I opened my mouth to gasp for breath and felt icy water gushing into my throat. I fought to reach the surface with my free hand, but somehow I couldn't find it.

I could feel the strength ebbing from me. Darkness closed in on me from all sides. There was no pain, just a sensation of cold and numbness.

The next thing I knew, I was on my back and vomiting, and the vomit was gushing over my face and across my chest. I was lying in the mud on the shoreline, and the woman Concha was kneeling on top of me, pumping my chest. Her body was blue with cold, and we were still handcuffed together, along with half our clothes.

'What the fuck happened?' I said weakly.

'A piece of wood, a log. It hit you on the back and you went under.' Her breath was coming in gasps. She had been giving me mouth-to-mouth. For a woman of her size, hauling me out of the water must have taken some doing. She climbed off me and I hauled myself on to my knees. 'Are you OK now?' she asked.

'Yeah, I'll be fine,' I told her, even though I felt weak and ill. My back was sore too, I was freezing cold and my heart was beating ragged. But I was coming out of it.

'What happened to our kit?' I asked.

'Kit?'

'The raft? Did we lose it all in the river?'

'Oh no, when you fell under the water I kept hold and the current pushed us in to the shore.'

I stood up and saw the raft with our trousers and stuff

still on it, bobbing among the flotsam at the edge of the water. A keen wind was blowing and Concha was shivering. 'Shake the water off yourself and jump around,' I told her. 'It'll warm you up.'

I reached for the raft and pulled it ashore. I was weak, but I had survived.

Concha was still standing shivering. I slapped her on the bottom to get her moving.

'*Cabron!* Don't you dare hit me!' she snarled, lashing out and catching me on the cheek with a bony fist.

At least I'd got her leaping about.

'Ahh!' she cried as the circulation began to return to her limbs. I told her the pain was a good sign. It meant she hadn't got frostbite. She said something savage in Spanish. 'I was calling on God to strike you dead,' she answered when I asked what it was.

'Get dressed,' I said. 'We've a lot of ground to cover and you can't do it naked. And if you want to take a piss, now's the time because we're not going to be stopping for a while.'

'*Hijo de puta!* I am not one of your stupid soldiers,' she said. 'Stop giving me orders.'

Before I could think of a response we heard shouts from the woods on the other side of the river.

THIRTY

I grabbed our clothes and pulled Concha towards the trees. Fifty metres in we found a hollow in the ground and flung ourselves down, out of sight. We dragged our clothes back on, yanking ill temperedly at one another as we struggled to button ourselves up.

The enemy seemed to have got on to our trail even more quickly than I had feared. Maybe someone from the main convoy had noticed the gap in the railings where the Jeep went over.

I peered between the trunks of trees, but couldn't make out any figures on the far bank. It looked as if the pursuit had moved away to the north, the direction they would expect us to take.

Taking Concha by the arm, I hustled her up the slope to the top of the ravine.

Then we ran on, stumbling over tree roots and dead branches, the handcuffs biting into our wrists, till we came to the edge of the wooded area where we paused to get our breath back.

My body was warming up again after the river, but I was feeling deadbeat. I'd had no sleep for twenty-four hours and little food apart from a few chocolate bars wolfed down on the march. Concha looked in bad shape too. She leaned her back against a tree and closed her eyes.

It wasn't safe to remain this close to the crash.

Sooner or later someone might take it into their heads to search this side of the river. But attempting to move across country would expose us to the danger of being spotted from the air. Already I could hear the thud of helicopter blades in the distance.

I studied the landscape beyond the wood – rolling pampas, tall grass and patches of scrub, with here and there a few isolated stands of crooked trees. The wind sighed in the long grass and made the stalks rattle. In the distance was what looked to be a fair-sized lake. Overhead the sky was darkening.

'There is a storm coming.' Concha had opened her eyes again.

'Can you be sure?'

She jerked her chin at the sky. 'You live down here, you recognise the signs. The clouds are full of snow.'

That was good news if it was true. A blizzard would give us cover to move and keep the searchers off our backs.

'We'll wait here till the snow begins,' I decided. 'Then move out. So long as it's falling it'll cover our tracks.'

She eyed me suspiciously. 'Where are we making for?'

I hesitated – I couldn't afford to give away too many details of my plan, such as it was. 'If you fall in with enemy civilians,' our escape-and-evasion instructor had emphasised, 'it's vital you establish immediate control.' I had engineered our escape from the Jeep; I had swum us across the river – it was necessary for me to demonstrate continuing leadership if I was to retain her allegiance. At the same time she knew the area far better than I did, and her help would be invaluable. That she was still talking about 'we' in this context was significant.

'We need to put ground between us and any pursuit,' I told her. 'The further we move out, the wider the search area becomes and the better our chances become.'

'And then what? Do we just run until we drop dead from cold? This is the pampas in winter. How long do you think we can last outdoors?'

If we could survive till nightfall, I told her, then I had a friend who would help us.

She took this on board. 'A friend. Someone who you have bought.' Her lip curled in contempt. 'Stupid English soldiers, what are you doing here? Don't we have enough troubles without you?'

This stung. 'So you're with those marines back there who are preparing to start a war?'

'War,' she sneered. 'War is all you people care about. What do you English want with the Malvinas anyway? A few fragments of rock 12,000 kilometres away.'

I was pretty much in agreement with her on that. All I said, though, was, 'You were happy enough to do your bit then. A lot of British sailors died in the air attacks you helped guide in.'

She glared at me. 'A lot of Argentinians died too. My brother lost his life flying a bomber – shot down by an American missile fired by an English pilot.'

'My brother was killed too. Fifty miles from here, across the border in Chile. He thought he had made it out safely. I saw him die.'

Her face twisted with bitterness. 'Your brother, my brother . . . I suppose you think that makes us equal. Well, it doesn't. It makes me hate you more than ever.'

'As soon as it starts to snow,' I told her. 'We'll move out from here and head south.'

The snow started a quarter of an hour later – thin, bitter flakes falling fast, driven hard by the wind. We buttoned up our clothes and headed out from the wood, striking a course for the lake I had spotted. Concha still had her parka, but the Argies had taken my jacket and I was down to my camouflage fleece. The snow fell on our shoulders and swallowed our tracks swiftly.

At first the going was not too difficult. There seemed to be narrow paths, possibly worn by sheep in the past, winding across the pampas and threading in and out among the scrub bushes. Occasionally there were streams to leap across and once we had to wade a small river, but nothing as large as the one we had crossed earlier.

Concha followed me like a prisoner, wrapped in bitterness. When she spoke it was only to vent her hatred at me, the British, and soldiers in general. 'We are pacifists,' she told me fiercely, 'me and my friends.' I did gather that the marine division had been deliberately stationed here to repress dissent. Concha's network was coordinating the southernmost resistance to the coup.

Her attitude pissed me off. Apparently it was OK for her group to interfere in the invasion plans, but not for the British. But to her, I presumed, I was just an ignorant soldier whose only purpose in life was killing people. Even if we could contact her supporters, there was no guarantee they wouldn't turn me in.

Twice we heard helicopters and burrowed into the grass till they had passed – but visibility was so poor there was little risk that we would be spotted. I could imagine the search parties cursing the weather.

With every hour that passed they would have to widen their search area. Once we heard the wail of a locomotive. According to Concha the line ran just west of the road – which suited us because we needed to find the emergency rendezvous, which was located close to the track.

The snow fell more thickly. The lake was further off than I had realised. Distances were hard to gauge in this flat landscape. I judged we had around two kilometres to go, and I worried about losing our direction. It's easy to become disorientated in snow when there are few reference points. We had to be able to navigate our way to the RV somehow, and that meant finding the railway track in the dark.

The suddenness with which the weather had worsened was alarming. The temperature was right down and we were burning up reserves of energy just trying to stay warm. It was so cold and dark. It was hard to believe it was the middle of the day. Concha was lagging behind; I had to tug her along like a dead weight. Then she started retching, a sign that her body was running low on sugar and starting to burn fat. She had reached the point that marathon runners call 'hitting the wall'.

At one point I stumbled on a tussock and fell. She flopped down next to me on the snowy ground, and I stooped to pick her up. 'I'm so tired,' she pleaded. 'I need to rest.' I was tempted – we still had about a kilometre to go. Maybe, I thought momentarily, if she had a short sleep she would get some of her strength back. But experience told me that she would never get up again if I let this happen. There is no warmth to be had outdoors. She would sink into a coma as the afternoon wore on, and die. With difficulty I got her up and we staggered on.

I was navigating by the wind on my face – as long as we were walking into it, I assumed we were going south.

I reckoned we were covering half a kilometre an hour at most. Probably we were not very far from the outskirts of the town, but it might have been a lifetime away as far as we were concerned. Ice was crunching under my boots and I could hardly feel my feet any more. The temperature was plunging. It was midday, and we were freezing to death out in the open. Combining the chill factor of a forty-mile-an-hour wind, no food and wet clothing, it was clear that neither of us would be able to endure much more. At this moment a prisoner of war camp seemed preferable.

I guess we had been walking about two hours when we hit the edge of the lake. I was half supporting Concha. She had had no sleep the previous night; she had been beaten and abused and forced to swim a freezing river. I was tired too, though I knew I could keep going all day if I had to. But she needed warmth and rest or I would be carrying a corpse by nightfall.

One option was to turn away from the lake, put the wind on my right side and try and make for the railway. It was possible we might find some sort of shelter nearer to the town, albeit with an increased risk of capture.

A while later on, while I was still supporting Concha, I crashed full-length into a pool. This was madness; we had to take shelter soon before one or other of us broke a leg – then we would be truly finished. I rubbed Concha's hands and slapped her face in an attempt to get her blood circulating. 'Come on, you stupid Argentine bitch! Are you going to let yourself be whipped by an Englishman?' I jeered.

'*Cabron!*' She pushed me away and tried to stagger on. She had guts all right – but within a few more minutes she was buckling at the knees once more. I picked her up, but she went down again.

The wind whipped round us, cutting through our damp clothes like knives. The snow was blowing almost horizontally; walking ahead into it was agony. My eyes were continually blocked, the skin raw from scraping away the frozen crusts that accumulated on the exposed flesh of my face. Concha's hair clung to her face in frozen streamers. The sheer effort of lifting our feet though the snow and the clinging canopy of frozen grass was draining us of energy. Time and again I thought I'd stumbled on shelter, but always what looked like a hut at a few metres in the swirling snow proved to be a clump of gorse or the stump of a wind-blown tree.

I had been half hoping that the lake would be fringed with trees and undergrowth, perhaps with some huts used by fishermen. Instead we found ourselves plunging through vast reed beds and attempting to detour bogs. Visibility was down to a few metres. By now I was having to carry Concha for ten minutes at a time, supporting her across my shoulders in a fireman's lift. Even though she was slightly built she weighed twice as much as a bergen. When I put her down to rest and stretch my back she'd be falling asleep on her feet. Her mind was wandering, and I knew she was in the first stages of hypothermia.

The shore of the lake traced a line towards the east – either that or the wind was veering westward, I had no way of telling. Still, instinct suggested that we were heading towards the railroad. We moved on, and I was stumbling along half-blinded by the snow when the ground in front of my feet suddenly fell away without warning. I found myself sliding down a slope into a wide ditch of some kind. I flung myself backward, clawing for purchase with my free hand. Concha hit the ground behind me and lay where she had fallen.

The grass on the bank was thickly overgrown. By

twisting on to my front and clinging on to a tuft I managed to save us both from sliding down into the ditch. But the snow was several inches deep and the ground was frozen hard. Concha was sprawled next to me and any movement I made only succeeded in making her slide further down into the ditch. The ditch probably contained at least a metre of water and liquid mud. She would never survive another immersion, and if I couldn't get her out she was done for. If she died on me I'd have no choice but to try and rip her arm off to free myself.

I was clawing on to the grass for handholds, but now her weight was dragging at my left wrist and the steel edge of the cuff was cutting into the numbed flesh. In another minute she would tear my hand loose and we would both subside into the ditch.

I kicked with the toecaps of my boots, trying to make a foothold. If I could take some of my own weight, then I could lift Concha and push her back up the bank. I got both hands under Concha and by brute force heaved her up the bank, the handcuffs cutting agonisingly into my wrist as I did so. I moved sideways and, after some fumbling about, found a secure footing against a stone. Wiping snow from my face, I now saw that further along some rushes grew up the bank. Transferring my left foot to the stone, I hacked another hole with the toe of my other boot and shifted closer. Another step or two and the rushes would be within grasp.

Stretching up as far as I could reach, my numbed fingers encountered the stalks of the nearest reeds and I dragged myself back up. It was only a momentary respite. Already I could feel the roots being torn out under my weight. I jabbed my feet into the earth bank and snatched another hold. Concha was leaning heavily against me. There were more reeds within my grasp now, and I found I could stand among the lower roots. Slowly I clawed my way up the slope, shoving Concha in front of me like a sack. It seemed to take for ever to reach the top, but at last I made the crest and squirmed over on to the flat again.

I felt shockingly weak. My feet were blocks of ice and the feeling had gone from my hands. My whole body was pleading for rest, but I knew that if I gave in I was finished. Either I got myself up now and carried on or we both lay down to die right here. Concha was too far gone to help me. She was a dead weight and I had to get her up if I was to save myself. I hunched myself on to all fours and dragged her into a sitting position against me. I let her flop on to my shoulder, and somehow staggered upright beneath her.

'Fuck you!' I shouted at her. 'Fuck all you bloody Argies! Fuck your sodding weather and your lousy country and your fucking Malvinas!' Rage was all that was keeping me going. Rage against the country and the mission that had gone wrong; above all rage against the useless, ungrateful lump I was shackled to.

I had no idea where I was headed now. I was past caring. All I could do was keep walking. Oddly, the handcuffs were a help for the first time; they kept Concha fixed over my shoulder and rested my left arm.

Together we staggered on into the blizzard.

How long we kept going I had no idea. It may have been a few minutes; it could have been as much as half an hour. I seemed to have left the lake behind, and now was following a path. The snow was blowing as thick as ever, and I was blundering along three-parts blind when something made me stop. We were in a fold in the ground, sheltered slightly from the worst of the wind. A stunted tree, bent almost double by the wind, loomed ahead. To one side, half hidden by drifting snow, was a shed of planks with a corrugated iron roof and a stove chimney sticking out of the side.

THIRTY-ONE

I don't know how long I stood staring. I was so convinced it was a hallucination, I hardly dared believe my eyes. But it was real. It was shelter.

There was a padlock fixed to the door, which burst open under a heave of my shoulder. At that moment I could have broken through a steel hatch, such was my desperation. I lowered Concha off my shoulder and dragged her in after me like a sack. The relief to be out of the wind and snow was indescribable. I stood shaking, revelling in the blessed silence. There was no window, but a dim light filtered through a snow-covered plastic panel in the roof, enough to make out the interior. It was larger than I had realised. There was a fold-out table against one wall with a crude bench beside it. At the rear was a wide shelf with some sort of bedding on it. In the other corner stood a crude stove made out of an oil drum. The floor was made of heavy timbers that looked like wooden sleepers looted from the railway. The general construction was solid and workmanlike. I guessed it belonged to a hunter; a place where he could shelter overnight before getting up at dawn to shoot duck on the lake.

I propped Concha against the wall and started searching for firewood with my spare hand. Eventually I located a store beneath the bunk, together with a supply of kindling. Thank God I'd had the presence of mind to bring away the major's cigarette lighter. The only paper I could find was damp, but there was a bundle of string on a hook that would serve instead. I laid the fire carefully.

There was a hand-axe beside the stove and I split a couple of logs. Everything had to be done one-handed. I toyed with the idea of trying to chop through the chain of the handcuffs but I decided the axe was too small.

I applied the major's lighter and the fire took hold. I nursed it carefully, adding more kindling and split logs as it grew. The stove may have been primitive but it gave out a good heat and cast a cheerful, flickering glow inside the hut. The wind and snow would dissipate the smoke, so for the present we were safe enough.

Outside it was still light. The marines had taken my watch, but at a guess it was between one and two pm – another couple of hours before dusk. And when night came the atrocious weather would continue to screen us from view. As the hut began to warm up I peeled off my soaked boots and set them to dry. I did the same for Concha. She was semi-conscious still, and her flesh was ice cold. I rubbed her hands and feet to aid the circulation.

What was needed was food to restore our strength. On a shelf above the table I found a rusting tin of corned beef and a bottle of what appeared to be Argentinian brandy, a quarter full. Both looked as though they had been there for months if not longer, but I was in no state to be choosy. I hacked the can open with the axe. The contents smelled good to me, and with luck the brandy would disinfect any bugs.

I put the opened tin on top of the stove to heat up. Tilting Concha's head back, I forced some of the brandy between her lips. She coughed and choked and opened her eyes. 'Drink,' I told her. The brandy would warm her stomach and get some life into her. She took a gulp and pushed the bottle away.

The tin of meat was warmed through. I scooped some out with my fingers and gave it to her. She eyed me suspiciously but accepted a mouthful. I took some myself. With brandy it wasn't too bad. We scraped out the tin between us and I started to feel better.

I poked around some more on the shelf and found a box of rusting tools. Among them was an old hacksaw blade. This was a stroke of luck.

I sat Concha down on the floor by the warming stove and put our linked hands on the bench. I fixed the blade into some pliers, gripped it tight, and set to work on the handcuff chain. I sawed in long steady strokes, trying to use the full length of the blade. It was difficult because the teeth kept slipping on the links at first, but after a while I got a groove started and it became a question of keeping at it.

The stove was getting hotter and I could feel warmth creeping slowly back into my limbs. After a while I broke off the sawing to put a couple of the drier-looking logs on to the fire. Concha's head was lolling stupidly. She was three-parts asleep. I took up the blade and returned to the sawing, running the makeshift saw back and forth like an automaton. I was beyond tiredness myself, functioning on my nerves, concentrating on the one task ahead of me.

Finally I cut through one side of the link, but the chain still held. I tried levering the link open with the pliers but couldn't get a proper grip. There was nothing for it but to set to work on the other side and cut through it completely.

It was discouraging but I stuck at it, stopping at intervals to build up the fire. I was about half-way through the second side of the link when the blade snapped.

Fuck, I thought, even though I had been expecting it. With the pliers I took up one of the pieces and continued using that for a while. It was much less efficient because the stroke was shorter and the saw teeth were getting blunt with the hardness of the steel.

In the end I threw the blade down and used the pliers to give a couple of hard twists of the chain. The link broke with a snap and the chain parted. We were free at last. The cuffs were still round our wrists, but we were no longer fettered.

The glow from the stove illuminated the bed. What I had taken to be a heap of blankets proved to be a heavy covering made up of several sheep fleeces sewn together into a single mat. The wool was inches deep and incredibly soft. I opened it out to air in the warmth of the stove, then set to work to strip the wet clothing off Concha. She made no protest as I undressed her, rubbing her down to get the blood flowing. When I had her completely naked I carried her over to the bed and wrapped her in the fleece. It was an enormous cover, and she curled up inside it like a baby.

I located the major's automatic and dried it off. There was an oil rag on the table, probably left when the owner last cleaned his own gun. I wiped the pistol over and checked the magazine. It was a Spanish Star, a copy of the Colt M1911A1, which had served the US armed services well for half a century and was only now being replaced by the Beretta Model 92. The magazine held seven rounds of the thick 230-grain slugs – whose stopping power made so many serving soldiers consider it the best weapon of its class, capable of stopping a charging man dead in his tracks. Though a heavy gun with a violent kick, lacking in many of the safety features of more modern pistols, in the right hands it was unbeatable.

The hut was heating up nicely now, and our clothes were steaming on the bench where I had spread them out to catch the heat. I found some old newspaper and stuffed it in the boots to draw out the damp. The wind was still howling outside. With luck now it would keep up till dark, when we could creep out and try and find our way down to the railway and the RV. Four or five hours' rest in the warmth should restore our strength.

I was squatting on the floor with only an undershirt

on. A draught was rushing in under the door, and it occurred to me that I would be a lot more comfortable on the bed. It was easily wide enough for two of us. Concha was as slight as a child, and there was enough of the sheepskin to cover both of us. I remembered something about hypothermia cases recovering faster when put in bed with someone. And animal heat made a good conductor.

'To hell with it,' I said to myself. I had carried her all this way. The least she could do was let me get warm. I climbed on to the bed and pulled the fleece over the pair of us. Concha gave a sleepy moan and snuggled up to me, wrapping her arms around my body for warmth.

The moment my head touched the wool I was conscious of a desperate urge to sleep. I had not shut my eyes for thirty hours. I had been continually in action since leaving the submarine. First there had been the trip in the boat, then the trek overland to keep the rendezvous with Seb. Together with Josh I had penetrated the base and made my way out again. Then had come the forced march out to the assembly point, the battle with the marines, capture and escape. The woman and I had swum the river and trudged through the snow to get here. All without respite and on virtually no food.

The stove was banked high. The wood would last several hours. The blizzard was set to continue till nightfall at the least. The chances of anyone stumbling on us were just about nonexistent. But just in case I put the gun under the fleece where I could keep a hold of it.

Concha was sleeping soundly, her chest rising and falling in a steady rhythm. The colour had returned to her face, and her skin had lost its icy chill. The food and liquor was putting energy back into her system and the warmth was reviving her. All she needed now was rest. We both did.

I knew I had to stay alert to keep watch, but my eyes kept closing. Each time they did I would jerk awake, but a few seconds later they would feel heavy again. I was terrified that if I did fall asleep I'd miss the rendezvous or dawn would arrive and the smoke from our fire would be visible.

I woke with a guilty start. It was fully dark outside. Shit! I wondered how long I'd been asleep. The stove was almost out. I slipped from the bed and threw in a couple more logs. Judging by the wood we had consumed I had slept for about four hours, which put the time at around five pm. The wind had dropped but I couldn't tell whether it was still snowing. I felt stiff and bruised from the various falls I had taken, but warm and much stronger. I climbed carefully back under the fleece, trying not to wake Concha. Her face was turned toward me, framed by a tumble of dark hair. In the half-light she looked oddly innocent, younger and more peaceful. I thought how near I had come to cutting her throat up on the hangar roof last night. I hadn't known it was her then.

Her eyes snapped open suddenly and narrowed as they took in the sight of me beside her. She pulled down the edge of the fleece with her now freed hand and a look of shock came over her as she realised we were both naked. 'Get away from me.' She squirmed across the bed.

'Calm down, can't you? Our clothes are drying by the fire. Of course I had to get into bed with you. Did you think I was going to freeze to death?'

'You took off my clothes?'

'No, I just whistled and they undressed themselves. What was I supposed to do? Let you catch pneumonia? Anyway,' I added, 'I owed you that much for saving my life back on the river.'

She snorted. 'That! I had no choice. We were chained together. I would have left you to drown otherwise!'

I felt suddenly angry. 'Fuck you, girlie! You'd be lying dead out in the snow right now if I hadn't carried you to this place. Which makes the second time I've saved your skinny hide – so a little gratitude on your part wouldn't be out of place.'

'And fuck you too, disgusting English soldier. I know why you brought me in here, took off my clothes. So you can rape me like that marine wanted. I know about English soldiers and how they raped our women during the war.'

'What are you talking about?'

'Your soldiers came ashore secretly and forced Argentinian girls for their pleasure. Everyone knows this.'

I shook my head in amazement. 'You're crazy,' I told

344

her. 'We never even set eyes on an Argentine female, let alone raped one. It's just propaganda and lies.'

She was silent for a moment. 'Tell me,' she said suddenly. 'That day on the ship when you discovered me. I was your enemy. Your countrymen had died because of me. Yet you came back to set me free when the bombs fell. Why?'

I had puzzled over that question many times myself. 'You were just a child.'

'Old enough to be the cause of many deaths.'

'What happened to you after the ship went down? How did you get ashore?'

'I pulled my hood up and climbed aboard a boat. It was dark. When we reached the land I jumped out and ran ashore. Later I was captured and taken on board one of the aircraft carriers.'

'And then?'

She shrugged. 'Interrogations. Questions. How did I get on board the *Northland*? Was I alone? What frequency did I transmit on?' She smiled sadly. 'I was a student at Imperial College in London. A man from the Argentine Naval Attaché's office in Vauxhall Bridge Road gave me the transmitter and asked me to smuggle it on board the fleet at Portsmouth. I never meant to stay with the ship but there were men everywhere and I could not get back to the land before it sailed.'

'And so you made a hiding place down in the hold in one of the trucks.'

'Yes, several places.'

345

'And after the bombing of the ship? You escaped in a boat?'

'They took me for a man, one of the sailors.' She gave a short laugh. 'When we reached the shore I jumped out and tried to make my way to the front line but some soldiers caught me next morning.'

So Jenny's story was right, I thought. 'And what happened after they had interrogated you? Did they send you back with the prisoners?'

She nodded. 'They sent me in a ship to Rio de Janeiro. The fighting was still going on. I was an embarrassment; they wanted to be rid of me.'

She wanted to know from me what I planned doing about the Globemasters on the airbase. 'Will you try to warn the English in Port Stanley?'

'If I can,' I told her. 'They'll send up fighters to turn the planes back.'

'And if the message does not get through?'

I looked at her. 'Then a lot of men will get killed – like last time.'

She nodded sadly. 'My brother and yours too. So many lives lost, and all for a few pieces of rock.'

I stroked her dark hair gently. She didn't seem to object. Four hours' sleep had restored some of my strength and I was suddenly conscious of how very desirable she was, a strange mixture of beauty and passionate anger. Lying naked beside her under the warm fleece was a severe test of my self-restraint.

I let my fingers slide down on to the soft skin of her neck. She sighed drowsily and stretched her back, her hip touching mine. I caressed her shoulder, skating over the upper slope of her chest. Her eyes were closed, her lips apart.

'Are you married?' I asked after a minute.

'For five years, to the son of a family friend – a businessman who was proud to own a war heroine for a wife. When I told him I was now a pacifist and that the thought of all the sailors I had killed filled me with disgust, he called me a traitor and divorced me. And you?'

I shook my head. 'I saw what it did to my brother's wife and kids when he was killed. I couldn't put a family of mine through that.'

'But it does not stop you being a soldier and killing other women's husbands!' she snapped, brushing my hand away.

Fuck her, I thought. It looked like my luck was out. She was a hard woman to figure – one minute warm and sexy, the next all spit and fury. 'Get yourself dressed,' I ordered. 'It's time we were moving out.'

She rolled over on her front. 'We are no longer chained together. You can go by yourself.'

I gave a grim laugh. 'No way, lady.'

'What are you planning now – to kill more Argentinian soldiers? Isn't that what you are here for?'

'I'm here to stop a war, for fuck's sake. Now put your clothes on.'

'No!' She twisted round suddenly, arched her shoulder and launched a straight-armed punch at my eye with all the strength in her wiry body behind it.

'Christ!' I yelled. That really stung. It was the first time in my life I'd been hit hard by a woman. 'You bitch! I'll teach you how to behave!'

I grabbed her by the shoulder and pushed her on to her front. She bucked and kicked, spitting at me like a wildcat and trying to bite my left hand. I ripped the fleece down, exposing her tail and gave her a smack on her taut backside that echoed round the hut like a gunshot. She shrieked and tried to kick me off the bed, but I flung my weight across her, pinning her down. She twisted under me like an eel, bringing up a knee into my groin, then she pulled herself away and drove both feet into my ribs with a strength that made me gasp.

I eased off, thinking maybe we had gone far enough, but she launched herself at me again in a flurry of kicks and scratching. It was like fighting with a wild animal; she was a whirlwind of teeth and heels and nails. She fought with a manic fury, stabbing at me with her elbows, slapping and biting. Somewhere along the line she had learned unarmed combat, because now she was attempting some vicious stabs to the eyes and windpipe. She whacked at me with the cuff on her wrist, using it as a weapon, and in my mind I was taken back aboard the *Northland* twenty years ago, the darkness of the truck. She was fighting now as she had fought then, gouging and punching accompanied by a stream of spits and curses in Spanish.

Finally I caught her hands, flung a leg over hers to block more kicking, and forced her back against the fleece. She gnawed at me with her sharp teeth till I managed to move my knee across her stomach and straddle her, holding her arms above her head. Even then she refused to give up and continued to struggle, snarling at me like a cornered dog. I gripped her left arm in mine. Her wrist was as slim as a child's; I could have snapped it like a stick.

'Enough!' I shouted.

She spat in my eye and arched her back, trying to throw me off. 'I will not go with you! *Vete so hijo de la gran puta!*'

With my free hand I slapped her a couple of times across the face, blows intended to bring her to her senses, and she spat at me again.

Her olive skin was shiny with sweat. Her pointed breasts rose and fell as her chest heaved, the dark nipples fiercely erect. Her eyes were blazing, her teeth bared at me in hate. 'Go on then!' she spat. 'Rape me! Isn't that what soldiers do to women? Or are you just a *maricon*?'

And by God I was highly aroused at that moment. She was a woman, all passion and heat, and I was still heady from the brandy I'd drunk. I could feel all the coiled strength of her body struggling underneath me, resisting and challenging me in the same breath.

'I'll show you what I can do!' And I flung myself down, crushing her mouth under mine.

She gasped and I felt her teeth grip my bottom lip. I let go her hands to grab her tits and her nails clawed my shoulders. Her body writhed under me. My skin was burning. I saw the muscles of her arms clenching, the veins standing out blue against the sweat-slicked flesh, her breasts rising under my hands. I rubbed them fiercely and she shouted aloud in Spanish. She was biting at my shoulders and chest. I could feel her hipbones sawing at my lower body, her legs clamping round my waist, heels drumming on my back.

Next instant she straightened with a jerk and she was fighting me off again, kneeing and punching like a boy. Then I pushed her down and kissed her again, forcing my tongue between her lips. Her nails dug into my back like spurs.

The glow of the fire made her skin look burnished. I sucked at her nipples. Her breasts tasted of salt. Her stomach was hard and flat; her pelvis thrust up at me and there were rivulets of sweat running between her legs. I scraped my hand down her back, feeling the muscles sliding over the bone. I pushed her legs apart and she clasped her hands behind my neck, pulling my head down. I kissed her on the mouth and with a cat-like squirm she was out from under me, laughing. I grabbed her again and we grappled, rolling among the wool. Her breasts swayed above me as she straddled my chest, taunting me. I could smell her hair and the heat of her body, and it was driving me wild.

We were beyond stopping now. I picked her up bodily and flung her down on her back, forcing her knees open. She clenched her teeth and pounded me with her fists. She cried out as I drove inside her, clawing at my back again, yanking at my hair. Again and again I plunged into her as she tightened her thighs around me. With each thrust I drove deeper and she gasped and dug her nails in, cursing me in Spanish. I could feel her hard pubis rising to meet me in spite of herself as her vagina clamped itself around my prick. She was shrieking and gasping and flinging herself about. Her body was plunging and thrusting with mine, sucking at me, drawing me deeper into her. Her legs were locked round me, her throat arched and she cried out in passion as I burst inside her like a volcano. Our bodies locked together and I felt the heat explode through me as her cries went on and on.

I rolled off her, and she turned away from me to lie facing the wall. I stroked her back softly, letting my fingertips glide over the satin-soft skin.

'Let me alone!' she snarled, shaking me off.

'Easy,' I said, pulling her towards me, and in a flash she rounded on me again, sinking her teeth into the flesh of my arm, her fingers clawing. Hot tears dripped on my face as we wrestled in silence on the fleece.

I held her tight against me, not speaking, while she clawed and bit by the flickering light of the stove, hitting me with her fists, hating me and hating herself, it was all the same thing. When she subsided I turned her on to her back again and stretched myself out on top of her. She struggled and kicked, and as I entered her once more she clung to me with despairing strength, sobbing and gasping in her hunger while I moved inside her, till at last we were both exhausted.

We slept again then. When we woke next I reached for her, and this time she came to me as sweetly as a bird, hung on to me and called my name as she came with me.

Afterwards we lay in each other's arms, content.

THIRTY-TWO

When we woke for the third time I told her it was time to be moving. It was fully dark now, the wind had dropped, and when I cracked open the door I saw the snow had stopped.

We dressed reluctantly. She kissed my neck in the process but there was no time for love now. 'Get ready,' I said. 'We have to keep the rendezvous.'

She grinned at me obediently. 'Yes, my enemy lover.'

Our clothes had dried out thoroughly, and so had our boots. We drank a final slug of the brandy each, then left our refuge. It was bitterly cold when we stepped outside, a clear night with a crescent moon riding up in the south-west. The lights of the town made a glow in the sky about a kilometre away.

'The old mine is near the railroad on this side of the town,' Concha said. 'It is not far.'

I led the way, my right hand on the pistol in my pocket. The snow was around a foot thick, but in places there were much deeper drifts. I went carefully, testing the ground at each step. There was enough ambient light to show up major obstacles, but I was wary of falling into a ditch again. We were leaving a clear track for anyone to follow, but with luck we wouldn't be coming back again this way. Still, if there were any patrols out they might spot us and it was essential to reach the RV quickly.

I was worried for the rest of the team, by now presumably under lock and key on the airbase along with Concha's companions. Maybe the British consul could negotiate their freedom. I wasn't very hopeful though. It would probably depend on how long the military junta remained in power.

The vital thing was to make the rendezvous and establish contact with Seb. He would be able to send a message to his controllers, telling them to warn Port Stanley of the impending assault. There was no time to lose. Judging by the haste with which the plane we had seen was being prepared, the attack was planned for the very near future, quite possibly dawn tomorrow.

We ploughed on through the snow for the best part of a kilometre. Several times we had to detour round frozen pools or thickets of gorse. Once I had to lift Concha over a wire fence.

The lights of the town were growing nearer. The long wail of a locomotive sounded in the distance and we heard the clank of wagons. 'That will be the evening train from Ushuaia,' Concha said. 'The track can only be half a kilometre away. The old mine is on this side, between us and the town.'

'That's good. We should be able to spot the workings against the lights.'

Another fifteen minutes of steady walking brought us to a shallow slope in the ground, and there ahead of us were the rails, gleaming in the moonlight. I pulled Concha down into a crouch and eased the pistol in my pocket.

'All we have to do now is walk in the direction of the town,' she whispered. 'The old mine is close to the track on this side. The railway was constructed originally to bring out the ore.'

Now that we were getting close to the RV I was worrying about letting Concha meet Seb. Even if Concha could be trusted it would blow his cover for good, and his bosses in the Firm would raise hell. I couldn't see that there was any other option, though. It was vital that I contact Seb to arrange for a message to be sent; blowing Seb was the price British intelligence was going to have to pay to avert a second Falklands War.

Our eyes were accustomed to the darkness now. Crouched down among the grass on the edge of the slope I could discern a tall chimney rearing into the sky some way off to our right.

'That is the mine,' Concha breathed in my ear. Her voice was deliciously husky. 'It is broken now, but it used to reach up nearly ten metres.'

I thought for a moment. Time was passing and it was urgent we reach the RV point without delay, but I feared walking into another trap. 'We'll wait here a few minutes,' I decided. 'Just in case there's an ambush party out there.'

We squatted, shivering, on the ground while the minutes ticked by. The train we had heard seemed to be stopped in the town and I was aware of a blend of different noises: a car horn, dogs barking, the thump of a stereo system carried on the wind.

'We'll move up slowly along this side of the track,' I told Concha quietly. 'Keep low. That way an enemy will show up against the sky and the light behind. If you see or hear anything drop flat and don't move.' She squeezed my hand in answer.

Side by side we crept through the snow along the edge of the track, probing the darkness. As we neared the chimney every nerve in my body was on edge. None of the rest of the team would have given away the location of the RV, not yet anyway. They were trained to resist interrogation and would hold out for a day or so at least. My worry was that Seb had been taken. The Argentines would not be squeamish about torturing one of their own caught working for the enemy. If he had been broken we could be walking straight into a trap.

The ruins of the old mine were visible now, mantled in snow. We moved cautiously from one patch of shadow to another. Against the whitened ground we were all too visible.

Concha stopped and squeezed my hand. I had spotted it too – close under a broken wall, moonlight glinted on metal. A vehicle, waiting for us.

We flattened ourselves in the snow. Our eyes searched the darkness, scanning for the telltale flicker of movement that would indicate a tensed marine waiting in ambush, finger on the trigger of his assault rifle, ready to blast us the instant we stepped into the open. The vehicle looked like Seb's Toyota at this distance, but if it were a trap that would be the bait to lure us in to capture or death.

I checked the track for footprints or tyre marks. If I were the officer leading an ambush platoon I would have brought my men silently up the railway and posted them among the ruins to cover all approaches, with orders to wait until we got to within five metres before triggering the ambush lamps. My ears strained for any whisper of static from a personal radio or the faint click as a safety catch was switched to automatic fire.

I couldn't make out if there was someone inside the Toyota or not. Seb could be waiting there, sitting with a gun trained on his spine and a promise of freedom if he co-operated.

We waited for at least ten minutes. The night stayed still. Under normal circumstances I would have waited until I was sure, but now there was nothing for it but to take a risk. It was either that or let the Argentine attack on the Falklands go ahead. I got Concha to her feet and we crept forward again. The automatic was in my hand, held low and ready to fire at the first suspicious movement. Two people and a single side-arm would stand no chance at all if it was a trap, but it made me feel better.

Grabbing Concha's hand, I ran with her across the intervening fifteen metres of open snow to the shelter of the wall, expecting any moment to have blinding lights flash in my eyes and hear the shouted command to halt.

We reached the wall and flung ourselves against it, our breath smoking in the frozen air. The Toyota was five metres away with its rear towards us. As far as I could tell it was empty. I counted to thirty and stepped forward, the gun held out and cocked. I had seven shots in the magazine. If we were challenged I'd save the last one for the girl. After what I'd witnessed of Argentine interrogation procedures I didn't want her to fall into their hands alive again.

Snow crunched under our feet as we approached the Toyota. If there was anyone waiting they must have heard us by now.

I was a metre from the vehicle when a metallic snick in my rear brought me up short. I sprang round and knocked Concha to the ground, out of the line of fire. My right hand was extended, finger on the trigger ready to shoot, heart hammering.

'*Buenas tardes*,' came a cool voice from the shadowed corner of the wall.

I crouched, taking aim. '*Que hora es?*'

'*Son las ocho.*' The correct response.

My heart rate steadied.

'You are late,' Seb remarked, stepping forward, lowering his own pistol – a heavy .45 automatic like the one I had taken from Oliveras, evidently the weapon of choice in this region. 'Lucky for you I decided to wait.'

'I have someone with me,' I said, indicating Concha's shadow at my side.

He sighed wearily. 'I was expecting the two of you. *Hola, Concha, como esta?*'

I heard her draw in her breath as she recognised his voice.

'You knew about us? How?' I asked.

'I am a friend to Concha and her group. M16 provides funding to the dissidents. I also have a source in the marine barracks. News of your capture and escape reached me at midday. I assumed you would try to reach the rendezvous, so I waited here.'

Concha let out a hiss of anger. 'You told us the money came from liberal businesses in Buenos Aires!' she burst out. 'All the time you are working for British intelligence!'

Seb laughed briefly. 'Don't be so naive. The rest of the group understood the source of the funds perfectly; they were not squeamish. They wanted to prevent a war, and so do the British.'

Before either of us could speak he went on, 'We must hurry. The marines are hunting everywhere for the two of you. Get into the car and stay down out of sight.'

Seb drove fast, talking as he went. 'They brought the rest of your comrades back to the barracks at the airbase. They are held there along with Julian and the others.'

'Have they been questioned yet, do you know?' Concha asked. By 'questioned' I understood she meant tortured.

Seb shook his head. 'I do not know. The whole area is in turmoil on account of the killing of Major Oliveras and his driver. The border is closed and there are roadblocks on all routes leading out of town.'

'Oliveras' death was an accident,' I told him.

'Possibly, but that is not how the Argentinians will view it,' he answered drily.

I told him what Josh and I had seen in the hangar the previous night. He seemed unsurprised. 'Yes, we have suspected for some while that an attack was being planned. We did not know the precise manner until now, though.'

I was still adjusting to the realisation that Seb and she were working together. Evidently Tierra del Fuego was a smaller place than I had realised. I supposed it made sense that a British agent would be in touch with dissident groups.

'Will they abandon the plan now, do you think?' Concha asked. Her voice was still tight with anger at being deceived by him, as she saw it.

Seb slowed to take a corner. We were passing down a wide, well-lit street. In the rear-view mirror I glimpsed tin-roofed houses and empty snow-covered sidewalks. Rio Grande was a depressing place, I decided.

'I did not know what they intended until you told me just now,' Seb replied. 'According to my informant, however, the marines are on stand-by for action, so we must assume the operation is imminent.'

Seb drove us to a single-storey house on the edge of town. He put the Toyota straight into the garage and pulled down the door. Climbing out, I saw a tool bench against the wall at the back.

'Right, let's get these cuffs off,' I said. More than

anything I wanted my hands free. It violated all my soldier's instincts to be chained. I needed to be able to fight again.

Seb nodded and plugged the cable of an angle grinder into an electric socket. For protection I wedged a strip of scrap metal between my wrist and the cuff. Seb put on a plastic safety visor and switched on the machine. The screeching disk bit into the bracelet amid a shower of sparks. It took only a couple of minutes to cut through the hardened steel. The cuff fell open and I slipped my wrist out.

'Now your turn,' I said to Concha. I held the handcuff steady and Seb bent to work again. When it was over she straightened up, rubbing her wrist and looking at me. I knew what she was thinking: we had worn the cuffs for more than ten hours; we had nearly died in the blizzard and we'd made love to one another. They were a symbol of something.

Seb wrapped the pieces in a newspaper and threw them into a bin. I guessed he would dispose of the incriminating evidence later. We followed him through into the house.

'Would you like food?' he offered. 'How long has it been since you both last ate?'

I looked at Concha and she nodded. We both suddenly realised how hungry we were again; the scraps of corned beef in the hut had barely kept us going. 'First though, we need to get a warning message out,' I said.

Seb was leading the way into the kitchen. He pulled

down the blinds over the window and beckoned us in. He poured coffee into a machine and switched it on.

'The message,' I repeated. 'It's important. The Argentines may be intending to strike very soon.'

Seb turned back to face me. His mouth was grim. 'There will be no message,' he replied quietly. 'I cannot send one.'

I took out my gun and cocked the trigger.

THIRTY-THREE

'Seb,' I told him, speaking carefully to hold on to my temper. 'I don't care what rules you have about security. Get on your radio and send that warning, and do it now.' I had worked with spooks before, and I knew their paranoia about having their communications networks compromised.

Seb sighed again and gestured at the fridge. 'Help yourself to something to eat. There are fillet steaks in the freezer or I can make an omelette if you prefer.'

'Didn't you hear?' I shouted. 'Send the message now.'

Seb fixed his dark eyes on me. 'There is no radio,' he answered calmly. I blinked at him. 'There is no radio,' he repeated. 'I do not even know how to use one.'

'Don't give me that shit. How the fuck do you make contact with your handlers?'

'I have a cellphone,' he explained patiently. 'When I need to meet a contact I drive up to the Chilean border till I am within range of San Sebastian and ask for a meeting.'

I lowered the gun. 'You must have an emergency

procedure, though. What happens if you need exfiltration in a hurry?'

He nodded. 'In an emergency I can phone a Chilean number and leave a text message.'

'So, do that. And hurry.'

He shook his head. 'That is not possible either. Cellphone calls between here and San Sebastian travel along the landlines beside the coast road. All telephone and radio links have now been cut by the military. Road, rail and air traffic has also been stopped. There is no communication between the Argentine sector of Tierra del Fuego and the outside world.'

'*Madre de Dios!*' Concha exclaimed. 'The attack must be for tonight!'

'What about satellite phones?' I suggested desperately. 'This is an oil town; the geological teams must use them all the time.'

'By law all such devices must be registered with the authorities. At four pm this afternoon the police, acting on the orders of the military governor, seized every satellite phone they could find. There may be a few out in the bush but we could never track one down in time.' Seb looked at us both seriously. 'Accept this, my friends, we are completely isolated here. There is no way we can send a warning in time.'

Concha stared at me, her eyes big with dismay as the full enormity of the position sank home. The Argentines had outwitted us at every stroke. They must have planned this well in advance and put their scheme into effect the moment they realised we had escaped. I looked at the clock on Seb's kitchen wall. It was almost nine pm. If the Argies were timing their assault to hit Mount Pleasant before dawn to catch the garrison asleep, the planes would be loading up shortly.

'We must do something,' Concha said. 'It will be war otherwise.'

'There is only one way we can do that,' I told her. 'We have to stop those planes taking off.'

'It's madness,' Concha murmured – but I could tell she was thinking about it.

We were sitting over steaks in Seb's kitchen. I had finished mine, while Concha was still toying. She seemed to have lost her appetite. Seb was in another room calling his contact at the base to find out the latest security situation.

'The odds are better than they look,' I said. 'The marines will be preparing for their mission; the last thing they'll be expecting is to be attacked. Seb and I will slip into the base and do the job. It's what we've been trained for.'

I went next door to see how Seb was making out. He was on a mobile phone, speaking in Spanish. He terminated the call abruptly as I entered, as if he did not want to compromise his source. 'Your comrades are being held in the guard post at the base. Julian and the others are in with them,' he said. 'As far as my informant knows they are unhurt; the enemy has been too busy hunting for you two to spend time questioning them.'

Concha had followed me through. 'I know the guard post,' she said. 'It is part of the main armoury. I will lead you to it.'

'Oh no, you won't,' I cut in. 'This is no job for a woman.'

Seb put a hand on my shoulder. 'Maybe it would be as well if she does come,' he suggested. 'She knows the base well. If we succeed and get out together, so much the better. If we fail,' he shrugged, 'what is there for her here?'

Capture and torture, I thought bleakly. Seb was right as usual.

'We'll need white sheets,' I said, 'for camouflage in the snow.'

Seb nodded. 'I will see to it.'

'Cut holes in the middle and we can wear them like ponchos. And pillowcases to put over our heads.' I turned back to Concha. 'Do you want a weapon?' Now that her friends were in danger I wasn't certain how deep her pacifism ran.

'I have a light hunting rifle that I use for deer, a .225,' Seb offered.

She nodded, her face pale and set. 'I will take that.'

Seb and I had our pistols. Given a choice I would have preferred a 9mm such as the Sig. The .45 was inaccurate and its magazine was small. It was a true man-stopper though, and would serve for close-quarter work. With luck we would all be able to swap our weapons for something heavier before the real action started. We would also take a selection of tools from Seb's workbench.

Seb was giving me funny looks, as if trying to work out whether or not I had been shagging Concha. Maybe he fancied her himself, I didn't know. Either way I ignored his glances and concentrated on the job in hand.

The plan was for us to enter the base, break into the guardhouse, free the rest of the team, along with Concha's friends if possible, and then with the weapons we found there attack the hangars and destroy the aircraft. The first thing to do was decide on a route into the base. I was worried that our previous method of entry, via the fence to the north and through the drain, might have been compromised.

'I know a way,' Concha said. 'Pedro and I used it last night. I will show you.'

It had come on to snow again as we climbed back into the Toyota, big soft flakes that drifted down out of the night sky. 'The wind will get up soon,' Seb remarked as he started the engine. He sounded nervous. I didn't blame him. I was feeling jumpy myself. This was a one-way mission; we might pull it off, but the chances of any of us coming out alive were slim.

I concealed myself under the blankets in the rear and gave Concha a quick kiss out of sight of Seb. I'd never gone into battle before with a woman, still less with one that I cared about. It occurred to me that we were going in to complete the self-same mission that Andy and I had aborted all those years before. Maybe this time it would be my turn to stop a bullet. I put that out of my head and concentrated on the business in hand. The first challenge was to reach the base without getting stopped by a patrol. Seb's vehicle was well known, but in the current state of tension everyone was a suspect.

Seb reckoned the roadblocks would be concentrated on the roads out to the north and west leading to the Chilean border. With Concha's agreement he cut eastwards across town. 'If we are questioned I shall say I am going to the station to meet someone off the train from San Sebastian.'

Beams of light swung through the cabin, as we crossed the main street. There were other cars around here in spite of the snow, and we felt safer. We passed a military truck, but it ignored us. We drove on into the industrial sector and along dark side-roads. Eventually Seb halted behind a large building. 'This is one of the cargo depots for the civilian airport,' he said softly. 'The main fence is only a short distance.'

I peered out of the rear window. The building was dark; there were no lights showing anywhere. Snow lay thick upon the ground.

'We need to move fast,' Seb whispered. 'Some of the premises here next to the base have night watchmen who will report anyone behaving strangely.'

We baled out quickly, carrying our camouflage sheets over our shoulders. Concha held her rifle by her side. The snow was still falling thickly and the wind was getting up; it was doubtful anyone would be able to make us out at twenty metres. Concha and I followed Seb along the road. After a short way it became a gravelled track and there were no more buildings. We were right on the edge of the town. Five hundred metres away in the distance were lights which could only be the airbase.

We were walking through virgin snow now overlying grass and heather. 'Better put on our cammies,' I told the others. I slipped the poncho sheet over my shoulders and pulled on the pillowcase. Concha had cut slits for eyeholes. I chuckled. 'You look like a ghost,' I told her.

A few minutes further on we came across deer-like hoofprints, recently made. 'Guanacos,' said Seb. 'Relatives of the llama. They come down to the edge of town in cold weather.'

Concha was staring at the snow and shivering. 'Suppose a patrol comes across our tracks?'

'In half an hour we'll be inside the base,' I reassured her. 'Once the shooting starts it won't matter anyway.'

She shivered and clutched her rifle.

She was better when we reached the wire, and it became her job to guide us. On this side nearest the town there was only one fence, and no minefield, she assured us. Evidently the Argentines did not fear attack from this direction. We crept along the wire till a tall shape loomed up ahead of us on the far side.

'What's that?' I whispered. 'A watchtower?'

'Julian says it is a navigational aid for aircraft using the base – a radio altimeter transmitter, something like that,' Concha whispered back.

'Is it manned?'

'No, automatic. A technician comes round to check it during the day. This is where we go in.'

She knelt down beside the fence and scrabbled at the snow. Soon she had uncovered the base of the wire and I saw that there was a scraped trench underneath the fence. 'Foxes,' she said. 'They come on to the base at night to raid the garbage. Julian and I made it bigger.'

Lying down, she pushed up the bottom of the fence and wriggled through on her back. Seb passed her rifle through, plus the bag of tools we had brought. He signed for me to follow. It was more of a struggle for me, but I managed it – at the cost of tearing my sheet. When it came to Seb's turn I held the wire up to make it easier.

Together we crouched in the shadow of the tower. We were on the southern side of the base, opposite to where our LUP and observation post had been last night. Seb had lent me a watch to replace the one the marines had lifted off me. I checked the time: 10.05pm. The marines would be boarding their aircraft soon.

We could see the tower, quite close and lit up. The main runway was almost dead ahead, the landing lights darkened again. The big hangars were invisible in the darkness on the far side.

I swept my eyes in a 360-degree search. 'All clear,' I whispered.

Concha nodded. 'Wait here for my sign, then follow.'

She ran bent double, flitting soundlessly across the

snow. Even as I watched she vanished into a dip in the ground. I caught a low whistle and Seb gave me a pat on the arm, signalling me to go. I scrambled along her tracks to find her fifty metres off, crouched in a concrete light well.

'Clever,' I murmured as we waited for Seb to join us.

'Yes, we can hide in these as far as the taxiway 300 metres down. Then we cut away to the left to a radar dome.'

It was a clever route she took us on, chosen by someone who had studied the base carefully. We darted across the open space from hole to hole like animals in the wild. From the radar installation we moved on to a clutch of fire hydrants.

'Where next?' I asked as we paused for breath. The wind was stronger out here, ripping across the bleak expanse of the field.

She pointed a sheet-draped arm right. 'Over there, about sixty metres. You can just make out some trucks against the lights behind. They are used to clean the snow off the runway.'

'I see them.'

I watched her run across the gap. She was almost on the trucks when the last in line suddenly switched on its headlamps.

Shit, I thought. She's been seen.

Concha dropped flat into the snow. The cough of the truck's engine bursting into life reverberated across the apron. The beams of the headlamps swung outwards and began to move. The huge tyres revolved, spinning off plumes of spray. I watched with clenched fists. It was heading directly for where she lay.

I flattened out myself, burying my face as the lights shone in my direction. The truck roared, picking up speed. It must be making for the intersection with the main runway. Maybe a flight was expected. Whatever the reason, Concha lay right in its path. Squinting through my eyeholes, I watched in horrified disbelief as the yellow monster ground down upon her.

'Run!' I yelled to her, but she didn't move. The engine noise drowned out my voice.

The truck was almost on her. Jesus wept, I thought, the driver must spot her. A huge dozer blade on the front was poised above her like an axe. If the driver chose to drop it, she would be cut in half. The glare of the headlights was so bright now I could no longer make out what was happening. I thought I caught a flicker of movement as the wheels reached her. Had she flung herself aside at the last moment? I pictured the giant ridged tyres crunching over her frail body, crushing and smashing.

The headlights swept over me and moved away as the truck turned on to the taxiway. I waited till the cab had drawn level and gone twenty metres past, then I ran as fast as I could along its track. I found the point where her track crossed the tyre marks, after that there was a confusion in the snow and I couldn't tell what had happened. 'Concha!' I whispered hoarsely.

A voice came back. 'Ssh, over here.'

I ran towards the sound.

She was kneeling against the brushes of a huge road-sweeper. 'Jesus, you almost got run over.'

'I know. I thought the driver would see me if I didn't leave it to the last minute. I waited and rolled between the wheels but it was turning and one of the rear tyres almost crushed me.'

Seb came up to join us, and Concha detached herself from me. By now we had penetrated into the heart of the base. There was the control tower rearing up, like a huge, illuminated head peering into the blackness. Nearby was a small plane, its wings blanketed in a thick covering of snow. It must have been there all day. Behind us the truck was grinding steadily out on to the runway and had lowered its dozer blade. 'They must be trying to keep the runway clear overnight,' Seb said.

We considered the implications behind that. 'Lucky for us they didn't start a couple of minutes earlier,' I said.

Concha put her hand to my mouth. 'Do you see that building over there?' She pointed to a row of lights on the other side of the roadway, about forty metres off. 'That is the guard post where the prisoners are being held.'

THIRTY-FOUR

'We'll try round the rear,' I said.

For several minutes we had lain under the trucks, watching the building. Time was pressing. If the planes were to hit the Falklands at dawn, then boarding must commence very soon. But first we had to get the others out and seize the guards' weapons. Two men and a woman with nothing but side-arms couldn't hope to knock out two big aircraft.

I could make out nothing through the windows of the guard post. At a guess the night guard would consist of a couple of men on watch, with half a dozen others on immediate call, probably dozing or watching TV. The prisoners would be held somewhere in the back with another man watching them in case of trouble. A sudden assault, carried out with brutal rapidity, would give the guards no time to organise resistance. It was the sort of action I had carried out many times in the past, both on exercise and in real life. Always before, though, I had been acting as part of a team. Tonight I was on my own with two civilians as back-up.

We worked our way round to the rear of the building, keeping to the darkness. A quick dash across a snow-covered parking area brought us to a door through which a light showed. Around the corner was a blank wall with a row of tiny barred windows set high up. It looked like the standard guard post layout – a main front office with the lock-up off it, and mess rooms and offices in the back.

'Pass me the tools,' I said.

The door had a reinforced glass panel in it. Inside, we could see another internal door, also with a window, and beyond that a cream-painted brick passage. There was no one moving about that we could see. Judging by the layout the prisoner accommodation was up the passage and to the right.

Above the outer door was an alarm box. I gave Seb a boost up. He unscrewed the cover, prised out the battery, then cut the wires. The alarm stayed silent. 'Okay,' he said. 'Done.'

He dropped down again. I took a crowbar, put the edge into the jamb of the door by the lock, and levered. There was a splintering of wood but the lock held. 'Fuck!' I said. There was no time to waste. I moved to the top hinge. Two hard jerks and the screws came out. I did the same at the bottom and the door fell outwards. I pulled it away and propped it against the wall.

The inner door was unlocked. I pushed it open and moved quickly up the passage, my gun at the ready. The only sound was a TV playing somewhere in the front of the building. On the left side were offices; opposite were what looked like cupboards. We moved up cautiously, checking each room as we went. I was nearing the far end when I heard the click of a door opening and a man appeared round the corner from the left. He was a young soldier of about nineteen, in battledress – one of the guard, presumably, come to investigate the noise. He carried an assault rifle loosely in one hand.

At the sight of three hooded and white-shrouded figures with guns trained on him he froze, his mouth dropping open. For a long moment he stood there, transfixed. Was he debating whether to raise his weapon and risk certain death? We were five metres from him, our guns trained on his chest. I moved up swiftly before he could pull himself together, jabbed the muzzle of the .45 in his ribs, snatched the rifle from him and bundled him into the nearest cupboard. It held cleaning equipment, mops and brooms, an electric floor-polisher. I banged him one on the head and dropped him like a sack.

'Rope,' I hissed to Seb. There was no telling how long the guy would stay out for. He passed me a hank of cord we had brought from the house. I cut off two lengths, bound the boy's hands and feet and stuffed a washcloth in his mouth for a gag. It would keep him quiet long enough for what we had to do.

I ripped off my shroud and checked his pockets. No keys, which was a blow. I picked up his rifle. It was an American M-16 without the grenade launcher. I checked the magazine and it was full. Immediately I felt more secure with a proper weapon in my hands once again. He had a bayonet, and I took that too – it might come in useful if there was any silent killing to be done.

I whispered to Seb to put the door we had destroyed back into position again while I kept guard. I didn't want any passer-by getting suspicious. Concha had thrown off her sheet too, and was waiting for orders. I checked the layout again in my head. The passage turned left and the soldier had come through a door. Most probably that door led directly to the guardroom, which must lie beyond the wall at the end. The prisoners were almost certainly on the other side of the wall to our right, accessible only through the guardroom for security. From somewhere close by I could hear a TV blaring and the sound of male laughter. With luck we would have a few minutes before it occurred to any of the soldier's buddies to wonder why he was gone so long and to come looking for him. Signing to the others to cover me, I moved out into the cross passage.

It ran for about four metres, ending in a wall with a fire extinguisher and two fire buckets, like military establishments everywhere. There was a solid door on the right, opening outward. I checked to see that the others were following and, turning the handle smartly, stepped quickly inside, rifle at the ready.

There was no one inside. It was a large room with whitewashed walls, and brightly lit. A swift glance took in two large desks and a number of notice-boards that looked as though they dealt with fatigue duties and orders of the day. An Argentine flag hung behind one of the desks, a Marine Division banner over the other. By the main entrance stood a water dispenser and a rack of useful looking M-16/M203 rifle-and-grenade-launcher combinations, ready for immediate use if the guard had to turn out. Otherwise the place was empty.

Immediately on my left was an open doorway into a darkened room, which had to be the mess room for the duty guard. Inside four men were seated around a TV, laughing over a porn movie, while a fifth, presumably one of those on watch, stood watching over their shoulders, his rifle propped against the back of a couch.

On the other side of the guardroom, on the same wall as the door I had come in by, was a metal grille that must give access to where prisoners were held.

Reaching inside the mess room, I snapped on the overhead light. Five faces blinked stupidly in the sudden glare, slowly taking in the M-16 pointed at them and the armed figures behind. I didn't give them a chance to recover. 'On the floor,' I said, pointing.

The standing man hesitated fractionally. His weapon was within reach and he was tempted to make a grab for it. But I was ready for him. Before he could move I swung the butt of the Armalite to catch him viciously in the small of the back. With a grunt of pain he fell forward across the couch, clutching himself. Seb moved forward and picked up the gun. Now there were two automatic weapons to cover five men, one of them disabled.

The rest of the Argentines had seen what might happen to anyone who didn't cooperate. They got down on their knees hurriedly, hands held skyward.

'Watch them,' I said quietly to Seb. He nodded and

took his stance where he could sweep the room. I went back out into the guardroom. Three strides and I was at the steel grille. There was only one guard on duty, a burly middle-aged Argentine with a narrow face like a rat who had evidently realised something was amiss and was scrabbling to unlock the door. He froze as he stared into the muzzle of the M-16, his mouth working soundlessly. I reached through the grille to twist the key in the lock and pulled the door open. The guard was trembling so much with terror he could hardly move; he must have thought I was going to shoot him on the spot. I took his gun and keys, spun him round and pushed him ahead of me to the holding cell.

There was just the one – a long chamber with a floor-to-ceiling grille like the one I'd just come through. The guys were inside, our lot and Concha's friends together, propped against the walls, bound and hooded. The floor was wet and there was an open-topped 45-gallon oil drum in the middle of the chamber, so it looked as if they'd been given the drowning treatment – having their heads ducked in a drum full of water with their hands bound behind them. Doug and I had watched that being done once on an op in Nigeria. It wasn't pleasant. Bastard Argentines.

I prodded the guard into a corner and made him squat with his hands on his head. Still keeping him covered, I knelt beside Doug. 'Doug, it's me, Mark. I'm going to take the hood off, OK? Watch your eyes.' He didn't respond. Probably he thought it was a new trick devised by the Argies. After ten hours of being blindfolded and bound he would be disorientated and exhausted. All his training would be warning him to trust nothing and nobody.

I rolled him into a sitting position and eased the hood up. He screwed up his eyes against the light and I guessed my face was just a blur to him. His torso was soaked, his body stank of sweat and urine, and he looked drained. I found a key in the bunch I'd taken off the guard which fitted his cuffs, and unlocked him. He gave a groan and eased his stiffened shoulders. He blinked again and cracked his eyes open. 'Fucking hell,' he croaked. 'Where'd you spring from?'

'Never mind,' I answered. 'Can you stand?'

He grunted and I heaved him up. He leaned against the wall, gasping. 'Jesus, I need a drink,' he said thickly. Denying water and toilet facilities was standard softening-up procedure before interrogation.

'Doug, we have to get you and the others out of here.' Briefly I explained. 'We're going to have a fight on our hands soon.'

Doug bared his teeth. 'As it happens, I've been wanting to kill some of the fuckers.'

I released Kiwi's hood and shackles. 'Fuck, am I glad to see you, boss,' he grunted when we got him free.

I handed Doug the keys and the guard's rifle. 'Turn Nobby and Josh loose, the Argentines too. Kiwi, you come with me.'

We ran back into the guardroom. Kiwi grabbed a weapon from the rack and gulped a long drink from the water fountain. Wiping his mouth, he joined me in the mess with Concha and Seb. 'Right,' I said, 'let's get 'em locked up and we can finish what we came here to do.'

The rest of the boys were staggering out from the cells, stinking and gagging for water. 'Fucking length of time you took getting here,' Nobby grumbled. Josh was groggy but anxious to show he could handle it. There were a few bruises but no one seemed to have been badly roughed up and everyone was capable of fighting. They snatched up weapons from the racks and took up positions to cover the windows. Kiwi found a big old American Browning M2 – a 0.5-inch heavy machine-gun on a massive tripod mount – and dragged it to the end of the passage we had come in by to command the rear.

Josh and I herded the guards into the cell and locked them away. Two of the four Argentine civilians were in poor shape. They were older men and had not had the training to resist interrogation or known what to expect. One of them was being dragged between Julian and Seb while Concha jabbered rapid-fire Spanish at them.

She grabbed my arm as I came past. 'This man cannot walk.'

I shook my head. 'He *must* walk or he'll have to be left behind. We're going to have a fight on our hands very shortly. We can't carry anyone.'

Doug interrupted. 'Hey, Mark, look what the fuck I got!' He had found a second weapons locker in the rear and come away with an armful of RPG-7 Soviet-made rocket launchers. The RPG-7 fires a rocket-boosted grenade capable of taking out a main battle tank at 500 metres. Fired into one of the hangars, it would turn an aircraft into an inferno.

'All prisoners squared away,' Josh reported. He had a cut on the side of his head, but was looking better already. 'I found the guy you locked in the cupboard. He was coming round so I brought him out and put him in the cells with the other lot.'

'OK,' I called. 'Everybody – check you've got enough ammo. We're moving out from the rear.'

Concha was still trying to attract my attention. 'It is a long way from here to the hangars where the aircraft are hidden,' she said urgently. 'More than 700 metres. What happens if we are seen and stopped?'

I shook my head. 'We'll just have to take that chance and fight our way through. Come on,' I said to the others.

'Wait.' She dragged me back. 'Why not take a truck? One of those out in front? Then we can put my friend in too.'

I hesitated. The idea made sense.

'Even if we were seen, people might not suspect,' she continued. 'They would think it was just part of the maintenance for the runway.'

She was right of course. A vehicle moving around would attract much less attention, particularly something like the snow clearer that had so nearly run her down.

I called to Nobby – he was our mechanical expert – and he came running back from the rear.

I took him to the window. 'See those trucks parked

out there? We need one of them.' I explained the plan. 'Something big and heavy that can take punishment.' I had in mind that we might need to ram the doors of the hangar.

'Sure, boss. No sweat.' He grinned. I'd never seen Nobby so happy. 'I'll scrounge a few tools and bring you back anything you want.'

While Nobby searched for the tools he wanted, I pulled back the shutter on one of the windows to check the front. The snowplough was still working on the runway, otherwise the scene was deserted.

Nobby returned with a long-bladed screwdriver and a pair of pliers.

'OK?' I said. He nodded and pulled on a coat that had been hanging on a hook by the door. I opened the handle to let him out. 'Walk normally,' I muttered. 'You'll attract less attention.'

'Aye, boss. Don't fret. I'll be back in a jiffy with the wheels.' He set off, shoulders hunched against the wind, the image of a reluctant man ordered out into the snow against his will. I watched him from the door, my rifle at my side. He reached the group of vehicles and I saw him move along the line, checking each one. Finally he climbed up into a cab. There was a pause.

Josh joined me at the door. 'Think he needs any help?'

'No. If Nobby can't start the fucker, no one can.' I remembered Nobby telling me that, in his teenage years, before he'd signed up with the Army, he'd been a tearaway joy-rider, whose greatest thrill had been breaking into high-performance motors then taunting the cops to chase him. There wasn't a vehicle built that could resist his assault for long.

We saw one of the vehicles switch on its lights, then heard the throb of a diesel engine as Nobby gunned the motor into life. We watched it pull out and make a wide turn to bring it round towards the guard post. It was a huge yellow truck with a massive dozer blade, like the one that had almost killed Concha.

'He's bringing it round to the car park at the back,' I said. 'Everybody get ready. I want everybody aboard sharply.'

We grabbed coats and anoraks belonging to the guards and gathered in the rear passage. There were eleven of us now, five SAS and six civilians including Seb. 'You get in the front,' I told Concha as the headlights illuminated the guard post. 'You can help navigate.'

The truck was enormous, built like a tank and almost as big. The others scrambled up into the massive tipper at the rear, dragging the semi-conscious Argentine with them. It was half loaded with sand for gritting, but at least that gave the injured man something to lie on.

Kiwi staggered down the steps from the guard post, lugging the Browning. I lent him a hand loading it up. The thing weighed a ton, but its huge armour-piercing bullets would make short work of an aeroplane if we could bring it to bear. Doug was throwing up the RPGs to Josh. I saw him add three or four medical packs too.

Kiwi settled the machine-gun so that it could fire over the rear lip of the giant scoop. 'What the fuck's happened to the rest of the Argies?' he grunted, already spoiling for a fight.

'I know. It's too bloody quiet,' I said. 'Maybe they're all busy with the assault force.'

'Well we're ready for the bastards,' he said defiantly.

The mood of the other men was the same; if it came to a battle they would go down fighting this time. No way were they going to endure another bout of capture and interrogation at the hands of the Argentines.

I saw everyone safely stowed, then ran round to the front and climbed up beside Concha and Nobby.

'Back on to the runway,' Concha told him, 'then to the left.'

With a grinding of gears we set off. The snow was still falling thickly. Nobby hunched over the wheel, peering through the screen. We reached the edge of the runway and turned north, following Concha's directions. I was tense with excitement. It seemed incredible to me that we could have come this far without being detected.

'There! Over there – that is the fuel depot!' Concha cried, pointing. 'The hangars are just beyond. You can see them now!'

I stared through the swirling darkness, and could just make out the familiar looming hulks of the giant hangars. We were almost there.

And at that moment a searchlight stabbed the night, illuminating us in its brilliant cone, and streams of tracer bullets tore towards us from every side.

It had been too easy. The enemy had been waiting for us all along. We had driven into another trap.

THIRTY-FIVE

Trapped in the searchlight beams from our left, Nobby Clark reacted instinctively. Flooring his foot, he sent the huge truck careering across the apron towards the hangar. A hail of gunfire opened up from every angle, and bullets pinged off the heavy steel sides of the vehicle. Our headlights lit a Jeep-mounted GPMG, firing at us from almost dead ahead. I could see the tracer glancing off the snowplough's blade like coloured beads. I wound down my side window, leaned out and aimed the grenade sight on my 203. I triggered the launcher and a huge flash engulfed the front of the Jeep as the round exploded on top of it. The gun stuttered into silence. A hit to us.

There was a screaming sound like tearing fabric, followed by a terrific bang. An armoured car was out there, throwing full calibre shells at us. It sounded like 105mm – a single hit from one of those babies would turn us into scrap metal. A second round cracked off, and this time we saw the shell burst 500 metres beyond and well behind. Nobby was swerving to throw off their aim. The gunners were shooting wildly, probably firing at their own side's gun flashes; in a night action with excitable troops, chaos is often likely to result unless officers keep a firm grip.

More tracer and cannon fire sprayed around. From the rear of the truck came a furious pounding as Kiwi opened up with the Browning. The steel-cored slugs were like cannon shells, smashing through light armour. I loosed off a couple more grenades towards the flash of infantry weapons ahead of us. From the number of shots I estimated half a company at least, maybe fifty men.

The rest of our team was firing from the rear. I could trust my guys to fire aimed shots and not just blaze away wasting ammunition like the Argies.

Something struck the roof of the cab a hammer-blow, and the truck rocked under the impact. Almost at the same moment the windscreen starred and cracked as two holes were punched through by bullets. I leaned back inside for a moment to slot in a fresh magazine. I was aware of Nobby gripping the wheel and shouting at the top of his voice, but the noise of gunfire was so loud I couldn't make out the words. He was steering straight for the hangar which was now less than a hundred metres away, looming at us like a huge wall. Dimly through the smoke of battle I became aware of Concha's face beside me. Reaching out, I pushed her head down below the level of the dashboard.

A spray of bullets rattled against the side of the truck – another machine-gun had found our range. I heard the squeal of tyres to our rear and a couple of quick-firing cannons opened up, sizzling round us like infuriated hornets. It felt like the entire Argentine army was shooting at us. A huge ball of fire flared up, away to the left – our guys in the back must have hit a fuel bowser or a tanker. The lurid flames belched upward and blazing fuel spewed out across the concrete apron.

The searchlight still had us in its beam. 'Fuck you,' I screamed at the top of my lungs. I worked the slide of my grenade launcher, ejecting the spent casing and slotting in a fresh round. The range was right at the limit. I aimed high and let fly. Someone in the back must have fired at the same time because I saw two bursts detonate just beneath the light source. The beam stayed on but swung round jerkily, pointing up at the sky. We must have knocked out the operators.

We were fifty metres from the hangar now. Another Jeep came roaring alongside, an Argentine standing up in the rear with an M-60 machine-gun, blazing away at us like a madman. A burst ripped through the roof of the cab, almost taking my head off. I fired back, aiming low to take out the driver. I saw him slump against the wheel and the Jeep swerved, hurling the machine-gunner around like a doll, his tracer cutting away through the night, scything towards his own side. The Jeep careered onwards, striking the snowplough's blade a glancing blow. The huge metal prow flipped the vehicle over and it vanished behind us in a cloud of dust and snow.

More rounds screeched overhead, and I saw an armoured car that had us in its sights, pursuing us from the left rear – one of those fast, lightly armoured tank-killers with an outsized cannon. Luckily for us, probably because the gunners were afraid of hitting the hangars, the shells were falling behind us.

I could feel Kiwi's big gun pounding away at the back, firing in short, aimed bursts. The immense bullets, based on a German anti-tank rifle round, have a muzzle velocity of almost 1000 metres a second, and the weight and speed of the rounds produce a devastating impact.

The flames and smoke from the burning fuel were spreading out among the attackers to our rear, and their fire was slackening off for the moment. The heavy cannon had stopped shooting altogether – either its gunners couldn't see any longer or they were afraid of hitting the hangar. Nobby was steering for the huge main doors with grim resolution. I saw a bunch of soldiers in front of us scatter as the huge truck thundered inexorably down on them. The doors were only thirty metres away now.

'Hang on!' I screamed out of the window. I might as well have been pissing into the wind for all the good it would do. We were travelling at over fifty miles an hour and bullets fired wildly from behind were punching holes in the side of the hangar like giant hail. A burst of 30mm cannon chewed up the apron right before our wheels, gouging chunks from the concrete.

In the last seconds before impact Nobby dropped the blade of the plough so it would take the full impact. He was steering for the centre of the left-hand door, aiming at the widest part where the thin metal covering would be more likely to give way. The door came rushing towards us like a cliff face. I braced myself for the crash.

Nobby was still yelling inaudibly as the point of the plough struck the sheet metal, ripping it back like a giant tin opener. With a shriek of tortured steel the truck tore on through. Nobby and I ducked our heads as flaps of broken sheeting clanged across the bonnet – but amazingly the windshield remained unscathed. A huge supporting beam bounced against the side of the hull with a boom that set my teeth rattling inside my head, as we burst inside the brilliantly lit hangar in a cloud of flying debris.

Directly in our path – and, seen from the ground, more enormous than ever – stood the huge plane. The soaring tail, as big on its own as a medium-sized airliner, reared up into the roof. The ramp was down and I could see straight into the cavernous hold. Amid the noise and smoke I was vaguely aware of hundreds of men in full battle kit with packs and rifles running like ants to escape the lumbering behemoth that had smashed in upon them – the marines, caught in the act of boarding for their mission! Only moments had passed since the shooting had erupted outside, and they stood wondering what to do as the world suddenly came crashing in around them.

We had burst in under the portside tail-fin. Immediately in our path was a mobile work gantry being towed out of the way by an electric tractor. Racing on, the point of the snowplough caught the tractor just behind the rear wheels, flipping it over like a toy. The fragile gantry toppled over, crashing down on to the outer tip of the wing like a heap of sticks.

Dead ahead of us gaped the exhaust of the inboard engine.

Our tyres shrieked on the slick flooring as Nobby spun the wheel desperately. The truck heeled over, skidding between the inner and outer engine pods. As the shadow of the wing passed overhead I held my rifle out of the window, muzzle upwards, and emptied the magazine into it.

The hammering sound of the Browning from the rear told me that Kiwi had brought his gun to bear. I pictured the heavy slugs ripping through the fuselage, tearing off great chunks, severing hydraulic lines and slicing through control surfaces. There was a swoosh and a deafening bang that echoed so loud through the hangar that for a second I thought the Argies had lost all control and were shelling us inside. Then I realised it was Doug with one of his RPGs.

I slammed in another magazine and raked the cockpit through the window as we shot by. 'Take that, you fuckers!' I shouted as I saw splashes of metal and glass fly.

There was another swish as someone else launched a rocket. This one I saw strike high on the fuselage, by the wing root – a terrific red flash followed by a spurt of flame that blossomed across the wing as a fireball sprouted upwards, mushrooming into the roof space. A wave of heat swept over us. The plane must have been fully fuelled up for the mission.

'Fuck, we've done it!' I shouted to the others in the cab, delirious with excitement and battle fury. No way could this baby be made serviceable again. The hangar was filled with men running for their lives to get out before the whole place went up – in another couple of minutes the flames would reach ammunition aboard the plane and we'd be done for.

Nobby was standing on the brakes and the truck's nose was slewing as the rear wheels broke away and we spun around like a rally car. Our tail smacked into another gantry, sending it flying into the hangar's rear wall. For a moment I thought we were going to follow it. I saw two soldiers running for their lives as we slid sideways on to them, smoke spewing from our tyres. Then they were gone, crushed into nothingness by the lethal blade of the plough.

The Globemaster's mid-section was a mass of flame by now, smoke belching up in oily clouds. Nobby was fighting to gain control of the wheel as we slid past the plane's bulbous snout. His clear intent was to circle right round the aircraft and drive back out the door again before the whole thing exploded on us. A hatch up on the flight deck was open and three figures were clawing their way down a ladder to the ground – the flight crew, trying to escape from the cockpit. Poor bastards, they stood no chance.

Nobby dropped down through the gears, pumping the throttle to get us moving round the aircraft's nose and down under the starboard wing to the hangar door a hundred metres away. I heard the thud of another detonation as a second fuel tank went up and the wingtip in front of us exploded into flame. The truck lumbered forward, engine racing. Billowing clouds of smoke rolled across the hangar, filling the cab with choking fumes. Everything went dark and the sudden heat was suffocating.

Jets of fire spurted up through the darkness as fuel lines burst in the heat. We were moving under the starboard wing now, Nobby desperately steering to avoid the burning engines. Smears of liquid avgas spattered the windshield. A fiery drizzle of flaming droplets shot through the smoke. Any moment now the whole wing could break up, drowning us in blazing fuel.

Our speed was picking up. Above the roar of the fires I could hear the note of the engine surging. There was the tail ramp ahead to our right now. Two hundred Argentine marines were struggling down it, throwing away their weapons and kit, frantic to escape the flames. I saw one, braver than the others, whip up his rifle as we passed, but the sound of his shots was swallowed up in the cacophony. Other men by the door of the hangar were firing their rifles at us, the bullets pinging off the truck's heavy structure.

A furious marine leapt up against the door on my side, thrusting his machine pistol through the window. The muzzle caught me in the face, knocking me backwards. Christ, this is it, I thought.

There was a deafening explosion in my ear. Concha had picked up my .45, the one I had taken from Oliveras, and fired it two-handed into the man's face. The marine's head burst into a bloody cloud and he flew from the truck. Concha had fired instinctively. Another second and the marine's weapon would have shredded me.

Nobby was swinging wide to build up speed. Through the smoke I could make out the shattered door of the hangar, hanging crazily from one end. Christ, I thought, how are we ever going to get through that without bringing the whole hundred-ton section crashing down on top of us?

Heaving on the wheel, Nobby wrestled the sluggish truck towards the gap. Fleeing marines scattered before the plough blade as we cleaved a path through the mob. An electric truck driven by a panicking Argentine powered past us, bowling men over without stopping.

As we neared the door I saw a great beam lying across the floor in front of us. A terrific blast shook the building and more wreckage crashed down from the roof. A mass of tangled metal sheeting blocked our path. Without slackening speed, Nobby swerved under the plane's giant tail. A marine plunged across our path, making for the hangar doors, risking being crushed in the desperation to escape. I grabbed the dash as the front tyres thudded over bits of debris, the truck's body lurching wildly.

Nobby was shouting to me. 'It's no use, the door's fucking blocked!'

'We must leave the truck!' Concha cried, her eyes round and staring at the destruction all about us.

'No way!' I shouted back. 'The marines outside have automatic weapons, they'd cut us down on foot. Try the rear again!' I yelled to Nobby. 'There must be another way out!'

Before I'd finished there was a boom from our rear followed by a devastating crash that split the apron under the wrecked doorway fifty metres ahead of us. Bits of concrete fountained upwards, spraying the hangar. An armoured car had found its range and was shooting at us regardless of its fleeing comrades. Nobby spun the wheel over to the right and swung round beneath the burning Globemaster's tail, ploughing through the smoke towards the rear of the hangar, heedless of the faces that loomed up before him. There was a second boom and another shell screeched by, exploding against the wall of the hangar. The Argentine gunners must have been raging at the destruction we were causing. They were obviously determined to stop us now whatever the cost.

There came another ear-splitting crash and a huge shell tore in through the wall beside us, missing the truck by inches. It skimmed past the tail of the aircraft and exited through the far wall, detonating outside.

At the same moment a hail of small-arms fire broke out in our rear. Bullets whined and skipped overhead. Another shell crashed through the hangar wall and plunged into the fuselage of the Globemaster, exploding in a fireball of burning fuel. The armoured car outside was now firing full-calibre rounds directly into the hangar and to hell with the consequences. An anti-tank rocket whizzed through the partly open door and detonated against a beam as the infuriated marines joined in with the clear intent of burning us alive.

THIRTY-SIX

The aircraft was a mass of flames now. We had cut across the tail, completing our circle of the plane and were running along the port side again, swinging wide to avoid the blazing wing. An RPG, fired from outside, whizzed overhead and slammed against the rear wall of the hangar, detonating in a shower of molten steel fragments. More volleys of automatic fire from the marines outside sprayed through the doorway and peppered the sides of the building. Underlying the rifle fire came the deeper *thud . . . thud . . . thud* of a 30mm cannon. An armour-piercing round struck the edge of the snowplough in front of me, slicing neatly through the steel. A lubricant cart caught in a burst of incendiary rounds was ripped apart, spewing torrents of flaming oil across the floor.

There was a terrific crash behind my head and the cab bounced under the impact of a direct hit as the windshield dissolved in a hail of fragments. I looked round to see a gaping hole in the bulkhead behind me. A cannon shell had smashed through the thick steel of the tipper's body and continued into the cab, punching through the back of the seat where Concha had been sitting, and blowing through the glass. If I hadn't pushed her down into the footwell she would have been torn in half.

Another thunderous explosion shook the hangar and flames spouted up towards the roof. I couldn't tell if it was another shell from the 105mm or the Globemaster's fuel tanks igniting. A tongue of roaring flame darted from the flight's deck hatch and a figure sprang out, burning like a torch. At least his end was quick.

Kiwi's Browning was still banging away behind. There was a crash from overhead and large lumps of debris came tumbling down. Either the wild firing or the heat from the blazing aircraft was bringing down the roof, trapping us in.

There was a shout in my ear. Doug had thrust his face into the hole smashed in the rear of the cab. 'Josh has stopped a bullet and one of the Argies has bought it.'

'We can't take the front,' I yelled back. 'The fucking door's blocked and that armoured car would cut us to pieces the moment we showed ourselves. Our only chance is to try the rear!'

The smoke was so thick it was almost impossible to breathe. I thought of telling everyone to bail out, but the chances of us finding a side door were a hundred to one. The Argies would shoot us down like rats – if the fumes didn't get us first. Well, at least we had destroyed one of the planes and probably torpedoed their plans for invasion. Back at Hereford our names would be inscribed on the clock tower and the Regiment would celebrate our stand against two battalions of Argentine marines.

But then, fuck it, I thought – we weren't finished yet. I shouted to Nobby: 'Crash through all that junk and try to gouge a big enough hole for us to crawl out.'

He nodded grimly. It was the only hope we had.

He revved the engine and swung the wheel over, and for a moment I thought he had misunderstood what I was saying. Then I realised he was circling us round to gain momentum. The truck heeled round, crunching bits of debris and pieces of equipment beneath its massive wheels. Nobby was squinting red-eyed through the smoke, trying to see beyond the end of the bonnet. The plane was no more than a wall of flames licking up into the roof. The roar of the fire was so intense that we no longer noticed the flying bullets. The heat made the paintwork on the truck blister and bubble before our eyes. Concha was gagging on the smoke somewhere down by my feet. I reached down to brace her shoulder as we stormed blindly onward.

A burning Jeep suddenly loomed in our path. 'Shit!' Nobby yelled and spun the wheel without slackening speed. The truck lurched, tipping sideways. Nobby caught it somehow, and we straightened up and pounded on. The smoke was pouring in so thickly that we couldn't even make one another out. If we hit the end wall of the hangar head on we might stand a chance, but if we struck one of the main beams we'd probably bounce off and the impact of the collision would very likely throw us all out.

Dimly I was conscious of more of the roof collapsing around us. Drops of burning fuel scorched our flesh and we seemed to be moving through a world of darkness shot with writhing flame. I felt my hair smouldering, and the skin on the backs of my hands blistered and shrivelled. My mouth and throat were scorched by the fumes and heat. I heard Nobby yell as a long finger of flame licked through his smashed side window, searing his face. The truck bumped over something unseen in the smoke and lurched on, engine roaring.

We saw fire ahead of us, crimson and blue flames feeding on the smoke. I never saw the wall coming. One moment there was nothing but leaping flames, and the next brought the loudest crash I had ever heard. I was flung back against the rear of the seat and my head bounced off the bulkhead behind me. Something huge and black smashed into the cab and the entire truck seemed to leap into the air, dropping again with a jarring thud that hurled me up against the roof, then forward on to the dash. The door beside me sprang open and I felt myself slide helplessly from the seat. I scrabbled at the dash to stop myself before an instant later the door was slammed shut again with incredible violence, knocking me across the cab into Nobby's lap.

I felt a draught of cooler air against my face and gulped breaths thankfully into my tortured throat and lungs. Still the truck ground onward, accompanied by the shriek of tearing metal. The smoke in front cleared momentarily and I glimpsed the snow-covered ground outside. The cab was out, and the rest of the body was scraping through the gap. Incredibly we had battered our way out of the hangar.

With a final lurch the truck heaved itself clear and our wheels scrunched over the carpet of snow. We were out of the hangar and crossing the parking area behind. It was still dark, but the flaming building cast a lurid light over the scene. The hangar was completely ablaze now. Part of the roof had fallen in, and flames were leaping out. Dense smoke was rolling across the airfield, but firing still persisted out on the apron and strings of tracer curved through the sky. I glanced across to the right and saw that the second hangar was burning. A stray shell must have set it alight too.

The truck was jolting forward over the grass as Nobby grasped the wheel almost in a trance. One headlamp was still functioning, casting a yellow-eyed glare upon the virgin snow. 'Kill it!' I shouted to him. 'Kill the light!' My voice sounded hoarse and faraway; I'd been partially deafened by the noise in the hangar.

Nobby pulled himself together and switched off the headlamp, and we drove on in silence. The smoke and confusion seemed to have masked our escape for the moment. Now we were in total darkness.

'The fence!' I shouted to Nobby. 'Try to make for the gates, it's the only way out through the minefield.' If we could only make it off the airbase, there was a chance we could run for the border in the truck.

Concha scrambled coughing out of the footwell. She stared round blankly at the shattered cab and the snowy airfield lit by the immense fires behind us. Still no shots came our way as we stormed on through the darkness.

'I'm going back to check on the others,' I said. I wanted to find out how badly Josh had been hit. I opened the side door and, clinging on to the cab, pulled myself round and up into the back of the truck. In the flickering red light I saw a number of sand-encrusted figures emerge. The sides of the truck were torn and gouged by bullet tracks, but the industrial-gauge steel had held the thing together.

'The worst hit we took was a thirty-mil round fired from behind,' Doug told me, wiping his mouth and eyes. 'The fucker penetrated the steel at the rear end and detonated at shallow depth. We took a shower of splinters. One of the Argentines copped it. Then as we were approaching the second hangar a burst of machine-gun fire ricocheted off the side wall and Josh caught one in the belly.'

A stomach wound was one we all dreaded. I knelt down in the jolting truck to talk to Josh. He was lying still on his back in the sand. A shell dressing was packed tight against his stomach to stem the bleeding and he was holding an intravenous drip bottle in his hand. 'How's it going?' I asked him gently.

'Not so bad, boss,' he answered tightly. 'Comes and goes.' He meant the pain. You can't do anything to sedate a stomach wound. Morphine makes you feel sick, and coughing or retching only does more damage. So you just have to take the pain as best you can. Josh's breathing was steady, and when I felt his pulse it was running around a hundred a minute – not too bad in the circumstances. As long as we could hold the bleeding and keep his fluid levels up he should last out. The pain would be the worst bit. Getting him to hold his own IV bottle at least gave him something to do and kept his mind busy. Also we would notice quickly if he lost consciousness.

'We're going to make a run for the border,' I told him. 'With luck we should manage it in a couple of hours and then we'll get you to a doctor. So just hang in there till then, OK?'

He grinned weakly. We both knew it couldn't be that simple. 'Sure, boss. Sorry I screwed up.'

'Don't be stupid. You did good. I'll see that goes in the report.'

I left him and saw that Julian had been hit too. His was a flesh wound to the shoulder. Ugly, but not dangerous. Seb had patched it up and Doug had given him a shot to deaden the pain. He was young and fit. If it came to a walkout he would probably keep up.

I checked the ammo supply with Doug. 'Still got three RPG rounds left,' he said happily. 'Two belts for the Browning or maybe three; Kiwi thinks one's buried round here somewhere. I've half a dozen mags for the 203, plus whatever Josh has left.'

Nobby and I had several magazines still up in front. We could fight another engagement if we had to.

I had another brief word with Josh and climbed back over into the cab again. We were nearing the fence by now. Nobby cut away towards the left along the perimeter road. As he did so there was a renewed burst of firing from 300 metres to our rear left flank, and rounds of tracer came arcing through the smoke.

'Step on it,' I told Nobby urgently. 'Looks as though they've rumbled our escape.' I wasn't sure whether those were aimed shots or just a general spraying in the direction they thought we might have taken, but moments later all my doubts were removed. There was a shriek overhead and a big shell burst against the fence fifty yards behind us.

'Fuck!' I shouted. 'They've got our range. Get moving!' With a terrific jolt we passed over the drain. The gates were about half a kilometre off and we were doing about forty kph. At this rate it would take us the best part of a minute, during which time the gun could get off three or perhaps four shots. One hit was all it would take.

Nobby had his foot flat on the floor and the truck shook as the speed built up. The armoured car carrying the gun almost certainly had infra-red night-fighting sights which would pick us out clear as daylight. The smoke might mask us a little, but I didn't count on it.

The next shell screamed across the bonnet in front of us. It burst with a deafening crash in the bush between the fences. Earth fountained up in a massive blast, spraying the sides of the vehicle with fragments. 'Shit!' Nobby cried. 'The bastard must've set off a mine!'

Flames crackled among the bush as we raced past. I was craning my neck into the night, trying to spot the gates while the wind tore at my eyes. We heard the *crack-thump* of the next shell and tensed, but when the blast came it was well behind. I twisted my head back and laughed. 'Fuckers saw the fire and thought they'd hit us! They're shooting at their own smoke.'

There was a long pause. Some cannon fire sprayed around, but nothing that came close. Probably the gunners thought they'd taken us out. Then I saw a dark object against the flames. It was moving rapidly and in a direction that would cut us off. Something about the shape triggered a memory – the AFVs we had seen outside the hangar the previous night. One of them had guessed our intention and was racing to intercept.

A stream of tracer reached out like a chain of coloured lights. The shells passed hissing overhead, detonating against the fence. We were almost at the gate now. 'Turn!' I shouted to Nobby, 'Turn!'

Another spray of cannon rounds burst around us. Fragments rattled against the sides of the truck. The punishment the old girl was taking was amazing. Nobby fought the wheel round but the nose was swinging too slowly. We were missing the gates and taking out the fence on the far side. Posts and wire crumpled like paper under the plough as we brushed through. We had missed the track by half a dozen metres. Christ, I thought, if the Argies planted their mines close to the edge we're done for.

But Nobby had control again. He was straightening up and was heading us back on to the track again. I waited for the blast of a mine under our wheels but none came. The outer gates appeared in front of us and we smashed them down, thundering out into the bush beyond.

More tracer crackled around us, sizzling in the snow-covered bush. The AFV was charging in pursuit. I heard the heavy rattle of the Browning opening up. At close range there was a chance Kiwi might do some damage or throw the gunner's aim off. Otherwise Doug might get close enough to use an RPG. With its eight-wheel drive the AFV would run rings round us in rough country. It could stand off out of range and pepper us. It would be only a matter of time before we took a vital hit. Then our only choice would be to ditch the wounded and take off on foot.

A heavy shell whizzed past, detonating in our tracks. The 105mm gunners had spotted us again. It was a competition to see who would get us first. Our pace was slowing as we started on the rise leading up to the main road. Looking back I could make out the AFV in the gap we had torn in the fence, its gun spitting fire after us.

Suddenly a mushroom of smoke burst from the earth under its front wheel. The explosion jarred the ground, flinging the vehicle on to its side across the track. For a moment I thought it had been hit by one of its own side's shells, then I realised it must have swung wide of our track and detonated an anti-tank mine.

THIRTY-SEVEN

'Fuck it, they're stuck in their own minefield!' Doug yelled from the back of the truck.

The AFV was lying on its side, pouring smoke. The heavy anti-tank mine had blown off one of the wheels and the front section was burning. I could see men struggling from the rear hatch. The vehicle was lying across the track, completely blocking it. With a minefield either side, the Argies would have to push or drag it out of the way before they could continue with the pursuit. The gunners in the armoured car had ceased firing, probably afraid of hitting their own people.

'Which way?' Nobby shouted, dropping down into low gear. The truck was struggling up the rise, pitching and rolling on the rutted surface. The snow was deep here and it was hard to make out the track, especially without lights.

Concha scrambled up from below the seat and the two of us peered out. 'Keep right!' she shouted. 'The ground is hard there and the slope is easier.' She evidently knew the road. I felt absurdly proud of her.

The truck was making heavy weather even so, its wheels spinning on the packed snow. Nobby eased off on the throttle and was crawling along in first gear. It was desperately important that we keep going. If we could only make it the kilometre up to the highway we stood a chance of reaching the border.

I heard a rattle of shots from the back. Argentine marines must have bypassed the knocked-out AFV and were pursuing us on foot. Kiwi and his machine-gun would keep them at a distance, if we could only make it up the steady rise towards the highway.

Snow was blowing straight into the cab, making it hard to see anything. Nobby was steering almost by instinct. I had only a faint memory of the route having walked along it in the dark twenty-four hours before, but that wasn't much help.

Luckily Concha seemed more confident. She yelled instructions in Nobby's ear, occasionally grasping the wheel and pushing it round when he seemed to be going off course.

The firing behind died away as we crested the last hump, and we were on the road before we realised it. Chips of gravel flew from under the tyres as Nobby swung us round and we plunged northward into the night.

'Boss, I gotta turn the lights on,' Nobby pleaded. 'I can't make out a fucking thing in this!'

I looked back. The horizon was brilliant with leaping flames and there were no more signs of pursuit. But it would not be long before the armoured car found another exit and came after us. It was vital we get a head-start. 'OK – but step on it.'

Nobby snapped the switch and our single headlamp stabbed into the swirling snowflakes. Snow was falling fast and I reckoned even with lights on we would be hard to spot at any distance. Luckily another vehicle had used the road within the past hour or so and the tyre tracks were still visible. Nobby shifted up the gears and our speed built slowly.

'How far to the border?' I bawled in Concha's ear.

'To San Sebastian? Eighty-five kilometres.'

I squeezed her arm. There was snow in her hair and on her face, but she looked beautiful. Eighty-five kilometres – that was around sixty miles: two hours, two and a half, say, in these conditions. 'How's our fuel?' I called to Nobby.

'Fine,' he shouted back. 'I chose this one because she had a full tank. I'm more worried about the tyres. I reckon at least one of the rear wheels has been hit.'

Fuck the tyres, I thought. The truck was a big eight-wheeler. If we had to we would drive on the rims to the frontier. I glanced at the speedometer needle. It was quivering around forty. The armoured car that had been shooting at us was a massive beast and its huge cannon must weigh some. Even so, it would be capable of matching our speed easily. Allowing for our lead, I estimated it would catch us up in ten kilometres or less.

I tried to remember what I knew of the route. I nudged Concha again. 'That bridge, the one we escaped from. How far off is it?'

She wiped the snow from her mouth. 'Not far, about four kilometres.'

I tried to guess what the enemy would do with the forces available. The obvious solution would be to send up a helicopter but the weather ruled that out. I knew they had at least one more tracked AFV of the type we'd seen outside the hangar earlier, in addition to the armoured car – and there were probably others. The tracks would make short work of the snow and they carried an entire section of troops, but they were slower. The armoured car with its eight-wheel drive would have the legs on the road, and its big gun had the range and computer-guided night-fighting equipment to pick us off. So I reckoned they would send that in first and use the AFVs to mop up any survivors afterwards.

This was a good section of road. Snow was flying by and our speed was holding. At this rate we should make the bridge in another ten minutes at the outside.

It was seven minutes flat before we glimpsed two red lights glowing through the murk ahead. 'That is the bridge,' Concha shouted. I shot a glance behind, and thought I could make out a glow of headlamps on our tail.

'Nobby, there's a left-hand bend immediately after the bridge. As soon as we're out of sight of the bridge, stop the truck but leave the engine running. We'll give the marines something to think about.'

'Gotcha, boss.' Nobby sounded positively cheerful at the prospect of further action.

We rattled over the bridge, past the spot where Concha and I had taken our dive in the major's 4x4 twelve hours ago. I wondered if the Jeep was still down there. Our trek through the snow seemed like another age. Our clothes were caked in snow, but we had too much adrenalin coursing through our bodies to feel the cold now.

Nobby braked the truck round the corner and cut the lights. He and I jumped down with our guns. 'You stay in the cab and make sure the engine doesn't cut out,' I told Concha.

I ran round to the back. 'We're going to set an ambush,' I shouted up to Doug and Kiwi. 'Bring the RPGs. I want to try and take out that armoured tin can with the cannon.'

'Fucking right,' Doug called back. He was always up for a fight.

'What about the Browning?' Kiwi asked.

'Negative. Take Josh's gun. We may have to bug out in a hurry.'

The Browning's awesome firepower would be an undeniable asset, but it weighed as much as a fully-grown man with its tripod and ammunition. Besides, I wanted to lure the Argentines on with a false impression of our weakness, not have them stand off and shell us to bits.

The two of them jumped down, leaving the Argies aboard and the injured Josh with Concha up in the cab. Doug was carrying the three RPGs with his 203 over his shoulder. He passed us one each to Kiwi and Nobby and together we ran back the hundred metres to the bridge. There was a drainage ditch on the left-hand side of the road that would provide cover for our withdrawal. We could see the headlights probing through the snow on the other bank of the river. We reached the start of the ironwork and Doug and Nobby flung themselves down in the snow. Kiwi and I took up positions by the parapet either side. We cocked our guns and chambered grenade rounds.

The approaching lights resolved themselves into a column of at least ten vehicles. It looked to me like a Jeep in the lead, which was what I was expecting. Behind it was the big armoured car with its enormous cannon swinging as it descended the rise on the other side. An AFV followed, with what looked like more Jeep-loads of troops in the rear. I reckoned maybe eighty men with two armoured vehicles, a formidable force.

We had been lucky once tonight, taking the guard post and fighting our way out of the ambush set by the marines. Yet an uneasy doubt nagged at me: how had the marines come to be in position? Why had they waited till we left the guard post to attack when they could have had us surrounded?

But there was no time to reflect. Already the leading elements of the column were drawing near. I could see the snow being thrown up by their wheels and tracks.

I gauged the width of the bridge – about 120 metres across. 'Let the truck get its front wheels on, then hammer it,' I said to the others.

The Jeep came on without hesitating; they could see from our tracks we had crossed. I guessed they must

411

have thought we were on the run and it was simply a question of chasing us down. The moment it drew level with the railings I stood up above the parapet, raised my 203, flipped up the leaf sight and squeezed the trigger of the launcher. The HE round shot out of the tube in a soaring arc, skimming towards the truck like a well-thrown egg. In the same instant Nobby fired from the other side and Doug let rip a burst from his rifle. One grenade exploded on the Jeep's bonnet with a bright flash, the other detonated under the wheels.

'Fucking on target!' Kiwi yelled, delighted.

The Jeep slewed across the road, two bodies spilling out into the snow. The four surviving Argies tumbled out, some screaming, and ran off back down the road. The remainder of the force crammed on the brakes and pulled off the road to take us under fire. They were hampered though by the steep bank and the bend in the river. A heavy machine-gun on the armoured car opened up, sweeping the approaches of the bridge. Then the 30mm cannon on the AFV joined in. We lay flat below the parapet and waited.

The enemy had two choices now. They could keep hammering away with automatic fire to keep our heads down while their infantry worked its way across the bridge to get to grips with us. If they did that they would have to accept casualties. Otherwise they could hold their men back and send in their armour to winkle us out. If we could do them sufficient damage to slow them up, maybe even block the bridge, there was still a chance we could make it to the border two hours away.

The firing continued for a few minutes. We waited quietly. Then I saw Doug stick his head round the edge of the parapet and fire a quick burst. There were screams from the far side and a storm of angry firing swept the bridge in response. Moments later I spotted the outline of a helmet moving along by the bottom of the parapet on the opposite side at about a hundred metres' range. He was wearing camouflage white but the gun flashes of the covering fire provided light enough to see by. I took careful aim and popped off a single shot. He rolled over and lay still.

The troops on the far bank were doing their best to outflank us, but the terrain was against them and we were well protected by the curve of the parapet. After a few more minutes' uncontrolled shooting we heard the growl of tracks moving up. They had opted for the armoured solution.

The AFV advanced slowly, pausing every few metres to search the end of the bridge with its machine-gun. It was fitted with a co-axial Hughes chain-gun in 7.62 calibre. The high velocity rounds smacked into the parapet above my head with an evil sound. There would be a section of infantry crouched in the back, anything up to eight or ten men, who would be ready to make short work of us when they disembarked. The closer it got the bigger it looked; it must have been all of three metres high and as wide across. Its full-up weight would be around twenty tons.

It crawled out towards the centre of the span, making the bridge shake and looking like a squat iron toad. The turret swivelled from side to side, as the chain-gun let off short bursts, and the hatches were buttoned down tight against sniper fire. The squeal of its tracks grated on my nerves.

I glanced across at Doug. He had his RPGs in his hand, and was waiting. I loaded another grenade round in my 203 and risked a quick look out to check on the range. The beast was just coming up to the slight hump in the centre of the bridge. That would put it at about sixty metres off. I signalled to Doug to be ready, counted to ten, then gave him the thumbs-up sign. I stepped out quickly and triggered the grenade, aiming for the gunner's vision block. My intention was to shatter the periscope or at the least throw the gunner's aim off so as to give Doug and Kiwi a clear shot with their rockets.

I jumped back under cover and in the same instant Doug rolled out into the snow to kneel on the roadway, the RPG on his shoulder. My grenade burst on one of the hatches and the infuriated chain-gunner swung the turret towards me. A hail of bullets flattened themselves against the heavy ironwork of the parapet, ricocheting off all around me. I flattened myself against the road, staring across at Doug.

The AFV was right on the crest of the hump. Its snout reared up momentarily, making it hard for the gunner to lower the barrel sufficiently and exposing its slanted belly. Doug settled the RPG on his shoulder, flipped up the sight coolly and flicked off the safety.

The vehicle tilted over the hump and came down on

the front of its tracks with a thump. The gunner, realising too late that it was a trap, was already swinging the turret round frantically, but he was too slow and now he was unsighted. Snatching his chance, Doug fired. There was a swoosh and a plume of smoke as the propellant ignited and the oversized grenade on its rocket shot from the tube. It struck the AFV full on the snout, right underneath the cannon and on the weak spot in the armour where the gun joined the turret ring. There was a small flash, followed by an incredibly loud bang that made my ears ring.

Now it was Kiwi's turn. As Doug rolled away, Kiwi sprang out and knelt in the snow, levelling his own rocket. Again there was the flash and smoke blast of the firing followed by the crash as the warhead detonated, this time on the turret. The AFV shuddered to a halt with smoke pouring from the hatches. I glimpsed sparks of fire, intensely bright – phosphorous incendiary ammunition burning inside.

The hollow-charge warheads had flattened on impact, igniting the explosive and instantaneously melting the steel liner to focus a jet of molten metal that bored right through the armour plate. It could penetrate up to half a metre thick. Inside the vehicle, the stream would've expanded into a cloud of superheated gas and fragments that ignited everything inside. The crew stood no chance.

'Pull out!' I yelled to the other two, signalling with my hand. We were still almost deafened from the blasts of the grenades. Picking up my still unfired rocket, I ran crouched across the bridge with Kiwi to join Doug. We dived into the ditch as the stunned Argentines on the other side of the river opened up with every weapon they had in a furious attempt to avenge their comrades. But the bridge was well and truly blocked. The AFV was burning with an intense heat and a deep roar that drowned out the screams of the crew. Exploding ammunition inside rocked the hull, showering flaming fragments and clumps of white-hot phosphorus over the bridge. The road was totally blocked; nothing could get past for several hours.

The smoke that was blowing back on us carried the stench of burning flesh, but there was no time to feel sickened at what we had done. We crawled along the ditch for 200 metres till we were out of range of all but the heavy weapons. Then we got up and ran through the snow and darkness up the road to join the truck.

I felt light-headed with tiredness and relief. We had stopped the pursuit. No helicopter could pick us up in this weather. There was nothing for it now but to press on to the frontier.

We jogged easily up the road through the snow for fifty metres. We were near enough to make out the truck's shape in the dark and hear the throaty rumble of the motor running when another sound stopped us in our tracks.

It was a pistol shot.

Oh shit, I thought, and broke into a run. As I did so the rear lights clicked on, the gears grated, and the truck lumbered forward into motion.

THIRTY-EIGHT

I sprinted up the road through the snow with every ounce of speed I possessed. My rifle thumped against my back but there wasn't time to dump it. At all costs I had to reach the truck before it could gather speed. It was twenty-five metres ahead of me. I had no idea what was happening. Could a bunch of Argentines have come down the road from the other direction and taken over the truck? Suddenly anything was possible. They might have shot Josh, Concha and her friends, but surely they would have waited to catch the rest of us?

The truck was still a dozen metres ahead. It slowed and there was another crash of gears. Whoever was driving was a novice with big trucks. The wheels were slipping on the gradient; he would have done better to keep his speed down and go for a steady pace. I pounded on, straining for the glow of the rear lights, the others tearing after me. If I could only reach the tailgate and grab a hold. What I was going to do then, I had no idea. The truck could be full of Argentine soldiers.

I'd left Concha in the cab. Was the shot I heard the one that killed her? Fury at the thought drove me on. I was so close now that the slush thrown up by the rear wheels was hitting me in the face. The engine was snorting and coughing as if the mixture was too rich. Any moment now it might cut out altogether. The driver obviously thought the same, because he changed down. There was a momentary hiatus as the engine disengaged and the truck's momentum slowed still further.

My breath was pounding in my lungs, my heart labouring. The tailgate was less than a metre away now, but the truck's speed was picking up again. It was now or never; I put everything I had into one final convulsive effort. In the glow thrown out by the rear lights I could dimly make out the rungs of a ladder up the near side. My fingers stretched for the lowest rung and found a handhold. The momentum of the truck plucked me forward. I clawed with my other hand and swung myself up. The truck's speed had picked up suddenly, and when I put a foot down to kick off it was whipped from under me. I bent my knees and tensed my biceps just as Josh had done on the beam back in the hangar, then snatched upwards in the dark, found the next rung and pulled myself up.

Now I could get a foot on to the ladder, and for a moment I hung there like a human fly, sucking air back into my lungs. The truck was rattling away up the slope from the river at a gathering pace. I had made it just in time. I didn't know what had happened to the others but I knew they would be racing in pursuit. If I could halt the vehicle I would have some back-up soon enough.

As soon as I had got my breath back I climbed to the rim of the tailgate. For a moment I paused. It was still pitch dark. Above me the muzzle of Kiwi's machine-gun gleamed faintly. If the truck had been seized by Argentines then I needed to work out a strategy. My rifle was still on my back but it was a cumbersome weapon for close-quarter fighting. Tucked into my waistband I still had Major Oliveras's .45 automatic. I dug it out and, wedging an arm through the ladder, cocked it and flicked off the safety. Then I gathered myself together, put a hand on to the rim and in a single movement heaved myself up and over into the truck body.

I landed awkwardly, caught my foot in the tripod of the machine-gun and fell forward into the sand with a clatter. I rolled over, bumping against someone in the dark and swung the automatic round, seeking a target.

There wasn't one. The darkness was total up here but from where I lay I could look upwards against the snow drifting down and there was no one else on their feet. I reached out with my free hand and encountered a leg. Was that Josh? I gave it a squeeze. There was no answering movement. My heart sank. The stillness around me told its own story.

Picking myself up, I crawled towards the front. I now recognised Josh's body by the field dressing against his stomach. One hand was still clutching the IV drip that had been his lifeline. There was sticky blood on his chest where he had taken another hit. Tears of rage came into my eyes. I swore I'd make the bastards pay for this –

gunning down a badly injured man who couldn't possibly have posed a threat.

Crawling on, I discovered the bodies of Concha's friends. One had been dead already but the others lay heaped where they had been shot. As far as I could tell each had been slotted with a single hit to the head. Whoever had done this had killed them first, then gone on to finish off Josh where he lay helpless to defend himself – and I swore again that I'd make the cunt suffer.

I knew who it was then, too. My God, I kept thinking, how could I have been so stupid all this time? The Argentines had been playing us for patsies all along, and I had never once suspected.

I moved cautiously up to the cab, careful to keep my shadow from falling on the driver, and peered through the hole in the back. The solitary headlamp cast its beam into the falling snow, the lights of the dash cast a dim glow inside, and I could make out the shape of the driver hunched over the wheel. There seemed to be no one else in the cab – no sign of Concha. A bend was approaching, the driver's head shifted as he hauled the steering wheel round and I caught the unmistakeable outline of a beard.

I waited till we were round the corner and the truck had straightened up again. Then I stowed the pistol away, unslung my rifle and pushed it through the hole. He was so intent on the road ahead that he didn't notice till I jabbed the muzzle into the side of his neck.

He stiffened and the truck's nose jerked round,

swinging outwards. 'Watch yourself!' I snapped. 'No sudden movements.'

Carefully he straightened up again. Keeping the muzzle pressed firmly against his neck, I reached a foot down through the gap in the rear bulkhead and kicked the gear lever into neutral. The engine roared as it spun free, the truck slowed, and Seb took his foot off the throttle.

'Put the hand-brake on,' I snarled at him. 'Put the hand-brake on or I'll fucking shoot you where you sit, you bastard!' I jabbed the rifle deeper into his neck. He gave a grunt of pain and reached out and jerked the brake lever up. The truck slithered to a halt on the gravel amid the empty pampas. 'Keep both hands on the wheel where I can see them.'

He obeyed, his big hands gripping the wheel tightly. Looking straight ahead, he spoke for the first time, his voice harsh and controlled. 'It isn't what you think,' he said.

'Shut the fuck up!' I told him. 'Open your mouth once more and I'll blow your head off your fucking shoulders!' I was so mad with hatred and fury it was as much as I could do not to kill him there and then. I squeezed through the gap that had been torn in the bulkhead, keeping my rifle in his neck and my finger on the trigger. I climbed down on to the front passenger seat and crouched next to him, resting against the nearside door.

I had kept the gun trained on Seb all the time. 'This thing is on full automatic. One move and you get the entire box in the belly. You'll die screaming. Now, take your pistol out by the muzzle and slide it across the seat. Do it slowly.'

He did as he was told. I took the weapon and put it in my pocket, then lowered my left hand into the footwell and touched something soft. Concha's hair. The scalp was matted with blood.

'She's still alive,' he said tersely.

'She would be,' I said. 'You climbed into the cab to speak to her and hit her on the skull with your gun when she wasn't looking. You had to do it quietly for fear of alerting the others. Then you went back into the rear and whacked the others one by one.'

'It is all war,' he sighed. 'You killed many of our people tonight. Those men who burned in the hangar – they suffered. We do what has to be done.'

'We?' I yelled at him. 'We?'

He was silent for a spell. Finally he replied, 'My father was British. My mother was Argentinian. When the war came I had to make a choice.'

'And you chose your mother's side?' I said bitterly.

He nodded slowly, as if he had been giving the matter much thought. 'The British approached me at the outset of the campaign, asking me to work for them. I reported the contact to our intelligence people and they told me to accept the offer.'

'So, way back in 1982 – you were a double agent then?' I asked. 'You met us at the border and deliberately guided us into the ambush? My brother Andy was killed because of you?'

'You were supposed to have been picked up at the rendezvous point. If you had surrendered, there would have been no shooting and you would all have been set free after the war.'

'Fuck that,' I told him. 'What about this time round? You met us off the beach and led us into the airbase, but first you wrecked our communications gear so we couldn't call in to report what we had seen. Then, when we contacted you over the phone, you told the marines the location of the RV point. When Concha and I escaped you waited for us at the emergency RV and brought us in. But then you helped us to take the guard post. What happened – did I interrupt when you were warning your pals on the base over the phone?'

'Yes,' he admitted. 'I only had a chance to tell them you were aiming to attack the planes.'

'And so they were waiting for us.'

'You were too good for us, though. You shot yourselves out of the ambush and destroyed the planes – and with them our hopes of retaking the Malvinas.'

I held the rifle on him. 'You shouldn't have killed Josh,' I said levelly.

He shrugged. 'He was a brave man. I was going to leave him but he grabbed me by the leg and threw me off balance. He fought like a tiger, even though he was dying. There was no time to lose. You might have come back any moment. I had no choice but to shoot him.'

Poor, brave Josh. He had fought till his last breath, and saved our lives at the cost of his own.

There came a groan from down in the footwell.

Concha was stirring, moaning softly. I squeezed her shoulder gently to let her know I was there. How long could she have been out? A few minutes only. With luck she would have suffered only mild concussion. She was fortunate to be alive.

I heard boots thudding outside, then a bang on the door. Doug and the others had reached us. They stood in a gasping circle, weapons trained on the cab.

'Get down,' I said to Seb. He climbed stiffly out into the snow and I followed him down. 'Watch him,' I told Nobby, who pushed Seb against the side of the truck with his arms out and kicked his legs apart.

'Jesus! What the fuck's been going on?' said Doug. 'Who topped the guys in the back?' He was bewildered. To the three of them it looked as if there had been a fire-fight between the Argentines and me, in which Josh had somehow got killed.

'It was him,' I told him, with a nod at Seb, adding, 'You were right all along not to trust him.'

'He killed Josh?' Doug couldn't have cared less about Julian and the rest. As far as he was concerned, the more dead Argentines the better. But killing a mate was something else.

His face went hard. 'You want to whack the fucker, or can I?' Doug meant what he said. He would have taken Seb into a ditch and let him have one in the head right then. Josh had meant a lot to me; I'd seen a bit of myself in him, and now a part of me was dead along with him. This had been my last mission; I'd fucked up, and Josh was dead because of it.

'I'll do it,' I said. I handed Doug my 203 and took out the pistol again. The others watched.

I grabbed Seb by the shoulder and spun him round.

'Wait!' he cried. 'I can still help you. I was a double agent, yes. So I have intelligence vital to your superiors. They will be very angry if you kill me now. You have to take me back with you.'

'Fuck to that, you arsehole!' Doug's anger boiled over. Swinging his gun like a club, he caught Seb in the gut. Seb fell to his knees, gagging, and Doug kicked him savagely in the ribs, knocking him into the snow.

'Leave it out, Doug,' I said.

Seb writhed in agony in the roadway. 'You'll never make it across the frontier without my help,' he gasped. 'The border is heavily garrisoned now. At first light there will be patrols out, helicopters searching.'

'Yeah, and you'll show us a way across like the last time, cunt!' Doug raged, launching another kick at him. 'I lost two mates in that show thanks to you, you bastard!'

Seb pulled himself back against the wheel of the truck. He spat blood from his mouth. 'MI6 has a helicopter on stand-by on the Chilean side. I have my phone. If I call in from the border it can pick you up.'

'You have the phone on you?' I asked.

He nodded. 'In the pocket of my coat.'

I patted him down and found the device.

'It has a GPS unit built into the receiver,' Seb went on. 'I transmit the position and the helicopter flies in to the rendezvous.'

I weighed the phone in my hand. 'You told me this thing only works within a short distance of the border.'

'Within two to three miles,' he agreed. 'We have to be within range of the base station at San Sebastian.'

'Fuck this!' Doug stormed. 'Don't listen to him. It's another of his tricks.'

I ignored him. 'So the deal is, we keep you alive and you send the code to bring in the helicopter to lift us out?'

'Don't trust him,' Doug snarled.

'If I am lying then you will kill me,' Seb countered. 'The road is bad from here on – it was washed out in a storm two weeks ago. It will take you most of the night to reach the border. Then I will make the call. What have you to lose?'

I wanted to get away from here – and until we were safely out of Argentina Seb might be useful, traitor or not.

I slipped the phone into my pocket. 'Put him in the back of the truck,' I ordered. 'Tie his hands and feet so he can't escape.'

Doug hissed between his teeth. 'OK, boss, if that's how you want it.' He sighed and jabbed Seb with his gun. 'On your feet, you.'

'And, Doug,' I called after him, 'don't mess him up. We need him in a fit state to make that call.'

THIRTY-NINE

Seb had been right about the state of the road. Within a couple of miles the hard surface had crumbled into a morass of loose gravel and mud in which the truck lurched and swayed, crawling along at a snail's pace. While I cradled Concha's head in my lap Nobby fought the wheel as we struggled northwards. The snow had changed to a light powdery dusting, which seemed to add little to the depth on the ground but made visibility next to impossible. If our single headlamp had given up on us we would have been finished.

We crossed several bridges – one of them spanning the river Doug and I had swum across on the mission twenty years before – and passed through two villages. Nowhere though did we meet any resistance; all the houses were shuttered against the storm. Perhaps the telephone lines were down – or perhaps the inhabitants wanted no part in the government's battles.

We met no other traffic of any kind. I assumed that the border had been closed and most local movements shut down by the weather. No one but madmen or desperados would be out in such conditions.

As the night wore on we changed over at intervals to

give everyone a chance to warm out in the cab. Only Concha was allowed to remain. She slept much of the time, but towards five o'clock, when I returned from a stint in the rear snow-covered and shivering, I found her sitting up and talking.

'We must be only twenty kilometres from the border now,' she told me. 'Another two hours perhaps at this speed.'

I told her of Seb's boast that the border would be strongly garrisoned and she shrugged. 'Usually there is only a small unit of customs and police. It is possible though that the military has taken extra precautions. In any case, there are ways around the town – smugglers' routes. They are long and slow, but I can lead you across.'

I glanced from the window. Time was running against us. The weather was moderating, and with it the likelihood of the Argies coming after us increased. If there was a helicopter, the sooner we could rendezvous with it the better.

Concha sighed. 'So many killings . . . Is anything ever worth dying for?'

'As a soldier you have to be prepared to give your life for what you believe in,' I said. 'That goes for all soldiers, Argentine or British. If your number comes up that's the way it has to be.'

'And you? Will you go on until your number comes up one day, as you put it?'

'No,' I told her. 'This is my last mission, me and Doug.'

'And will you be sad?'

'Sad to leave the Regiment,' I answered. 'It's been my whole life.'

'Tell me about it,' she murmured, leaning her head against my shoulder.

So while we ground on through the night I told her about Northern Ireland and the battles to contain the terrorist bombers; of fighting drug lords in Columbia and lifting war criminals out of safe havens in the Balkans. I described storming hijacked aircraft, and Nobby told her of the time he had parachuted on to a cruise liner in mid ocean that was being held by fundamentalists.

'Do you have a girlfriend?' she asked me when I had done.

'No,' I told her with a grin. 'Not right now.' I thought about Jenny as I spoke, but that was all in the past now.

She had fallen asleep again by the time seven o'clock approached. The snow had changed to a light powder that hung in the air, glistening in the beam of the headlamp. The road condition had improved, and we appeared to be running more or less on a hard surface again.

After a while the snow stopped altogether. Nobby eased off the throttle.

I sat up. 'What's wrong?' I hoped it wasn't a problem with the truck.

'I think I can see lights ahead.'

'Cut the headlamp.' I reached for my gun and we stared across the pale snow at the scattered pinpricks in the distance. 'Looks like a small town. Probably San Sebastian. We must be close to the border.'

'About fucking time too,' Nobby said. 'The engine's starting to run hot.'

I leaned over to squint at the gauge. It was hovering at the edge of the red zone. 'Oil or water leak?' I hazarded.

'Could be either. With the treatment the old bus has had these past few hours it's amazing she's got this far.'

'Well, try to keep her going. The border can't be more than four or five kilometres off.'

I crawled through into the back and shook Doug alert. 'I'm going to take Seb up front to try contacting Chile.'

'Aye,' he said. 'If the fucker gives you any trouble, let me know and I'll give him some persuading.'

I pulled Seb up and untied his hands and feet. We had given him his turn inside during the night, but now he was so numbed he could hardly stand. It took two of us to get him up and push him through into the cab.

He rubbed his fingers and blew on them. Ice had congealed in his beard and eyebrows, and his eyes were red with fatigue and pain. 'Where are we now?' he asked.

I told him that – judging by the odometer reading – we had done eighty kilometres and must be close to the border. I took the phone out. 'Tell me the code and I'll punch it in.'

'The code to switch the phone on is simple: 241982,

the second of April 1982 – the date for Operation Azul, the occupation of the Malvinas.'

I tapped in the numbers and the display came alive. I showed it to him.

'The signal is very weak. It would be better to drive on a while till it improves.'

Ten minutes later the signal bars indicated some reasonable reception. 'What's the number?' I asked him.

'First we have to find our position with the GPS.'

This part of the device was more or less standard with others that I had used. I obtained a fix and noted down the co-ordinates. 'OK, give me the number to call. And remember – play any tricks and it's your life you're fucking with.'

Seb rattled off a ten-digit figure. I committed it to memory and punched the buttons. To my relief the display showed a connection. 'Right, we're through. Now what? You said a text message.'

'Condor, like the eagle.'

'That's all?'

'That is the code-word for requesting an immediate extraction. Then you add the GPS coordinate. That is enough.'

I did as he instructed and pressed the send button. The display told me the message had been sent.

'Leave the phone on. If we shift our position we will have to update the GPS fix. When the helicopter is in the air it can interrogate the unit and home in on us.'

That was ingenious. 'A clever bit of kit,' I told him. 'How long do we have to wait?'

'They will be waiting for the call. To get the aircraft into the air, half an hour – then we are only a few minutes' flying time away.'

I retied Seb's hands. 'Might as well stop here and let the engine cool down,' I said to Nobby. 'No sense in driving any further than we have to.'

We sat in the darkness, listening to the tick of the engine block cooling while the wind played about us. Kiwi got down to have a pee. 'Don't stray too far,' I warned him. 'If anything comes along we may have to take off in a hurry.'

Faint fingers of grey were creeping over the eastern horizon, and the darkness thinned so that the outlines of objects became clearer. We could almost make out one another's faces. Concha sat up and looked about. 'I know this place. The border is only two kilometres away. We could walk it easily even in the snow.'

I shook my head. 'You heard what Seb said – the border will be sealed tight and the Argies will be waiting for us. They'll have patrols out, helicopters, the works, and they won't be taking prisoners. Tabbing out is a last resort.' We were all of us tired. The thought of stepping into a nice big helicopter and being whisked back to the warmth and safety of Port Stanley was hard to resist.

Time crept past. I looked at the watch Seb had lent me – half-past seven. Maybe there was no helicopter. Suppose it was just a ploy of Seb's to delay us here? It would be dawn in another hour. If we were to try for the border on foot I knew we had better leave soon, before it got light.

I eased Concha's head off my shoulder and turned to the rear to talk to Doug. 'We can't hang about here much longer. I think we should start footing it across the border and call the helicopter again from the other side.'

Doug grunted. I could tell he didn't like the idea. 'You're the boss,' he said.

At that moment the handset in my pocket emitted a beep. 'What's that?' I said to Seb.

'The helicopter is interrogating the GPS receiver. It must be airborne and on its way.'

Everybody cheered up.

We waited a few minutes more.

I was getting edgy again when Kiwi said, 'Listen!'

We all sat up. Faintly, from the distance, came the regular thump of helicopter blades.

It grew stronger as we listened.

'Coming from the west,' I said.

'South of west,' Doug countered. 'He's overshot and flying a search pattern.'

We listened some more. The noise of the helicopter grew steadily and the handset beeped again, making us jump.

'He's come in to the south of us, picked up the road and he's following our tracks,' Doug said eagerly.

'Everyone get ready,' I ordered. I turned back towards Seb. He was sitting bolt upright in the middle seat between Nobby and me. His eyes were closed and his lips were moving silently. 'Seb.' I nudged him. 'Come on, get your arse in gear.'

The noise of the blades was much louder now.

'Twin-engine job?' Nobby suggested, puzzled. Seb still wasn't responding. His eyes were squeezed tight shut as if in pain. The helicopter sound was suddenly deafening.

Then it hit me. 'Christ!' I shouted. 'That's no civilian bird, that's an attack chopper! Everybody out!' And I flung the handset from me. 'You bastard!' I yelled at Seb. 'You set us up again!' He didn't move. 'Well, you can stay here and get what's coming to you!' Grabbing his bound hands, I used the tail-end of the paracord to lash him to the steering wheel.

Concha looked scared. I reached across her to open the door, pushed her out and jumped after her into the road. Kiwi and Doug were baling out of the rear. 'Run!' I bawled at Concha, grabbing her arm and hustling her across the road.

We plunged into the snow on the far side, our feet sinking thigh-deep into the grass and heather underneath.

'Faster! Keep going!' I shouted. 'Get away from the vehicle!'

The other three were sprinting ahead, leaping through the snow and bush in great bounds. We could hear the roar of the helicopter engines blasting up the road towards us, and I looked back. Concha was gasping for breath. I dragged her ruthlessly on. We were 200 metres from the truck when a searchlight beam blazed suddenly out of the sky in the south.

'Down!' I shouted, flinging myself flat, throwing Concha into the snow. 'Burrow underneath and lie still!'

I wriggled into the long grass, then worked myself round, rifle at the ready. Lifting my head slightly I saw the monstrous, blazing eye skimming up the road from the south. Just visible in the backwash of the search-light was the stubby outline of an attack helicopter, like a huge predatory insect, cannon barrel projecting from its snout and menacing rockets slung beneath the winglet pylons. Fucking hell, I thought, an Apache!

The Apache was the US Army's primary attack helicopter, designed to operate day and night and in all weather. 'Flying tank' would be a more accurate description. The fuselage is invulnerable to ordinary rifle and machine-gun fire – it would take a lucky hit from a 23mm cannon shell to bring it down. The leading edges of the main rotor blades are plated in stainless steel to survive impact with trees and metal fragments during low flight, and the pilot and gunner sit in Kevlar-armoured seats for protection over the battlefield. The armaments comprise a 30mm Hughes chain-gun, thirty-eight 70mm unguided explosive-head rockets, and eight Hellfire anti-tank missiles. In short, it is fast, heavily armed, and near impossible to knock out.

It swung in dead along the centre line of the road. I heard the swoosh of a missile and ducked my head again. There was a shattering explosion and the ground heaved underneath us. Snow and debris rained from the sky. I risked another look. The truck was burning from a direct hit.

The Apache spun round on a wingtip, and passed directly over where we lay crouching. Christ, I thought, we're much too close. A near miss with an anti-tank missile or rockets could take us all out.

I saw the pilot line up along the road again. There was a burst of flame from under the starboard wing-stub and a pod of unguided rockets streaked towards the ground like burning arrows. The ground heaved again and the truck vanished in a cloud of smoke and fire.

The Apache was circling round again. I held my breath. The truck was lying toppled over on its side, a mass of flames. The bodies of Josh and the four Argentines had fallen out and lay strewn in pieces in the snow. I prayed it would look to the crew like they had got us all. I couldn't see Seb, but he must have been dead too. The road was cratered for fifty metres either end of the truck. If the gunner launched his second load of rockets from the western side of the road, we were done for.

The helicopter lined up from the north this time. Its searchlight blazed through the smoke like an evil eye as the gunner loosed his other pod. The nineteen 70mm folding-fin rockets spread out in a fan formation, rushing towards us in a cloud. I wedged myself down into the earth, clutching Concha's hand.

The explosions seemed to go on and on. Something struck the ground nearby with incredible violence; metal fragments fell hissing all around us. One of the rockets had run wide and ploughed into the snow metres away.

Snow whirled round me in a cyclone as the machine thundered overhead. The truck was still on its side, burning fiercely.

The Apache pivoted, there was a shattering sound, and a solid stream of red light stabbed out from the helicopter into the truck. The gunner was letting go with his Hughes chain-gun. The 30mm rounds ripped into the wrecked truck, slicing through the metal like a giant chainsaw, tearing it apart, obliterating it in a cloud of flying pieces.

Jesus, I thought – if he turns that thing on us we're done for.

The helicopter buzzed around the wreckage like a hungry wasp, giving occasional squirts from the cannon, while we cowered in the snow. Abruptly its nose lifted and it soared skywards, its tail spinning around.

Uh-oh, I thought. It's going to check around for survivors.

The Apache held the hover for a minute. I watched the turret swivelling from side to side as the gunner scoured the ground through his heat-sensitive goggles to locate us. Against the snow we must have stood out like fireflies in the dark.

I readied my 203 – not that it would be any use. The bastard was on the far side of the highway, the burning remains of the truck between him and us. He could sit up there at a thousand feet and rake us with the chain-gun from a safe range.

If only he would come closer, we might get a shot at him.

The red light in the chin turret winked and a burst of shells blasted over our heads. Snow and earth rained down on us. The gunner took another burst, chewing up the bush to my left, then evidently decided to take a closer look. The Apache's nose dipped and it came skimming in towards us, moving fast, chain-gun rattling as it came.

I could feel the rounds hosing closer and closer, kicking up debris as they detonated in the snow; I could smell the phosphorus from the tracer in the base of each round. The noise of the twin engines was intensely loud, the rotor thudding almost directly over where we lay, whipping up the snow into a blur around us. The gunner was firing in short bursts, but he was shooting behind us.

Now was the moment. I jumped up from the snow, my weapon vertical, and swung the grenade launcher towards the dark shape overhead, aiming for the centre of the main rotor disk. It would take an extraordinarily lucky shot to penetrate the Apache's armour with the 23mm grenade. I was shooting at extreme range, but there was a chance I might frighten the pilot off. If not, I had definitely given away our position to the gunner for his next pass.

Where the round went I didn't see but there was no flash of an explosion. I worked the slide swiftly, chambering a fresh round; rifle fire was useless against the Apache's thick armour.

The helicopter swung back round in a tight circle, put its nose down again and came swooping back for the kill, angered by the infantryman who had dared to fight back with his puny weapon. Cannon shells burst around me as I sprinted forward in a desperate attempt to lead the firing away from where Concha lay.

Then I saw Nobby jump up from where he had been lying away to my left, the last RPG tube clamped to his shoulder. Hardly pausing to aim, he squeezed the trigger. There was a swish and the rocket grenade scorched upward, trailing smoke. The pilot must have seen it, because the Apache banked violently on to the starboard wing-stub. I thought the grenade was going to miss, but then I saw the flash of an explosion as the warhead detonated under the tail rotor.

The Apache was already banking hard over. It climbed for a moment, then, deprived of the stabilising thrust of the tail rotor, it spun round several times, flipped over on to its back and fell away from us, plummeting downwards.

There was nothing the pilot could do. In another instant the craft struck the ground a hundred metres away with a terrific impact, exploding violently into flames.

I ran back to where Concha lay. 'Are you OK?' I cried.

She got to her feet and nodded shakily as she stared at the horror of the blazing crash. The crew never stood a chance of getting out.

'The phone?' she said.

I nodded. 'I was stupid. Of course the Argentines would be monitoring the phones. Seb must have told them the system. They homed in on the GPS signal and ran us down. He didn't care if he died so long as he took us with him.'

Nobby was stumbling jubilantly through the snow to join us, Kiwi and Doug following him. Amazingly none of us had been hit by the shelling or the rockets. The burning helicopter was throwing off a fierce heat and spare rounds from the chain-gun were popping off like firecrackers. In the lurid light of the fire, choking smoke drifted across the snow-covered ground.

'We need to move out fast,' I said. 'This lot will bring out everyone in the neighbourhood. We've an hour before dawn to make the border.'

'The border is not far from here,' Concha said, 'and I know a way across.'

Dawn had reached us, and a keen wind was blowing from clear skies. The snow was crisp and hard along the path. I had lost count of how far we had walked. According to my watch we had been going two hours. The country here was unchanging – featureless pampas with clumps of long grass, heather and gorse. The reaction from the attack had set in and we were drained. I felt as if I had been walking all night.

Led by Concha, we had circled round the border crossing and were making for a village on the Chilean side. There were no markings that I could see, unless we had passed them earlier in the darkness. We might be anywhere.

'Someone's coming,' called Kiwi, who was scouting in front. 'Looks like a kid with a bike.'

'Hide yourselves,' Concha said. 'I will ask for directions.'

Wearily we ducked down behind a clump of grass and waited. The boy approached slowly, pushing his bicycle through the snow. He wore a red hat and was singing a little tune to himself. He greeted Concha politely, and they spoke in Spanish for some minutes. Concha seemed to be questioning him animatedly. The boy pointed down the track. Shit, I thought, we've still a way to go.

At last they bade one another farewell and the boy trudged on.

Concha came leaping through the snow to join us. Her face was beaming.

I stood up. 'How much further?'

She laughed. 'Half a kilometre – to the village. But it is OK, we are in Chilean territory. We are safe!'

There were whoops of relief from the others. 'About fucking time!' Doug said as he sat down in the snow.

Concha was still smiling. I looked at her. 'There's something else, isn't there?' I said. 'What else did the boy tell you?'

She nodded. 'The boy was an Argentine but living in Chile. He was on his way to catch the bus to Rio Grande. He said that on the news half an hour ago it was reported from Buenos Aires that the military junta has fallen. Argentina is free again!'

'So the fighting is over,' I said. My mind was so dulled with fatigue I could hardly take it in.

She flung her arms around my neck. 'The fighting is over. You have fought your last mission, soldier.'